BOOK TWO OF TIMELESS LOVE SERIES

JADA WEST

First Edition
Paperback ISBN: 978-976-655-171-1

Disclaimer: The story, characters, and plot are the original work of the author.

BEFORE DAWN:

Editor: Avery Jensen at Ink & Insights, Catherine Oni, Kenna Serein at Kenna.authorservices

Proofreader: Ashley Vaccaro

Cover Designer & Interior Formatter: (E-Book & Paperback): TheBookJedi

Translator: Edward

Acknowledgements

Before I dive into acknowledgements, I just want to take a moment to say thank you. This journey has been incredible, filled with highs and lows, but one thing that has remained constant is the love and support from so many people. To every single person whose excitement, support, and love has brought me here—thank you from the bottom of my heart. I wouldn't be here without you.

First and foremost, I want to thank God. I have had so many down moments writing and editing this book. There were so many times I really wanted to give up, but when I prayed, God held my hand and brought me through this. It's not by chance that I'm here and doing all these amazing things, so I want to thank God.

Next, I want to thank myself—because girl, you really did that! You wrote your second book, which you're so proud of, and you told a story that you have always wanted to tell. One that isn't just about love, but also about healing and how real and raw certain things are.

To my mom and grandma, thank you for believing in me and constantly yapping to everyone, *'Did you know my daughter/granddaughter wrote a book?'* I always strive to make you both proud, and I'm so happy to know that I have.

Next, I want to thank my alpha readers (Chloe, Emily, Lexy, Missy, and Rachel). You guys helped me develop this baby so much, and you stuck by me! Thank you.

To my beta readers (Ashley, Lexi, Rachel, Stephanie, and Zoë), your comments and corrections gave me life, and I honestly couldn't have done it without you. I appreciate how much you all stayed within the deadline (even when it was sometimes too short, lol), and how you hyped me and this book up so much.

Ashley— you're my manager/assistant/proofreader/everything in one, lol. I couldn't do it without you—from literally talking me through meltdowns to reacting to everything with me to helping me sort out ARCs and forms. The time, love, and dedication you have shown me haven't gone unnoticed, and I really appreciate it.

Next is Yapper (she gave me permission to use this name). Thank you for all your insights and helping me fix chapters from a reader's POV. You've done so much for this book and Mikkel's character, and I want to say THANK YOU!

Avery—I didn't even know what manuscript critique was until you told me! But girl, thank you. The insights you gave on Before Dawn and the way you helped me to perfect and fix everything were amazing. Even when I had doubts and texted you about them, you helped me through, and I need to say thank you to you.

Catherine, my editor—thank you for your insights and editing this manuscript.

To my character artists, Fran, Stephy, and K, thank you. You brought my babies to life in the most beautiful way, and I'm still in awe at how PERFECT THEY ARE.

My cover artist and interior formatter, TheBookJedi—if I could write an entire essay about you, I WOULD. You have brought out such creative parts in me, as well as literally taken all my ramblings and the billion messages I've sent you (which could've easily been one thing, lol) and turned my vision to life in a timely manner. I cannot wait for us to work on the rest of this series, and I am never letting you go!

To my street team, you guys held me afloat, especially when I was in Insta jail and had a million crises a day, lol. Thank you all SO MUCH for always hyping me up.

To my ARC readers—whether you loved this book or not, thank you for taking the chance on me, signing up, and reading my babies. I appreciate it.

Kenna, you edited a sample, and thus, your love for Mikkel grew, lol. It was perfect, and I appreciate it.

Next, I want to thank Anya. You have been one of the best people I've met in the book community. You've never missed a post, and in more than one way, you've kept me SO organized. Thank you, especially in the days leading up to release—you've been a listening ear and a sounding board.

Sunny, you've been here from day one, actually, and I honestly couldn't be happier to have you as my friend. THANK YOU.

Victoria, thank you for listening to me yap about this book (plus all the others) and for believing in me when I couldn't believe in myself. I could also write an essay about how valuable you've been.

And to everyone else who has been part of this journey, I thank you! Your love and support mean the world to me.

To everyone who struggles with anxiety—you are not alone. Your strength lies in showing up, even on the days when it feels impossible.

To those who've been told they were too much, hear this: you are more than enough.

To anyone who's ever believed the lie that they were the problem—I need you to know, you never were.

To every soul longing for a love that's calm, patient, and fiercely passionate—I can't promise when that love will find you. But I can give you Mikkel. Here's a taste of what you deserve.

And finally, to those brave enough to put themselves first, even when it broke them—you are unstoppable. I'm proud of you, and Abigail-Ann is too. Keep standing tall.

Content Warning

Anxiety (Generalized Anxiety Disorder)
Assault (Mention)
Blood
Endometriosis
Graphic Scenes
Infertility (Mention)
Mature Content & Language
Miscarriage (Mention)
Past Relationship Trauma
Revenge Porn (Mention)
Sexually Explicit Scenes (including Bondage)
Violence

Dicktionary

This section includes all the sexually explicit chapters for reference, in case you'd like to skip them, avoid them, or approach these chapters with caution before reading them in their entirety.

Chapter 34 – Mild
Chapter 35
Chapter 39
Chapter 50
Chapter 51
Chapter 60
Chapter 61

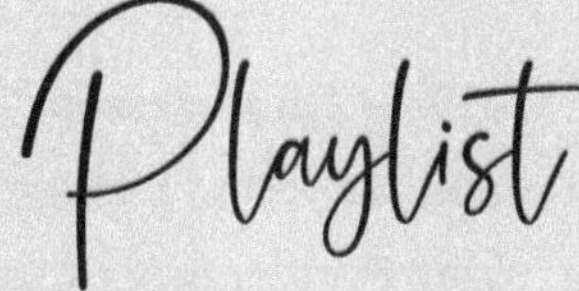

"Falling" – Harry Styles

I'm falling again, I'm falling again, I'm falling

"Delicate" – Taylor Swift

Is it cool that I said all that?
Is it too soon to do this yet?
'Cause I know that it's delicate

"Into You" – Ariana Grande

A little bit dangerous
But, baby, that's how I want it
A little less conversation and a little more touch my body
'Cause I'm so into you, into you, into you

"Better" – Khalid

Nothin' feels better than this

"One" – Lewis Capaldi

You broke her heart down with ease
Now I'm pickin' up every piece
I'm sayin' thank you to the one who let her get away, away

More Than Friends – 24kGoldn

Cute face, thick thighs, put it all on me
'Cause I'm dying inside, baby, can't you see? (Ugh)
You the one on my mind, take a chance on me

WOW – Zara Larsson
And you make me feel so f*cking pretty
Take loving me to a new extreme
If I can't have you, I don't want no one

"September" (Acoustic) – James Arthur
My crush on you has never faded
Let's go back to bed until we break it
I'm gonna love you for the rest of my life

"Fight for Us" – Masicka & Fave
Here comes my knight in shining armor
Show me a girlie who's luckier
A kiss? No really
I need two or three to heal me

"Can I Be Him" – James Arthur
You walked into the room and now my heart has been stolen
I wanna dry those tears, kiss those lips
It's all that I've been thinking about

"Dive" – Ed Sheeran
I have traveled the world, there's no other girl like you
No one, what's your history?
And I could live, I could die
Hanging on the words you say

"Finally Feel Good" – James Arthur
When I broke free from the old me
I was singing, "I finally feel good"

"Capital Letters" – Hailee Steinfeld & BloodPop
We put a crack in the shadows
And you tell me it's okay to be the light

And not to swim in the shallows
And we don't care who's watching us, baby

"calgary" – Tate McRae
And the best of me right now is looking a lot like a mess
I thought I had my shit together
I thought that I was getting better
No, I got better at pretending

"Don't" – Bryson Tiller

Bed Chem – Sabrina Carpenter
Who's the cute boy with the white jacket
And the thick accent?

"Sad Eyes" – James Arthur
And baby, even when your troubled tears are falling
Darling, you should know you still look beautiful

"Video Games" – Lana Del Rey
It's you, it's you, it's all for you

luther – Kendrick Lamar & SZA
I wouldn't give these nobodies no sympathy
I'd take away the pain, I'd give you everything
I just wanna see you win, wanna see

"Purple lace bra" – Tate McRae
I'm losin' my mind, I'm losin' my head
You only listen when I'm undressed
Hear what you like and none of the rest
I'm-I'm losin' my mind 'cause giving you head's
The only time you think I got depth
Hear what you like and none of the rest

QR Codes for Streaming: This playlist is available for streaming on Spotify and Apple Music. QR codes can be found in the book for easy access—simply scan to listen!

Apple Music

Spotify

Watchlist

Throughout this book, you'll find nods to various movies (some serve as inspiration, while others reflect the themes explored in Abigail-Ann & Mikkel's story). While not all of these films are directly mentioned, they resonate with the emotions, struggles, and journeys my characters experience. Themes like anxiety, loss of control, perfectionism, and emotional burnout are woven into the narrative, much like they are in these films.

That said, you **don't need** to have seen any of them to enjoy the book! This is just a fun way to blend some of my favorite movies with the world of my characters. Some references are subtle, some are direct, but all are meant to add an extra layer to the story.

Whether you're a movie lover or just here for the journey, I hope you enjoy these cinematic connections!

Beauty and the Beast (1991, 2017, Belle's Magical World (1998), Enchanted Christmas (1997))
The Holiday Calendar (2018)
Clueless (1995)
Me Before You (2016)
Legally Blonde (2001)
Say Anything... (1989)
Endless Love (2014)
The Notebook (2004)
Black Swan (2010)
Whiplash (2014)

SYNOPSIS

Abigail-Ann Asher

New York City was supposed to be my fresh start—a chance to leave behind the ghosts of San Francisco and the insecurities that refuse to let me go. I came here to rebuild myself, to prove that I am more than my past.

Then I meet him.

Mikkel Suarez is powerful, magnetic, and heartbreakingly handsome. He's everything I should avoid—yet every time he looks at me, my walls begin to crack. He makes me want to believe in something I swore I'd given up on. Love. The kind that consumes you. But trusting him feels like a risk I can't afford.

Because if I fall, I might not survive the landing.

Mikkel Suarez

My life is built on control. Everything in its place. I never questioned what I wanted—until I saw her.

Abigail is a contradiction—strong yet guarded, confident yet wounded—and I can't stay away. She doesn't see what I do—her brilliance, her strength, the way she lights up a room. I want to be the man who proves she's worthy of love.

But she's not the only one afraid. There are parts of me I never let anyone see… but with her, I want to.

I just have to convince her to stay before she decides she's better off alone. Because losing her? That's not an option.

AUTHOR'S NOTE

(Please Read)

The narrative of this story spans two timelines, shifting back and forth to converge into the present moment. It intersects with the events of the previous book in the series, *After Hours*. This book is divided into two parts: Part I and Part II, with Part II starting ten weeks after Part I ends.

While it's recommended to read *After Hours* first for a deeper understanding, it's **not necessary** to enjoy this story.

Please take a moment to read the content warnings and additional notes before proceeding. This book may appear long due to the chapter count, but the chapters themselves are not lengthy. If you know that spice isn't your thing, please refer to the dicktionary for specific chapters that may require caution.

Endnotes are provided in the e-book, and footnotes are included in the paperback for easier reading, as Spanish is used throughout.

PART 1

This section precedes the timeline that overlaps with *After Hours,* book one in the Timeless Love Series. All the events happening take place up to the Epilogue of *After Hours.*

PROLOGUE

You and I both know how love works. It's messy. It's beautiful. It makes you feel like you're on top of the world, only to tear you apart in ways you never imagined. Love isn't always kind, and it sure as hell doesn't always heal. It hurts. It can break you and leave you questioning everything you thought you knew.

I've felt that pain. I've stood in the wreckage, wondering if I'd ever find myself again.

For the longest time, I thought my story ended with Joshua. I thought that broken, twisted version of love would be the one I'd carry with me forever. That I'd be haunted by it, forced to live with the shadow of a man who took more from me than I could ever give.

Some nights, I'd wake up gasping, my heart racing, as if I could still feel his presence, his words echoing in my mind. The things he or even his family said about me; that I was too much, never enough or trying too hard. It played on a loop in my head, and I couldn't find the off switch.

But you know what I learned? Sometimes a man is so insecure that he'll break you just to make himself feel whole. He'll make you doubt everything about yourself because he hates what he sees in the mirror. And when he's done tearing himself down, he'll tear you down, too. And to make matters even worse? He'll end up blaming you for everything, sadly enough, you may even believe him. Because when you're already questioning yourself, it's easy to think the problem lies within you. I've been there. I've sat with those thoughts, feeling like my chest might cave in under the weight of them. But I'll be the one to tell you—it's NEVER your fault.

I know what it's like to feel like you're not enough. To look in the mirror and barely recognize the person staring back. To wake up each day with a pit in your stomach, bracing yourself for the next thing to go wrong. Or to stay up late, with tears running down your face as you pray and ask: *'Why me?' I* know the feeling of being consumed by that ache, the one that sits in your chest and steals your breath when you least expect it.

But I'm here to tell you this: *no one, no man, no heartache should ever steal your light because you have the power to shine too brightly.* Even when your thoughts are screaming at you, telling you otherwise, you're stronger than you think.

It wasn't until Mikkel—*God, Mikkel*—that I even started to believe I could be whole again. He didn't just save me; he reminded me that I could save myself. When I felt like I was drowning, he became the anchor that kept me afloat. He didn't brush off my moments of panic or my need for reassurance. He didn't tell me to just "move on" or "get over it." He stayed. He listened. He held me when I couldn't hold myself together. And most importantly, *he saw me.*

Mikkel had pulled me out of my darkest moments, showing me what love truly meant—how it felt when someone wanted to build me up, not break me down. He had become my strength when I thought I had none left. He hadn't come into my life to sweep me off my feet. No, he had stood beside me and straightened my legs so I could run.

I know you've felt it too—that fear, that doubt. The intrusive thoughts that creep in, whispering that it's all too good to be true, that this person might hurt you just like the last one. I know what it's like to over analyze every word, every look, every pause, trying to prepare yourself for the moment it all falls apart. I know what it's like to wonder if you'll ever feel whole again.

But I'm telling you, there's light at the end of that tunnel. Sometimes it doesn't look the way you expect, but when it comes, it's blinding.

Mine just happened to come in the form of a handsome, tattooed 6'5" Hispanic gentleman who positively changed my whole life. And if there's light for me, then there's light for you, too.

So, keep going.

Don't give up.

Your story isn't over yet.

And in the meantime, sit tight and read mine.

CHAPTER ONE

Abigail-Ann

"Love is not something you find; love is something that finds you."
~ Loretta Young

THREE WEEKS EARLIER

"Get it together, Abigail," I muttered, blinking hard to keep the tears at bay.

The terminal at San Francisco International Airport hummed with the electric mix of eager anticipation and heartfelt farewells. Travelers flowed like a restless tide, each swept up in their own journey of goodbyes and new beginnings.

I sat amidst the crowd, eyes fixed on the departure board as a knot tightened in my stomach. Tears blurred my vision, turning the glowing letters into a watery haze.

Flight AA17638 to John F. Kennedy Airport.

Yet, despite the urgency, my mind lingered in the past, replaying memories like a broken record. The flicker of overhead lights matched my racing heartbeat, amplifying my anxiety.

Five years.

Five fucking years.

That's how long I spent in a relationship that slowly suffocated me. The first ten months with Joshua had been decent—a love I tried to believe was enough. But the last four years? A nightmare.

His drinking became a storm that never passed. I told myself it was just a phase we'd get through. I was wrong.

I begged, cried, pleaded for him to see what it was doing—to us, to me, to himself. I stayed up countless nights, watching over him as he stumbled in, reeking of alcohol, mumbling empty apologies. I dragged him to therapy, got him into AA, stood by his side through every failed attempt to sober up. But nothing changed.

He always found his way back—to the bottle, the drugs, the bad habits, and most painful of all, the women who weren't me.

It broke me to watch him slip further away, the man I once loved buried under addiction. I tried to pull him out, but he resisted, blaming me for things beyond my control. He said it was the alcohol speaking, that he didn't mean it—but the damage was done.

How many times can you try to fix something broken before realizing it will never be the same?

The final blow came when I discovered he'd been cheating. He didn't even deny it, brushing it off like it meant nothing. *Like I meant nothing.*

But it meant everything to me.

I wasn't just fighting his addiction or his infidelity—I was fighting the man he had become. The one who once called me his world now treated me like an inconvenience. Every time he hurt me, he found an excuse, never taking responsibility. I had been drowning in his demons, but it was time to save myself.

Once, he would have held my hand tightly on our adventures. Now, his bright hazel eyes only stirred fear. His touch, once a comfort, sent shivers down my spine.

Those moments were gone. Now, every touch from him filled me with nothing but disgust.

And just when I thought the pain couldn't get worse, my phone buzzed.

> **Joshua**
>
> Where r u? Need u here now. Can't believe u r leaving without saying goodbye. U r good for nothing but running. Typical. Just forget about us, huh? Fine. Enjoy ur little adventure. Just don't expect me to be here when u get back.

Tears burned my eyes as I read his message, each word cutting deeper into an already shattered soul. I needed to break free from his suffocating grip.

Was moving to New York the right choice?

What if I ended up stuck in the same cycle?

What if I couldn't make it on my own?

Lost in my spiraling thoughts, a deep yet soothing voice broke through the chaos.

I looked up, and froze.

"Hey, are you okay? What's a pretty woman like you doing here crying?"

Fuck that. I didn't just see a man. *I saw him.*

Towering at least 6'3, he had a muscular build and the most mesmerizing tattoos I'd ever seen. His rugged features—a hint of stubble, defined jawline, and piercing honey-brown eyes that seemed to hold entire galaxies—only added to his allure. He carried himself with effortless confidence, his gym-sculpted frame dominating the space beside me. Behind his glasses, his gaze was warm yet laced with concern.

I tried to respond, but my emotions betrayed me, leaving me speechless.

Sensing my struggle, he sat beside me, his presence oddly grounding. The rich scent of grapefruit, patchouli, and ambergris wrapped around me—*impossible to forget.*

"Whatever has you crying isn't worth it." His words slipped past my defenses, stirring something deep within. "Someone as beautiful as you shouldn't be shedding tears of hurt; those green eyes should only light up with pleasure."

"T-Thank you," I managed to murmur, heat rising to my cheeks as I met his understanding gaze.

His lips quivered with amusement. "I'm glad I could be the one to tell you."

Before I could respond, the overhead speakers crackled to life, announcing my flight. I turned to share a grateful glance, but he was already gone, leaving nothing but the memory of his kindness and a small but undeniable flutter in my chest.

As I made my way to Gate 37, I felt a mix of trepidation and liberation.

New York City, here I come.

CHAPTER TWO

Abigail-Ann

"Sometimes the heart sees what is invisible to the eye."
~ *H. Jackson Brown, Jr.*

THREE WEEKS LATER

I should've known better than to let Azzy talk me into this. But when has she ever taken no for an answer?

Before I get into that, let me tell you about my birthday three weeks ago. I turned twenty-three. It was perfect—triple chocolate cake, terrible singing, Chipotle bowls, and barbecue Lay's (the best snack on earth). Quiet, but the good kind of quiet. No Joshua, no criticism, just me existing for myself.

The only downside to being in New York City was missing my parents and my sister, but I bombarded them with calls until they had no choice but to answer. Still, the best part was waking up every day in the presence of Azzy and her mom, Auntie Leann, who always made me feel loved and cared for.

That night was everything I could've asked for. Tonight? Not so much.

Standing on the dance floor of Midnight Mirage, I felt my stomach tighten. The club pulsed with energy—lights flashing, bass vibrating through the floor, bodies swaying to the beat. It should've felt exciting, but my hands felt clammy, and my pulse pounded for all the wrong reasons.

The night had started fine—until the bartender stared a little too long at my cleavage. Azzaria didn't hesitate. "Eyes up here," she snapped, her voice sharp, cutting through the noise. The bartender flinched.

Azzaria Willis—my brown-haired, sexy-as-hell, slightly overprotective best friend of nearly a decade—was the kind of woman who wasn't afraid to step up and fight for me. It was part of what made her so irresistible and exactly why I loved her like a sister.

After more than a few rounds—*okay, maybe ten*—of scotch and whiskey, she convinced me to head straight for VIP. And now, here we were, standing before the red rope, where the best bottles gleamed behind it like exclusive trophies.

And once again, I found myself thinking, I should've never let Azzy talk me into this.

This was a bad idea. I knew it. But at this point, there was no turning back.

"You can't enter without a pass," the security guard said firmly, his deep voice as serious as the all-black suit he wore.

"How much?" I asked, already reaching for my purse.

"No cash," he said, tone sharpening. "A pass."

"You don't have to be an ass," I shot back, raising my voice enough to turn a few heads. A hint of embarrassment crept in, but the liquor in my system made it easy to ignore.

"You need a—"

"Let them in," a distinct masculine voice interrupted, commanding and sharp.

The guard stiffened, spinning around in surprise. "But, sir—"

"I said let them in."

A man strode toward us, his presence so powerful it seemed to quiet the air around him.

I turned to Azzaria, ready to mutter a quick thanks to whoever this savior was, but the expression on her face stopped me short. Her eyes widened, and her lips parted slightly as if she couldn't quite believe what she was seeing.

"Holy shit," she whispered, her voice barely audible over the music.

My heart kicked up a notch as I took in the man standing before us. "Isn't that—"

"Yes," she said, breathless, her voice trembling with equal parts disbelief and something else I couldn't pinpoint. "Yes, it is."

Sure enough, it was Dillon Xander—billionaire, playboy, walking tabloid scandal. *But why was he here?* More importantly, why was he looking at Azzaria as if she was the only person in the room?

"I can hear you both. No need to whisper." His lips curled into a teasing grin. "Hello to you, too."

Azzaria froze, her usual quick wit apparently short-circuited. Her cheeks flushed, and her shock melted into something softer. *Warmer.*

I smirked, leaning in just enough to stir the pot. "Am I interrupting something?"

She shot me a look that promised retribution, but her gaze quickly darted back to her boss. Their eyes locked again, the intensity between them so thick it felt like the room had tilted slightly.

"Shall we?" he gestured toward the entrance, his voice smooth as the guard stepped aside with a reluctant grunt.

Azzaria stepped past the rope, her arm barely grazing his—but the way Dillon's gaze flicked to hers, you'd think she set him on fire.

I followed, unable to shake the buzz of excitement in my chest.

The VIP section was a world of its own—glittering chandeliers, plush velvet couches, sleek metal accents, and the hum of money in the air. Warm lighting bathed the space, where exotic flowers adorned glass tables. Large windows framed by silk drapes showcased breathtaking views of the city skyline, a detail I loved most.

But my focus wasn't on the surroundings. It was on Azzaria and Dillon, whose every glance and subtle move seemed charged with something electric.

I leaned closer to Azzaria, nudging her lightly as we walked further. "You need to go talk to him," I whispered, trying to sound casual despite the growing grin on my face.

"What? *No!*" Her wide eyes darted toward Dillon, who was busy chatting with a sharply dressed man near the bar. "I can't leave you here by yourself."

I rolled my eyes, waving her off. "Yes, you can. I'll be fine. Go get your billionaire."

She froze, her jaw dropping slightly as her cheeks deepened to an even darker shade of pink. "He's not *my* billionaire," she mumbled, looking everywhere but at me. "He is my boss."

"Not yet," I teased, crossing my arms as I tilted my head toward him. "He's clearly interested, or he wouldn't be looking at you like that."

Azzaria hesitated, chewing her bottom lip as her gaze flickered between Dillon and me. "But I don't want to abandon you. What if you—"

"I'll be fine!" I cut her off with a soft laugh. "Look around. This place is crawling with potential distractions. I'm not going to die of boredom."

"But you will die of anxiety."

"I'm plied with enough whiskey to survive. Go."

She studied me for a moment longer, searching my face for any sign of hesitation. When she didn't find any, she exhaled a shaky breath. "Okay... but if anything happens, come get me. I mean it."

"Go." I gave her a playful shove in Dillon's direction. "Don't waste this."

Her steps were slow at first, hesitant, like she was walking a tightrope. But then, as if something clicked into place, I saw the shift—the way her shoulders squared and her chin lifted just slightly.

Dillon turned toward her almost immediately, his gaze locking onto her with an intensity that made my stomach flip. *Yeah. My best friend was in for a very interesting night.*

I sank into the plush red sofa, the deep fabric wrapping around me like a cocoon. I was just starting to relax when a familiar scent curled into my senses—something warm, rich, and unmistakably male.

I looked up.

And there he was.

The guy from the airport.

And damn, he was already heading my way.

I'd thought he was handsome before, but tonight? He looked like sin wrapped in white linen. His pants fit perfectly, tailored just enough to hint at powerful legs, and the matching short-sleeved shirt was tucked neatly into his waistband. The undone top button revealed a glimpse of his chest tattoos—most notably, a compass inked over his skin like it had been drawn by fate itself.

The contrast of his golden skin against the crisp white was almost criminal. His chiseled jawline, the groomed stubble, the sharp angles of his cheekbones—everything about him screamed untouchable.

And yet, all I wanted to do was touch him.

What the fuck was wrong with me?

"Is it a blessing that I've seen your face twice in one month?"

His voice cut through my haze, the deep Spanish lilt making my pulse stutter.

I blinked, his words pulling me back to the present. *He remembered me?* After nothing but fleeting glances at the airport? My fingers gripped the edge of the sofa as I fought the urge to look away, to hide the way my nerves twisted inside me.

"Most definitely," I said, forcing a small, awkward smile.

His honey-brown eyes studied me, warm and unreadable, like he was trying to figure me out. "Would you like to have a seat with me, Red?"

Something about the way he asked—like it wasn't just an offer, but an invitation to something deeper—made my chest tighten.

Red.

I blinked at him, my brows pulling together. "Red?"

His lips twitched, a slow smirk tugging at the corner.

"Is it because of my shoes?"

As soon as the words left my mouth, I mentally cursed myself. *How fucking stupid did that sound?*

Get a grip, Abigail.

"No, your curly red hair," he replied, amusement glimmering in his eyes.

I blinked, surprised. With my hair tucked in a bun and the dim lighting, I hadn't expected him to notice its color—let alone that it was curly. Most men's eyes usually went straight to my tits or ass, like the bartender earlier who couldn't seem to tear his gaze from my cleavage.

But I wasn't about to overthink this. It was... refreshing.

"As for the seat, you lead the way."

I glanced at Azzaria, who looked perfectly content, her head on her boss' shoulder, his arm around her like he belonged there. So much for pretending she wasn't into him.

I took a deep breath, straightening up before following him.

"Here we are."

He gestured to the seat, waiting for me to sit first.

"Would you like a drink?" he asked, crossing his leg at the knee. The movement pulled his shirt tighter across his chest, and—Jesus Christ.

I forced my eyes up. "Water is fine."

He handed me a bottle, and our fingers brushed. A small, ridiculous jolt shot up my arm. I told myself it was just the chill of the bottle. That was all.

Still, my grip wasn't as steady as I wanted it to be.

"This is nice," I managed, though the words felt inadequate, trailing off into nothingness as I struggled to think of something else to say.

I felt my face warm as I realized he was watching me again.

"Are you feeling better?"

"Better?" I asked, confused.

He cleared his throat, taking a slow sip of his drink. The way his lips barely touched the glass—delicate, controlled—was mesmerizing. Like a scene straight out of a movie.

"The airport," he clarified.

My eyes widened. "I didn't think you'd remember that."

He chuckled. "I always remember a pretty face."

I sat upright, bringing the bottle to my lips to hide my smile. "You've seen quite a few, then?"

"None have been in my memory as much as yours, Red."

My stomach flipped. *Oh, he was smooth.*

"Flattery will get you everywhere," I murmured.

He chuckled, his eyes crinkling with amusement, dimples deepening on his cheeks.

"Jokes aside, though—are you better?" His voice was softer now, laced with something real. Genuine.

I exhaled slowly, nodding. "That was so embarrassing," I admitted. "But, yes. I'm better."

"You were upset and showed emotion," he noted, tone calm and matter-of-fact. "There's nothing embarrassing about that."

He was right, but I rarely let my emotions show—especially in public.

"Thank you for that," I replied, my voice softer now, more relaxed. "Sure you're not sparing my feelings?"

"Lying isn't my thing." His steady gaze locked onto mine, and something about the weight of it made my heart stutter.

I tried to hold his gaze, but my cheeks warmed again. "I've heard that before."

"You've never heard it from me," he countered, a sly grin tugging at his lips. "So, it counts, right?"

Ridiculous. This was ridiculous. I didn't even know his name, and yet my pulse was doing a whole damn sprint.

Focus, Abigail.

"Your girlfriend must adore you," I blurted, unable to stop myself.

He adjusted his glasses, scanning the room with an exaggerated glance. "I don't see her, do you?"

His lips curled into a teasing smile, but his voice dropped just slightly when he added, "And if I had a girlfriend, I wouldn't be anywhere near another woman—let alone spending my Friday night in a club, Red."

I blinked. *Okay, damn.*

"No girlfriend?" I mused. "You don't seem like the single type."

He arched his brow. "What type do I seem like, then?"

My stomach twisted as I scrambled for a reply. Before I could recover, he leaned in slightly, his grin turning more playful.

"I'm not the type to settle for less than what I want." His gaze locked onto mine, slow and deliberate. "And what I want is to spend the rest of my night with the beautiful woman in front of me."

My breath hitched.

Oh.

Well.

Shit.

He sat back, picking up his drink again, clearly enjoying my reaction. "So, no girlfriend," he added, taking a slow, casual sip.

Trying to steer the conversation away from my reckless thoughts, I asked, "Do you… own here?"

He shook his head. "Dillon does. I own a luxury transport service."

Hot, Hispanic, and an entrepreneur? Great. As if he wasn't already unfairly attractive.

"So, is this your ideal Friday night?" I asked, curiosity creeping into my voice. "Hanging out at a club?"

He tilted his head slightly, considering my question. "Not exactly my usual scene," he admitted. "I'm just here for moral support." His fingers tapped against his glass, his lips curving. "And a good drink while he does business."

Yeah, business *clearly* named Azzaria Jane Willis.

I leaned in a little, letting the dim lighting mask the smirk tugging at my lips. "Sounds like a lot of dedication."

His eyes sparkled with mischief as he met my gaze. His next shrug was slower, more deliberate. "Dedication?" he echoed, his voice dipping just enough to add a flirtatious edge. "I just enjoy good company."

I raised an eyebrow. "Good company?"

He chuckled softly, leaning back, his elbow resting lazily on the sofa's arm. "I'm here talking to you, aren't I?" His gaze flickered down, tracking the lazy circle my finger made against my thigh before lifting back to my face. His next words were smoother than silk. "I'd say that's a pretty clear sign."

The heat rose in my cheeks, but I played it off with a light laugh, refusing to let him know he was getting to me. "You're smooth," I admitted, shaking my head as I took a sip of my drink. "Is that how you get your clients? Or is this just for me?"

His grin widened, flashing just enough teeth to be dangerous. *God help me.*

"You think I talk to my clients like this?" He gave a mock look of offense. "You must have me confused with someone else." Then, he leaned in closer, his voice dropping into a deeper, more intimate tone.

"You say that to all the girls, don't you?"

"You're a woman," he corrected smoothly. "Not a girl."

The word struck like a spark—sharp, deliberate, and electrifying. It hung between us, sending a slow, unexpected heat curling in my stomach. There was something about the way he said it—steady, laced with a hint of admiration—that made me feel seen in a way I hadn't in far too long.

"But to answer your question," he murmured, his eyes holding mine hostage, "only the ones I meet in airports."

A thrill sparked down my spine. *Oh, hell.*

"You must meet plenty of girls—I mean women—in airports, then?" I asked, trying to keep my voice even as my pulse raced.

He shook his head slowly, a half-smile tugging at the corner of his mouth. "Just an unforgettable redhead I saw three weeks ago—about 5'5", striking green eyes, a sprinkle of freckles—five or six at most, and a floral maxi dress."

My breath hitched as the memory crashed over me.

He remembered everything.

Not just the moment—*me*. My height, my clothes, my eyes, even the freckles I barely acknowledged myself.

This wasn't just flirting.

This was far more dangerous.

"Unforgettable redhead, huh?" I murmured, meeting his gaze with a flirtatious smile, even as my heart hammered in my chest. "Lucky me."

"Luck?" He gave a slow shake of his head, his voice dipping just enough to draw me in. "Nah. I'd say blessed."

With a tap of his glass on the table, my thoughts scattered.

"Right," I whispered, trying to get a grip.

"Do you work?" he asked casually, but the way his gaze locked onto mine made it impossible to focus on the question itself.

"I'm almost done with school."

His expression shifted—just barely, but enough for me to catch it. A flicker of something unreadable. Was that… shock? Did he think I was younger? How old was he?

He couldn't be over twenty-six—not with that face, or that body.

"I'm twenty-three, by the way," I added quickly, hoping to clarify.

His eyes flickered, an emotion passing too fast for me to catch. Relief? Amusement?

"And you?" I asked, aiming for casualness, though my pulse pounded harder than it should. "How old are you?"

He hesitated. His gaze dropped to his glass, then lifted back to mine.

"Thirty-three."

Thirty-three.

The number settled between us, heavier than I expected. A ten-year gap. Was that supposed to bother me? Maybe. But somehow… it didn't.

He watched me carefully, the playful glint in his eyes momentarily replaced by something more serious.

"Is that okay with you?" His voice was lower now, cautious. "If you're not comfortable, we don't have to continue this conversation."

The question caught me off guard. There was something rare in his tone—*vulnerability.*

Most guys his age would brush off concerns, assuming they knew best. But him? He was giving me a choice. *And damn, that was unfairly attractive.*

A slow smile crept onto my lips. "It doesn't bother me." I held his gaze, steady. "Besides, if I did have a problem with it, I wouldn't still be sitting here, would I?"

His shoulders relaxed, and the corner of his mouth curved into that devastatingly charming smile again.

"Fair point. But I just wanted to make sure you're comfortable, Red."

Something fluttered in my chest. He just kept making himself more attractive, and that was going to be a problem.

I leaned forward slightly, a spark of boldness flickering through me. "I'm comfortable. Maybe we can get back to enjoying this conversation."

He watched me for a beat, then took another slow sip from his glass. When he set it down, the glint in his eyes was back, sharp and playful.

"So, Red," he murmured, tilting his glass toward me. "What's your major?"

"Real estate and business, with some electives in architecture."

He nodded, clearly impressed. "My sister's a realtor. She enjoys it for the most part. Sounds like you've already got your path figured out."

I let out a soft laugh, taking a sip of water. "Congrats to her. I wish I had it all figured out, but hey, I've made it this far. That counts for something, right?"

His gaze softened, locking onto mine. "It counts for *everything*. You should be proud of yourself." His voice was warm, reassuring. "Final year?"

"Yep. Did you go to university?"

He chuckled, leaning in slightly. "My parents would've had a heart attack if I didn't. I have my bachelor's and master's in business."

I tilted my head, intrigued. "How'd you know I was going to ask what you studied?"

He shrugged, an effortless smile curving his lips. "Just a hunch."

"Good guess."

"I'm good at reading people." His gaze didn't waver. "Especially when I'm interested."

I bit my lip, warmth flooding through me. Was it normal to feel this drawn to someone I barely knew? Probably not. But after weeks of stress and exhausting exams, this was the most at peace I'd felt in a while.

"Your accent…" I trailed off, eyes searching his. "Where's it from?"

"Dominican Republic." He paused. "Wasn't sure if you'd notice."

"Very noticeable." I leaned in just a fraction, caught in the way his presence filled the space between us. "Are you fluent?"

A mischievous glint appeared in his eyes. "*No lo sé, ¿verdad?*"[1]

The words rolled off his tongue, smooth and rich, sending an unexpected thrill down my spine.

Dear God. Why was this turning me on?

I swallowed hard, steadying myself. "I'll take that as a yes."

"Bingo." He grinned, his confidence unwavering. "I grew up there. Moved to California when I was about nine. English was a challenge at first, but I figured it out."

"Do you still speak Spanish often?"

"When I'm upset or with my family. They insist on it."

"Learning quite a lot about you tonight, aren't I?"

His lips curved, slow and deliberate, as he slid off his glasses, locking eyes with me.

"I don't mind. I've got interesting company."

Before I could respond, a guy—who almost resembled the one from the entrance—walked up and murmured something in his ear. I couldn't make out the words, but I caught one: Mikkel.

Of course. The hot stranger had a name just as devastating.

His expression shifted, more serious now as he turned back to me. "That's my cue to leave, Red. You're good company, and if you forget everything else I said tonight, don't forget this."

I blinked up at him. "Huh?"

His gaze softened. He leaned in, his voice dropping just enough to make my pulse skip. "Whoever or whatever made you cry isn't worth a

---

1 *I don't know, do I?*

single tear. And they sure as hell don't deserve to be in your life."

That made my night. Possibly my whole damn month.

He pulled his keys from his pocket and walked out—practically gliding through the door.

So fucking unreal.

So goddamn majestic.

I downed the rest of my water, sitting there, letting the music soak in, trying—and failing—to wipe the Mikkel-induced smile off my face.

I couldn't forget this night.

I couldn't forget our conversation.

I couldn't forget him.

Oh, this wasn't gonna end well.

CHAPTER THREE

Mikkel

"The soul always knows what to do to heal itself. The challenge is to silence the mind."
~ Caroline Myss

R*ed.*

Those striking green eyes I had the privilege of gazing into Friday night.

That captivating woman I'd had the pleasure of seeing not once, but twice.

Que Dios me ayude[1].

The black fitted romper hugged her in all the right places—a masterpiece of temptation. The fabric clung like a second skin, tracing every curve and dip with maddening precision. She was perfection—art in a museum I had no right to admire. But that didn't stop me.

---

1 *God help me*

Then there was her hair—a fiery halo of deep copper-platinum curls, pulled into a loose bun, stray strands teasing the nape of her neck. I spent hours last night scrolling through Pinterest and Google, searching for the perfect shade. I couldn't get it out of my head—the most stunning color I'd ever seen, on the most beautiful woman I'd ever laid eyes on.

And her skin. Rich. Dark. Luminous. The contrast against the black romper was breathtaking, her beauty timeless. Untouchable. My glasses weren't enough to frame the sight of her; she was a masterpiece, and I was helpless—completely undone by the very thought of her.

I couldn't stop thinking about her all weekend. Each rep at the gym felt heavier. Her laughter echoed in my mind, throwing off my rhythm. At the office, I caught myself staring out the window, wondering if I'd ever see her again. Even while cooking, the scent of rosemary and thyme reminded me of her—but no meal could compare to those fleeting moments with her.

The weekend slipped through my fingers like sand, and now, as Monday morning dawned, memories of her clung to me, igniting a quiet, reckless hope that I'd see her again.

My phone buzzed incessantly, snapping me out of it. The group chat. Unsurprisingly, Arnoldo and Ronan were already bickering.

Reyes
When are we hanging out again?

Alex
Ask Ronan. he's too busy being a hero.

Ro
My apologies for saving lives. Won't happen again.

Me
When you aren't saving lives, you're soul searching in Italy.

Ro
stronzo.

Luci
dio mio.

Dill
Why are you all awake so early?

Ro
Why are you still in bed, Mr. Busy?

Dill
One night out drained my social battery. Need a week to recover.

And there it was, the goddamn catalyst. One message was all it took for everyone to start typing.

Alex
you willingly went out?

Ro
what?

Reyes
I'm on my way to your house.

Luci
what a revelation.

Dill
Everyday I contemplate muting or exiting this chat.

If you all must know, I went to have a drink with Mikkel.

Dill
Arnoldo, don't come to my house; I don't want to see you.

Reyes
I love you too, and I'm still stopping by.

Dill
Wouldn't be Arnoldo Reyes if you didn't.

Ro
I love you, Arnoldo.

Dill
Is this your attempt to get attention?

Ro
fuck off.

Reyes
Yes, Ronan. I love you too.

Ro
great. just checking and including myself.

Alex
what about me? do i not deserve love?

Luci
do not enable them, Alexander.

I chuckled at the banter, knowing that beneath the jests lay genuine affection among us.

We met in university, thrown together as roommates by chance. At first, it was chaos—Dillon, the quiet thinker; Ronan, the heart; Arnoldo, the blunt realist; Lucio, the ghost who barely spoke; and Alex, the self-appointed 'dad' of the group. And me? The adaptable one. The perfectionist. The one who never said no. Somehow, that messy start turned into something unshakable—*brotherhood*.

I pushed the silk sheets aside as sunlight poured through the windows of my penthouse at Central Park Tower. Every corner was filled with white and cream—from the marble countertops to the thick rugs underfoot—offering rare moments of calm in a life that never slowed. The view of Central Park shifted with the seasons, always changing yet somehow constant.

After a quick shower, I threw on a white shirt and jeans, running a hand through my hair as I moved through the kitchen. The cool marble under my fingertips helped steady me for a moment, clearing my head before the day began.

Just as I was about to leave, my phone buzzed—Dillon asking if I could stop by later. I sent a quick reply and headed out, ready to see Alex.

"Good morning, Mara," I greeted chirpily, my face breaking into a bright smile.

Mara Xander-Williams—Alexander's wife, Dillon's sister, and a surrogate sister to the rest of us.

"Mikkel!" she exclaimed, her face lighting up as she walked over to me. "I had no idea you were coming today! How are you?"

"I thought Alex would've told you, but I'm good. How are you?"

"I'm great," she said, her hand instinctively resting on her baby bump.

"Thought Alex would've told you what?" Alex asked, stepping into the room.

Alexander Williams—a tall, handsome figure with a warm smile that reached his dark brown eyes.

"Told Mara I was coming over."

He shrugged, heading for the fridge.

"Want anything, angel?" His voice was soft with affection, his gaze fixed on her like she was the only person in the room.

She shook her head gently. "No, thank you. I'll make lunch after my nap."

"I'll make lunch. Get some rest," he replied, his tone firm yet tender.

She rolled her eyes, a playful smirk on her lips. "Pregnancy doesn't mean incapability."

"True," he agreed, his expression softening with a gentle smile, "but I'm here to take any and every form of pressure off you. Take your nap."

"Ugh," she groaned, but there was a hint of pleasure in her voice. "But Alex, I ca-"

"I'll take you shopping after your nap."

Her face lit up. "At Hudson Yards?"

"Anywhere you want, angel," he confirmed, his eyes twinkling.

"Want anything, Suarez?" Alex asked as Mara headed upstairs.

"Whiskey, thanks."

He poured a drink, and we made our way to the living room.

"You good?" I asked, noticing the uncertainty in his expression. Something was off.

He exhaled, clearly frustrated.

"I'll take that as a no. What happened?"

"Mara's smiling, but trust me, it's just a cover for the crime she's plotting." Alex exhaled, rubbing a hand over his face. "I swear, one of these days, I'm waking up with a pillow over my head because my schedule is only getting worse."

He took a sip of his scotch, and only then did I realize we were drinking before midday.

"Have you told her about it yet?"

He took a slow sip of his drink. "Not yet."

"Didn't you just get back from a trip?"

He nodded. "I got in this morning around three, and Mara had a few unpleasant words to exchange with me. I didn't even get a welcome home kiss."

"Yikes." I winced. "That doesn't sound great."

He let out a sigh, rubbing the back of his neck. "She's been upset at everything lately, and I can't blame her."

I leaned back, eyebrows raised. "Everything? Or just you being gone all the time?"

He ran a hand through his hair, clearly worn out. "A little of both. She's frustrated I'm not around, but it's not like I can just snap my fingers and fix it."

"Have you thought about scaling back?" I asked. "You've been flying nonstop for years. Maybe it's time to take a breather."

He chuckled dryly, shaking his head. "Scaling back would mean leaving money on the table. Not happening."

"You're rich, Alex. Money isn't everything," I said pointedly. "Your marriage? Your son on the way? Those *should* be your priorities."

"They *are* my priorities," he admitted, his voice dropping. "But it's not that easy."

I whistled low. "You're playing with fire, Alexander."

He groaned. "Tell me about it."

I sipped my drink, considering him for a moment. "So, what's the plan? Besides getting yelled at and possibly murdered."

He hesitated, then smirked, a mischievous glint in his eye. "I'm buying the airline."

I choked on my drink, coughing as I set the glass down. Was he serious? Out of all the ways to fix a marriage, buying an entire airline was nowhere near the list of sane options.

"WHAT?"

"Look, it sounds crazy, I get it," he admitted, rubbing his jaw. "But I can't keep promising Mara I'll be home and then breaking that promise. If I control the damn thing, I can make sure I'm there when it matters."

I stared at him. "How much?"

"About forty million dollars," he admitted with a laugh. "But it's a long-term investment. I can restructure the flight rotations, make sure I'm home more often. Everybody wins."

"You think Mara's just going to forget about everything once you hand her an airline?"

He shrugged, that same smug grin tugging at his lips. "It's a start. Besides, this airline's been on my radar for a while now. The timing just lines up."

"When do you plan to tell her this?" I asked, raising an eyebrow.

He gave me a sheepish smile. "Once the deal is finalized. You know, save her the stress."

I stared at him, incredulous. "Yeah, because nothing says stress-free like dropping *'Angel, I bought an airline'* into casual conversation."

He laughed, the tension easing from his shoulders. "You think she'll be mad?"

"Mara's unpredictable," I smirked. "But if you play your cards right, it might just be the thing that saves your ass."

"I like your optimism."

I shook my head. "Only you would try to solve a marriage problem with a business acquisition."

He raised his glass. "They should name an award after me if this works."

He tapped his glass thoughtfully, then shifted the conversation. "How was Friday night with Dillon?"

I hesitated, then admitted, "I met someone." My voice wavered between excitement and hesitation, but the grin pulling at my lips gave me away.

"You meet people all the time. What's different now?" His tone was casual, but his raised brow told me he was already suspicious.

I leaned back, my gaze drifting. Copper curls. A quiet confidence. Unparalleled beauty. The way she looked at me like she saw right through the bullshit.

"I sat with her for about an hour. We talked, and…" I exhaled, shaking my head slightly. "I haven't stopped thinking about her since."

His eyes widened, curiosity flickering through his usual stoic demeanor. "What's her name? What does she look like? Did you get her number?"

The words tumbled out before I could stop them. "She's got this hair—fire and gold mixed together, like you can't look away. And her beauty…" I shook my head, a soft laugh escaping. "Man, she's breathtaking. I could listen to her talk for hours."

His expression turned pointed. "What's her name?"

I winced, scratching the back of my neck. "I don't know."

He blinked. "You *don't* know?"

"I don't know," I repeated, sharper now. "We started talking, got caught up, and before I knew it, we were interrupted."

Silence stretched between us before he asked, "Does she live in the city?"

"I don't know that either," I admitted. "I saw her at the airport three weeks ago, then again last weekend."

He stared at me like I'd lost my mind. "Three weeks ago? And you ran into her again? That's gotta be divine intervention."

"Maybe it is," I murmured, the thought oddly comforting.

"If she's in New York, there's a ninety-nine percent chance you'll see her again."

I clung to that number like a promise, even as doubt pressed in.

He let the silence linger, a smirk tugging at his lips. "Alright, lover boy, we'll call this fate. Now, I need a driver for Mara."

I blinked, switching gears. "A driver?"

He leaned back into his pristine white couch. "Someone safe. Reliable."

"All my employees are reliable, but I'll handle it." I already had the perfect person in mind.

His tone turned serious. "I don't doubt your business—it's number one in the damn state. I just need my wife protected."

"Consider it done." I laid out the process, and he nodded.

"All settled."

A glance at my watch—9:04 a.m. Time to get to work.

I left and headed to Lower Manhattan, where my empire awaited.

Elite Rides started with a bank loan and my parents' support, and now? A multi-billion-dollar enterprise, New York's leading luxury transport company. Two hundred and eighty drivers, reserves on standby—precision and efficiency at its core.

Stepping into my office, I acknowledged my staff with quick nods, keeping the momentum going.

Morison, my ever composed assistant, greeted me. "Good morning, Mr. Suarez."

"Morning. Let Sapphire know I need to see her."

Minutes later, she walked in, her posture crisp, her expression sharp.

"Good morning, Mr. Suarez," Sapphire Stone greeted, settling into the chair across from me. Tall, light brown hair, the backbone of operations. Without her, none of this ran smoothly.

"There's a request from Alexander Williams in the company email. I need you to handle it."

Sapphire nodded, handing me a thick brown spiral-bound folder. "These are thirty new applications that need vetting."

I flipped through the pages. "I'll get on it. Speaking of vetting, don't forget your trip to Chicago next week. We need to kick off the expansion integration, and I want you to assemble a solid team."

Her expression sharpened with focus. "I've been preparing. I'll finalize the itinerary and coordinate with the new hires to run the BETA system."

"Good. Mr. Reyes will be there for a day to assist with the transition. He knows Chicago better than anyone, so use his expertise."

"Already done, sir," she replied, her tone firm. "This is our chance to get the expansion off on the right foot."

"Perfect." My mind was already racing ahead. The stakes were higher than ever.

She gave a small nod before walking off, leaving me alone with the folder. I opened it, but my focus wavered. Exhaling sharply, I shoved it aside and pulled up the expansion details instead—numbers, logistics, projections. Every figure had to align, every risk accounted for. I scanned each line thrice, then again, hunting for gaps, errors—anything we might've missed.

I adjusted the papers, straightened the edges, and rechecked my calculations. *This has to work.*

Failure wasn't an option.

Then, it hit me—an invisible fist squeezing my chest, the weight pressing down. *What if this fell through?* The thought dug in, tightening its grip.

I reached for my phone. "Morison, push my meeting back. I need a few minutes."

He nodded and stepped out. The moment the door shut, I locked it. Slumping into my chair, I pressed trembling hands to my face. *Breathe.*

A sharp inhale. A slow exhale.

I wiped my face, forcing myself to get it together. *Focus.* I paced the room, deep breaths keeping the panic just barely at bay. It wasn't gone, but it was manageable. Just enough.

Straightening my shirt, I walked into the meeting, letting Morison take the lead. I nodded when necessary, my expression unreadable. But the weight never lifted.

By the time it ended, I needed an escape.

The gym. The only place where the pressure eased, even if just for a moment.

With each rep, each set, my pulse steadied. The tension unwound, little by little.

And then—*her.*

Copper platinum curls. A smile that wouldn't leave my mind.

Jasmine and amber, lingering in my senses.

Everything else faded. The gym, the weights, the pressure.

For one fleeting moment, there was only her.

WARNING

The following chapter contains heavy mentions of mental health/physical health issues. Please refer to the content warning list to be reminded of any potential triggers. Your well-being is important to me, so please take care of yourself while reading.

CHAPTER FOUR

Abigail-Ann

"We are shaped and fashioned by what we love."
~ Johann Wolfgang von Goethe

What was the saying? Ah, yes—*disappointed but not surprised.*

I sat in the living room, staring at the last message Joshua sent three weeks ago. No calls. No texts. Not even a simple: *Did you land safely?*

My sister, Aurora, had always told me one thing: Never let a man show you he doesn't want you more than once.

I should have listened.

Regret settled deep in my chest, the kind that felt like a weight pressing down on my ribs. My eyes burned, but then I remembered Mikkel's words.

"Whoever or whatever made you cry isn't worth it."

He was right. Joshua wasn't worth it.

Dr. Green, my therapist, always said that sometimes, happiness requires cutting people off. Maybe it was time I finally did.

"Abigail!" Auntie Leann's voice snapped me from my thoughts. I looked up at the woman who was practically Azzaria's twin.

"You look upset. Is everything alright?"

I nodded. "I just have something difficult to do."

She sat beside me, her voice gentle. "I know it's hard, but you're strong. It might hurt now, but you'll get through it."

I turned my phone toward her. "Do you think I should respond to this?"

She gasped, eyes widening. "I don't think he deserves a response. But do you?"

I shrugged. "I don't know."

She stood, grabbing her bag. "Then wait until you're sure. If you don't feel like talking to him until you get back to California, then don't. Do what makes *you* happy. He can go fuck himself."

A laugh bubbled out of me at her bluntness.

She kissed my forehead. "I love you, my dear Abigail. *Always.*"

As she left, clarity settled over me. I was done being afraid. Done wasting time on someone who barely cared if I existed.

Then, he returned to my mind—the man whose presence lingered like a melody I couldn't forget.

Every time I closed my eyes, Mikkel was there.

Tall. Imposing. That voice, smooth and deliberate, making every word sound like a promise. The way he looked at me—like I was someone—sent my heart into a sprint. And that cologne…spicy, warm, and all-consuming.

Curiosity got the best of me.

I didn't even know his last name, but a quick Google search for "luxury transport companies in New York City" gave me more than I expected.

His face was everywhere.

Mikkel Suarez.

Owner of Elite Rides, the top luxury transport company in New York. Billionaire. Businessman. And insanely fucking handsome.

How had I not known this?

I scrolled past article after article—interviews, business expansions, and, most surprisingly, not a single photo of him with a woman. My stomach twisted. This man wasn't just successful—he was one of the biggest names in the city.

Just as I was about to close the tab, my phone pinged.

Joshua.

Joshua
?

I sighed. Since I had already opened it, I decided to respond.

Me
What?

Joshua
I texted u like three weeks ago.

Me
And how was I supposed to respond?

Joshua
Idk. You could just answer.

Me
What do you want?

Joshua
Missed u, send tit pics.

I nearly gagged.

Me
You didn't even check to see if I landed safely, but now you're asking for nudes?

Joshua
?? That's what you're here for. Making me feel good. Are you planning to fail at that too?

The phone slipped from my hands. A single tear escaped.

"That's what you're there for."

"Are you planning to fail at that too?"

I thought he had broken all of me, but I was wrong.

Something else just shattered—something deeper, a part of me I didn't even know was left to break.

I felt useless. I felt disgusted. I felt fucking defeated.

Placing my phone on the table, my fingers trembled as I let it go. I sat there in complete silence. For an hour, maybe more, I just… shut down. I couldn't move. Couldn't think. Nothing.

The only thing I was certain of was how disrespected I felt. How utterly hollowed he'd left me. My stomach churned, nausea creeping in, but I swallowed it down. No tears came—maybe I was too broken to cry anymore. Or maybe I just refused to let him have that part of me too.

The hurt was overwhelming, crashing over me in waves. Every second that passed, it sank deeper into my bones. How little he thought of me. How he tore me apart and left me to pick up the shattered pieces, as if they were meaningless.

I forced myself to push it all aside, shoving the knot of frustration down. There'd be time to deal with all of that later—maybe. Right now, Azzaria had texted, asking me to meet her for drinks at Jimmy's Corner.

I needed the distraction as much as she did.

Whatever was weighing her down seemed heavy. Mine? Well, mine could sit in the dark a little while longer.

When I got there, she was already at the bar, downing shots like water. One after another, no pause, no hesitation.

"Keep them coming," she told the bartender, her voice laced with anger and something deeper, something sharper. *Desperation.*

Sliding onto the stool next to her, I studied her face. "I think you should do something else instead of drinking," I said cautiously, not wanting to come off as preachy but needing to say something.

She shrugged, her shoulders slumping as if the weight of the world had settled there. "Like what? I don't really have many other interests."

"What about that gym you used to go to? You were really into it before."

For a split second, nostalgia flickered across her face, but it faded just as quickly, replaced by regret.

"Yeah, it's still there, but I've got a teensy balance I need to clear off. Plus, you know I'm cutting expenses."

Her words settled uncomfortably in my chest.

I reached out, giving her hand a reassuring squeeze. "You should go back, even if it's just for a little while. I can help you out if you need it."

Her eyes darted toward me, wary. I added quickly, "Or maybe you could switch to a college plan? Most gyms have special rates for students."

"Maybe." Her tone was reluctant, her eyes still clouded with uncertainty.

"Good!" I grinned, trying to lift the mood, even if just a little. "It'll help you burn off all this pent-up anger and frustration. And trust me, you've got plenty of both right now."

That earned me a sigh and a faint, grudging smile. "Yeah, I guess it couldn't hurt to go back."

And then, she shrugged and downed another shot.

I gave her a moment before pressing. "What the hell happened today?"

She hesitated, but then the words spilled out anyway, raw and bitter.

"I apologized to him out of courtesy for Friday night. *You know what he told me?* That it was a mistake on both our parts and we should keep things professional."

She let out a bitter laugh, but her fingers clenched around her glass, knuckles turning white. For a second, I swore I saw something in her eyes—hurt, regret—but then she blinked it away, masking it with indifference.

"I don't even know why the fuck it bothers me."

Her words hit me like a sucker punch.

I froze, my grip tightening around the water bottle I didn't even remember picking up. *When did I even get this bottle?*

"You're lying," I blurted, disbelief ringing in my voice.

"Oh, I'm *very* serious."

"Are you sure he only said that because you apologized?" My heart pounded. "Why did you even say sorry?"

Mistakes? Every smile, every touch? *Bullshit.* No way in *hell.*

"Either way, it's not that serious," she said, licking the salt off the rim before downing another shot. "I just didn't expect that response from him."

"It's serious to you," I pointed out, my voice steady but insistent. "Because you enjoyed the conversation. And you like him."

"I *don't* like him," she shot back, glaring at me. "I'm *attracted* to him. I think he's hot."

I raised a brow. "What's the difference?"

She groaned, rolling her eyes. "Shut up." Her voice was sharp, but it lacked any real bite. Then, just like that, she pivoted. Azzaria Willis' classic deflection.

She tapped her nails against the shot glass, a telltale sign she was about to dodge something uncomfortable. Then, like clockwork—"Why aren't you doing an internship?"

"I did mine last semester," I said with a soft laugh despite the tension. "And when I suggested you do the same, you said you had all the time in the world."

She groaned again, this time at herself. "I can't believe I said that," she muttered, taking another sip of her drink. "Anyway, it's fine. How are you?"

That question, which I'd been dodging since I arrived, now hung between us, unavoidable.

How was I?

Hurt. Broken. Useless. Confused. Anxious.

But I couldn't say that. Not here. So I took a deep breath, swallowing the truth like a bitter pill. "I'm fine."

And just like that, I became a hypocrite.

She looked at me, lowering the shot glass from her lips. "I'm going to pretend you didn't lie to me. So I'll ask again, how are you?"

I exhaled, feeling the weight of her stare pressing into me. "Confused, mainly," I admitted, the words leaving me heavier than when I had started.

"About what?" she asked, her tone measured but edged with curiosity, like she already knew the answer but needed me to confirm it.

I hesitated, glancing at her glass, then at the chipped tabletop. "It's a long story."

She glanced up at the clock on the wall, then back at me with raised brows and a knowing smirk. "What a relief that time is all we have."

The corners of my lips twitched at her sarcasm, but the laughter in me was buried under layers of unease. With a deep inhale, I admitted, "It's Joshua." The name tumbled out like a stone, sharp and unyielding.

Her posture stiffened, and I saw the beginnings of anger bubbling beneath her calm expression. "What did that little bitch boy do now?"

I let out a hollow laugh, shaking my head. "He's being… very dictating. And rude," I muttered, my words reluctant, almost like I didn't want them to be real. "With the stuff he asks me to do."

Her brows furrowed instantly. "What kind of stuff?" she pressed, her tone protective but simmering with frustration.

I swallowed hard. My throat felt tight, like the words would suffocate me before I could get them out. "He asked me to send him *pictures*."

I tried to sound nonchalant, like it wasn't as big of a deal as it felt, but my voice betrayed me—shaky, strained.

Her expression darkened. "Wait. *Pictures*?" she echoed, voice colored with disbelief, tinged with disgust. "Of your p—"

"Yeah." I spat out bitterly, my lips curling like just the taste of the word was revolting.

Silence stretched between us, thick and heavy.

Then she leaned forward, her voice low, but the anger now unmistakable. "I'm so sorry you had to deal with that, but let's forget about Joshua. If you don't want to send him explicit pictures, then don't. No means no, and if he can't respect that, he's a piece of shit."

I clenched my fists under the table, nails pressing into my palms. My chest felt too tight, like my ribs were caging in something I couldn't quite name. It wasn't just disappointment—it was grief.

Azzaria's voice softened, but it held an edge of steel. "And if he ever makes you feel like your worth is tied to whether or not you send him pictures, then he's even worse than I thought."

I nodded, biting my cheek to stay composed. "It's just very disappointing." My voice cracked, and I hated how weak it sounded, how vulnerable I felt.

"Five years down the drain, you know?"

I sighed.

Five years of love, loyalty, waiting for him to treat me like I mattered. Five years of thinking I was building something real, only to realize I was the only one putting in the effort.

"I get it," she said softly, sliding her glass of alcohol toward me. "But look at it this way—you're basically done with him. We're going to make the most of our time here before you leave. We'll document everything, find you a great man. Not a boy—*a man.*"

A small laugh broke through my lips.

"And most importantly," she continued, a smirk playing at her lips, "you'll discover who you are and realize how incredible you are, with or without anyone."

I exhaled, the tightness in my chest loosening ever so slightly. Maybe she was right. Maybe, for the first time in years, I had the chance to finally be me.

And maybe that was worth more than any relationship ever could be.

"Are we really?" I asked, doubt clinging to my words like smoke.

"Yes, we are," Azzaria declared, her confidence so unwavering, so genuine, that for a moment, I wanted to believe her. "Nobody messes with my best friend and gets away with it. You deserve the sun, the moon, and the fucking stars, Abigail."

A small smile tugged at my lips, gratitude unfurling in my chest. "Are we going to find you a man too?" I teased, my voice lighter now, even though the ache still lingered beneath the surface.

She chuckled, rolling her eyes. "Let's not get ahead of ourselves."

And then I froze.

The faintest hint of fresh wood, warm ambergris, and spicy cedarwood curled into my lungs, rich and familiar. My skin prickled, as if someone had whispered my name in the dark.

It was him.

"The special for Mr. Xander and Suarez, please," a deep, velvety voice spoke, smooth yet rugged, laced with an accent that sent a shiver down my spine.

I turned slowly, my pulse thrumming wildly.

Mikkel.

His honey-brown eyes locked onto mine, and in an instant, the noise of the bar faded into a dull hum, the world dimming at the edges. That grin—equal parts mischievous and devastating—spread across his face, knocking the air straight out of my lungs.

"Hey there, gorgeous," he greeted, his voice low and warm, like a secret meant only for me.

Heat flooded my cheeks. I felt them flush, a shade so bright it could rival the setting sun. My lips parted, but for the first time in a long time, words failed me. He was standing here—again—like some sort of cosmic joke. Or maybe… fate.

Before I could lose myself completely, I noticed Azzaria.

Her head was down on the table, her entire posture screaming: *don't look at me*. My brows furrowed as my gaze followed hers.

A man. Staring at her from across the bar.

Not just a man. Her boss.

What the fuck?

So much for Friday night being a mistake.

I barely had time to process before Mikkel's voice pulled me back.

"Three times in one month…" His smirk was lethal, cocky and lazy in a way that made my pulse stumble. He leaned in just slightly, eyes locked on mine like he could hear every single thought in my head. "Are you following me, Red?"

I recovered fast, arching a brow. "I should be asking if you're the one following me."

His laugh—*deep, rich, intoxicating*—wrapped around me like warm silk. My body betrayed me, leaning closer without permission, as if gravity itself had shifted in his direction.

"If only, Red." His voice dropped just a fraction, something unreadable flickering in his gaze. "If only."

I opened my mouth to respond, but before I could, a hand clamped around my arm.

Azzaria.

"Let's go. Now."

Her voice was tight, urgent. Her fingers dug in, her eyes flickering toward her boss like he was a hunter and she, his prey.

I didn't want to leave. Not with the warmth of Mikkel's laugh still brushing against my skin. Not with his gaze still holding mine like I was the only person in this room.

But I had to.

For the third time, I left without a proper goodbye, rushing with Azzaria through the evening crowd, heart pounding, Mikkel's scent and voice lingering long after we disappeared into the first taxi we could find.

CHAPTER FIVE

Mikkel

"If one day the moon calls you by your name don't be surprised, because every night I tell her about you."
~ Shahrazad al-Khalij

You've got to be fucking kidding me.

One minute, I was in my office, fine-tuning a contract. Dillon and Arnoldo sat before me, bickering as usual, their voices blending into an unintelligible hum. The next thing I knew, Dillon and I were speeding through the city, tailing a cab his intern was in.

I should have questioned it. I should have told Dillon he was being fucking ridiculous. But I didn't.

Because the second I saw her, I forgot about everything else.

Red.

That fiery copper-platinum hair. The kind that made her impossible to miss, impossible to forget. My chest tightened, my steps quickening as if drawn by some invisible force. And then I heard it—her voice. Melodic. Hypnotic. It twisted something inside me, something I didn't have time to figure out.

And just like that, she was gone. Again.

The moment shattered too fast, slipping through my fingers like every other time we crossed paths. It was starting to feel like a cruel fucking joke.

Dillon kept talking beside me, his tone laced with frustration and uncertainty. He was fixated on his intern, trying to work through whatever the hell he was feeling. "Show her you're human," I muttered, barely paying attention. "Drop the grumpy asshole act and make her feel safe."

His eyes tracked the cab like a man watching something slip away, and I almost laughed. Look at us. Two men standing in the middle of the street, watching women disappear into the evening, wondering what the hell just happened.

But I wasn't focused on Dillon.

I was thinking about her—the way her cheeks flushed when I called her gorgeous. The way she smiled, wrecking me in the process.

I barely made it through the rest of my day, and week to an extent. Board meetings dragged on, filled with the same repetitive bullshit: projections, strategies, arguments over numbers. I powered through, but my mind wasn't in it. Not completely.

By the time I was done, I needed a damn break.

A text from Arnoldo reminded me about game night at Dillon's. I should have asked him to reschedule, but instead, I ended up walking through Hudson Yards with Alexander.

What was supposed to be a quick trip stretched into nearly two hours of aimless wandering. My patience ran thinner with each passing minute, but at least I walked away with a new Patek watch. A small victory.

Alexander, on the other hand, still had nothing.

"We've been walking for two hours," I said, exasperated. "And you still haven't bought Mara's gift."

He let out a long sigh, rubbing a hand over his face. "She has a list, but I need to think outside the box."

I eyed him, considering his words. "You know your wife best. Let's look at it this way." I paused, waiting for him to meet my gaze. "What have you already planned? Once we see what you've got, we can figure out what's missing."

Alexander nodded slowly, mulling over my words.

He opened his notes and read aloud, "Floral arrangements—five thousand dandelions—arriving by eight. Private brunch at Sea Gate Beach. Oh, and I bought her a vacation home in Bali because she likes the sunsets. Then we'll be back in time for her birthday party."

I blinked. "A vacation home?"

Alexander looked up, unbothered. "Every time we travel somewhere she loves, I get her a place there."

"Husband of the century," I muttered.

He laughed, but the gleam in his eyes told me he was dead serious. "As long as it makes her happy. But I still need to get her something else."

I thought for a second. "Book a spa appointment at Lucio's spa upstairs. And if you want, make it a couple's thing."

A deep sigh left him, one of pure contentment. "Great idea, but I'll make it all about her. She deserves it. Carrying a baby is no joke." Then, his gaze sharpened, his lips tugging into a smirk. "You'll see what I mean once you hit it off with the redhead." He nudged my shoulder playfully.

A grin pulled at my lips despite myself. Her image flashed across my mind, unbidden. "Her hair is copper platinum, not red."

Alex's brows shot up. "And how do you know that if you've only spoken to her twice?"

"Three times," I corrected. "I saw her earlier this week, but our conversation got cut short." My voice dropped slightly. "And I know because it's impossible to forget a color like that. Or a woman like that."

His smirk deepened. "Three times? And something interrupts every time?"

"At this rate, I might have to start hanging out at bars, clubs and airports more often."

His teasing faded, replaced by something quieter—curiosity. "What is it about her?" He tilted his head, watching me closely. "I get that you're attracted to her, but do you actually know her?"

"All I know," I admitted, "is that I want to."

Alex studied me in silence, brow furrowed. "Isn't that a bit risky?"

"Maybe," I said, voice softer. "But isn't everything worth having a little risk? I don't know her yet, but I can't get her out of my head."

His expression turned thoughtful. "If you had the chance, would you take it?"

I nodded without hesitation. "Why let it slip through my fingers?"

"Good point," he said, then exhaled, running a hand down his face. "Just promise me you'll be careful with your heart."

A faint smile tugged at my lips. "Someone's worried about me."

He rolled his eyes. "When your thirty-three-year-old best friend hasn't had any romantic action in nearly a *decade*, worry's inevitable."

I placed a hand on his shoulder. "Love you too, Alex."

Arnoldo leaned back in the chair, a nostalgic smile playing on his lips as he poured himself a glass of gin. "What a life we're living."

We gathered in Dillon's living room for our usual hangout, the atmosphere relaxed despite Ronan and Lucio's absence.

"Lucky bastards, the lot of us," Alex chimed in, raising his glass.

Dillon turned to him, curiosity in his gaze. "Are you ready for fatherhood?"

Alex took a slow, deliberate sip. "I don't think I'll ever be ready, but I'll wake up every day trying."

Arnoldo's expression softened. "I've always wanted a kid, you know? Never really worked out that way for me."

I smirked, reaching for a handful of pretzels. "I wonder why."

Arnoldo frowned. "I'm not following."

In unison, we all chimed in, "Manwhore."

He threw up his hands. "Raise your hand if you've only slept with one woman," he challenged.

No one moved.

"Unfair question," Dillon said with a smirk.

"What's unfair is picking on me because I'm open about it," Arnoldo argued.

Dillon arched an eyebrow. "Maybe you could be more discreet."

Arnoldo scoffed. "Mikkel sleeps around, so does Ronan, even you, Dillon."

"Fuck off, Reyes," I said, rolling my eyes. "Not that it's any of your business, but I've been celibate for years."

"That's true," Alex added.

"Vouching for him?" Dillon and Arnoldo asked in unison.

"Always," Alex smirked. "Jealous?"

"Of course I am. Times like these, I miss Lucio," Arnoldo muttered. "He would've been on my side."

Alex laughed. "Sure, he would've."

Dillon took a slow sip of his scotch. "I'm not interested in sleeping around anymore."

Arnoldo shrugged. "How convenient."

Their bickering faded into the background as I leaned back, absentmindedly tracing the rim of my glass. The noise around me dulled, replaced by the image of her.

Next time, I had to get her name.

"Suarez," Alex's voice cut through my thoughts.

I blinked, clearing my throat. "*Qué*?"[1]

---

1 *What*

"We've been calling you. What's on your mind?"

Arnoldo smirked. "Or should we say, who's on your mind?"

I rolled my eyes. "*Métanse en sus propios asuntos.*"[2]

They exchanged a look, clearly not buying it but letting it go. For now.

"You know what I think about often?" Arnoldo blurted.

"What?" we asked in unison.

"Mara," he said, lifting his glass for a slow sip. "I fee—"

Alex straightened, eyes narrowing. "Should I be concerned that you're thinking about *my pregnant wife*?"

Arnoldo sighed, waving off his concern. "You didn't let me finish, dumbass. I was saying I think about how you married her."

I tilted my head. "I'm not following."

Arnoldo exhaled sharply. "*Idiotas*[3]. I mean, wasn't there a rule about best friends and their sisters?"

"There is," Dillon said, swirling his drink. "But this is Alex. As annoyed as I was, he met Mara when he was celibate in his twenties. Not much to worry about."

Arnoldo and I burst into laughter as Alex's face turned slightly pink. "And yet, here I am—happily married to the most gorgeous woman on the planet, with a baby on the way."

"Would it weird you out?" Dillon asked suddenly, shifting the conversation with a glance in my direction.

I frowned. "What?"

"If one of your best friends dated your sister," he clarified.

A shudder ran through me. "I don't even want to think about Emilia with Arnoldo." The thought alone made my skin crawl.

Arnoldo raised his hands in mock surrender, but the mention of my sister clearly unsettled him. "Why me—oh, right. Everyone else is taken." He leaned back with a smirk.

There was a beat of silence before we all cracked up.

---

2 *Mind your own business*

3 *Idiots*

Alex shook his head, exasperation laced with amusement. "You guys are ridiculous."

"Anyway," I said, steering the conversation away. "What are we playing?"

"Poker. You in?" Alex asked, mischief glinting in his eyes.

I shrugged, settling back in my chair. "Why not?"

Dillon shuffled the deck with practiced ease. "Alright, ante up—one grand, winner takes all."

Arnoldo scoffed. "What if I'm broke?"

Laughter erupted.

"Then you wouldn't be Arnoldo Reyes," I shot back.

Arnoldo grinned. "Fair enough. Let's make it two grand. I'm feeling lucky."

"Deal." We all tossed in our money, and the game began.

As the night wore on, the stakes climbed, and tension rose and fell with each hand.

"*Maldita sea*,[4]" Arnoldo muttered, glaring at his dwindling stack of chips. His frustration was palpable and hilarious. "I'm getting slaughtered here."

"Luck running out?" I teased, earning a sharp glare from Arnoldo.

Across the table, Dillon smirked, his chip stack growing. "Looks like Lady Luck's on my side tonight."

I chuckled, trying to ease the tension. "Relax, Reyes. Plenty of game left—anything can happen."

"Bullshit," Dillon scoffed. "He's just a sore loser."

Arnoldo let out a frustrated sigh. "*Joder esto*,[5]" he muttered, raking a hand through his hair.

What a group of friends I had. And the funniest part? This would've been even more chaotic if Ronan and Lucio were here.

---

4 *Damn it*

5 *Fuck this*

WARNING

The following chapter contains heavy mentions of mental health/physical health issues. Please refer to the content warning list to be reminded of any potential triggers. Your well-being is important to me, so please take care of yourself while reading.

CHAPTER SIX

Abigail-Ann

"The greatest thing you'll ever learn is just to love and be loved in return."
~ Nat King Cole

F*ailure is not an option.*

The words looped in my mind, tight as a noose. I had chosen this path, and my future depended on passing this exam. It was either a 3.8 or higher GPA, or nothing. But as I sat surrounded by the chaos of textbooks, half-eaten bags of barbecue Lays, and scattered notes, it was hard to believe.

The storm of my final exam loomed heavily, and the marketing and finance course was tearing me apart. My mind, though, refused to cooperate, drifting far from the papers and formulas spread out before me.

Joshua's name flashed on my phone screen again: *Text me back, I miss you.* More pleas for attention I kept ignoring. It wasn't guilt that kept me from replying. It was exhausting. The kind that settled in my bones after years of feeling unseen, unheard. It was as if he thought I was a switch he could turn on and off whenever it suited him.

I stared at the screen, my thumb hovering over the reply button before shaking my head and tossing my phone aside. I wasn't going to do a back-and-forth with him again.

I wasn't supposed to be thinking about Mikkel. But he had a way of slipping in anyway. His face, his laugh, his voice—everything played on a loop in my head.

What was it about him that made me want to see him again? Maybe it was the way he looked at me, as if he truly saw me, or his deep, rumbling laugh that felt like sunlight breaking through my storms. Or maybe it was how his words brought out a smile—not polite or forced, but one that felt like it was meant to stay.

I sighed and ran a hand over my face, trying to shake him off. *God, just focus on something else.* But even as I tried to block the thoughts, they lingered, like the smell of fresh rain on a summer night—impossible to forget.

Did he think of me too? That question, so simple but so frustrating, buzzed in my mind. Did he replay our encounters the same way I did? Were his thoughts just as tangled? I felt myself getting lost in the idea of him, and it was maddening. Especially when I had Joshua's texts sitting there, unanswered, taunting me.

This felt so wrong, so complicated—but I couldn't seem to stop myself.

What kind of person did that make me? Daydreaming about some sexy stranger I'd spoken to only thrice while ignoring my "boyfriend's" attempts to get my attention? The logical side of me screamed to snap out of it, to stop letting my thoughts drift. Joshua and I had been together for almost six years, and while the spark was as dead as a doornail, we still hadn't ended things—not yet. But here I was, fantasizing about someone else—and it felt so good.

Maybe this was the beginning of something I didn't even understand. *I really need a distraction.*

But oh wait, I was supposed to be studying.

Focus, Abigail.

With a heavy sigh, I glanced at my notes filled with market analysis and investment strategies as they blurred together. Highlighting key phrases to ground myself, I spent the rest of the night trying to master the course.

At least, that's what I told myself.

I awoke to the sound of Azzy crowing the lyrics of "Uh Oh" by Tate McRae. My head throbbed, my body heavy with exhaustion, but the relentless singing gave me no choice but to pry my eyes open. Rubbing the sleep away, I forced myself out of bed, dragged my feet to the bathroom, and brushed my teeth before making my way to the kitchen—where Azzy's voice only seemed to grow louder by the second.

"Morning, Azzy," I mumbled around a yawn. "You're suspiciously happy. Should I be worried?"

She twirled around, beaming. "Good morning! Did I wake you? I'm leaving in ten minutes, and no, you don't need to worry."

I chuckled, reaching for a bottle of water. "Your crowing is quite the alarm."

"*Crowing?* Rude." Azzy grinned, but her expression softened. "Sorry, though. I know you were up studying late last night. Good luck with your exam today."

"Thanks," I said, cracking open the bottle. "And remember, I'm leaving this weekend."

"Ugh. I wish you could stay forever." She groaned, glancing at her phone. "I've got to go, but we'll definitely talk later. I love you."

"Love you too!" I called after her as she hurried out the door.

The second she was gone, the weight in my chest returned. A tight, suffocating knot that made every breath feel just a little too shallow.

I knew what I had to do this weekend. The decision had been made. But that didn't make it any easier. The thought of it pulled me down like a rock sinking to the bottom of the ocean. No matter how much I braced myself, the anxiety still clawed at my ribs, my brain already spiraling through every possible outcome.

Breaking up with someone after years together—years that had shaped so much of who I was—wasn't just difficult; it felt like an unraveling. Like stepping off a ledge and not knowing if there would be anything to catch me.

I pressed my palms against the counter, my fingers curling against the cool surface as I inhaled deeply. The dread wasn't about losing him—I'd checked out long ago. It was the uncertainty that followed. What did this mean for my future? What if I never found someone who truly loved me? What if I ended up alone? My thoughts tangled together, looping into a cycle of worst-case scenarios. My chest grew tight, my pulse hammering, my stomach twisting into knots that refused to unravel.

Stop. Breathe. Focus.

I squeezed my eyes shut and exhaled slowly, forcing myself to pull away from the spiral. There were things I had control over, and right now, that was my exam. I had studied all night for it, and no amount of anxiety was going to make me fail.

Pushing past the nerves, I grabbed my bag and hurried out the door, my mind still buzzing as I made my way to NYU. The city blurred around me, my brain too consumed with overanalyzing everything to process my surroundings.

By the time I sat down in the exam room, my heart was already racing. My fingers curled around my pen, too tight, my breath short and uneven. The questions stared back at me, the letters almost blurring together as my mind blanked for a terrifying second.

This is it. What if you fail? What if you read the questions wrong? What if—

I clenched my jaw, forcing myself to take another breath. I had studied for this. I knew the material. One question at a time. I grounded myself, focusing on the paper in front of me, and slowly, the answers started to come.

The moment I handed in my paper, a wave of relief washed over me, so overwhelming that I nearly stumbled on my way out of the room. It was done. No more late-night cramming, no more lectures, no more deadlines hanging over my head. I could finally breathe—or at least, I thought I could.

Then my phone buzzed.

The second I saw Gianna Mendez's name, my stomach twisted into something ugly.

Gianna Mendez
I know things between you and Joshua are messy, but he needs a second chance. He misses you.

My grip tightened around my phone. My jaw clenched so hard my teeth ached. She had some fucking nerve.

I stared at the message, my pulse pounding in my ears. The way my chest constricted made me feel like I couldn't take in a full breath. My brain immediately latched onto every possibility—Was he trying to manipulate me again? Did she seriously think I'd fall for this? How many other people had he lied to? How many times had he spun some sob story about me just to play the victim?

No. No more.

My fingers flew across the screen.

Me
Ride his dick for as long as you want. Never text me again.

I blocked her number before she even had a chance to respond.

Joshua was a lying, cheating, manipulative, toxic whore, and Gianna was nothing more than a backstabbing bitch. I didn't have the time or energy to entertain either of them anymore.

Closing the chat, I exhaled sharply and hailed a taxi to Common at the Reserve, where I was meeting the realtor. My chest tightened with a mix of dread and cold determination—the sooner I moved on, the better.

By the time I arrived at the apartment complex, Emilia was already waiting in the lobby, scrolling through her phone. As I stepped inside, the sharp click of her heels echoed against the tile. She glanced up, flashing a bright smile. Emilia was one of my sister's friends—more out of convenience than true connection—but I couldn't deny my gratitude for how quickly she'd found this place.

"Abigail! Hey, how are you?" She greeted me.

I forced a smile. "I'm okay."

"Ready to see your potential new home?" she asked, her enthusiasm unwavering.

"Yeah, let's do it."

The building itself was impressive—clean lines, neutral tones, a sleek modern aesthetic that felt polished without being cold.

"Aurora said you wanted something simple," Emilia noted as we walked down the hallway.

I nodded. "One-bedroom, spacious but not excessive, with plenty of closet space."

"We've seen a few duds," she admitted with a small smirk. "But I have a good feeling about this one."

So did I. Eight apartments in, and all of them had been underwhelming. Too dark, too cramped, too outdated. One was practically a shoebox with a kitchen that barely fit a microwave. Another overlooked an alleyway that reeked of garbage. I was starting to think I'd have to settle.

When we reached the last door on today's list, Emilia shot me a knowing look before pushing it open.

"Okay," she said, stepping aside. "Tell me what you think."

I walked in and stilled. Sunlight spilled through floor-to-ceiling windows, washing over the open-concept living space. Light gray walls and warm hardwood floors stretched out before me, the furniture modern yet cozy. The kitchen had sleek countertops, new appliances, and—thank God—actual storage. The bedroom was spacious, the bathroom spotless, and the closet? Massive.

My shoulders sagged, the tension in my chest loosening.

"This is exactly what I was looking for," I murmured, running my fingers over the cool kitchen counter.

Emilia beamed. "And the best part? It's fully furnished, so you can move in immediately."

I exhaled, already picturing it. A soft throw draped over the sofa, candles flickering in the dim light, *Beauty and the Beast* playing in the background while I curled up with a bag of barbecue Lay's.

"This feels like home," I admitted, surprising even myself.

She grinned. "That's what I was hoping you'd say. The rent is thirty-six hundred a month, but since you're a student, I pulled some strings—you'll get a twenty-five percent discount for the first three months."

I hesitated. "What's the catch?"

"No catch," she said, then paused. "Well… you drive, right?"

I frowned. "Yeah. Why?"

She gave me a knowing look. "Parking in this city is a nightmare. Having a car is both a blessing and a curse."

I shrugged. "Not a dealbreaker. What else?"

Emilia leaned against the counter, glancing toward the window. "You're in a prime location. Restaurants, parks, nightlife, and shopping all within walking distance."

I nodded slowly. "And the noise levels?"

She hesitated, just long enough to make my stomach tighten.

"A bit during the day," Emilia admitted. "It's close to Central Park, so you'll hear traffic."

Something I could live with. "Safety?"

"Very secure," she emphasized, leaning in. "ID at the front desk, swipe card access, and each floor has a personalized door code."

I nodded. "Good. My parents would freak out otherwise."

She chuckled. "Aurora made that clear." Then, with an encouraging smile, she added, "This place is a steal. Rent only goes up around here."

"Perfect."

She handed me a folder—brochure, property rules, fee breakdown. "Review this. To lock it in, you'll need the first month's rent as a deposit. That covers admin, security, and taxes. Cleaning's optional for an extra fee."

"I'll handle the cleaning. What's the lease process?"

"Six-month or one-year lease, then renewal. If you decide to leave, give a month's notice. Once the deposit is paid, you can start moving in." She tilted her head. "When are you thinking of moving?"

"Next month." I exhaled, feeling the weight of reality settle. "Just need to sort out my car and finish packing."

"That works. Gives you time to get everything in order."

I tapped the folder against my palm. "I'll run it by my parents and confirm."

She stood, signaling the end of our conversation. "Sounds like a plan. Just text or email when you're ready."

We exchanged pleasantries, and I stepped outside. Warm air wrapped around me as I paused, absorbing the moment.

I was really doing this. Moving. Starting fresh.

The thought settled in my chest—not heavy, but firm.

First things first—call my parents.

I pulled out my phone and dialed, but they were busy. "We'll call you back," my mom said, her voice hurried.

Figures.

Slipping my phone into my bag, I hailed a cab for my nail appointment.

I let the nail tech, Kody, freestyle, and she chose almond-shaped nails with a soft ombré base, yellow floral accents, and gold foil. My toes matched with a delicate floral design, and the end result was stunning. I'd tried convincing Azzy to come, but she wasn't in the mood.

Afterward, I checked the time and headed to therapy.

Dr. Green and I usually met over Zoom, but since I was in town, I figured an in-person session would be better. I'd been introduced to her through Azzaria, who had stepped back after feeling overwhelmed.

Therapy was something I never thought I'd need. But here I was, sitting in the waiting room of Dr. Green's office on Eighth Avenue, preparing to lay myself bare once again.

Each session cost three hundred dollars, but thankfully, Azzy and I had the cost covered through our student health insurance. Still, no amount of money could put a price on what it had given me—a lifeline, a place where I could unravel without judgment.

I had a great upbringing, filled with love and support, but even the best foundation wasn't enough to shield me from the monsters in my mind. I struggled far more than anyone knew. A lot of it stemmed from Joshua—hell, I was pretty sure that was where most of it came from.

For a long time, I thought I was fine. Or at least managing. Until it all unraveled in front of the people I cared about most.

The day my parents, Aurora, and Azzy walked in on me breaking down was just the tip of the iceberg. They found me sobbing uncontrollably, struggling to breathe, consumed by the unbearable weight of my own existence. I wanted to disappear. The thought of enduring another day in my own skin felt impossible.

At first, I didn't understand what was happening to me. The panic attacks. The overwhelming dread. The constant, racing thoughts that never let me rest. My mind was never quiet. Eventually, I was diagnosed with Generalized Anxiety Disorder (GAD), but even with a name for it, coping wasn't easy. Some days, the anxiety was so loud in my head that I could hardly think straight. Other days, I felt like a 'normally' functioning human being.

I hated how I looked. I hated the way I was treated because of my body, my skin tone, my weight. The world never let me forget that I didn't fit in. People told me to ignore it—*"Don't let their words affect you."* But how could I not? Every snide remark, every cruel comment about my weight or complexion cut deeper than they realized. It wasn't just about my looks; it became about who I was at my core.

A memory clawed its way to the surface, sharp and unrelenting.

I was standing in front of the bathroom mirror, tears streaking down my face, hands gripping the sink until my knuckles turned white. Joshua's voice rang in my ears, thick with disdain and casual cruelty.

"You need to take better care of yourself."

"It's just tough love."

But it never felt like love. It felt like a slow, deliberate breaking of something inside me. I stared at my reflection, wondering if I would ever see myself as enough.

A sharp inhale pulled me back to the present. I swallowed hard, pushing past the lump in my throat as Dr. Green called me in.

Her name was displayed in crisp white vinyl on the glass door. Inside, the sterile scent of lavender and chamomile filled the air, but the warmth of the room softened its clinical edge. The sunlight poured in through wide windows, reflecting off the shelves lined with books and thriving green plants.

She sat poised in her usual chair, her green eyes kind yet probing. Her short blonde hair framed her elegant features, making her look as put together as always.

She gestured toward the sofa. "Abigail, it's good to see you. Please, have a seat."

I sank into the cushions, smoothing my hands over my lap. "I just wanted to update you on everything since I got here."

Dr. Green nodded, her hands resting gently in her lap. "That's something to be grateful for—being here and being alive. Tell me about your stay. How's the city been treating you?"

I inhaled deeply. "It's been good, really. I'm staying with Azzaria and Auntie Leann, and I haven't done much except exams. Azzy and I went out the other night, but that's about it. I took my last exam today—went better than I expected. I met with a realtor since I'm moving here, and got my nails done."

A flicker of nostalgia crossed her face. "How's Azzaria?"

"She's okay. I'll tell her you asked about her."

Dr. Green smiled faintly, though there was something else there—a quiet longing, maybe, to see Azzy heal, too. "I'd appreciate that. But now, let's focus on you. It sounds like you're making big changes, taking control of your life. But I want to know—are you feeling any pressure through all of this?"

I hesitated, choosing my words carefully. "Not with moving, at least. I'm actually excited for that. But…" I exhaled slowly. "I'm ending things with Joshua this weekend when I go back."

Dr. Green leaned in slightly, her expression gentle yet unwavering. "How are you feeling about that?"

I stared down at my hands, my fingers twisting together. "Relieved… and scared."

She waited, letting me fill the silence on my own.

"For so long, I stayed because I thought that was what I deserved," I admitted. "He was always good at making me believe that. But now… I don't know. I'm afraid of being alone."

The words hung between us.

"I know I don't want to be with him anymore. But I also don't want to be alone."

It wasn't just the loneliness itself—it was what it meant. Like I was slowly fading into the background, watching as everyone else had someone to pull them into focus. And I wanted that.

I wanted someone to see me.

Really see me.

Someone who looked at me like I was the only person in the room. The one whose thoughts they couldn't wait to hear. The one whose mere existence lit up their world.

But I wasn't sure I'd ever have that.

"I don't love him anymore, and I can't afford to lose any more time. Or worse—lose myself again."

Dr. Green's expression softened, her hands resting lightly on her notepad. "That's something we've talked about before, Abigail—how you tend to put others before yourself, even when it hurts you. But this? This is growth. You're finally prioritizing your well-being."

I exhaled slowly, absorbing her words. I hadn't thought about it that way before, but she was right. For the first time in a long time, I was putting myself first. It was overdue, but better late than never.

"Thank you, Doc."

"You're so welcome." A small, encouraging smile touched her lips. "Is there anything else you'd like us to talk about today?"

I hesitated. The words formed in my throat but refused to come out. My fingers curled around the couch cushion, gripping the fabric like an anchor. No one knew. Not Azzy. Not anyone. And saying it out loud felt like giving it power.

But it already had power, didn't it?

"There's something I haven't told you yet," I admitted, my voice barely above a whisper. "It's… embarrassing, but also terrifying."

Dr. Green didn't rush me. She never did. She just waited, her presence steady and grounding.

I swallowed hard. "Joshua has something on me. Something he's been holding over my head for years."

Concern flickered across her face. "What does he have?"

I forced myself to meet her gaze. "Videos. Pictures. He compiled them without my consent. Stitched together sexual moments I didn't even know he recorded." The lump in my throat swelled. "I don't know if he'll threaten to release them or just let the fear of it be enough."

Dr. Green's face remained calm, but I saw the subtle shift in her posture—the quiet fury behind her professional composure. "Abigail, I'm so sorry you're going through this," she said gently. "What he's done is a violation. If he releases them, he can be held accountable. Distributing intimate content without consent is a crime, and there are laws to protect you."

My nails dug into the cushion. "It just makes me feel… powerless."

"You are *not* powerless." Her voice was firm but kind. "That's what abusers want you to believe. But you have options. And you have people who will stand by you."

I wanted to believe her. But fear had settled into my bones, deep and unmoving.

"Let's try something," she said, her tone soft but guiding. "Close your eyes. Count backward from ten."

I did as she asked. "Ten… nine… eight…"

With each number, I focused on my breath, on the weight of my body against the couch, on the warmth of the room.

"Seven... six..."

The pressure in my chest began to ease, the sharp edges of panic dulling.

By the time I reached one, my breathing had steadied.

When I opened my eyes, the world hadn't changed, but the storm inside me had quieted, just a little.

Dr. Green studied me for a moment before speaking again. "I know that fear doesn't disappear overnight. But you are taking steps forward, and that matters."

I nodded, shifting in my seat. The silence settled around us, thick but not suffocating this time. I let it sit for a moment before blurting out, "Do you think fate is real?"

Dr. Green blinked, caught off guard by the shift. "Fate?"

"I need a distraction," I admitted. "Yes. Fate. Do you believe in it?"

She tapped her fingers lightly against her chair. "I believe there's a reason for everything, but I'm not entirely sold on the idea of fate."

I exhaled, steady now. "Three weeks ago, I was at the airport, crying, and a stranger comforted me. And then I saw him again at a club. And again, just the other day, at a bar. I don't know if it means anything or if I'm just overthinking it."

Dr. Green's lips twitched into a small smile. "Well, that's new."

I huffed out a short laugh. "You don't think it's fate?"

She shrugged. "This is New York. People cross paths. But maybe instead of focusing on why it's happening, you should focus on closing the Joshua chapter first."

I nodded slowly. "You're probably right. It's nothing anyway."

But deep down, I wasn't so sure.

I left her office feeling lighter, like I'd finally put something down I'd been carrying for too long. Maybe life wasn't just about endings—maybe it was about what came next.

Even if—though I seriously doubt it—it had anything to do with a stranger I met at the airport.

CHAPTER SEVEN

Mikkel

"You don't love someone for their looks, or their clothes, or for their fancy car, but because they sing a song only you can hear."
~ Oscar Wilde

By the time I wrapped up at the office—confirming fleet checks and schedules, finalizing the start date for Alex's new driver, and completing three back-to-back interviews with *The New York Times*, *The Washington Post*, and *USA Today*—I was ready to call it a day. But Dillon and Arnoldo had other plans, dragging me to a tech seminar at the Park Avenue Armory.

The moment we stepped inside, chaos erupted. Cameras flashed in relentless bursts, microphones shoved into our space as reporters shouted over each other for a comment. The air buzzed with desperation—like a feeding frenzy, each journalist trying to sink their teeth into the next big headline.

Arnoldo and I exchanged a glance. Unspoken agreement. We sidestepped, letting Dillon bask in the attention.

He thrived on this. Always had. My friends loved the glitz, the spectacle, the constant spotlight. I tolerated it. Avoided it when I could. Perfectionism made me my own worst critic, and the fear of saying the wrong thing—the wrong anything—kept me steering clear of the press. But escaping the spotlight was never truly an option.

"You're practically hanging on the reporter's every word," I murmured to Arnoldo, watching the gleam in his eye.

"She's good-looking," he replied with an easy shrug, voice rich with indifference. "That's all."

I rolled my eyes. Right. Like it was ever just that with him.

Arnoldo's reputation wasn't just well-earned—it was legendary. Women gravitated toward him like moths to a flame, and he basked in their attention without hesitation or apology. It was an art form to him, one he'd perfected with alarming precision.

"Do you ever not think about sleeping with women?" I asked, only half-joking.

He shook his head, expression mock-serious. "All the time."

I huffed a laugh. "Could've fooled me."

His eyes widened in exaggerated shock, lips forming an amused 'O' before shifting his attention back to the reporter. The way she blushed under his gaze, the coy smile playing at her lips—it didn't take a genius to figure out they'd already hooked up.

Dillon wrapped up his interview just as Arnoldo made his move. One hand on the small of her back, a few murmured words in her ear, and just like that, she was grinning like she'd won the lottery.

"He's definitely fucked her," Dillon muttered.

I didn't disagree.

Arnoldo returned with a smug grin—one Dillon and I had seen a thousand times before. We exchanged a glance, silently acknowledging the routine.

"You really have a way with the press, don't you?" Dillon drawled, amusement flickering in his tone.

Arnoldo shrugged, unbothered. "Comes with the territory, Xander."

Dillon smirked before I threw in a jab. "Manwhore."

Arnoldo smirked. "At least I'm not alone."

"Does sleeping around count as having company?" I quipped.

"Yes," he said without hesitation, then leaned in like he was about to share something profound. "And for the record, I don't sleep around. I can admire a woman without wanting to fuck her."

Dillon snorted. "That's a first, and at least we don't have to worry about catching anything."

Arnoldo scoffed. "First of all, I get tested every three months. Second, I never go without protection. And third—" He pointed between us. "Both of you are single. Lucio and Alex are the only ones taken."

"And Bryce," Dillon added just to push his buttons.

Arnoldo groaned, waving a dismissive hand. "He's barely our friend."

Feigning innocence, I asked, "Why do you hate Bryce again?"

He exhaled sharply. "He's reckless in business and, worse, ungrateful. What rich man complains as much as he does?"

"He'll always be a distant friend," I said, attempting to lighten the tension.

Arnoldo shook his head. "Let's not forget he cheated on my former law student with the girl he's now engaged to. And I know he's cheating on her too."

Dillon raised a brow. "Law student?"

Arnoldo smirked. "You don't know your friend as well as you think."

I leaned back, recalling something. "He had a thing for my sister last year."

Arnoldo's expression flickered—just for a second. The smugness faded, his face going a shade paler. "He had a what?"

I watched him, noticing how the mention actually seemed to bother him. Not just irritation—something deeper. But I didn't think much of it.

Arnoldo pretty much hated everything Bryce did.

Dillon, ever the pragmatist, shrugged. "As long as Bryce doesn't screw up a business deal tied to any of our empires, I couldn't care less."

Arnoldo and I exchanged a glance and nodded. "Fair enough."

But just as quickly, Arnoldo's attention drifted—his gaze locking onto the journalist again, lingering without shame.

Dillon chuckled, shaking his head. "I cannot wait for the day you fall flat on your ass in love, Reyes."

Arnoldo adjusted his jacket with a smirk, confidence unshaken. "Very low chance of that happening."

I was about to throw in my own jab when a flash of red curls near the bathroom caught my eye.

The color and volume seemed different, but maybe she'd changed it. My pulse kicked up—a sharp mix of hope and nerves tangling together.

"I'll be back," I muttered, already moving before they could ask questions.

As I closed the distance, anticipation crackled through me like a live wire. If she was here, this would be the fourth time our paths had crossed—and this time, I wouldn't let her slip away without learning her name.

"Hey there," I greeted, keeping my tone easy.

She turned.

And my breath caught—for all of one second before realization hit.

Not her.

Fuck me.

"Oh, I—I'm sorry," I stammered, heat creeping up my neck. "I thought you were someone else."

She let out a warm laugh, amused rather than offended. "No worries."

A relieved chuckle escaped me, and we shared a brief nod before parting ways.

I rejoined Dillon and Arnoldo just as their debate over Arnoldo's nonexistent love life reignited. The conversation only paused when the seminar shifted to awarding scholarships, then picked up again once the formalities were over.

By the end of the day, we had celebrated with the recipients, participated in a panel discussion, and capped it off by writing additional $20,000 checks to further support the program.

"Let's get out of here," Dillon said as we walked to the parking lot.

Sliding into the driver's seat, I glanced at Arnoldo. "Home or your office, Reyes?"

"My office," he replied. "I need to go over a case with Melissa for tomorrow."

Dillon leaned back in his seat. "Equinox for me."

That caught me off guard. He rarely went there—too many memories of his grandfather. I didn't push, just nodded and drove in silence, respecting whatever was on his mind.

We barely made it past the receptionist's desk before chaos erupted. Raised voices. An argument unfolding.

Wait.

Holy shit.

"Isn't that yo—"

"My assistant," Dillon cut in, irritation lacing his voice. "I'll be back."

As he strode toward the commotion, my phone pinged—a flight reminder. I took the opportunity to check in with my sister.

Me
Have you booked the ticket for you and Eli yet?

Emilia Suarez (Hermana)
Elijah isn't coming. He's staying with Ashley. Book mine, I'll pay you back.

Me
Send me your passport.

Emilia Suarez (Hermana)
You're the best big brother when you feel like it.

Me
Te amo también.[1]

I shut off my phone just as Dillon approached, a too-cheerful grin on his face.

"Mikkel, let's go," he called out, voice light, almost too upbeat.

I frowned. "Weren't we checking upstairs?"

He waved off my concern. "I've seen and done all I needed to."

We headed to the car, and as soon as we settled in, he let out a deep, relieved sigh.

"I got the girl," he announced, satisfaction dripping from every word.

---

1 *I love you too*

I raised a brow. "Got the girl?"

"Azzaria," he clarified, eyes twinkling. "My intern."

I shot him a knowing look. "Don't screw it up."

Dillon's grin didn't waver. "I won't."

I studied him for a beat. "How do you feel about it?"

His expression softened, but the gleam of triumph remained. "Accomplished. You wouldn't believe how damn hard it was just to get her to talk to me."

I smirked. "Sounds perfect for you. You thrive on challenges."

"For sure." His voice brimmed with satisfaction—like, for once, everything in his world had lined up just right.

Switching gears, I mentioned, "I'll be out for about two weeks starting Friday."

Dillon turned to me. "Where to?"

"Sacramento. My cousin's engagement party. Then Chicago for an investor meeting."

His face lit up. "Investor meeting? That's huge!" He leaned back, grinning. "I told you from day one that your business would take off. You've worked your ass off for this, Suarez."

I chuckled. "Yeah, but it's not just me. I've got a great team. Now, I need these investors to see that."

"What's the pitch?"

"Expansion. I want them to see the potential in other cities. We're changing the way people think about transportation."

"Morison or Sapphire going with you?"

"Neither. Just Emilia and me for the engagement party."

Dillon nodded. "Good luck with the meeting, and send my best to your parents."

"Will do."

He gave me a firm nod. "You've got this, man."

And for the first time in a while, I actually believed it.

CHAPTER EIGHT

Mikkel

"Where there is love, there is life."
- Mahatma Gandhi

The fluorescent lights buzzed overhead, washing the stack of profiles in a sterile glow. I traced the edges of the papers absentmindedly, but my thoughts were miles away.

The thought of her sent a charge through me, sharp and electric. From the moment I saw her, the rest of the world faded. Her twinkling green eyes held a thousand secrets—ones I ached to uncover.

In my thirty-three years of life, no one had ever done this to me.

I'd only seen and interacted with her three times, yet she consumed me. *Completely.*

Insane. Obsessive. But if losing my mind meant feeling this alive, I'd gladly unravel.

"*Contrólate*, Mikkel,[1]" I muttered, trying to focus, but it was useless. Red's image lingered in my mind, her laughter echoing in my ears.

A familiar voice cut through the haze. "Mr. Suarez? You look distracted."

I looked up to see Sapphire standing in the doorway, her brow furrowed. She'd just returned from Chicago, and I was surprised to see her back in the office so soon.

"Everything's fine," I said, forcing a smile that felt hollow. "Did you need something?"

She stepped inside, her heels clicking against the floor. "Actually, yeah."

"Go ahead."

"We've got a problem with Alexander Williams," she said, exhaling sharply. "No response on client follow-ups."

I clenched my jaw. "I'll take care of it. How's everything else?"

"All our drivers are out and assigned. No complaints so far, sir."

Exactly what I wanted to hear. I let out a breath, my chest easing. "Great. I'll be out for a week or two starting tomorrow, so it's the usual protocol until I'm back."

"Okay, sir. Safe travels." She hesitated. "I met some potential hires in Chicago. One stood out—Laura Ellison. Strong background in logistics and tech integration. Could be a major asset."

I leaned forward, intrigued. "Did you go over our goals with her?"

"Yes, and she's already full of ideas to improve efficiency. I also scheduled meetings with local tech firms to explore partnerships. If it works out, we'll streamline operations significantly."

That was exactly the kind of initiative I valued. "Perfect. Keep me updated as things progress."

"Of course, Mr. Suarez. Everything will run smoothly while you're away, and I'll have the documents ready for your approval." Her confident smile left no room for doubt.

---

1 *Get a grip, Mikkel*

"Good. I'll expect a detailed report when I return."

She turned to leave, but I stopped her, grabbing the folder from my desk. "I reviewed the profiles. Some candidates look promising, others not so much. We'll get a clearer picture during the in-person interviews."

She took the folder with a nod. "Got it."

As the door clicked shut behind her, my phone lit up with a string of messages from the group chat.

Reyes
I'm headed to the gym, who's coming?

Alex
i'll be there.

Dill
Busy, sorry.

Ro
i'm coming.

Me
Wrapping up at the office. I'll be there soon.

Luc
i'm with my wife, so no.

Ro
we KNOW you're married, fratello.[2]

2

stop rubbing it in.

Luc
Never.

Reyes
Perfect.

Dill
Why do you all go to the gym anyway?

Ro
we go to your gym.

Dill
I don't recall asking that. I was alluding to the fact that you are all in perfect shape but never mind.

Ro
oh. love you.

Dill
I truly wish the feeling was mutual.

Ro
you're missing out.

Dill
Sure I am.

---

2 *brother*

I swiped out of the group chat just as Morison walked into my office, a thick folder in his hands.

"You've got that meeting with the investors in Chicago after you leave California," he said, dropping the folder on my desk. "Final list came in."

I leaned back in my chair, glancing at the folder but not reaching for it yet. "Anyone I need to worry about?"

Morison smirked. "Damon Ashford's there, along with Cataleya Nguyen. And Marissa Lyle, from Sterling Ventures."

That caught my attention. "Lyle? She's in media and tech. Why's she suddenly interested in transport?"

"She's pivoting," Morison said, crossing his arms. "Wants a foothold in transportation. She's got big money and is itching to spend it."

I picked up the folder, flipping through the profiles. Ashford, Nguyen, and Lyle—they weren't small players. This was the type of crowd that wanted more than just numbers; they needed a guarantee that our expansion wouldn't fall apart.

"They're going to push hard," Morison continued. "Ashford especially—he's big on timelines. He's already questioning whether we can pull it off with everything else on our plate."

I set the folder down, looking up at him. "We've dominated New York. They know that. They just want to see if we can scale."

"Just be prepared. They'll look for cracks, Mr. Suarez. They want security." Morison's expression was steady, but there was a hint of concern in his voice. "You know how these guys operate. They're not just here to invest—they're here to control."

"Taking orders has never been my thing." I smirked, leaning back in my chair. "I've handled worse than Ashford. Lyle's the real key. If she's serious about transportation, we get her on board, and the others will follow."

Morison nodded, though his brow stayed furrowed. "You've got this," he said, heading for the door. "Just keep your cool, and most importantly, don't lose your temper, sir."

I leaned forward, my gaze sharpening as I watched him leave. "I won't," I muttered, though the fire in my gut was far from cold. I'd make this work, and if anyone tried to stand in my way, they'd regret it.

Once he left, I spent the next hour perfecting the pitch and had to call in the team to fix an issue—nearly losing my temper when some of the numbers didn't add up.

By the time I made it to Equinox, the familiar scent of sweat and determination filled the air as weights clanked and treadmills hummed. I spotted my friends already deep into their workouts.

"Suarez, over here!" Ronan called from the bench press, sweat glistening on his forehead.

"Took you long enough," Arnoldo smirked, effortlessly repping pull-ups.

I dropped my gym bag beside them, rolling out my shoulders. "Traffic. And perfecting an expansion pitch."

Arnoldo groaned. "You need to get that perfectionism under control."

I shot him a dry look. "Says the guy who rewrote a contract clause eight times last week."

Ronan snorted as Arnoldo muttered, "Not the same thing, and you know it."

Alex racked his weights and turned to me. "Suarez."

"Arm day or freestyle?" I asked, already stretching.

"Leg day," he said, loading plates onto the squat rack. "You're just in time."

I exhaled sharply. Fantastic. My least favorite.

As I stepped forward, I noticed Alex's phone on the bench. "Did you not see the company calling you?"

"Nah. Just got that phone," he muttered.

"What happened to the old one?" Ronan asked.

"Mara threw it at me."

Arnoldo and Ronan burst into laughter.

"What the fuck did you do?" I asked.

Alex groaned. "A flight attendant messaged me about an upcoming flight. Mara didn't like it. So she broke it."

"Stop irritating the pregnant woman," Arnoldo teased, still laughing.

Alex gestured around. "How am I the bad guy?"

Arnoldo clapped a hand on his shoulder. "When a beautiful woman, especially your wife, tells you that you're wrong, then you're wrong."

Alex huffed a laugh, nudging him. "That's rich coming from you, Reyes."

Arnoldo just shrugged. Then, turning to me, he said, "Speaking of work, you know the Astar family?"

"Yeah. Didn't you represent them?"

"Still do. Their parents need a personal driver for their daughters. I recommended Elite Rides. Just a heads-up."

I nodded. "Appreciate it. I owe you a beer."

He waved it off. "No big deal."

"By the way, I'll be out of town for a week."

Reyes raised a brow, smirking. "Honeymoon?"

I chuckled. "Engagement party."

"Ahh," he said, his tone playful. "Have fun. Oh—about the expansion? Morison sent me the investor list."

I stretched my arms, my mind shifting back to business. "We'll be good."

"Never doubted you." Arnoldo grinned. "Keep me updated."

"Same time next week?" Arnoldo called out as we parted ways, each of us heading off to our post-gym routines.

"Maybe," Alex said. "We'll see."

"I'll be out of town," I reminded them. "But after that, sure."

"Great. See you."

When I got home, I wasn't expecting to find Emilia standing outside my door, Elijah fast asleep in her arms and a bag at her feet. Her eyes were locked on her phone, brows furrowed like she was lost in thought.

I dropped my gym bag. "Why are you out here?"

She looked up, slipping her phone into her pocket. "Waiting for you."

I frowned, unlocking the door. "Why didn't you just go in? Management knows to let you inside."

She shrugged. "I don't barge into people's homes."

"You're my sister." I pushed the door open, holding it for her.

She didn't respond, just picked up her bag and stepped inside, the silence thick between us.

Emilia had always been different—lighter, more at ease in a way I never was. Our parents were affectionate, loving, but they clung to their traditional Caribbean values, even more so after we moved to the States. The language barrier had hit me hard. They never pressured me, but I still felt it—the weight of expectation, the responsibility of being the oldest.

So, I made sure everything was perfect. My grades. My behavior. If I kept everything in line, maybe they'd ease up on her, let her be herself. But the need for perfection never faded. It sat under my skin, tightening every time things slipped out of place.

I exhaled, snapping out of my thoughts as I found her standing stiffly by the couch, glancing around like she wasn't sure where to settle.

"The chair isn't going to burn if you take a seat, Em."

She looked at me, hesitated, then shifted her weight. "I don't want to just… make myself at home."

I frowned, walking over. "Emilia, you're my sister." My voice softened. "Mi casa también es la tuya."[3]

She hesitated, her gaze flickering with uncertainty, but after a moment, she gave a small nod and sat down, settling Elijah beside her.

I walked to the kitchen, grabbing a bottle of water, but as I reached for the fridge, I glanced back at Emilia. She looked out of place, like she wasn't sure if she belonged, and it tightened something in my chest.

Then I heard it—the soft, steady breathing of my nephew. His tiny fingers curled against her shirt, and she instinctively smoothed a hand over his back. The tenderness in her expression was something I'd never seen

---

3 *My house is also your house*

before. Motherhood had changed her, softened the sharp edges, and for a moment, all the stress lining her face disappeared.

I took a sip of water, letting the moment settle before clearing my throat. "We leave at nine in the morning, so we need to be at the airport by seven-thirty to check in. There's a two-hour layover in Salt Lake City, and we'll get there around one in the afternoon."

She lifted her gaze from Elijah to me. "Muchas gracias."[4]

"You don't have to thank me." I studied her for a beat before asking, "You okay?"

She nodded, her voice soft. "Yeah, I'm fine."

"I don't believe you."

She exhaled, finally meeting my gaze. "I'm fine, Mikkel. Really."

I let it go, though something still felt off. Just as I turned back toward the fridge, she reached into her bag and pulled out an envelope.

I frowned. "What's this?"

She held it out, avoiding my eyes. "I told you I'd pay you back for the ticket."

I sighed, shaking my head. "It's not a big deal."

She frowned. "I ca—"

"Emilia." My tone left no room for argument. "I'm not taking money from you."

She hesitated, fingers tightening around the envelope before slipping it back into her bag. "Alright, but I'm paying you back someday."

I leaned back against the counter, arms crossed. "You know I'll always be here, right? For you and Elijah. Doesn't matter how old we get or whatever happens, *hermanita*."[5]

She glanced at me, her expression softening just a little. "I know. I just… I have to do this on my own sometimes."

I nodded, my voice quieter now. "I get it. But if you ever need anything, I've got you, Emilia."

---

4 *Thank you very much*

5 *little sister*

Her fingers toyed with the hem of her sleeve, like she wanted to say more but couldn't find the words. Then finally, after a pause, she spoke.

"Thanks, Mikkel."

I gave her a small smile. "De nada."[6]

---

6 *You're welcome*

CHAPTER NINE

Abigail-Ann

"The best love is the one that makes you a better person, without changing you into someone other than yourself."
- Unknown

I woke up to an email from Emilia, the payment receipt attached along with a few other documents. After quickly skimming through them, I slid out of bed and dressed in my favorite pair of high-waisted, light-wash blue jeans that hugged my curves just right, pairing them with a crisp white bodysuit blouse. One last glance in the mirror, I ran my fingers through my hair, letting the curls fall loosely around my shoulders.

"Well, Azzy," I said, stepping forward to hug her, "I'll see you in about two weeks."

My Uber was on its way, and though Azzy had wanted to come to the airport with me, work had other plans.

"Be safe, and make sure to call or text me," she said, pouting as she pulled me into another hug. Then, with far too much volume, she added, "I love you! And don't forget the goal of this trip!"

"The goal?"

"Abigail-Ann." Her tone was scolding, but her eyes twinkled with amusement. "You're going there to break it off, not give him a good-bye fuck."

I scoffed. "I don't want his penis anywhere near me."

"Make sure," she said, narrowing her eyes. "As a matter of fact, sleep with no one. Keep your dry spell going."

"You're no fun since you've been hooking up with your hot tycoon," I teased, rolling my eyes.

She grinned, unable to hide her happiness, and launched into a recap of her latest moments with him—awkward office encounters, insane amount of spending, his thoughtful gestures, and a certain turning point in an alleyway.

From the way she spoke, it was clear: he was the one.

"I kissed a guy once, or ten times, and now you think I'm hooking up?" she said, feigning innocence.

She couldn't fool me.

I laughed. "You should break *your* dry spell. You want him, and he sure as hell wants you."

She rolled her eyes. "This isn't about me. This is about you and that bitch boy. Break it off, no sex, and then you can pursue Mikkel."

I think I stopped breathing.

How the hell did she even know about Mikkel?

What was even there to *know*?

I had deliberately never mentioned him because there was nothing to mention—just fleeting, short-lived moments and an undeniable, magnetic pull.

Yeah. No. Big. Deal.

"I'm not going to pursue Mikkel," I said, forcing my voice to stay even.

"Sure," she replied, too casually, but skepticism danced in her eyes.

"What?"

"Nothing." She shrugged. "Just please remember the goal."

I could have argued, but the last thing I wanted was to drag this conversation out.

"Got it. Bye, Azzy," I said, turning to leave.

"Call me!"

"I will," I replied, my voice softening as I disappeared through the doorway, my luggage rolling behind me.

But just as I stepped out, something struck me. Without thinking, I ran back inside.

"Azzaria!"

She groaned, rubbing her temple. "You're gonna miss your flight at this rate."

"Let magic happen between you and Dillon," I said, a hopeful smile tugging at my lips before dashing off again.

The ride to the airport felt longer than it was, frustration simmering beneath my skin as Joshua's relentless texts flooded my screen. *If only he was this persistent while we were dating.* My fingers stabbed at my phone, muttered curses slipping out as I silenced notifications one by one.

But the unease didn't fade.

The anxiety of flying pressed in on me, tightening like a fist around my lungs. Every step closer to my gate made my chest heavier. My palms were damp. The overhead announcements buzzed in my ears, blending with the rush of travelers. My mind spun through worst-case scenarios. What if the plane hit turbulence? What if something went wrong midair?

My breaths quickened.

It was always like this before a flight. Always this battle against thoughts that refused to quiet.

Then, out of nowhere—bam.

My shoulder collided with something solid, jolting me backward. My bag slipped from my grasp, items tumbling to the floor.

"Shit," I muttered, bending down to gather my things, barely sparing a glance at the person I'd crashed into—until a familiar scent wrapped around me.

Clean, masculine, with a crisp hint of something dark and intoxicating.

I knew that scent.

A sinking feeling settled in my stomach.

Slowly, I lifted my gaze.

And there he was.

Towering over me, tousled hair a perfect mess, casual attire that somehow only made him more irresistible. His tattoos—God, those tattoos—snaked down his arms, bold against his tanned skin. Each intricate line dared me to trace them.

Our eyes locked.

Frustration. Surprise. And something else—something unspoken—flashed between us.

I took a slow, steadying breath, my heart hammering as I braced for whatever came next.

"Mikkel," I said, my voice sharper than intended, the annoyance from Joshua's texts still lingering. "What are you doing here?"

"You know my name." His crooked smile was all mischief, eyes tracing over my disheveled state like he was committing it to memory. "I have a flight," he said easily, though the glint in his gaze told me there was more to it. "Been hoping to see you, Red."

"Hoping to see me? Why?"

Silence. Thick, charged, full of something unsaid.

Then, without breaking eye contact, he crouched down, reaching for the things I'd dropped. "Let me help you with that."

His fingers brushed mine, sending a jolt through me, and I cursed how easily he got under my skin. The airport was loud, but somehow, in that moment, the noise dulled, everything shrinking to just him.

"Thank you."

He studied me, lingering just long enough to make me squirm. "I still don't know your name. I can't call you Red forever."

He absolutely could.

And before I could stop myself, I muttered, "I wouldn't mind if you did."

The corner of his lips twitched. "*A mí tampoco me importaría, Red.*[1]"

I had no idea what he just said, but it was quite possibly the sexiest thing I'd ever heard.

"Abigail-Ann," I mumbled. "But most just call me Abigail."

"Abigail." His voice wrapped around my name like it belonged to him. And fuck, I don't think my name has ever been said that attractively in my life.

"Pretty name for an even prettier face."

I rolled my eyes, but the warmth spreading through my chest betrayed me. "Smooth as ever, Mikkel."

He chuckled, the sound rich and unhurried. "Can't blame a guy for trying." A beat of hesitation, then—"Would it be weird if I asked for your Instagram?"

I blinked.

Not my number. *My Instagram.*

My fingers curled around the strap of my bag before I even realized it. Men rarely asked for anything other than my number—because they thought they were *entitled* to it. I'd had a man grab my wrist once, yanking when I refused, slurring insults in my ear as I wrenched myself away. Another had followed me for *blocks*, shouting how I was stuck-up, ugly, a tease.

So no, it wasn't weird at all. It was… a relief.

"Not at all," I said, surprising myself. "It's abi_asher."

He nodded, his expression unreadable. *Thoughtful.*

"Thank you," he mused. "So, where are you off to, Abigail?"

"San Francisco for a bit," I said, adjusting the strap of my bag.

He hummed. "I'm headed home, too. My cousin's engagement party, then business in Chicago."

---

1 *I wouldn't mind either, Red.*

"Home as in?"

"Sacramento." He tilted his head. "And I hope your trip is great, Red."

"I hope you enjoy yours too, Mikkel." A soft chuckle escaped me. "Thought you were calling me Abigail now?"

He shrugged. "Depends. How many people call you Red?"

"A couple," I teased.

He gave an exaggerated pout. "Really?"

"No," I admitted. "You're the first."

Something flickered in his expression—pleased, almost smug—but it softened into something else when he murmured, "I hope to be the last."

The words were so quiet, I almost convinced myself I imagined them. "Huh?"

"Nothing at all, Red." His grin was slow, teasing, and dangerous.

Before I could press him, the intercom crackled to life, announcing my flight's boarding. I exhaled, a part of me reluctant to leave this conversation unfinished.

"Well," I sighed, adjusting my bag, "looks like that's my cue. It was nice seeing you again, Mikkel."

His smile held something unreadable. "The pleasure is all mine."

I turned, stepping toward the gate, but the moment I disappeared into the crowd, I knew.

This wasn't over.

Not even close.

The plane touched down with a jolt, and I exhaled, relieved to be back in San Francisco after that turbulence-filled flight.

Stepping into the arrivals area, I scanned the sea of travelers until my eyes landed on Aurora, her bright smile standing out even in the crowded terminal.

"Abigail!" she called, waving me over.

I rushed to the car and pulled her into a hug. "Aurora, I missed you."

The porter loaded my luggage while we climbed into the car, the city lights streaking past as we pulled onto the highway.

"You hungry?" she asked, throwing me a knowing grin.

I groaned theatrically. "I'm starving."

"Good, because Mom and Dad are cooking dinner."

I squealed at the thought. Nothing compared to a home-cooked meal, and it was one of the things I'd miss most when I moved.

Pulling out my phone, I quickly texted Azzy.

Me
I landed.

Azzy:
Perfect! Be safe and call me if you ever need me!

Me
I will.♥

Aurora glanced over. "How was New York?"

"Exciting," I admitted, grateful. "And thank you again for setting me up with the realtor."

She smiled. "You're moving three thousand miles away. I needed to make sure you'd be comfortable."

"Still, I appreciate you."

Her brow creased slightly. "Are you feeling okay about all this? I know it's a lot to handle."

I hesitated, then shrugged. "It is, but I think I'm managing just fine."

"Just take it one step at a time," she said softly. "And call me if it feels like too much."

"Thanks. I probably will—more than you think."

She smirked. "What will you do for work until you graduate?"

"Not sure yet, but I'll look for something when I get back."

Her eyes lit up. "My friend works at Book Culture—they're always hiring. I'll ask her."

I gasped. "Seriously, what would I do without you?"

"Suffer," she teased.

I laughed, the weight of the move momentarily forgotten.

The rest of the drive was quiet, with small moments of sleep in between. But as we pulled into the driveway of our parents' home in Presidio Heights, familiarity wrapped around me like a warm blanket.

The house, with its tall arched windows, intricate molding, and the glow of a chandelier over polished floors, looked exactly the same. And the comforting scents of wood, fresh flowers, and my mother's cooking filled the air.

"Parentals!" Aurora shouted as we stepped inside. "We're home!"

The tap of my mother's heels and the steady sound of my father's shoes echoed down the hall before they appeared, arms already open for hugs.

My mom, Alicia Asher, exuded effortless elegance—her gray-streaked curls and warm brown eyes often making people mistake her for my sister instead. My dad, Daniel Asher, with his salt-and-pepper hair and kind smile, still carried the same quiet confidence he always had.

And just like that, the stress of the past few weeks melted away. I was home.

Before I could take another step, she was already fussing over me.

"How are you? How was the flight? Are you hungry? You look flushed... Are you tired, Princess?"

I flopped onto the living room sofa, grinning. "Calm down, Mom," I said. "I'm fine. I'm hungry, and the flight was turbulent, but I made it."

"Great," Dad replied. "We've got much to discuss, but we'll talk after you've settled. Glad to have you home, Princess."

The one thing I always loved about being with my family was their love. No matter where we were or what we did, it never wavered. I was beyond grateful to have them.

"Angel," my mom called out to Aurora.

"Yes, Mom?" Aurora replied, heading toward the kitchen.

And that was the last thing I heard before sleep pulled me under.

CHAPTER TEN

Mikkel

"The best love is the one that makes you a better person, without changing you into someone other than yourself."
~Unknown

Hours of delays and turbulence had me gripping the armrest in frustration. By the time we landed, I swore I'd never fly Delta again. The car our parents sent was waiting, but even as we drove through the city, my mind wasn't on the familiar streets or the frustration of the flight. It was on Abigail.

I caught sight of her while waiting for coffee, and before I knew it, I was walking toward her, drawn by something I couldn't name. A small, deliberate brush of shoulders—and then she turned, eyes locking onto mine, and suddenly, the world wasn't so loud anymore.

Her beauty wasn't just skin deep. It was in the calm confidence she carried, the quiet command in the way she moved. Even the smallest details—like the soft yellow floral accents on her nails—stayed with me. Who was she? What made her tick?

The questions spun in my mind like a song on repeat. She was unlike anyone I'd met, and I couldn't shake the need to find out why. So, I got her Instagram. Asking for her number felt too bold, too soon, but this? This felt like the perfect way to get to know her without overwhelming her.

Even as the car slowed in front of my parents' house, her name still echoed in my mind.

Tahoe Park stretched out before us, the house nestled among towering pines and bathed in the afternoon sun. It stood tall and impressive, with elegant details and large bay windows that reflected the light just right.

"*Mamá*," I called out.

I heard her footsteps approach, familiar and comforting. Valeria Suarez, my mother, appeared, radiating warmth like the Mediterranean sun. Her caramel-toned skin glowed, and her deep brown eyes met mine, offering reassurance.

"*¡Hola, mis amores!*"[1]

I leaned in for a hug. "You look radiant as always, *Mamá*.[2]"

She smiled and kissed my cheeks. "*Mi hijo*[3], you're so handsome," she said, her voice warm, before walking over to my sister. "My beautiful Emilia."

"Mamá,[4]" Emilia greeted her, her tone flat.

"I wished you brought my grandson," Mom added, her eyes lingering on Emilia with a hint of disappointment.

Emilia sighed, the sound heavy with annoyance. *Here we go.* "Hopefully, I'm good enough company," she said lightly, though the tightness in her voice gave her away.

Mom's face shifted to one of shock. "Em—"

---

1 *Hello, my loves*

2 *mom*

3 *son*

4 *mom*

"Don't worry, Mamá[5]. I'll take him next time," Emilia said, her voice tight, though she tried to stay calm.

I glanced between them, sensing the tension thickening like an approaching storm. Emilia's clipped tone and Mom's lingering disappointment were a familiar dance, one I wasn't about to sit through this weekend.

Wanting to steer the conversation elsewhere, I shifted my attention. "Where's Papá?[6]" I asked, scanning the house.

Mom adjusted her apron. "He's at the restaurant. He'll be home later."

Emilia's shoulders sank slightly, a sign of her frustration, but she didn't push further. Hoping to keep things from escalating, I reached for our bags. "I'll take these upstairs."

She nodded, though her gaze lingered on Emilia, who was already pulling out her phone to call Elijah.

Just as I turned toward the staircase, Mom's voice followed me. "Mikkel! Be down by eight for dinner. I'm making *La Bandera. Su favorito*![7]"

It felt like all my prayers were being answered today.

I could already taste the fragrant rice, red beans, and perfectly seasoned chicken, each bite carrying a hint of nostalgia.

"*Te quiero mucho, Mamá*,[8]" I called over my shoulder.

"*¡Yo también te quiero, hijo!*[9]"

Upstairs, I dropped the bags in my old room, took a quick shower, and got settled in. When I checked my phone, the group chat had exploded—Arnoldo, Dillon, and Ronan arguing over something completely pointless as usual.

Then, a message from Alex caught my eye.

---

5 *mom*

6 *dad*

7 *Su favorito-Your favorite*

8 *I love you so much, mom*

9 *I love you too, son*

Alex
you landed?

Me
Yep. Just got to my parents' house.

Alex
great. how was the flight?

Me
A bunch of fucking delays.

Alex
why don't you just buy a jet?

Me
It's not on my high list of priorities.

Alex
of course, it isn't.

Me
I saw her at the airport.

Alex
this has to be fucking fate. tell me you got her name.

Me
I got her name and her Instagram.

Alex
keep me updated.

Me
Will do.

Alex
it's your year of love, brother.

He was right. It was definitely my year of love.

Two hours later, the smell of dinner woke me, and as I headed downstairs, everyone was already seated at the table.

"*Buenas noches a todos*,"[10] I greeted, pulling out my chair. "*Hola, Papá*."[11]

Manuel Suarez, my father, looked up at me, sharp as ever in a white T-shirt and brown cargo pants. He was an older version of me—same

---

10 *Good night everyone*

11 *Hi, Dad*

strong features, same presence that commanded attention. It was almost eerie how much I resembled him, like my parents had copy-pasted his face onto mine the moment I was born.

"*Me alegro de verte, hijo,*"[12] he said, rising slightly to clasp my shoulder before pulling me into a brief hug.

I returned it, feeling the familiar weight of his strength. "How are you?"

"I'm good, Papá,"[13] I replied, meeting his gaze with a smile. "Busy as always, but things are going well. I'm headed to Chicago after the party."

He nodded, approval flashing in his eyes. "Let's eat."

As dishes of *La Bandera* were passed around, my mother's voice carried over the table. "How's the business, *hijo*?[14] I see you making headlines."

"It's great," I said, scooping rice onto my plate. "We're currently working on expansion."

He nodded. "I'm proud of you for following your dream." Then, after a beat, his gaze sharpened. "You're happy, right?"

I met his eyes, knowing the question ran deeper than just business.

A slow smile stretched across my lips.

"Exceedingly happy."

"*¿Alguna mujer?*"[15] mom asked, her tone laced with curiosity.

I smirked, spearing a piece of chicken with my fork. "Whenever there is, you'll be the first to know."

"I hope so." She gave me a pointed look before turning to Emilia. "How are things with you, *mija*?[16] Are you enjoying it there?"

Emilia nodded, chewing her food carefully before answering. "Things are fine. When Elijah is older and more settled, I'm planning to move into a bigger apartment."

---

12 *Good to see you, son*

13 *dad*

14 *son*

15 *Any women?*

16 *my daughter*

Mom's smile faltered, her fingers tightening around her glass. "Are you sure you can handle moving with a toddler? It's not easy when you—"

"*Mamá*."[17] My voice came out sharper than I intended, but I didn't regret it.

Emilia's fork clattered against her plate. She exhaled, slow and measured, but I caught the flicker of irritation in her eyes before she turned to me. "I don't need you to defend me, Mikkel." Her voice was steady, but the tension in her shoulders told me otherwise. "I got through pregnancy on my own; I'm sure I can handle moving."

Dad reached across the table, his weathered hand covering hers. "*Mi querida*,"[18] he said, his voice calm but firm. "You don't have to handle anything on your own. We'll all be there when you decide to move."

Emilia swallowed hard. She nodded, her chair scraping softly against the floor as she stood. "I'm going to call Ashley and check on Elijah. Goodnight."

"Em–" Mamá started, but dad touched her arm, silencing her with a small shake of his head.

"Let her go, Val. She'll come back when she's ready."

I leaned back, gripping the edge of my chair, willing my voice to stay level. "Cut her some slack, Mamá."[19]

Her frown deepened, and for a moment, she looked like she wanted to argue. But instead, she simply pressed her lips together, lowering her gaze to her hands. I knew my mom meant well, but sometimes her words came off a lot more critical than she intended.

The tension stretched between us, thick and suffocating, until my dad shifted the conversation to something safer. "The summer menu is a hit, and we're busy as usual," he said, his voice lighter. "The habichuelas con dulce keeps selling out by lunchtime."

Mamá[20] exhaled, the tension in her shoulders loosening. "We're

---

17 *Mom*

18 *my dear*

19 *Mom*

20 *Mom*

thinking of adding another dessert to the menu. Something light and fresh, maybe with mango or passion fruit."

"I already have the chef working on options," dad added, nodding thoughtfully.

I let their conversation wash over me as they discussed the restaurant they had poured their hearts into for years—El Sabroso Delicia. Their words blended into the background as my mind drifted upstairs. Emilia's voice, the tightness in it, the way she'd practically fled from the table—it weighed heavy in my chest.

Pushing my chair back, I stood. "I'm going to check on Emilia."

Mom waved me off, her voice softer now. "Go on. She might talk to you."

I took the stairs two at a time, stopping in front of Emilia's door. The light beneath it was dim, flickering slightly.

For a moment, I hesitated, pressing my fingers against the wood.

I knocked lightly. "Emilia?"

Silence.

I waited, listening for movement, for a shift, for any sign that she wanted to let me in.

Nothing.

I knocked again, a little firmer this time.

Still no answer.

I cracked the door open, the dim glow from the bedside lamp casting soft shadows over Emilia's sleeping form. She was curled up on her side, her breath slow and steady.

Carefully, I grabbed the blanket from the chair and draped it over her. She stirred slightly, mumbling something unintelligible, but didn't wake. I lingered, watching the way her fingers twitched against the pillow, as if grasping for something just out of reach.

With a quiet exhale, I stepped out and shut the door behind me.

Back in my room, I pulled off my shirt, swapping it for a fresh one before slipping into a pair of joggers. But even as I moved through the motions, my mind was elsewhere.

Abigail.

I sat on the edge of the bed, grabbing my phone without thinking. My fingers moved on their own, typing her username into the search bar.

She'd been on my mind all fucking day.

Her profile popped up instantly, and my thumb hovered over her picture for a beat too long before I clicked.

The first thing I noticed—her smile. Warm. Effortless. The kind that made my chest feel too tight. Her copper curls framed her face perfectly, catching the light in a way that made them look almost golden.

I scrolled.

Each photo was a glimpse into her world. Candid moments frozen in time—laughing with friends, standing against a city backdrop, eyes alight with something unspoken. Then there were the selfies, the ones where she was looking straight into the camera, like she was seeing right through me.

My grip on the phone tightened.

She was gorgeous, yeah. But that wasn't it. Wasn't why my stomach twisted every time I saw her face.

She wasn't just someone you looked at.

She was someone you felt. *Someone you couldn't look away from.*

My thumb hovered over a picture, then double-tapped. One like turned into another. And another. Before I knew it, I'd scrolled through every photo—eighty-three to be exact—she'd posted, my pulse quickening with each one.

When I reached the end, I hesitated.

Then I hit *Follow.*

Setting my phone on the nightstand, I leaned back against the pillows, rubbing a hand over my jaw. The room was quiet, but my thoughts weren't.

Her laugh. The way her name felt rolling off my tongue.

I closed my eyes.

Sleep came eventually.

But not before she followed me into my dreams.

WARNING

The following chapter contains heavy mentions of mental health/physical health issues. Please refer to the content warning list to be reminded of any potential triggers. Your well-being is important to me, so please take care of yourself while reading.

CHAPTER ELEVEN

Abigail-Ann

"Love looks not with the eyes, but with the mind."
*~ **William Shakespeare***

The night blurred by in a haze of exhaustion, my parents rushing off to an emergency and leaving behind a warm tray of lasagna. I ate, hoping to find comfort in the rich, familiar flavors, but the loneliness crept in anyway.

And then, out of nowhere, it hit.

My chest tightened, breath coming too fast, too shallow. The air felt thick, unsteady, like I was sinking into something I couldn't escape. Tears welled up and spilled over, hot and relentless, and no matter how much I tried, I couldn't stop them.

It felt endless.

I squeezed my eyes shut, forcing myself to focus. Inhale. Exhale. Count backward. Again. Again.

Slowly, the world steadied. My pulse slowed. My body sagged with exhaustion.

I climbed back into bed, curling into the sheets, hoping sleep would dull the lingering ache in my chest.

Morning came with the sound of Aurora's voice carrying through the hallway, light and unbothered.

What was it with the women in my life singing before the sun had even fully risen?

Stretching, I groaned softly, the weight from last night still lingering, though lighter now. Rubbing my eyes, I felt the mess of my curls—of course, I'd forgotten my bonnet. *Thank God for silk pillowcases.*

I reached for my phone, skimming my notifications, when one stopped me cold.

"Oh my God!"

The words tumbled out in a squeal as I clutched my phone to my chest, as if I needed to physically hold on to the moment to make it real. A giddy laugh bubbled up before I flopped back against my pillows, eyes wide, heart pounding.

My fingers moved on their own, opening Instagram, scrolling with purpose until I found his profile.

And then I froze.

He liked my pictures.

Every. Single. One.

Heat rushed to my cheeks. I could see it—Mikkel, scrolling through my posts, lingering, taking in each photo.

Then my gaze snagged on something else.

Seventy million followers.

"What the fuck?"

I shot upright, gripping my phone tighter as the number looped through my mind.

Seventy million.

My pulse roared in my ears as I stared at his profile picture—the same face that had left me dazed the first time we met. There were only two posts on his page, both minimal, yet enough to leave an impression that felt impossible to shake.

This man was a phenomenon.

The first photo showed him on a beach at sunset, bathed in molten gold. His tousled hair, black glasses, and white linen shirt—unbuttoned just enough to tease the intricate tattoos on his chest—made him look effortlessly striking.

Did he always wear white?

I thought back to the times I'd seen him. He had. Every single time. It fit him, though. There was this quiet control about him, something steady and unshaken, even in the way he dressed. But here, in this photo, that control was tempered by something untamed. Barefoot in the sand, the ocean behind him like it was his to command—he looked like he belonged to another world.

God, he was sexy. But not in some polished, Hollywood way. No, this was something raw, almost mythical. The kind of allure that felt unreachable.

The second post was entirely different, but just as magnetic. Mikkel at his company's opening, sharp in an all-white suit. His honey-brown eyes locked on the camera, confident, unreadable. Power radiated from him—unshaken, untouchable. The proud set of his shoulders, the ghost of a smirk, the ease in his stance. *Look away if you dare.*

I swallowed.

He looked like he could own the world if he wanted to.

And with seventy million followers, maybe he already did.

Why was I reacting like this?

I *should* have been overthinking. Normally, I'd be dissecting every detail, every like, every possible meaning. But I wasn't. I was just letting the moment exist.

And why the hell was I overthinking the fact that I *wasn't* overthinking?

I huffed, shaking my head, and scrolled back to the first photo. Then the second. Then the first again. My fingers hovered over the edges of my phone, my gaze tracing every inch of him, every hint of the life he lived.

Ridiculous. It was ridiculous, the amount of time I spent staring. But I couldn't stop.

A restless, electric thrill zipped through me—the kind I hadn't felt in ages.

With a deep breath, I tapped the *follow back* button.

The screen shifted, registering the action.

I stared at the bolded text. *What did I just do?*

What if that was a mistake? What if it made me look too eager? Should I have waited longer? Played it cool?

Before I could spiral, a new notification popped up.

A message.

From him.

My pulse leapt.

I froze, my eyes locked on the tiny preview of his words.

What did it say? Should I open it now? Wait? Did the timing even matter?

Stop. Just open it.

With trembling fingers, I tapped the notification. My heart slammed against my ribs as the message unfolded.

@mikkelsuarezofficial:
Good morning, Red. I hope I didn't scare you off with the liking spree. I couldn't resist.

I sat there, fingers hovering over the keyboard, fighting the urge to overthink. I typed, deleted. Typed again. Deleted.

God, why was this so hard?

Finally, I settled on something simple. Something that wouldn't make me sound like I was trying too hard.

Good morning! I don't mind at all.

I hit send and tossed my phone onto the bed, exhaling. *Distraction. I need a distraction.*

The phone buzzed immediately. My pulse jumped.

@mikkelsuarezofficial reacted ♥ to this message

@mikkelsuarezofficial:
How are you?

My stomach dipped. A slow, ridiculous smile tugged at my lips as my fingers flew across the screen.

I'm good. A little tired, but good.

Why the fuck am I so awkward?

Get some rest today, okay? Traveling can be exhausting.

I stared at the message, warmth pooling low in my stomach. My fingers hovered over the keyboard, tapping out a response—

A knock at the door interrupted me.

"Breakfast is ready, Princess." Dad's voice.

I sighed and quickly typed:

I have to go now, but we'll talk later.

@mikkelsuarezofficial:
Looking forward to it, Red. Have a great day.

I locked my phone and headed downstairs, the scent of pancakes and chamomile tea wrapping around me like a hug.

Dad stood by the dining table, flipping through a newspaper. As soon as he saw me, he kissed my cheek.

"Morning, sweetie."

"Morning, Dad," I said, sliding into the seat beside Aurora. "Morning, everyone."

He leaned over to kiss Mom before grabbing his lab coat. "I've got a patient in an hour, so I'm headed to the clinic." His tone shifted, more serious. "Listen, you need to finish packing today, but I don't want you alone with that boy."

I rolled my eyes. "I'll be fine, Dad. Just a few things left to sort out."

Aurora barely looked up from her phone. "Don't worry, Pops. We're going together, so she won't be alone with Joshua."

Dad's frown didn't fully ease, but he nodded. "Alright. Just be careful, and if you need anything, call me."

"We will."

With one last look, he kissed Mom again before heading out.

Mom, who had been uncharacteristically quiet, finally spoke. "The movers will be here this weekend, so we need everything packed by then."

Aurora and I nodded.

"Oh, and we picked up some clothes from your apartment yesterday."

"Thanks, Mom."

She smiled, grabbing her purse. "Alright, I'm off to work. Love you girls."

The front door closed behind her, leaving the kitchen quiet except for the distant hum of traffic outside.

I poked at my pancakes, appetite suddenly waning.

Aurora set down her fork. "You ready for this?"

I let out a slow breath. My chest felt tight. *No, I wasn't.* But that didn't matter.

"I have to be."

The moment the car rolled to a stop, my stomach twisted with unease. My hands were clammy. My pulse raced. The gnawing dread refused to let go.

I had no idea if Joshua was inside or what to expect. The uncertainty was unbearable. Forcing myself to breathe, I grabbed the empty boxes and tape from the trunk and made my way toward the lobby.

Inside, the familiar faces of the security guards offered a small but fleeting sense of stability, anchoring me amid the storm brewing inside.

"Good afternoon, Miss Asher," one of them greeted, his voice kind. "Welcome back."

I forced a smile and nodded, but my mind was already racing ahead, bracing for what lay beyond the elevator doors. As Aurora and I stepped inside, the polished marble floors seemed to stretch endlessly, making the journey to the third floor feel like an eternity.

Bittersweet memories, heartbreak, and countless nights spent crying and hating myself swirled in my mind.

A soft ding signaled our arrival.

We stepped into the hallway, and with each step toward Apartment 50B, the weight of the moment pressed down harder.

Aurora turned to me suddenly, pulling me into a hug so fast I barely had time to react.

"Shut up and let me hug you," she muttered before I could protest.

I frowned slightly. "But you don't like hugging."

"You're my sister, dumbass."

Her arms tightened around me, grounding me in the warmth of her presence. It was more than just a hug—it was a silent promise. A reminder that no matter what, she'd be there.

Steeling myself, I stepped inside.

Sunlight poured through the windows, but the apartment felt anything but bright. An overwhelming darkness seemed to seep into every corner.

I moved down the hallway, deliberately avoiding the living room. The bedroom door was slightly ajar, and despite myself, I peeked inside. The bed was unkempt, covers tossed aside. The room felt cold, unfamiliar—just a shell of what it once was.

Then, I turned to the living room.

And stopped.

The sight before me was worse than I imagined.

Empty bottles littered the floor. Beer cans, half-smoked cigarettes, and scattered pills formed a chaotic mess, mingling with dirty dishes and leftover food that had long started to decay. The air was thick with the stench of alcohol and something sour—rotting, forgotten.

"Holy shit," Aurora whispered.

She looked at me, wide-eyed. "This is…"

She didn't have to finish.

"A fucking mess," I hissed.

Aurora turned to me. "Do you want to come back later?"

Her voice was soft, but the weight of the question hit hard.

I swallowed, glancing back at the wreckage of what had once been my home. My past. My pain.

"No," I said finally, my voice steady despite the storm inside me. "I need to do this now."

"You sort, and I'll pack and label so we move faster," Aurora suggested.

"Sounds good."

I dove into packing, but the weight of the moment pressed down on me like a heavy fog.

I was really leaving.

I was really moving on.

Sadness, anger, relief, and fear tangled inside me as I wrapped each item in paper or bubble wrap. Every piece carried a weight beyond its physical form—the coffee mug from our first vacation, the blanket we once curled up under, the books we read late into the night. Ghosts of a past I was finally ready to leave behind.

For the first time, I let the reality sink in—he would never have me again.

But instead of breaking me, the thought settled like quiet closure, lighter than I expected.

Time blurred, and before I knew it, two and a half hours had passed. We were still at it.

"We've been at this for a while," Aurora murmured, stretching with a soft yawn. "I'm grabbing us lunch."

"Where?"

"Shake Shack!" She grinned. "I've been dying for a burger. Your order's the same, right?"

I nodded. "It is. Thank you."

As she left, I focused on packing the last two boxes, letting Mikkel's interview play softly in the background. It had popped up as a suggested video—probably due to my recent searches—but I didn't mind. His voice was steady, assured, and… comforting in a way I couldn't explain.

Sorting through my clothes and shoes, I set aside anything in good condition to donate. Then, stretching my sore muscles, I wandered into the hallway. My gaze landed on a framed photo of us—an illusion of happier times. But that was never our reality.

Just a façade I had clung to.

I had settled for scraps of affection, convincing myself they were enough when I deserved so much more.

With a quiet exhale, I placed the photo back on the wall, but a voice behind me made me freeze.

"What's going on, babe?"

I turned.

Joshua stood in the doorway, his brow furrowed in confusion.

"I'm leaving," I said, forcing myself to sound casual despite the irritation crawling up my spine.

"Leaving?" His gaze flickered around the room, as if just now realizing the half-packed boxes. "You're going on another trip?"

I swallowed the lump in my throat. "A permanent trip."

Something in me expected a reaction. Shock. Regret. Maybe even a sliver of sadness. But his face remained unreadable.

And then, to my utter lack of surprise, he shrugged.

"I'll see you later, then." He stepped past me, grabbing a coat off the hook. "Came to get this."

A bitter scoff escaped before I could stop it.

"This is why I'm leaving." The words were out before I could second-guess them, heavy with the sorrow I could no longer bear.

Joshua finally looked at me, confusion creasing his forehead. "What do you mean?" His voice wavered, the slightest tremor of unease creeping in. "Aren't you leaving to see Azzaria?"

I stared at him, something in me breaking and hardening all at once.

Taking a deep breath, I found the strength to say the words that had been festering inside me for far too long.

"I'm moving," I said, my voice steadier now, despite the storm raging inside.

His expression shifted, lips parting slightly, but no real understanding dawned.

"Is this a joke?"

"The only joke here is you," I continued, the memory of betrayal still fresh in my mind. "Five years and *you* threw it all away. *You* ruined us. *You* don't care. *You* let me feel like a burden. *You* broke everything. I gave *you* everything that I couldn't afford to lose. Every time I would pull myself together and want to leave, you came out of the blue saying you'd change and I believed you and you'd go right back to square one. What more is there to give you? The only time I matter is when I'm spreading my legs as you told me the other day. That's what I'm there for, right? I made you who you are. When you couldn't do shit yourself, I did it and now, I'm fucking done."

He was speechless, his eyes darting away from my accusing gaze, searching for a way to shift the blame, to justify his actions. But there was no justification, no excuse that could erase the hurt he had caused.

"This is unfa-"

My anger flared, fueled by years of silent suffering, by the pain of knowing I had been deceived. "Don't you dare try to shift the blame," I spat, my voice dripping with venom.

"Why now?" he pleaded, reaching out for me as if hoping to hold onto what had already slipped away between us. "I'll do better."

But I recoiled, the distance between us widening with each passing second. "Why now?" I echoed, my voice hollow with resignation. "Because I can't do this anymore. Because I deserve better. Because this should've been done the first time you showed me you didn't want me. Because the cheating and the alcohol and bars with your friends were more important. Because I'm nothing more than an easy way for you to get yourself off. Because you're never there when I need you."

He leaned in, his lips seeking solace, and I stepped back, my demeanor hardening as disgust washed over my features.

"You know all those times when you blamed your dad?" I said softly, my voice trembling, but firm. "When you said you hated him?"

He stopped, a subtle tension creeping into his shoulders. He didn't look at me, but I could feel the heaviness of his silence.

I took a deep breath, trying to steady my voice. "You're just like him."

His body stiffened. His eyes flashed with a flicker of anger, and I could see the fire building inside him. But it didn't stop me. "Go ahead, Joshua." My voice suddenly sharpened. "Break the vases. Be your daddy's son."

He didn't move a muscle.

Finally, he took a step back, the anger draining from his face. His breath came in sharp bursts.

The words escaped me in a whisper, the finality of them cutting through the air like a blade. "You came to grab your coat, do it, and leave."

And with that, I turned away, leaving him to grapple with the burden of his regrets, alone in the silence of our shattered love.

By the time Aurora returned with lunch, I was nearly done packing. Her bright smile faded the moment she stepped inside, her gaze sweeping over the last few boxes and then landing on me. She didn't have to say anything—the weight in the air spoke for itself.

We ate in relative silence, the only sounds coming from the rustling of paper bags and the occasional hum of conversation from the interview in the background. The Shake Shack burger should have been comforting, but it tasted like nothing.

Before we knew it, night had fallen. Our parents' calls became incessant, checking in, worrying. With the final box sealed and stacked by the door, we finally left.

Aurora was unusually quiet as we drove, but I could feel her watching me, concern radiating off her in waves.

"Abi," she called softly. "Are you o—?"

"I will be." My voice was steadier than I expected, but my chest still ached. "I just needed to put that part of my life behind me."

She exhaled slowly, gripping the steering wheel a little tighter. "I get it, but don't beat yourself up over it. It was five years, yeah, but you have an eternity ahead of you. You have no idea what the future holds."

The moment her words settled, Mikkel immediately came to mind, and I hated myself for it. A fresh wave of guilt crashed over me. I had just left someone, and yet my thoughts were tangled with someone else.

Fuck me.

"I wanted him to want me," I whispered, the admission stinging like salt on an open wound. "But he never did, and that's where I went wrong."

Aurora sighed. "No," she corrected gently. "It all went wrong when you thought you had to teach him how to love you. The right man won't need lessons."

I swallowed hard, blinking rapidly as a tear slipped down my cheek.

"For now, love yourself more than you could ever hate him," she continued. "And I promise you, everything will be okay."

Her words sat heavy in my chest, pressing against something I wasn't ready to name.

The rest of the ride was quiet. The hum of the car, the distant glow of streetlights flickering past, the city still alive despite the ache settling in my bones—it all blurred together.

When we finally pulled into the driveway, the house was warm and lit up, golden light spilling through the windows. The scent of home hit me the moment I stepped inside—my mom's perfume, hints of something baking, the subtle freshness of linen. It was familiar, safe. But right now, it only made the ache worse.

Mom and Dad were waiting in the living room. The moment she saw me, her expression softened, her concern barely masked beneath the warmth of her voice.

"Do you have everything you need?" she asked.

I forced a small, tired smile. "Anything I don't have, I can buy later."

"We're getting ready to eat soon," she offered gently, an unspoken invitation.

"I'm not hungry."

I turned toward the stairs, and as I walked away, I heard her whisper to Aurora, "What happened?"

"She just needs some time, Mom."

"I'm going to see what's up." Mom's footsteps followed, her worry evident in every step.

Aurora stopped her before she could climb. "Mom, let her have tonight. She needs space."

I paused on the stairs, my fingers curling into the wooden railing, feeling both gratitude and sadness.

Finally, in the quiet of my old bedroom, I let out a slow, shaky breath and collapsed onto the bed. The mattress was familiar, and the blankets still smelled faintly of home, but everything inside me felt foreign, like I was drifting somewhere in between the past and the unknown.

Just as I shut my eyes, my phone buzzed.

I almost ignored it. I should have. I was too tired to deal with anything else, too emotionally drained to open myself up to more.

But when I glanced at the screen, my breath caught.

Mikkel.

I hesitated. My fingers had tingled as I unlocked the phone, my pulse had picked up even though I had told myself it shouldn't have.

Despite everything—the exhaustion, the heartache, the weight of the past—I felt warmth bloom in my chest. And I hated how much I wanted to read whatever he had sent.

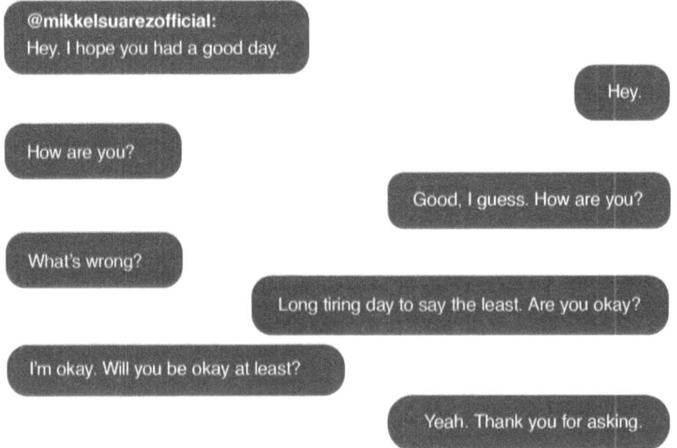

This might sound weird coming from someone you barely know, but if you need to talk, I'm here.

Thank you.

You're not crying, right?

No? Why?

Good. Remember I told you that you're too pretty to cry.

You were right.

Huh?

It wasn't worth my tears.

I'm glad you saw that.

Also, how was your flight? I forgot to ask.

It was good. I have a bit of flight anxiety but I survived.

Aerophobia or something else?

Not aerophobia, I just hate crowded spaces and airplanes are very crowded.

This is depressing lol. Distract me?

Alright. Let's play a game.

If you could have dinner with any three people, dead or alive, who would they be and why?

Marilyn Monroe because she's an icon.

That's one, two more.

Aurora (my sister) because she LOVES Marilyn.

Lana Del Rey because Lana would just have to be there.

Terrence Loves You.

WAIT… Wait… Did he just—

You listen to Lana???

I do.

What three songs would have to be on the aux if we were in a car?

Million Dollar Man, Video Games and Venice Bitch.

Impressive.

You KNOW Lana.

Shocking?

Very.

Your three?

Born to Die, Bartender and Cinnamon Girl

Top 10, I'll give you that.

They're classics! And Lana's voice is just…

Mesmerizing? I've seen her live, and it was incredible.

I've always wanted to see her perform live but never got the chance to.

Maybe someday I can make that happen.

I'd sob so hard if it did.

@mikkelsuarezofficial reacted ♥ to this message

It's getting late. I'm going to head to bed.

Before you go, how was the distraction?

I felt a warmth spreading through me.

As great as the company.

Happy to be of service.

Goodnight, Red.

Goodnight, Mikkel.

Sweet dreams.

I smiled at my phone, feeling lighter, and drifted off to sleep.

CHAPTER TWELVE

Mikkel

"In dreams and in love, there are no impossibilities."
~ Janos Arnay

Meetings drained me.

One after the other, my morning had been spent smoothing out errors, perfecting documents, and ensuring no detail was out of place. I sat through a quarterly Zoom meeting with the board—same formalities, same pleasantries, same recycled concerns about market trends and expansion. I had answered their questions with ease, laid out projections, and reinforced Elite Rides' dominance.

Still, frustration lingered. I had combed through everything at least thirty times, and each time, I found something that didn't sit right. It grated on my nerves, an itch I couldn't scratch, a flaw I couldn't unsee.

The only thing keeping me sane was texting Abigail.

I never thought I'd be the guy lounging around the house, phone in hand, waiting for a reply like some lovesick teenager. But here I was, *a lovesick adult*, checking the screen between emails, a grin tugging at my lips every time her name popped up. The way she texted—sometimes quick, sometimes drawn—had me hooked. I swore I was past the age of getting giddy over a text, but every time my phone lit up, my heart kicked up a notch.

I liked it.

A little after noon, I finally pushed away from my desk. My suit was ready for pickup at Wilkes Bashford, and I needed a breather.

Just as I was about to head out, my mother stopped me at the door.

"*Hijo,*[1] the engagement party is canceled."

I frowned. "Canceled?"

She nodded. "*Tía* Rosalina[2] called. It's off, and I already called to have your suit sent to New York instead."

"Alright then." I kissed her cheek, not pressing for details. "*Gracias, Mamá.*[3]"

With my evening suddenly free, I turned toward Emilia's room, knocking once. No answer. I knocked again, then pushed the door open. Empty.

Hm.

Shrugging, I retreated to my room, grabbed the remote and flipped on *You*. I had cleared my schedule for this damn party, and now I had nothing to do but lounge around and let TV fill the silence.

Then, my phone buzzed.

Abigail.

The canceled party, the annoying meetings, the nitpicking—all of it faded as I opened her text, already feeling the grin forming on my face.

@abi_asher:
You forgot me already? Lol.

---

1 *Son*

2 *Aunt Rosalina*

3 *Thanks, mom*

Forget her? That was becoming more and more impossible.

God's on my side.

"You look happy."

I turned around. Emilia stood in the doorway, arms crossed.

Quickly, I texted Abigail

I'll be back, my sister's here.

Then, I laughed.

"What happened?" Emilia asked, stepping into the room. "You're normally deep in a proposal."

I rolled my eyes. "Are pigs flying, or are you *actually* talking to me, *hermana*?[4]"

She scoffed. "I just had about three *Palomas* from Mamá y papá restaurant, so I'm plied with enough alcohol."[5]

---

4 *sister*

5 *Mom and Dad*

"Risky. Never knew you drank."

She rolled her eyes and moved to sit on my bed, letting out a deep sigh.

"¿Qué pasa?[6]" I asked.

She hesitated, then met my gaze. "I don't hate you, Mikkel."

I blinked. "What?"

"I don't hate you," she repeated, then paused before continuing. "Sometimes, I can't handle my emotions, and I only turn to myself. That's why I come off the way I do, but I don't hate you. I couldn't, *hermano*."[7]

Without thinking, I pulled her into a hug. "I know you have a lot going on. Sometimes, I just worry about you. *Pero te quiero mucho*."[8]

She nodded against my shoulder, hugging me back.

As we pulled apart, my phone rang. Morison.

I was about to decline when Emilia nudged me. "Go on. I'm going to help Mamá bake."

While left, I stepped by the window, pressing the phone to my ear. "Morison, what's up?"

"Payroll issue," he said, frustration laced in his voice. "There's a miscalculation, and I need your approval to override it."

I sighed, rubbing my temple. "Send it over. I'll look at it now."

After reviewing the issue and signing off on the necessary adjustments, exhaustion hit me like a freight train. I barely made it onto the bed before sleep pulled me under.

When I woke up, the first thing I did was check my phone. Abigail had sent a message saying she was going to finish packing, to which I replied, *Sorry about the abrupt pause earlier, I fell asleep. I hope packing isn't too tiring.*

I stretched and made my way downstairs, finding the house unusually quiet, with no one around. On the counter sat a bowl of *rabo guisado* and a plate of *buñuelos*—leftovers from whatever Mamá and Emilia had been

---

6 *What's wrong?*

7 *brother*

8 *But I love you very much*

cooking earlier. I ate in silence, the warm flavors settling comfortably in my stomach.

Back upstairs, Arnoldo and I sifted through legal documents, handling contract revisions and ensuring that everything was solid for the expansion pitch.

Then, finally, my phone pinged with a message from Abigail.

@abi_asher:
I gave up halfway.

You tried, that's all that matters.

Trying to make me feel good about my failures?

Hardly a failure, Red.

I'll take your word for it.

You should. I don't say things I don't mean.

Smooth.

Always.

How's your trip going so far?

It's good.

My mom made lasagna, so that made it even better.

Lasagna's one of my favorites, by the way.

Noted.

I'll keep that in mind.

In mind for what?

The future.

Bold.

Too much?

There was a pause before she responded, and I smirked at my screen, wondering what was going through her mind.

Nope.

Just enough, actually.

I didn't know if it was my words or the fact that she wasn't shutting me down, but my pulse picked up.

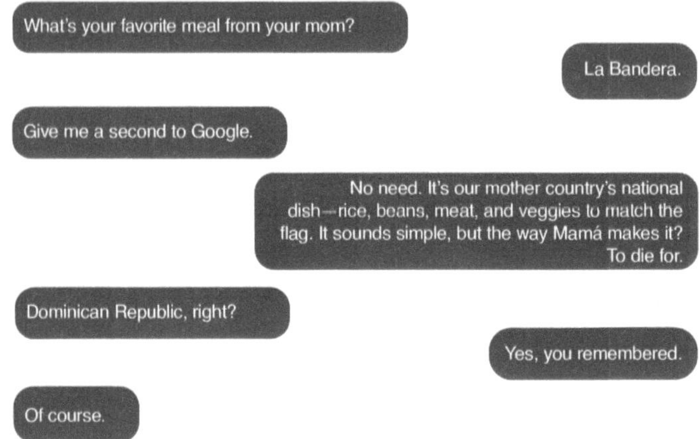

A warm satisfaction settled in my chest. She'd remembered.

As the night went on, our messages became more frequent, the conversation flowing effortlessly. We swapped favorite songs, debated over music genres, and tossed recommendations back and forth.

At some point, her responses slowed.

A lie.

I should've been sleeping for my flight tomorrow, but instead, I spent nearly two hours scrolling, searching for the perfect pictures and fonts for the playlist cover. Canva was a pain to deal with, but I finally managed to put something decent together. Unsure whether she used Apple Music or Spotify, I made versions for both, then started building the playlist until sleep finally overtook me.

The steady rain pattered against the car window as I joined an impromptu Zoom call with my team en route to the investor meeting. The city outside was blurred in streaks of water, matching the exhaustion tugging at me. Sapphire had sent a last-minute reminder about key discussion points, so I listened as we reviewed last week's performance—an uptick in bookings, high customer satisfaction ratings, and seamless execution of our latest promotions.

Leaving Sacramento this morning had been a struggle, and the back-to-back travel was wearing on me. Chicago had its charms—hotdogs, deep-dish pizza, architecture—but I wouldn't be here long enough to enjoy any of it.

By the time I entered the boardroom, the low murmur of conversation died instantly. The air was thick with calculation. Damon Ashford sat rigidly, his sharp gaze assessing, jaw clenched like he was already preparing a counterattack. Cataleya Nguyen was poised, exuding quiet authority, her pen tapping against the table in measured beats. And Marissa Lyles—the wildcard—was reclined, one arm draped over the chair like she'd already decided how this would go.

I took my seat at the head of the table. Calm. Controlled. Owning the room.

"Good afternoon," I began, adjusting my cuffs. "Let's get started. Elite Rides is expanding. We've perfected New York City, and now it's time for the next step."

Damon didn't hesitate. "I've reviewed the numbers, and Chicago's projections are ambitious. Do you really think you can maintain your edge, Suarez?"

I met his gaze without blinking. "We're not aiming to 'handle' Chicago, Ashford. We're aiming to own it. Just like we do New York. Our edge isn't a question—it's a guarantee."

His expression didn't shift, but I could see the wheels turning.

Cataleya leaned forward slightly. "And scalability? Expanding too fast can be a death sentence. How do you avoid stretching your resources too thin?"

I nodded, already anticipating the concern. "We've built an expansion team dedicated to each city—separate from New York operations. Every location has localized strategies, key partnerships, and infrastructure in place before launch. We don't stretch thin—we scale smart."

Marissa cocked her head, a smirk tugging at her lips. "Ambition is great, but speed kills. Scaling too fast can dilute exclusivity. How do you keep quality high?"

I leaned forward, voice even but firm. "Elite Rides doesn't sacrifice quality. Ever. Our exclusivity is built into the experience—from rigorous driver training to customer personalization. Our data-driven approach refines the service as we expand. The bigger we get, the better we get."

Damon snorted. "Bold words. I want specifics. When will Chicago go live?"

"Four weeks from today. Beta testing is already underway. On launch day, we'll be fully operational and dominating the market."

Cataleya arched her brow. "And if Chicago doesn't go as planned?"

I didn't miss a beat. "We don't hit roadblocks, Cataleya. We pivot. Chicago is just the start—we're already laying the groundwork in our next locations. We don't enter markets to participate. We enter to disrupt and win."

Marissa studied me, her smirk deepening. "Sounds like you've got it all figured out."

I held her gaze. "I do. And let's be clear—investing in Elite Rides means investing in the future of urban mobility. Either you're on board, or you're standing in the way of progress. This is happening—with or without you."

Silence.

They were calculating, but I knew they saw it. This wasn't a risk—it was an inevitability.

Damon exhaled slowly, then leaned back, nodding once. "I'm in."

Cataleya followed. "Same here."

Marissa's smile widened. "Looks like you've got yourself a deal."

I stood, shaking their hands. "Good choice."

As I exited the room, adrenaline still hummed in my veins. The deal was done. The expansion was locked in. Another city in my pocket.

I reached for my phone to share the update with Sapphire, but before I could, my pocket buzzed.

I glanced down.

Abigail.

An involuntary smile tugged at my lips.

Her text was brief—letting me know she'd be unavailable today because of a family trip and packing—but it meant more than she probably realized. She didn't have to tell me. But she did.

I exhaled, leaning against the cool marble wall. The sharp focus of the boardroom was already softening, shifting into something else entirely. She lingered in my thoughts like an unshakable presence. And I was completely at peace with that.

CHAPTER THIRTEEN

Abigail-Ann

"Love is the bridge between you and everything."
~ Rumi

I never truly considered what moving meant. I was starting over in a new city, away from my parents and sister, and I knew I'd miss our late-night talks, Mom's lasagna, and the comfort of having family nearby. I would miss San Francisco and the familiarity it brought, but I knew I had to keep moving forward.

You'd think my years with Joshua would haunt me, but my thoughts were consumed by Mikkel instead. His words made me feel alive and understood, like he knew exactly what I needed to hear. Conversations with him were effortless, as if we'd known each other forever. His small gestures made me smile, and his genuine interest in my passions surprised me—especially when I found out he was a true Lana fan, not just name-dropping her for the sake of flirting.

When I shared that *Born to Die* was my comfort album, he texted, “Same here. Especially *Video Games*. It’s like living in a memory that’s both beautiful and painful.” Then, I joked about *Norman Fucking Rockwell!* being my study music, and he sent a breakdown of why *Venice Bitch* was the perfect escape. His thoughtful responses kept me hooked, but the sound of the movers closing the truck doors snapped me back. They finished loading and waved goodbye, the delay caused by Mom repacking everything after criticizing our packing—*typical Alicia.* I took a deep breath and made my way to the back patio, where my family was waiting.

“Sweetheart,” Mom’s voice was gentle, a soft smile touching her lips as she patted the space beside her. “The movers finished?”

I nodded, exhaling as I sank onto the couch. “They just left.”

“Perfect. We need to talk.”

A knot formed in my stomach. “What’s up?”

“You’re moving, and we need to know you have a plan. If not, we’ll help make one.”

I nodded again, trying to ignore the creeping anxiety. “I mean, I plan to get a job, but right now, I’m focused on getting everything moved first. Then graduation.”

“What kind of work are you thinking about?” Dad’s voice was calm, but concern lingered beneath it. He clasped his hands together, leaning forward.

Before I could answer, Aurora chimed in, her voice full of certainty. “She’s going to work in a bookstore. I called a friend at Book Culture—they need staff, so I recommended Abi.”

I blinked, warmth spreading in my chest. Time and time again, Aurora had my back without me even asking. She made life feel easier, like I wasn’t constantly scrambling to figure it all out alone. I turned to her, mouthing a silent “Thank you.”

She winked in response, as if to say, *Always*.

“Perfect. And after the degree?”

“*Pops*,” Aurora interjected, firm but affectionate. “Don’t pressure her. When she graduates, things will fall into place.”

Dad's shoulders loosened slightly, but the worry didn't fully fade. "I just need to know she'll be okay."

I met his gaze, hoping to ease his concerns. "After graduation, I'll apply for apprenticeships and focus on building my career."

He nodded, satisfied, but not before asking, "Speaking of graduation—your fees are settled, right?"

"Yes, Dad."

Without another word, he pulled out an envelope and handed it to me. Inside was a bank card.

"Six thousand a month for rent and expenses, until you're on your feet. Consider it an early graduation gift."

I sucked in a breath, my fingers tightening around the card. A lump rose in my throat, the weight of their unwavering support pressing into my chest. "Thank you. How will I ever repay you?"

Mom placed a gentle hand on my thigh, grounding me. "You've made us proud, Princess. We promised to always support you and your sister."

Emotion thickened my voice. "You're amazing parents."

The heaviness in my chest eased, replaced by something softer—reassurance, love.

For the rest of the evening, we stayed right there. Talking, laughing, just *being*.

Later, Azzaria and I texted about her hot billionaire, whom she still couldn't wrap her head around, my packing progress, and her plans for the week. We chatted until she had to get ready for a night out with her mom.

I purposely avoided mentioning my breakup. It wasn't something I wanted to discuss over the phone.

As I settled in for the night, my phone vibrated on the nightstand. Mikkel's name lit up the screen, and an involuntary warmth spread through my chest. My stomach did a little flip—annoying and impossible to ignore.

Lately, he was everywhere. A *New York Post* article. A *Good Morning America* interview. His confidence was magnetic, the way he spoke—sharp, controlled, relentless. And *maybe* I wasn't actively keeping up with him, but the algorithm sure thought I was.

I hesitated before opening his message, but before I could fully process why, another thought snuck in.

Shouldn't I feel more after leaving Joshua?

The guilt crept in, slow and insidious. Shouldn't I feel heartbroken? Shouldn't I be wallowing in regret?

But I wasn't.

And that scared me more than anything.

I let out a slow breath, staring at the phone in my hand. Maybe I didn't have all the answers yet. Maybe I was still figuring it out.

But for the first time in five years, I felt *free.*

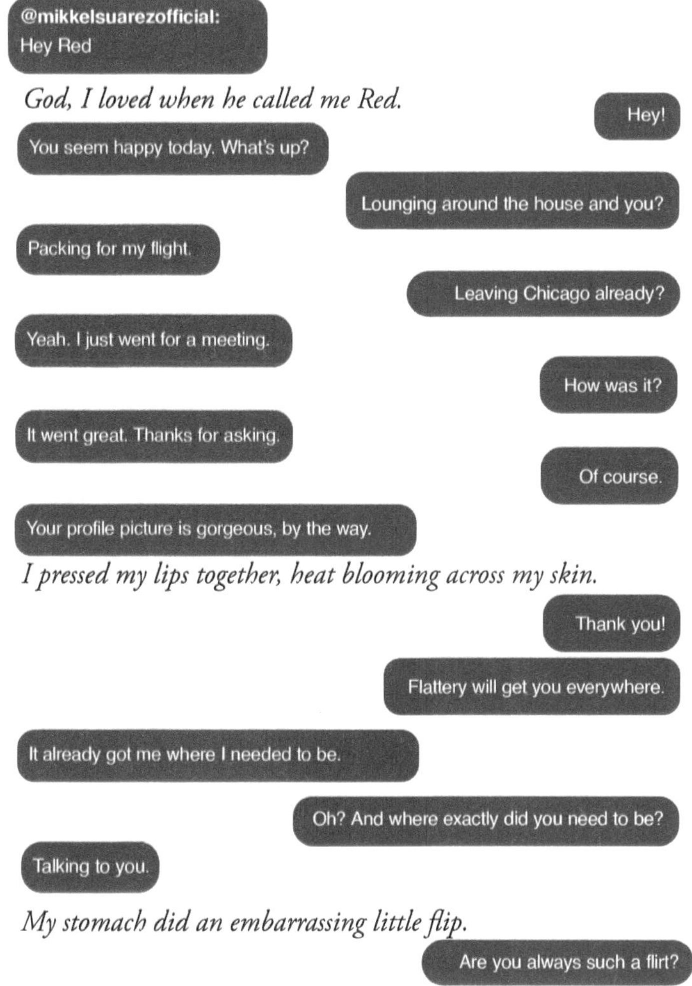

That would imply me flirting with others, and I tend not to.

I only flirt with you, Red.

I stared at my screen, heart hammering. He was too smooth for his own good.

You really are smooth.

Will smoothness get me everywhere too?

Smoothness, sincerity, and a good sense of humor. That's a winning combination.

I've got at least two out of three, right?

I'd say you're batting a solid three for three, Mikkel.

Flattery will get you everywhere too, huh?

When it's deserved, why not?

Well, in that case, I'll keep trying to earn it.

And I'll keep appreciating it.

@mikkelsuarezofficial reacted ♥ to this message

What's next for you to do today?

Get to the airport. You?

Sleeping because I spent all week packing.

Also, you wouldn't believe what my mother did!

What happened?

She unpacked the boxes my sister and I packed because it apparently wasn't done properly.

That's some serious commitment to getting it done her way. 🤣🤣

Right? She's impossible to deal with sometimes.

Well, at least you don't have to worry about it being done wrong.

I'm just glad it's over because moving is exhausting.

I bet. Especially with all those boxes... What time did you finally finish?

Around 9. I might sleep for a week.

You deserve it after all that. Get some rest, cariño[1] and text me whenever you're up.

I reacted to the message, then translated what he said, and nearly fell off the bed.

Sweetheart.

He called me sweetheart.

I set my phone down to charge, Mikkel's texts still lingering in my mind, a smile tugging at my lips. Curling up in bed, the soft sheets wrapped around me like a warm embrace. With thoughts of him drifting through my head, I closed my eyes, letting sleep carry me into a world where anything felt possible.

---

1 *Sweetheart*

CHAPTER FOURTEEN

Mikkel

"Love is a meeting of two souls, fully accepting the dark and the light within each other, bound by the courage to grow through struggle into bliss."
~ Unknown

The city pulsed with energy, the familiar hum of honking taxis and distant chatter welcoming me back. After landing and checking in on Emilia, I crashed for a quick nap before heading to Alex's house.

"How was the trip?" Alex asked, lifting an eyebrow as he took a sip of his beer. "Arnoldo said you hit the Windy City."

I leaned back, stretching my arms with a contented sigh. "Sacramento was good. Chicago? Even better. Secured all three key investors."

His grin widened. "Look at you, making moves."

I shrugged. "All in a day's work."

He let out a low chuckle. "Yeah, yeah. Like it's nothing." He studied me for a moment before smirking. "How's your girlfriend?"

Heat crept up my neck before I could stop it. My lips twitched—too much of a smile, too fast. "She's not my girlfriend yet." I paused, as if saying it aloud would make it true. "But we've been texting. She had a headache earlier, so she's resting."

Alex leaned in, eyes narrowing slightly. "Does she text you every day?"

"Yeah," I said, but it came out almost like a question, a shrug slipping in for cover.

"Do you guys flirt?"

I exhaled through my nose, shaking my head with a knowing smirk. "Yes."

"Does she tell you what she's up to?"

"Yeah."

His smirk deepened. "Then she's your girl."

I huffed out a laugh. "It's not that simple."

"Are you gonna ask her out?"

This time, my answer came without hesitation. "Yes." My voice was firm. "I'm waiting until she's back to make my official move."

Alex nodded, something unreadable flickering in his expression before it settled into approval. "I think this can be good for you."

I met his gaze. "I think so too."

"Mikkel!"

Mara's voice rang out from the hallway, full of surprise. I turned just as she stepped into the room, her eyes widening.

"I thought you were away."

A grin spread across my face as I stood, pulling her into a hug. "I was. But I'm back now."

I grabbed the two gift bags beside me and handed them to Mara. "The lilac one's for your birthday, and the blue one's for the baby shower. I'm sorry I missed both."

She waved it off. "If you could've been there, you would've. And thanks for the gifts."

Alex, standing beside her, studied her face. "You okay, angel?"

She yawned, rubbing her belly with a contented smile. "I'm fine. Just hungry. And my belly dropped."

Alex's head snapped up. "Dropped? Are you okay? Is the baby okay?"

Mara's laughter filled the room, her eyes dancing with amusement. "Relax, babe. It just means my body's getting ready for birth."

Alex let out a breath, raking a hand through his hair. "Damn. Had me worried for a second." He recovered quickly. "Alright, what do you want for dinner?"

She hummed, considering. "I don't know."

Alex was already reaching for his keys. "You want me to grab something? Or I can cook."

Mara shook her head. "I'll just DoorDash."

Alex pulled out his Amex, holding it out to her. "Get whatever you want."

She took it with a smile, eyes softening. "Thank you, baby. You spoil me."

"That's what I'm here for." His voice was warm, genuine.

As Mara walked out, my phone buzzed.

Dill
I know you're on a trip, but can I get a driver to pick up Azzaria in an hour?

Me
I'll do it. I'm back.

Dill
You sure?

Me
Yeah.

I locked my screen and slipped my phone into my pocket. "Sorry about that. Dillon texted."

Alex nodded. "Everything good?"

"Yeah, just a favor."

He gestured toward his liquor tray. "You want a drink?"

"Sure."

He poured whiskey into two glasses and handed me one. I took it with a grateful nod, the familiar burn grounding me back into the moment.

"How deep have you guys gotten?"

I shrugged, thinking it over. "Surface level. We're becoming friends, getting to know each other."

Alex smirked. "You could ask Arnoldo to do a little deep digging. Or hire a PI."

I gave him a dry look. "I'd rather get to know her myself, Alexander."

He laughed. "Always the better one of us."

I arched my brow. "Did you hire a PI for Mara?"

His grin turned sheepish. "She's my best friend's sister. I knew what I needed to do."

"Yes or no?"

Alex exhaled. "Yes." Then, with a smirk, "Even Lucio had someone look into Marina, and they're high school sweethearts."

I shook my head, chuckling. "You all are some possessive sons of bitches."

Alex lifted his glass in a lazy toast. "Women love it."

I huffed a laugh. "Maybe. But I like to think it's more about showing you care."

He nodded. "Touché. Always the better one of us."

I smirked. "So, what's the plan for the weekend?"

"Not much. Just spending time with Mara before the baby comes. You?"

I shrugged. "Catching up on work. Talking to Abigail."

Alex studied me for a second before taking a sip of his drink. "It's good to see you taking things slow with your redhead. Shows respect."

I nodded. "I don't want her to feel rushed."

Alex's lips quirked. "Just don't wait too long. Someone else might sweep her off her feet."

I chuckled, but the thought sat uneasily in my chest. "I'll keep that in mind."

A glance at my watch told me it was time to go. I downed the last of my whiskey and stood. "I should head out."

Alex stood, clapping me on the back. "Thanks for stopping by. Gym tomorrow?"

"Definitely." I moved toward the door. "Take care of Mara and the baby."

His expression softened. "Always. And good luck with your girl."

I smirked. "You know I don't believe in luck."

Alex chuckled. "Yeah, yeah. See you soon."

People often wondered why I prioritized my friends, but the truth was simple: when I had nothing, I had them.

Dillon, especially, had done more for me than I could ever repay. He never made me feel like I owed him, but I still found ways to show my gratitude. That's why, without hesitation, I took Azzaria to the beach for their date. It was rare to see Dillon like this—calm and collected on his wedding day but now jittery over every last detail.

"Thanks, Suarez," Dillon said as I brought Azzaria over to him.

"Anytime." I smiled, giving him a reassuring pat on the back.

With a final nod, I got back into my car. The engine roared to life just as my phone buzzed with a text from Abigail.

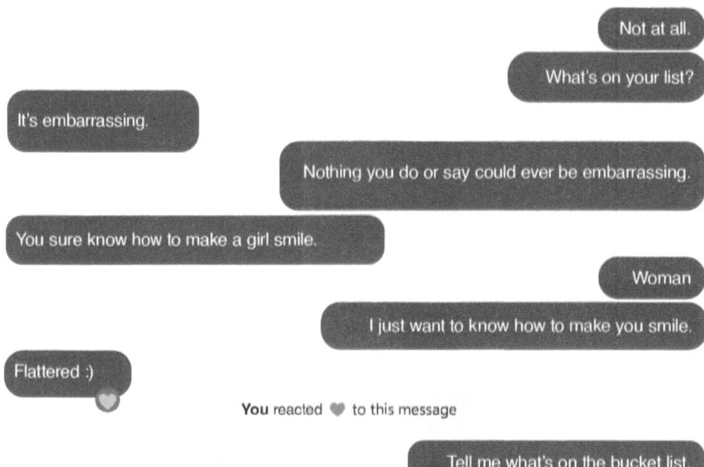

Her next message was a screenshot of her notes. I immediately saved it before she could change her mind.

- [ ] Helicopter ride - BD
- [ ] Feed sharks/dolphins/whales
- [ ] Play with/see a sea lion (I never get to see them in San Francisco)
- [ ] Empire State Building
- [ ] Explore a Farmer's Market
- [ ] Camping at a beach / Night Beach
- [ ] Visit somewhere new (new state or country)
- [ ] Take a class
- [ ] Lana Del Rey concert (A MUST BEFORE I DIE)
- [ ] Flower garden (I spent hours daydreaming of Longwood Gardens or Keukenhof)

BD?

Before Dawn.

Very specific.

Watching the sunrise from a helicopter feels like something I need to do at least once in my lifetime.

It's also my favorite time of day.

I get that. What a view it'd be.

My EXACT point!

I chuckled. I could just picture how wide her smile was right now.

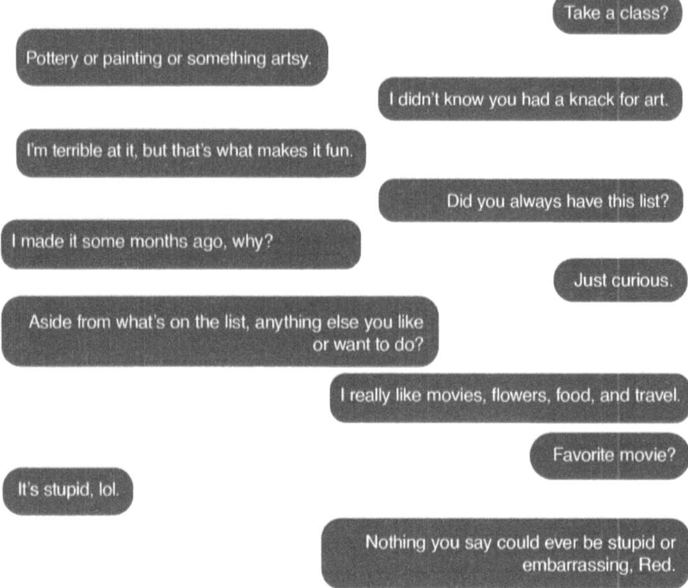

I meant it. Everything she said was important to me. Even if she told me she loved watching paint dry, I'd still think it was the best thing I'd ever heard.

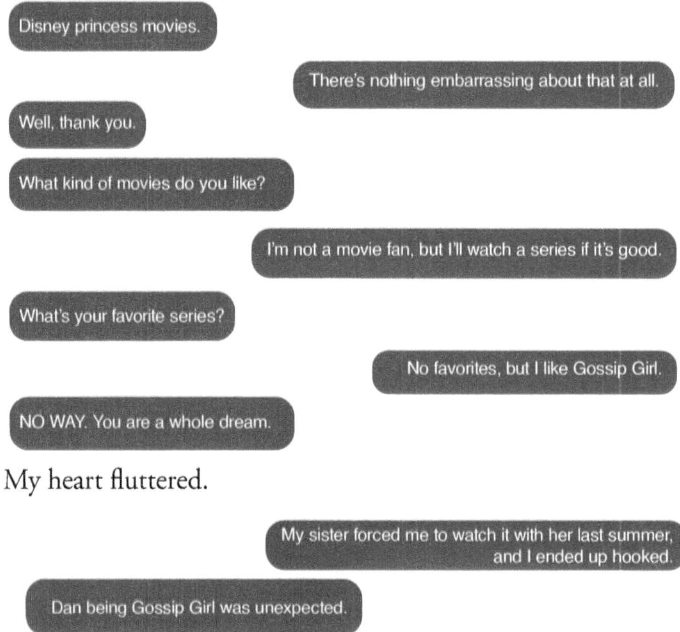

My heart fluttered.

I thought it was Dorota, but she had too much loyalty to Blair.

You're right. Plus, Dan was the 'outsider,' so it made sense.

Oh, fuck. I'm so sorry.

For what?

I asked about your favorite movie, then sidetracked into Gossip Girl.

I'm so sorry for that.

Mikkel, it's totally fine. I don't mind talking about Gossip Girl.

Are you sure?

10000% sure.

Okay.

Is there a specific Disney princess movie?

Beauty and the Beast!

Note to self: watch Beauty and the Beast when you get the chance.

That's a classic.

It's my comfort movie.

I'll be sure to remember that.

Keeping mental notes on me?

What kind of man would I be if I wasn't?

A true gentleman.

You reacted ♥ to this message

What's your favorite flower?

Primroses. Specifically yellow.

I smiled.

Birthday?

March 25, you?

February 20th.

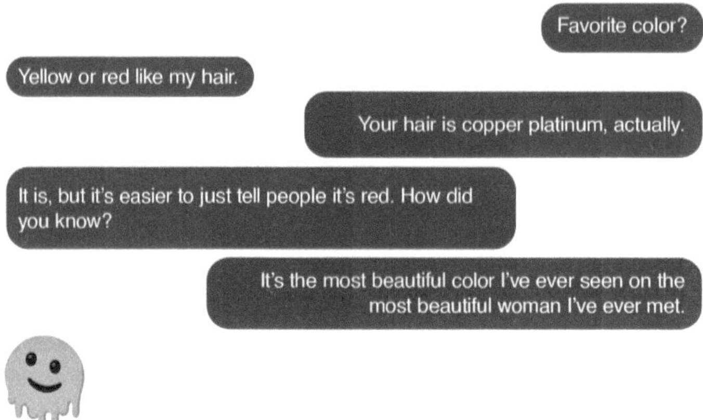

MELTING EMOJI?

I stared at it, grinning like an idiot. *I made her melt? Dreams do come true.*

My hair is naturally brown, but I dyed it at 16 and never stopped.

It compliments you well.

You think so?

I know so.

Thank you. I always wondered if people could tell it wasn't natural.

It suits you perfectly, and you're beautiful, so others' opinions don't matter.

That's sweet of you to say :)

Do you ever think about going back to brown?

Nope. I'm so used to this version of myself in the mirror that it's become part of who I am.

It makes you stand out in the best way.

You always know just what to say, don't you?

It comes naturally when talking to you.

I think this is the first time I've talked about that.

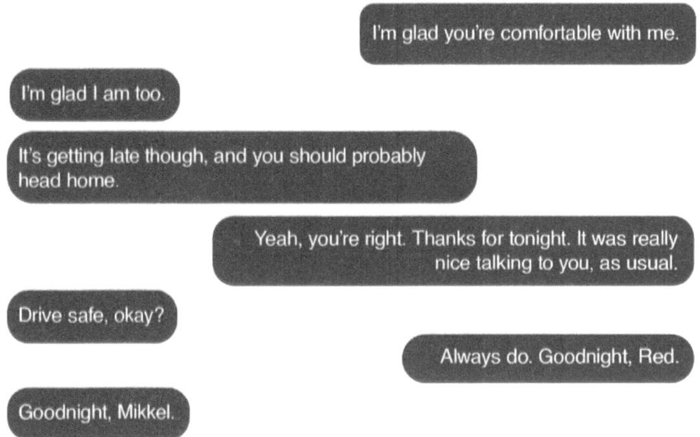

I slipped my phone into my pocket, took a deep breath, and drove off. Her smile and the way she opened up played on a loop in my mind, turning the drive home into a blur.

CHAPTER FIFTEEN

Abigail-Ann

"When we are in love, we open to all that life has to offer with passion, excitement, and acceptance."
~ John Lennon

Copper platinum. My hair color. I knew that. My sister and Azzy knew it too, because they'd helped me color it a few times. But Mikkel knowing it? That definitely wasn't on my bingo card for this year. In fact, Mikkel himself wasn't on the bingo card, or any other card, for that matter. And yet, here he was, texting me, casually dropping it into our conversation like it was no big deal.

"It's the most beautiful color I've ever seen on the most beautiful woman I've ever met."

What? Seriously? I couldn't shake the feeling of disbelief. It was like he could see these little details about me I hadn't even noticed, and we hadn't even hung out yet. My heart raced, and my stomach twisted.

Why was I freaking out over this?

Just me and my copper platinum hair, and suddenly, I was someone being noticed. Someone *he* noticed enough to remember. What was happening? I wasn't sure if I should feel flattered or scared. What did it mean that he knew something so... personal?

How could something as simple as a comment about my hair send me into this spiral? What did that say about me—about what I was used to? I shook my head, trying to quiet the voices of doubt.

My phone glowed softly in my lap as I messaged him:

"Boarding soon. Talk when I land."

The reply came instantly. *Was he waiting for my message?*

Safe travels, Red.

Below his message were a few links. Curious, I clicked one—videos on managing flight anxiety.

I stared at the screen, caught off guard. *He remembered.*

The PA system crackled overhead, announcing the next boarding call, but I barely heard it. My mind was too busy untangling the what-ifs.

Would we go any further? Did I want u-

"Abigail!"

My heart dropped as I turned to see Joshua striding toward me with a look of sheer desperation. Did he have a flight? How the hell had he gotten this far? In his hand, he clutched a bouquet of lilies.

My stomach churned.

Lilies.

He should've known better.

"What are you doing here?"

"Abigail, please, don't go." His voice cracked. He thrusted the flowers toward me, and I took an instinctive step back. "We can fix this. *I promise.* I can be better."

"This is pathetic," I said, my irritation barely contained. "I'm allergic to lilies, *remember*?"

He looked down at them, confusion flashing across his face. "Allergic? But… I thought you loved flowers."

"Primroses, *not* lilies." My voice broke, the mix of frustration, embarrassment and sadness bubbling to the surface.

He dropped the bouquet to the floor, his hands trembling. "I know I messed up. But we can make it work. Just give me another chance. Don't leave me alone."

Tears welled up in my eyes as the embarrassment of this encounter washed over me. I had once believed in those chances, but that hope had been shattered too many times. "This is why I'm leaving," I announced, my voice shaking. "You never listen. You never understand. Everything is always about you."

His face contorted with pain. "That's not true. I love you, Abigail. I need you."

My tears spilled over. "You love the thought of me. You've never loved me and you never will."

He reached out, and I took another step back, the distance between us growing. "Please," he whispered, his voice breaking. "Don't leave me."

The final boarding call for my flight echoed through the terminal, each word a dagger to my heart. I wiped my tears, steeling myself. "Goodbye, Joshua."

"Abigail, please!" he shouted, but I turned away, every step forward breaking my heart a little more.

I handed my boarding pass to the attendant, my hands shaking, and glanced back one last time to see him standing there, utterly defeated, the wilted lilies discarded at his feet. He didn't deserve me, and with that thought, I boarded the flight with absolutely no regrets.

Stepping off the flight, I let out a relieved sigh. After what felt like an eternity of cramped seats and endless delays, I was finally free. Surprisingly, the videos Mikkel had sent helped keep me calm for most of the flight—

soothing nature clips, ASMR-style rain sounds, and a guided breathing exercise.

I booked an Uber and headed straight to the apartment, grateful Emilia had handled everything while I was away.

When I arrived, I spotted her in the lobby, holding her curly-haired son.

"Abigail! Hey! Sorry, his babysitter canceled."

I smiled, approaching them. "Emilia, there's no need to apologize. Plus, he's just so adorable."

She grinned. "Thank you. How was your trip?"

"It was fine, but I'm happy to be here."

She handed me three swipe passes. "These are the smart passes for your apartment. There are also keys if you'd rather use those."

I took them with a grateful nod and stepped inside, immediately noticing the neatly arranged boxes. Emilia had already taken care of everything.

"Thank you, you're a lifesaver."

"It's my job," Emilia replied, handing me a folder. "This document includes your lease details and important contact numbers. If you ever need anything at all, don't hesitate to reach out to me."

I thanked her again before calling my parents to let them know I'd landed and settled. After that, I rang Azzaria, who immediately offered to help me unpack. We hung up, and I texted her the address before notifying the lobby she'd be arriving soon.

With a moment to breathe, I unlocked my phone and opened Instagram. While I knew Mikkel and I would exchange numbers and meet up eventually, I was enjoying our flirty chats and the way he took his time getting to know me.

I hesitated, then tapped on our messages. He was online.

My stomach fluttered.

Hey, I'm all settled

Perfect. How was the flight?

The flight was good and your videos helped! Thank you, again.

I'm happy they did, and you're always welcome.

My stomach did a little flip. The way he said things always felt personal, even over text. Like he meant them.

The words left me feeling bold, but I didn't regret them.

I wouldn't mind.

I'd never felt such a pure connection with a man before. Talking to him was effortless—no second-guessing, no hesitation. *Just right.*

Somehow, he quieted my anxieties, which was rare for me. I usually overthought everything, picking apart every word, every interaction. But with him? I felt at ease. Maybe a little *too* at ease.

Before I could spiral deeper into my thoughts, Azzaria's voice rang through the apartment, calling my name. I blinked, snapping back to the present, and rushed to open the door.

"You got here fast. Where were you coming from?" I asked as she stepped inside.

Kicking off her black pumps at the door, she dropped her purse onto the table, a broad smile lighting up her face. "I was like ten minutes away with Dillon, so he just dropped me off."

"You and your billionaire tycoon," I teased, nudging her playfully.

"Shut up," she shot back with a grin. "Now, tell me how San Fran was."

I shrugged. "It was fine. Just packed, spent time with my family, and broke up with Joshua."

Her smile faltered. "Are *you* okay?"

"Yeah." I sighed in relief. "But *oh my gosh*, he made a whole scene at the airport."

Her brows shot up. "What the fuck did he do?"

I recounted the humiliating moment—how he showed up, begging and pleading like we were in some cringy rom-com, and even brought me lilies.

Her face twisted in disbelief. "You're allergic! Five years together and he still doesn't know that?"

"He said he thought I said I liked flowers," I muttered, rolling my eyes.

"Dumbass."

We said it in unison, then burst into laughter.

"I was kinda down because it was so fucking embarrassing, but honestly? I'm over it now."

Azzaria gave me a knowing look. "It's gonna take a while to be fully over it, but with time—"

"No," I cut in, laughing as I shook my head. "I mentally checked out after the first fuck-up. I loved him enough to try fixing things, but the more I tried, the more I realized I wasn't Bob the fucking Builder. I stayed because I didn't want to feel like I wasted all those years."

Her eyes widened slightly. "Loved? As in, past tense?"

"Yep." I nodded, firm in my decision. "I won't stay where I'm unwanted."

A slow, proud smile spread across her face. "I'm happy for you, and I'm really proud of you, Abi."."

Before I could respond, my phone buzzed with a notification from Mikkel. The moment I glanced down, a smile tugged at my lips.

"Who's texting you?"

I quickly switched off the screen and set my phone in my lap, trying to sound casual. "No one. Just a notification."

Her skeptical look told me she definitely wasn't buying it. Azzaria could sniff out a secret from a mile away, especially if it involved a guy.

"So, a notification pops up, you start grinning, and it's nothing serious?" she pressed, one eyebrow raised.

"Exactly."

"Hmm," she muttered, clearly unconvinced. "Whatever you say."

I wasn't hiding anything on purpose, but I didn't want to jinx things by talking about Mikkel before we even had a chance to hang out in person. Some things needed to be solid before I let her in on them.

"Are you here to grill me, or are we gonna unpack?"

"Well then, let's get to unpacking," she said with a smirk, leading the way into the bedroom.

We spent the next three hours unpacking, but only managed to get through one and a half rooms. Between sorting boxes, we took a break for pizza—and I had to admit, Mikkel was right. The pizza here was the best I'd ever had.

As Azzy was about to leave, she paused by the door, purse in hand, and gave me a concerned look. "Are you sure you're good to stay by yourself tonight?"

I pulled her into a hug. "I'll be fine, and thank you so much for today."

She hugged me back tightly. "You're always welcome."

I walked her down to the lobby and watched as she climbed into a car that Dillon had sent for her. I thought about tackling some more unpacking, but the pull of sleep was too strong—until a call from Aurora interrupted my plans.

"I was seconds away from falling asleep," I groaned into the phone.

"Sorry! Are you free next Thursday at 9am?"

"What's up?"

"Can you head to Book Culture? You just need to meet with the manager so you can start as soon as possible."

"What do I need to bring?" I asked, now fully awake.

"I texted you all the details, but when you get there, ask for Adeline."

"Got it, thanks."

"And you'll be there, right?" she pressed.

"Yeah, of course. I'll be there," I confirmed.

"Perfect! How are you, sis?"

"Exhausted," I admitted, pushing myself out of bed. "Spent all day unpacking, and I'm still not done."

"Take your time, Abigail," she said softly, her tone calming.

"I've got to run errands tomorrow, too. Need to stock up on shower stuff and skincare," I replied, mentally making a list.

"Didn't Mom pack you a box with all that?"

I nodded, though she couldn't see it. "Yeah, but it's basically empty now. Anyway, goodnight. Love you."

"I love you too," she said warmly before hanging up.

Before finally drifting off, I sent a quick text to Mikkel.

Sorry for the lack of communication today. I was unpacking. Sweet dreams!

And as always, he replied almost instantly.

Hey Red.

I figured you were. Dulces sueños,[1] Red.

Do you always answer messages this quickly?

When you're the one messaging me, then yes.

I blushed so hard my cheeks started burning.

Get some rest. We'll definitely talk tomorrow.

1 *Sweet dreams*

CHAPTER SIXTEEN

Abigail-Ann

"Love is a canvas furnished by nature and embroidered by imagination."
- Voltaire

I pushed open the door to *Book Culture*, a charming indie bookstore nestled in the heart of the city. The scent of fresh paper mixed with the familiar musk of old books wrapped around me as I stepped inside. Tall bookshelves lined the walls, and cozy reading nooks with plush armchairs were scattered throughout. A staircase in the corner led up to a mezzanine level, giving the space an inviting, layered feel. Soft indie folk music hummed from the speakers, blending seamlessly with the occasional beep of the register and the quiet rustle of pages turning.

I inhaled deeply, trying to steady my nerves. This job was supposed to be a fresh start, a way to regain control over my life. But standing here, gripping the strap of my bag a little too tightly, I realized just how much working in public meant *interacting* with people. And that was the part I wasn't sure I was ready for.

I shook the thought away and took a careful step forward. *One thing at a time, Abigail. Just breathe.*

The young woman at the front desk glanced up and gave me a friendly smile.

"Hi, I'm Abigail-Ann Asher, and I'm here for an interview with Adeline," I said, my voice betraying a mix of excitement and nerves.

She nodded, still smiling. "Sure, just a moment." She picked up the phone and made a quick call. "Adeline will be right out."

I shifted on my feet, exhaling slowly as I tried to shake off the tightness in my chest. A moment later, a tall woman in her early thirties approached. Her dark purple hair framed her warm, professional expression as she walked toward me, dressed in a striped dress and black ankle boots.

"You must be Abigail," she said, extending her hand with a welcoming smile. "I'm Adeline."

"That's right," I replied, shaking her hand. "Nice to meet you."

"Wonderful. Come on back to my office."

I followed her through the store, my gaze flickering over the well-stocked shelves and tucked-away reading corners. It was the kind of place I could easily get lost in—if my nerves weren't buzzing loud enough to drown out the comfort of my surroundings.

Adeline's office was cozy but cluttered, with stacks of books piled on almost every available surface. A framed *Pride and Prejudice* quote hung on the wall, and a steaming cup of coffee sat precariously close to a stack of sticky notes.

"Please, have a seat," she gestured. I sat down, shifting slightly as I tried to relax.

"The position is for a bookseller—customer assistance, organizing books, and helping with events. Your schedule is Monday to Wednesday, 9am to 5pm; Saturday, 10am. to 2pm.; Sunday, 4pm. to 10pm. Thursdays and Fridays are your off days."

I nodded, pulling out my phone to jot down the details. *Focus on the facts. Don't overthink this.*

"The pay rate is $17.95 an hour, paid biweekly," she continued, handing me a clipboard. "Fill out this form when you're ready."

I took the form, my fingers tightening slightly around the pen before I forced myself to relax. *It's just paperwork, Abigail. You've got this.*

"The dress code is casual, with a few restrictions," she added.

"That sounds perfect. Thanks so much," I said, smiling despite the flutter in my stomach.

Adeline grinned, tucking a stray strand of purple hair behind her ear. "We're excited to have you! You'll start Monday. If you need anything, feel free to call."

I handed the form back, relief washing over me in slow waves. *Okay, that wasn't bad. You didn't screw up. Everything's fine.*

"Thank you, Adeline. I'm really looking forward to it."

"See you Monday!"

Stepping out of *Book Culture*, I pulled my coat tighter against the afternoon air. The nerves from my interview still lingered, but beneath them, something else stirred—relief. Maybe even a spark of excitement.

A fresh start. A new routine. It wasn't so terrifying when I thought about it like that.

As I walked down the street, my phone buzzed in my pocket.

Aurora
How did the interview go?

Me
Really well!

Me
I'll send you my schedule later.

Aurora
Great! Are you excited?

Me
I'm a little nervous, but I'm okay. It's perfect until graduation. I've started my apprenticeship applications.

Me
Once I have my degree and transcripts, I can submit them.

Aurora
I'm so proud of you! If you need anything, just let me know.

Me
Thanks, sis! Ttyl.

I smiled, tucked my phone away, and walked into the nail salon, where Kody greeted me with her usual energy.

"What are we doing today?" she asked, already settling me into the chair.

"Something simple but cute," I said, showing her a soft pink design with delicate white lines.

Kody grinned. "Love it. You always go for the classics."

As she worked, I let my body sink into the chair, the week's stress slowly fading. When she finished, she lifted my hands for me to admire.

"What do you think?"

"I'm obsessed."

Kody chuckled. "That's the goal."

After admiring my nails for a few more moments, I left the shop feeling… lighter. Like, for the first time in a while, things were actually falling into place.

Not ready to head home just yet, I stopped by *The Cozy Corner Café* down the street. The warm scent of freshly brewed coffee and vanilla wrapped around me as I stepped inside. I ordered a lavender latte and found a quiet corner by the window, ready to sit, sip, and breathe.

Just as I settled in, my phone vibrated.

Mikkel.

I smiled before I even opened the message.

For the past few weeks, we'd been texting every day, and I didn't mind one bit. Yesterday, he surprised me with a playlist of Lana Del Rey songs he thought suited me—including a few love songs. He titled it *Songs for You*, and I grinned like an idiot when I saw it. The cover was a mix of Lana's pictures and soft florals, and it felt so thoughtful. I was genuinely taken aback by how much he noticed the little things.

I'd hesitated to give him my number at first, unsure if his interest would fade. But it didn't. If anything, he grew more consistent, more engaged.

I couldn't remember the last time a day felt complete without hearing from him. He listened to my endless voice messages, responded to every detail. He watched all my vlogs and even sent some back. If it weren't for his constant traveling—England, China, California, Seattle—I was sure we would've hung out by now.

The sound of a spoon clinking against a cup pulled me out of my thoughts. I blinked, realizing I'd been staring at his name on the screen the whole time. Shaking off the daydream, I opened his message, already knowing it would make me smile all over again.

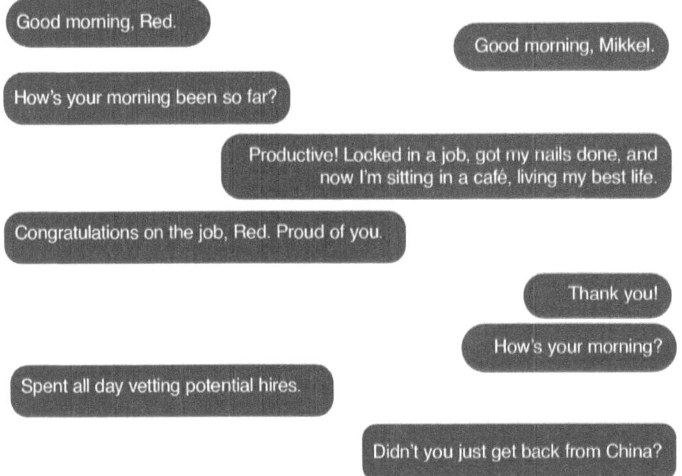

If I thought traveling between San Francisco and New York was exhausting, I couldn't imagine how wiped he must have been, hopping between back-to-back trips. And then heading straight into work like he was immune to exhaustion? His dedication was impressive—annoyingly so. Something told me he wasn't just hardworking; he was relentless.

Duty calls, cariño.[1] Hitting the gym later too.

Aren't you tired?

I'll sleep when the work is done.

---

1 *Sweetheart*

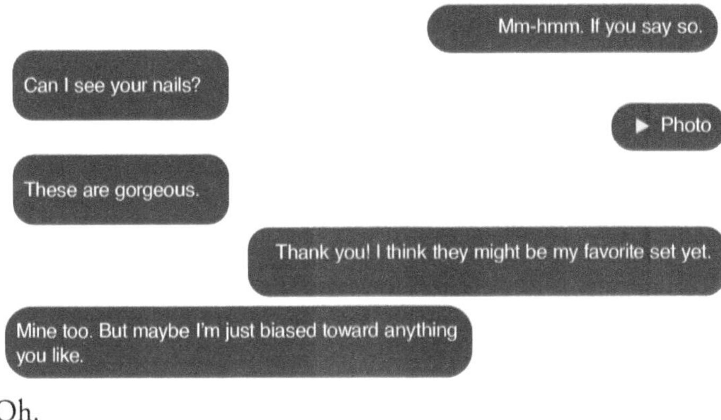

Oh.

Okay.

A warmth bloomed in my chest, spreading all the way to my fingertips. He was smooth—*too smooth.*

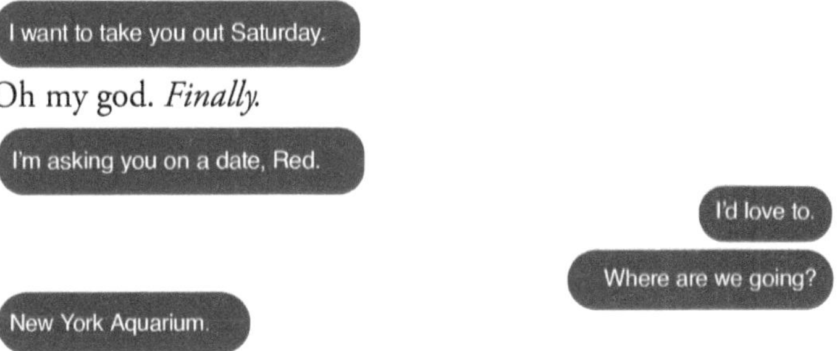

I stared at my phone, a slow grin tugging at my lips. Not a restaurant? Was he heaven-sent?

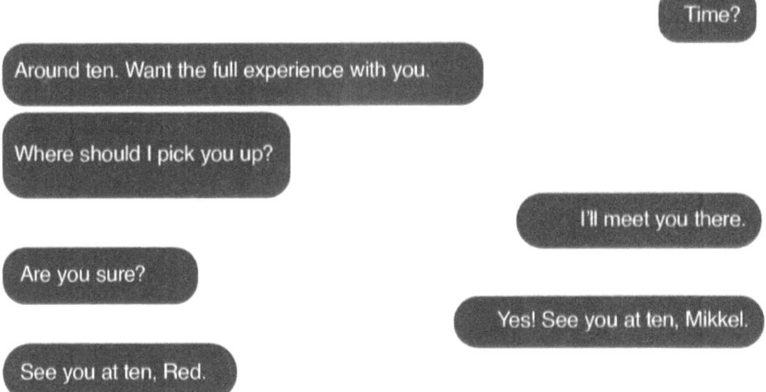

It was like he'd read my mind, sensing my doubt about whether we'd ever actually meet in person despite our constant texting. But this? This was real. My heart did a giddy little flip at the thought of spending an entire day with him—not just dinner, but an experience.

An adventure.

Sea creatures. Ocean tunnels. Touch pools. Maybe even sea lions if they were in season.

Excitement and nerves tangled in my stomach, but mostly, I just felt happy. Happy that he asked me out. Happy that we weren't doing something cliché. Happy about him.

It felt right.

It felt dangerously real.

CHAPTER SEVENTEEN

Mikkel

"To love is nothing. To be loved is something. But to love and be loved, that's everything."
~ T. Tolis

Saturday arrived faster than I expected.

Thank God.

The week had been a whirlwind of back-to-back investor meetings, expansion plans, endless travel, and a mountain of vetting. Work consumed my days, leaving little room for anything else. I still forced myself into the gym a few times, but even that felt more like an obligation than an escape.

The highlight? Texting Abigail every chance I got.

Even when I was knee-deep in a summit in Shanghai, rewriting a proposal for the thirtieth damn time, frustration clawing at me, one message from her was enough to cut through the noise. She was the one thing in my life that didn't feel like work.

But today? Today wasn't about business. It was about her.

I'd been counting down the days—hell, the hours, minutes and seconds—until this moment. I didn't want our first date to feel formal or suffocating in some overpriced restaurant where we'd sit across from each other, too aware of the moment. I wanted something real. The aquarium felt perfect—not just because it was fun, but because she'd once told me seeing sea lions was on her bucket list.

Maybe she hadn't realized I'd tucked that piece of information away.

But I did.

Because everything about her stuck with me.

I knew she loved ice cream, but only in certain seasons because of her sensitive teeth. That she wasn't a huge fan of sweets, but chocolate cake and the occasional donut were her kryptonite. That Lay's chips held a sacred place in her heart, but barbecue flavor ruled all.

And then there was her favorite color—yellow. It made sense. Yellow was warmth. Comfort. Sunlight spilling through a window, touching everything in its path.

But the thing that had stuck with me the most?

She told me that if she could be a time of day, she'd be just before dawn.

That quiet, extraordinary moment when the world holds its breath—full of promise. Not quite day, not quite night. Just… in-between.

She was right.

There was something about her that mirrored that moment. That feeling. She was the calm before everything changed.

Maybe that's why I couldn't stop thinking about her.

Every couple of weeks, she'd get her nails and toes done and send me pictures of her latest designs. At first, it was just a casual thing she did. Now? I looked forward to it like a fool. My heart kicked up whenever I saw her name pop up with an attachment. A glimpse into her world, into the little things that made her feel like herself.

Most days, she lounged around her apartment, hair in a messy bun or tucked under a silk bonnet. And yet—she was still the most beautiful person I'd ever seen. Her dedication to her hair, her routines, her care—it pulled me in.

She talked a lot, about everything and nothing. And I could listen to her for hours. She didn't believe I did sometimes, which pissed me off more than I'd like to admit. *Who the hell made her feel unheard?* I wanted to track them down just to let them know I'd spend a lifetime proving her wrong.

I even started watching *Beauty and the Beast*—both the original and live-action. Work swallowed me whole before I could finish the holiday specials, but I would. Because she loved it. And I wanted to know what made her heart ache in the best way.

I didn't just like her—I felt her.

She reminded me of fall. Not because of its fading beauty, but because of how it lingered—soft, steady, unforgettable. Fall didn't rush. It held onto its warmth, its colors, until the very last leaf fell.

She did the same to me.

Changing me in ways I couldn't stop, even if I wanted to.

And then I saw her.

The world seemed to stop.

She walked toward me in cargo pants and an oversized T-shirt, her hair pulled back into a black bow, a silver necklace with a flower pendant catching the light. Simple. Effortless. And yet, I was seconds from forgetting how to breathe.

I'd thought my glasses had failed me before, never quite capturing the full picture of her. Now, I knew for sure. No lens could do her justice.

And the worst part? I didn't even care.

Because nothing—not my vision, not the city blurring behind her—could pull my focus away from her.

And God help me, I didn't want it to.

"Hey," she greeted, her smile radiant, stealing the breath from my lungs.

"Hey," I murmured, my heart flipping like a gymnast at the sight of her. "You're really beautiful."

A blush bloomed on her cheeks, making my grip on reality even more precarious.

"These are for you, Red." I offered her a bouquet of yellow and blue primroses.

She stilled, her fingers brushing the petals with the kind of reverence that made my chest ache. "You remembered."

"I always will."

"Thank you." Her voice was soft, almost like she didn't trust herself to say more.

"I know you prefer yellow, but they didn't have enough, so I mixed in blue."

Her lips parted, eyes glistening with something unspoken. "They're perfect."

Not just the flowers. Her.

We stepped inside the aquarium, greeted by the cool hush of water and the distant hum of sea life. The air smelled of salt and something timeless, the kind of place where the world slowed down just enough to make you believe in magic.

The receptionist beamed at us. "Good morning! Welcome to the New York Aquarium."

I handed her my ID. "We have reserved tickets."

She scanned them, then glanced at Abigail's bouquet with an apologetic smile. "I'm sorry, but the flowers can't go inside. Would you like to leave them here?"

Abigail nodded, and I set them carefully on the counter, reluctant to part with something that had made her smile like that.

"Enjoy your visit!"

We wandered deeper into the aquarium, the light shifting like ripples in water. Schools of vibrant fish darted past, their scales catching the glow, and Abigail's awe was almost palpable.

"This is amazing," she whispered, pressing her hands against the glass. "It's like stepping into another world."

Her wonder was intoxicating.

We explored every corner, marveling at stingrays gliding like shadows, bioluminescent jellyfish pulsing with an eerie glow, seahorses drifting in slow-motion elegance. At the touch pool, we trailed fingertips over starfish and sea cucumbers, our laughter echoing when a feisty crab waved a claw in her direction.

"Oh my God! Did you see his expression? I think I scared him."

I chuckled. "He probably doesn't see women as beautiful as you very often."

She rolled her eyes but failed to hide her smile. "You're smooth in person too. Noted. But I'll stick with the friendlier sea creatures for now."

My grin widened. "Your loss. I think he was smitten."

We drifted from exhibit to exhibit, and I couldn't stop looking at her. The way her eyes sparkled, the way she lit up with every new discovery—it pulled me in like gravity.

She gasped, pointing to a tank full of clownfish weaving through coral. "They're so cute!"

I nodded, distracted by her more than the fish. "They are."

The truth? I agreed with everything she said, but she could've been pointing at a rock or coral and I would've still been mesmerized.

Her presence made everything feel lighter. The exhaustion I'd carried all week evaporated, replaced by something I didn't dare name yet.

We turned a corner, arriving at a towering tank where sea otters somersaulted through the water, playfully nudging each other. Abigail's laughter rang out, filling every hollow space inside me.

And just like that, I knew I was completely, hopelessly gone.

We followed the guide through dimly lit corridors, anticipation crackling between us like static electricity. The deeper we went, the quieter the world became, until we arrived at a secluded viewing area overlooking a massive shark tank.

The water stirred. A sleek shadow emerged, slicing through the depths with an effortless, lethal grace.

"Wow," she breathed, her eyes wide with awe. The glow of the tank reflected in them, making them shine even brighter. I should've been watching the sharks, but I found myself watching her instead—completely caught up in the quiet wonder on her face.

A trainer appeared at the tank's edge, carrying a bucket of fish. With practiced precision, he tossed the morsels into the water, instantly drawing the sharks' attention.

"They're so graceful," she murmured. "It's weird since sharks are violent."

I glanced at her, a faint smile tugging at my lips. "It's all about perspective. Even the most dangerous creatures have their own beauty."

She turned her gaze to me, and for a second, I forgot where we were. There was something about the way she looked at me—curious, open, like she was trying to figure me out.

The trainer approached us with a friendly smile. "Would you like to feed the sharks?" he asked, gesturing toward the bucket.

"Really?" Her face lit up, excitement flickering across it like sunlight over water. "Yes, please!"

With gentle guidance, she tossed a piece of fish into the tank, and her laughter bubbled up when the sharks rushed forward to claim it. I captured the moment on my phone, like I did with every other moment where her smile burned itself into my memory, where her joy softened something in my chest.

I liked seeing her like this. Completely in the moment. Happy. Calm.

After leaving the shark exhibit, we entered the aquatheater, where a crowd had gathered to watch playful sea lions perform acrobatic tricks. We found seats near the front, and I couldn't stop sneaking glances at her—the way her hands clutched the edge of her seat, how she leaned forward, completely absorbed.

"It's like a dream come true," she whispered, her voice soft with awe.

I grinned. "I can imagine, *cariño.*[1]"

A trainer approached us with a warm smile. "Would you like to learn some tricks to communicate with the sea lions?"

---

1 *Sweetheart*

Her eyes widened, and she nodded eagerly. “Of course!”

I watched as she learned the hand signals, her movements careful and focused. There was something about her that got to me. Maybe it was how she threw herself into things, how she let herself feel without hesitation. I’d spent years around people who calculated their every move, but Abigail was just herself.

“Growing up, my parents always took my sister and me on adventures.” She paused, her smile soft. “As I got older, I promised myself I’d do things like this, but I never got the chance. Being here today reminded me to appreciate life even more.”

I nodded, warmth spreading through my chest. “Experience is everything. I’m all about adventure, and growing up in the Caribbean, there was no shortage of it.”

“I bet there was,” she said, smiling up at me.

As evening approached, we grabbed her flowers and headed toward the exit.

“Did you have fun?” I asked.

“The most fun!” she exclaimed. “Today was amazing. I love sea lions, and feeding the sharks was unforgettable.”

“And let’s not forget your grumpy crab friend.”

She burst into laughter as we reached my car. “I’d never forget him.”

I opened the car door for her, pausing for just a second as she slid in. It wasn’t just about the way she looked—it was the way she fit into this day, into this moment, beside me.

She settled into the seat, then tilted her head. “Is this the part where you take me home?”

“This is the part where I take you to dinner, Red.”

She raised an eyebrow, amusement dancing in her eyes. “How much do I owe you—”

“As long as you’re with me, don’t worry about paying for anything,” I interrupted, my voice firm but gentle. “I should’ve told you to leave your wallet at home.”

Her eyes widened slightly, something flickering in them before she gave me a soft, appreciative smile. "You're too kind." Her voice was quiet, almost uncertain. "I'm sorry, it's just a bad habit to ask."

I shrugged, playing it off like it wasn't a big deal, even though her reaction settled in my chest. "It's nothing, Red."

But her words "bad habit" stuck with me.

Had someone actually made her pay for dates before?

The thought irritated me more than it should have.

As we settled in, I reached into the back and pulled out a small pillow. The front had a crocheted book, and the back read: *Congrats on your job, Abigail.*

Her eyes widened, and she gasped. "Oh my gosh! Mikkel! You didn't have to do this!"

I grinned, watching as she hugged the pillow close. "Whether you think your wins are big or small, they deserve to be celebrated."

She blinked, and for a second, I swore I saw a shimmer of tears in her eyes.

"This means so much to me. Thank you."

And just like that, my entire day felt worth it.

The warmth of the moment lingered between us as I pulled onto the main road. The city lights flickered across the windshield, casting soft, shifting hues inside the car. A comfortable silence settled in, broken only by the low hum of traffic. I reached for my phone and tapped the screen, queuing up the playlist I'd made just for her.

When she noticed, her smile widened, and she leaned her head to the side, a soft, knowing look in her eyes. That look always did something to me—like she saw straight through me and liked what she found.

Before long, we pulled up to Nathan's Famous, a cozy-looking restaurant, its windows glowing warmly.

"Here we are," I announced, turning off the engine and turning to her with a grin. "Hungry?"

"Starving."

"Then we're definitely in the right place," I responded, the warmth of her excitement contagious.

"I've never been here before. Is it good?"

I chuckled softly. "I wouldn't take you here if it wasn't." With a reassuring smile, I held the door open for her.

We slipped into a cozy booth, the rich aroma of grilled meat and sizzling fries hanging in the air. I stole glances at her, captivated by the neon lights reflecting in her eyes as she animatedly talked about the sea lions and sharks. She had this way of making the smallest details feel like the biggest wonders, and I'd listen to her talk about anything just to watch the joy light up her face.

"What are you looking at?"

I felt a flush rise to my cheeks. "You."

A soft blush bloomed on her cheeks, mirrored by the gentle curve of her lips. "You're too sweet."

Before I could reply, the waitress appeared at our table, a pad and pen in hand. "What can I get for you folks today?"

"Two classic hot dogs, fully loaded with mustard, ketchup, relish, and onions," I said, glancing at her for confirmation. "Barbecue sauce on the side."

"And a large order of fries to share," she added.

"Anything to drink?"

"Sprite and orange juice," I said, and the waitress smiled as she scribbled down our order before hurrying off to the kitchen.

"I cannot thank you enough, Mikkel."

"You never need to thank me." A smile played at the corners of my lips. I would've done this a thousand times over, just to see her look at me like this.

"It turned out to be everything I had dreamed our first date would be."

"You dream of me?"

"It takes me days to recover from a dream with you in it, Red."

She took a sip of water, her head dipping slightly, but when she looked back at me, I saw another tear welling up, her green eyes shining brighter, reflecting every emotion she felt.

"You mean that?"

I leaned in closer, my expression serious. "I wouldn't have said it if I didn't mean it."

She whispered, almost as if she was speaking more to herself than to me, "Right." Then, she looked up, trying to steady herself, and said, "Sea lions have always been on my must-see list, and seeing them today felt surreal."

"I know."

"You know?" she repeated, her voice tinged with surprise, as if she hadn't expected me to understand something so personal to her.

"Number two and three on your bucket list."

She looked at me with a mixture of softness and confusion. "I forgot about that. You remembered."

"What did I tell you earlier?" I prompted, a teasing glint in my eyes.

"Hm?"

"I told you that I'll always remember everything about you. I pay attention to detail."

Or, I should've said, I pay attention to everything related to you.

"I'm starting to realize that." She chuckled. "What else have you noticed about me?"

I leaned forward. "The green in your eyes gets deeper, like emerald or pine green, when you talk about your favorite things. Like today, when you saw the sharks or the sea lion interaction."

Blush crept onto her cheeks, but she couldn't hide the happiness shining in her eyes. "You noticed that?"

"What kind of man would I be if I didn't, *cariño*?[2]"

Her smile softened, a warmth spreading through her features. "You've got such a sweet mouth."

Before our conversation could continue, the waitress returned with our food.

"This looks so good," she said, her eyes widening as the steaming hot dog was placed in front of her, piled high with mustard, ketchup, relish, and onions.

---

2 *Sweetheart*

"Just wait until you try it."

With a playful grin, she drizzled barbecue sauce over her hot dog, took a bite, and let out a soft moan of satisfaction.

"Oh my gosh," she mumbled, covering her mouth as she chewed. "This is amazing."

"Told you," I teased, taking a bite of mine.

She leaned in slightly, her eyes bright with excitement. "You were definitely right." Her gaze flickered over my arms, lingering there. "You know, I've been meaning to ask you about your tattoos."

I raised an eyebrow, intrigued. "What about them?"

"They're so…" She bit her lip, her expression thoughtful before breaking into a smile. "They look incredible on you. What do they mean?"

I rolled up my sleeve, revealing a detailed lotus flower on my forearm. "This one represents new beginnings. Fitting, after moving from one country to another."

"Wow," she breathed, tracing the ink with her eyes, as if memorizing every line.

"And this one?" I pointed to the compass inked across my chest. "It's about finding my way. The journey being just as important as the destination."

She grinned. "You've got this whole mysterious vibe going on." Then, her voice dropped slightly, playful but firm. "Not to mention, you're really hot."

I huffed a quiet laugh, feeling my pulse spike under her gaze. "Hot?"

"Definitely," she confirmed, her lips curving as she wiped a bit of mustard from the corner of her mouth. "You *know* you are. The tattoos, the way you carry yourself… It's all part of the package."

I smirked, nudging her shoulder. "Careful now, *amor*,[3] you might just make me blush."

She laughed, a warm, melodic sound that wrapped around me. We finished eating in easy silence, the kind that didn't need to be filled with

---

3 *love*

words. Once I closed out the bill, we walked back to the car, and as soon as she slid into the passenger seat, she synced her phone to the Bluetooth. Lana Del Rey's voice spilled through the speakers, sultry and hypnotic.

As I started the engine, she shifted toward me, her expression suddenly serious. "Before we go any further, I need to tell you something."

I turned to her, giving her my full attention. "What's up?"

She hesitated, tucking a curl behind her ear. "I recently got out of a relationship. I'm over it now, but I felt like it was worth mentioning."

He must've been a real dumbass to lose a woman like her.

Was he the idiot making her pay for dates?

"I appreciate that," I said. "Everyone has a past, and whatever you did before me, doesn't matter."

She let out a soft, breathy laugh. "I just wanted to be upfront because… I don't think this will be our last date."

A slow, knowing smile tugged at my lips. "It won't be our last date."

She exhaled, relieved by my reaction. "I know it's not exactly first-date conversation, but—"

My chest tightened as a memory flashed through my mind—her crying in the airport, that lost look in her eyes.

"Was he the reason you were upset that day?" I asked, my voice gentler now. "Or why you asked about paying me back earlier?"

She nodded slowly, her gaze dropping to her lap. "If I wasn't paying for something, I wasn't getting it. And if I did get anything, I'd be reminded of it. Over and over."

A sharp, protective rage coiled inside me. *Es un maldito imbécil.*[4] I clenched my jaw, trying to keep my anger in check. The last thing she needed was for me to explode over something she'd already walked away from. Taking a deep breath, I forced the tension from my shoulders.

"There's nothing I appreciate more than honesty," I told her, voice steady. "And I know that no matter how 'over it' you are, talking about it still isn't easy."

---

4 *He's a fucking moron*

She met my eyes, the gratitude there hitting me straight in the chest. "I know… but I appreciate you listening."

Without thinking, I reached over, my fingers brushing against hers in a slow, deliberate touch. The moment they met, a spark shot through me—sharp, electric. Her breath hitched, and her eyes widened slightly, like she felt it too.

"Is this okay?" I murmured.

A small smile curved her lips as she gave my hand the lightest squeeze. "It's perfect."

I exhaled, something inside me settling. I hadn't planned on touching her, but now that I had, I knew I wouldn't want to stop.

I'd make damn sure she felt the difference between what she had before, and what she deserved.

As our hands lingered, I noticed a flicker of unease in her eyes. It was subtle, but it was there—something on her mind. Before I could ask, she broke the silence.

"Can I ask you something?"

"Of course," I said instantly, though I could see the hesitation in her expression. Without thinking, I pulled the car over and turned to face her fully. "What's bothering you?"

She took a slow breath, like she was choosing her words carefully. "When you were talking about China last week… and coming back to work…" She trailed off, and I sighed, already knowing where this was going.

"You're wondering why I push myself so hard, aren't you?" My voice was quieter than I intended.

She nodded.

I exhaled, running a hand over my jaw. "I just can't afford to lose track of anything. Or fall behind." The words were heavy, but there was more to it than that—more than I was ready to say. Not tonight. Not yet.

Her gaze softened, full of understanding. "I get it. But you know… it's okay to slow down. You don't want to burn out."

Her quiet concern settled over me, unexpected yet grounding. I held her gaze. "You're right," I admitted, feeling the truth of it more than I expected.

She gave me a small smile. "I'm sorry if I made you uncomfortable, I just…"

"You didn't," I reassured her, my voice steady. "But I needed to hear that. Thank you, Red."

"You're welcome."

The rest of the drive passed in a comfortable silence, her presence filling the space in a way that soothed something in me. When we pulled up to Common at The Reserve, I wasted no time getting out and opening her door. She stepped out, cradling the flowers and pillow against her chest.

Her smile was warm, bright enough to pull me in. "Thank you again for today, Mikkel. The flowers are absolutely beautiful, and this pillow? It's going right on my couch."

I smirked. "The pleasure will always be mine."

Her brow furrowed slightly. "Aren't you tired from… everything?"

I shook my head. "I am, but I'll be good."

She studied me for a moment before nodding, her lips curling into a smile. "Goodnight, Mikkel."

"Goodnight, Red."

I watched her disappear into the lobby, waiting until my phone lit up with her message: *I'm home. Thank you again for today.*

Only then did I drive away.

The day had been perfect.

She was happy. And that was all that mattered.

I was hers, and I'd wait until she was ready to be mine.

CHAPTER EIGHTEEN

Abigail-Ann

"Love doesn't make the world go round. Love is what makes the ride worthwhile."
~ Franklin P. Jones

How could one man be so thoughtful?

My gaze drifted to the primroses on my counter, their soft petals a quiet reminder of how much he paid attention. He listened—not just to my words, but to the little things, the details I barely realized I'd shared. From the moment we met, he made me feel comfortable. Like what I had to say actually mattered.

I hugged the pillow he'd given me, warmth spreading through my chest. It wasn't just the gift—it was the thought behind it. He made me feel safe. Valued.

I'd been to Pier 39 in San Francisco countless times, always missing the sea lions, but he made sure I didn't this time. And Nathan's Famous was the perfect way to end the day. The hot dog was good, but what stayed with me was how happy he was just watching me enjoy myself.

"I told you that I'll always remember everything about you. I pay attention to detail."

"Numbers two and three on your bucket list."

Joshua had been in my life for five years and still never got it. He'd shown up with lilies—the very flower I was allergic to—in a half-hearted attempt to win me back. He never even asked what I liked.

Mikkel, though? He'd known me for a fraction of that time and remembered my favorite flower after asking once. Joshua had laughed at my bucket list, dismissing it with a careless "Why bother?"

Mikkel made sure I checked things off it.

He remembered. And in doing so, he made me feel cherished in a way I never thought possible.

After a quick trip to Ulta and Walmart, I collapsed onto my sofa, my eyes drifting over the unpacked boxes. I reached for my phone, hesitated for only a second, then texted him back.

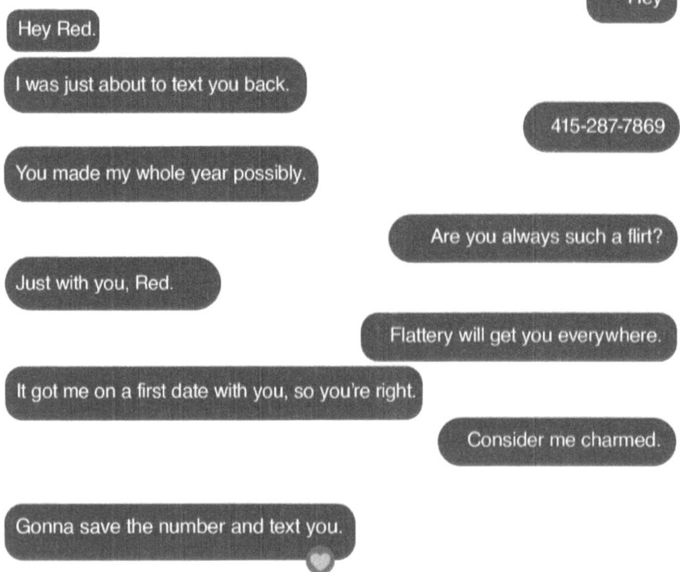

I liked the message and waited. When my phone buzzed with an unknown number, I saved it as "S" and opened it, my fingers trembling.

S
How was your day, hermosa dama?

Me
Hermosa dama?

S
Pretty lady.

Me
You certainly know how to make a woman blush.

S
I only want to make you blush.

Me
Officially charmed.

S
That was my goal.

S
How was your day?

Me
It was calm.

More like I had a day thinking about him.

S
You gotta gimme more than that.

S
I want details.

Me
You're interested in details?

S
I'm interested in everything you do.

Me
I ate, unpacked a bit then went to Walmart and Ulta.

S
Sounds like a cozy day. What did you get?

Send me a haul. I wanna see.

This was one of the very times I wondered if he was real. Never have I ever come across a man this interested in me.

Me
Okay!

Video

And as I expected, he watched and responded to every single thing I bought which had me kicking my feet and squealing into the pillow he got me.

Me
How was your day?

S
Exhausting. I had meetings all morning and then rushed to finish signing some paperwork in the afternoon, went to the gym with my friends then had an interview.

I'm home now, so I get to unwind for a bit.

Me
That sounds hectic but, I'm glad you're finally getting some downtime.

S
Me too, but talking to you is definitely the highlight of my day.

Me
Flattery I tell you.

S
I aim to please you.

Me
My dad sold my car, btw.

S
How are you feeling about that?

Me
It feels like I've finally let go of a part of me I should've a long time ago.

S
Here's to a new start, then.

Me
To a new start.

S
What's next on your agenda for the evening?

Me
Probably just more laziness. Maybe order some takeout and see where the night takes me.

S
Sounds tempting.

Me
It's really not.

We talked until he had to leave for a meeting, and I was amazed at how he could leave me speechless yet make me feel like I could talk to him forever. With just a sentence, he made me smile, slowly mending the brokenness in my heart. Still, a worry lingered—would he turn out like Joshua? Once had been hard enough; I couldn't bear another heartbreak. But I pushed the thoughts away, reminding myself that, though love and loss were daunting, it was worth the risk to open up again.

WARNING

The following chapter contains heavy mentions of mental health/physical health issues. Please refer to the content warning list to be reminded of any potential triggers. Your well-being is important to me, so please take care of yourself while reading.

CHAPTER NINETEEN

Abigail-Ann

"At the touch of love, everyone becomes a poet."
~Plato

The bookstore was quiet, the kind of stillness that amplified every rustle of a page and every sigh I let escape. It was my third week working at Book Culture, and though I was getting the hang of it, anxiety still gripped me tightly. Was I shelving books too slowly? Did I smile enough at customers? Did my coworkers think I was weird?

This week's struggle wasn't just anxiety—it was a whole new level of hell. My period arrived, bringing the full wrath of endometriosis with it. The cramps clawed at my insides like a monster, my lower back felt like it was being pummeled by a jackhammer, and nausea, bloating, fatigue, and a complete loss of appetite formed a relentless symphony of misery.

At least this month, I could get out of bed. That wasn't always the case. Some months, it left me paralyzed, helpless as my body waged war against itself.

Pushing through a shift while feeling like death was an accomplishment in itself. Just making it in was a victory. At least I didn't have to explain an absence to my new boss—dodging that conversation in my first month was a small mercy.

If anyone would've noticed something was wrong, it was Mikkel. He always checked in, asked questions, and never took 'I'm fine' at face value. Even when I brushed him off, he'd still call or text just to make sure. But today, he was in Chicago for business, and I didn't want to burden him with this.

Halfway through my shift, I heard a familiar voice.

"Abigail-Ann!"

I turned, and saw Azzaria, grinning like she'd won the lottery. My spirit lifted immediately.

"Azzy! What are you doing here?"

"You're way too hard to catch these days, and I thought I'd come and say hi on your break."

During lunch, we sat in Central Park with sandwiches and sodas, catching up. I vented about work, my period, and the urgent need for locks on my apartment since my parents kept nagging me about safety. She had a knack for making everything feel less overwhelming.

"Abi," she said between bites of her sandwich, "you need to get those locks before they book a flight from California to do it themselves."

I laughed, grateful for her. "I'm gonna do it."

After lunch, I called my parents during a lull in customers. My mom warmly asked about work, while dad joked about helping with "heavy books," though we both knew he'd just be checking up on me.

"I'm fine, Dad," I reassured him. "But seriously, locks are happening soon."

The rest of the shift passed in a blur. By the time closing rolled around, the cramps had dulled to an ache, and I was ready to crawl into bed.

Stepping into the cool night, phone in hand to book an Uber, I spotted a familiar white Rolls Royce idling at the curb.

My heart stuttered. *No way.*

The driver's side door opened, and Mikkel stepped out, his tall frame as composed as ever, but his face showed a genuine, soft happiness as he walked toward me.

"Mikkel?" My voice broke with surprise.

"Red," he replied, his tone like a caress.

I stopped in front of him. "You're supposed to be in Chicago."

He grinned, a boyish tilt to it that made my chest ache. "Came back earlier."

"Why?"

He looked down at me. "I had better things to do."

I couldn't stop the smile spreading across my face. "Better things?"

He tilted his head toward the car. "Come on, let me take you home."

I nodded, unable to resist the tenderness in his gaze. As he opened the car door for me and I slid in, he handed me a bag.

Inside were a bag of barbecue Lay's, a slice of chocolate cake, a bouquet of primroses, and—*holy fuck*—a heating pad.

I looked up at him, stunned. "Mikkel…"

He rubbed the back of his neck, suddenly looking shy. "It's your time of the month, so I thought these would help. If it's too much—"

I placed my hand over his, stopping him mid-sentence. "This is the sweetest thing anyone has ever done for me. Thank you." My throat tightened, but I fought back the tears threatening to spill.

His smile softened, and the overthinking thoughts that usually plagued me faded into the background.

As he started the car, he glanced at me. "Have you eaten?"

I shrugged. "Not really. I was thinking of ordering Chipotle when I get home."

"Alright," he said with a nod.

As we drove, music began to play softly through the speakers. It didn't take long to recognize the playlist—it was the *Songs for You* playlist he'd made for me. I smiled, the ache in my body melting away, replaced by something softer, more comforting.

Out of nowhere, I blurted, "What's your middle name?"

He chuckled, glancing at me briefly before focusing back on the road. "Andrés."

My eyebrows shot up. "That's…hot."

He laughed, a deep, rich sound that filled the car. "What's yours?"

"Charlotte," I said, feeling shy for some reason.

He nodded, a small smile playing on his lips. "That's beautiful."

I smiled back, a comforting sensation spreading through my chest. For once, I didn't overthink it; I just let myself feel. With that thought in mind, I kept asking him random questions, and he answered without hesitation.

Favorite color? White.

Favorite hobby? The gym.

Favorite song? *Video Games* by Lana Del Rey.

Favorite season? Fall.

Biggest pet peeve? "No offense" after an insult or dirty dishes in the sink.

Fun fact? He speaks four languages fluently: English, Spanish, Italian, and Mandarin.

I glanced out the window and realized the car was pulling into a Chipotle parking lot. I turned to him, surprised.

"You didn't think I'd actually let you order in, did you?"

I laughed, unsure of what to say.

We both stepped out, and I walked eagerly toward the door—only to find it locked. My shoulders slumped.

"It's closed," I muttered, disappointed.

Mikkel stood beside me, unfazed. "I know of another one if you're up for the drive."

"Are you sure?" I met his gaze.

He shrugged with a small smile. "Let's go."

"Okay," I said, following him back to the car.

As he started driving again, the conversation shifted. I asked him how Chicago was, and he told me about the meetings, mentioning his assistant's antics and how he was ready to be back. He turned the questions back on me, asking about my day at the bookstore. It felt natural, the ebb and flow of our exchange.

"For once, there's no traffic," I commented, staring out at the unusually clear streets.

"It's usually smooth sailing around these times," he replied, adjusting the playlist.

I fidgeted with the box containing the slice of chocolate cake, unable to resist running my fingers over the edges.

"You can eat it, you know," he said without taking his eyes off the road.

I shook my head. "I'm saving it for when I get home."

"Red," he said, his tone playful but firm, "if you want to eat it, eat it. I can always get you another slice."

I laughed, shaking my head. "Alright then."

I gave in, carefully opening the box and taking a bite. The rich, chocolate flavor melted on my tongue, and I sighed in satisfaction.

I really love chocolate cake.

The car grew quiet, and before I knew it, the cake was done and my eyes grew heavy. I must've dozed off, because the next thing I knew, we were slowing down, and I opened my eyes to see we were pulling into Chipotle.

"The other two before this were also closed," Mikkel said, his voice soft. "We're in Brooklyn."

I froze, turning to him. "You drove to Brooklyn?"

"You wanted Chipotle," he said with a shrug, like it was the most obvious thing in the world.

"Mikkel…"

"It's what you deserve," he cut me off, his tone teasing. "Are you coming, or should I pick for you?"

I laughed, shaking my head. "I'm coming."

After we ordered, I couldn't stop thinking about it. He'd driven over an hour just so I could have a burrito bowl. *Who does that?*

Back in the car, he glanced at me as I hesitated to dig into the bag.

"You can eat if you want."

"Most people freak out about crumbs in their car," I said, amused.

He grinned, glancing at me. "I'm not most people."

That silenced me in the best way, and I began eating. The heat of the food, combined with his quiet presence, made me feel at ease.

He pulled into a small parking lot, breaking the silence. "I have to make a quick stop," he said, stepping out.

I kept eating, a small laugh escaping me. He was so…unpredictable. A moment later, he returned, carrying another small box.

"Is that—"

"Another slice of chocolate cake." He handed it to me with a wink.

"You are something else," I said, shaking my head.

"As long as it's something you want me to be."

The ride back to my building was quiet but comfortable. We arrived just before midnight, and as he pulled up to the curb, he asked, "How are your cramps?"

"They're better," I said, and after a pause, I added, "It's endometriosis. I don't think I've told you before."

He glanced at me, his expression shifting to concern. "Do you want to talk about it?"

I nodded. "It's… a lot, but it's irregular, so I don't get twelve periods like most women. Sometimes it's less; sometimes it doesn't come at all. But when it does, I can barely get out of bed. It's not just the pain—it's the nausea, exhaustion, bloating, everything. I feel like it controls my life sometimes. But this isn't so bad, which I'm grateful for."

He listened intently, his hands relaxed on the steering wheel. "That sounds incredibly hard, Red, but you're strong for handling it."

I smiled faintly. "Thanks. Most people don't get it."

"I want to," he said softly.

I looked down, my voice quieter. "Is this pace too slow for you?"

"What?"

"Us. The pacing."

He let out a soft laugh, shaking his head. "Anyone who rushes you doesn't deserve you."

My chest ached, but in the best way. "Are you sure?"

"I'm sure."

He got out of the car and came around to open my door, helping me gather my things. "Thanks for the drive, the Chipotle, the snacks, and the cake," I said as I stepped onto the sidewalk.

"My pleasure, *amor.*"

I hesitated, before once again asking, "Why'd you leave Chicago early?"

"The girl I like wasn't feeling well. Thought I'd make sure she was okay in person."

I froze, his words sinking in. My heart raced as my mind started to spiral, but then he gently took my hand, bringing it to his lips.

"You deserve more than just a text," he murmured, pressing a kiss to my knuckles. "Or a call."

"Buenas noches, *cariño*[1]."

I smiled, a little breathless. "I know that one."

His chuckle was low, rich. "Sweet dreams."

I stepped toward the door, then hesitated. "Aren't you going to drive off?"

"Not until you're inside."

Something in my chest pulled tight—unexpected, lingering. I turned away before he could see it.

Once inside, I sent a quick '*I'm in*' text and barely blinked before his reply popped up.

I set the flowers in a vase, tucked the cake into the fridge, then collapsed onto the couch. But the moment I stilled, emotions crept in—thick, consuming. My stomach ached, my body drained, but my mind refused to quiet.

My phone buzzed.

---

1 *sweetheart*

S

There's a possibility you've already seen this, but I still wanted to share it.

I'm going to do more research when I get home.

A link followed. Remedies for endometriosis. Simple. Thoughtful. The tears came, unchecked. But for once, they weren't heavy.

WARNING

The following chapter contains heavy mentions of mental health/physical health issues. Please refer to the content warning list to be reminded of any potential triggers. Your well-being is important to me, so please take care of yourself while reading.

CHAPTER TWENTY

Abigail-Ann

"Love is like the wind, you can't see it but you can feel it."
- Nicholas Sparks

Curiosity—or maybe self-preservation—had me Googling Mikkel again.

The usual rumors surfaced. A man who kept to himself, thriving in the shadows while the world speculated. Headlines buzzed about his latest deal in Chicago, his name tangled with power and mystery. For someone so private, I couldn't help but wonder—where did I fit into all of this? Did he guard his personal life as fiercely as the rest of him?

I pushed the thought aside. It wasn't my place to pry. Not yet, anyway. But anxiety had a way of ignoring boundaries.

With one last glance at my freshly organized living room, I allowed a small smile. Unpacked boxes, framed photos, DVD's lined up just right—it finally felt like home. Maybe staying up all night on FaceTime with Mikkel had given me the energy to power through. Or maybe I just needed the distraction after two days trapped in Ticketmaster hell, only to watch Lana's concert tickets slip through my fingers.

Frustration lingered, but I shook it off and hurried to work, the scent of books lifting my mood.

While sorting through a box of new arrivals, I spotted a young woman scanning the shelves, eyes bright with curiosity.

"Looking for something in particular?" I asked, offering a warm smile.

She turned, excitement flickering across her face. "I'm just getting back into reading and hoping to find a good romance. Any recommendations?"

I nodded, already reaching for a fan favorite. "If you're into sweet and swoony, *The Dating Playbook* by Farrah Rochon is a great pick. But if you want something spicier, Sylvia Day never disappoints."

Her grin widened. "Thank you so much!" She dove into browsing, and I returned to stocking the shelves, until my phone buzzed.

Mikkel.

My stomach flipped as I quickly stepped into a quieter corner to check the message.

S
Are you free Friday?

Me
I am. What's up?

S
Our second date.

Me
Is that so?

S
It is so.

Me
Where to this time?

My heart stuttered. Coney Island. The words fizzed in my chest like champagne bubbles.

S
Coney Island.

Me
It's definitely a date.

S
Perfect. We'll talk later because I know you're at work.

Have a good day, bonita.[1]

I bit my lip, the warmth of his words lingering even as I slipped my phone back into my pocket.

Me

Mikkel's text echoed in my mind as Adeline called me into her office. She complimented my work ethic, which was a nice boost. After thanking her, I wrapped up my shift and headed home, exhaustion creeping in. Just as I sank into the couch, a knock at the door yanked me back to reality.

Azzaria's cheerful voice rang out. "Hey, it's me!"

I dragged myself to the door, finding her holding a beautifully decorated chocolate cake. "I baked this for you!"

"Sweet heaven, thank you!" I grinned, taking the cake as she walked in.

We settled in the living room, the cake's aroma filling the air as I cut us each a piece. "You look wiped," Azzaria remarked.

"You think?"

"How was work?" she asked, taking a bite.

"It was good. Adeline gave me some positive feedback from customers. Felt nice to hear."

"I knew you'd kill it there," she smiled. "You're great with people."

"Thanks, Azzy. How about you?" I asked, savoring the cake.

"It's good! Had fun baking and started a new project at work, but we'll talk about that later," she said, leaning back.

"I'm glad. And seriously, this cake is amazing. You should open a bakery."

She laughed. "Dillon says the same thing."

I raised an eyebrow. "You baked for him? That's next-level."

She chuckled, but there was a hint of hesitation in her voice. "Yeah… he's amazing."

---

1 *beautiful*

"What's going on? You sound off."

"It's just... sometimes I wonder if it's all gonna crash."

"I get it, but you deserve happiness. Life's been tough, but don't sabotage it if he makes you happy."

She sighed, looking down at her hands. "I needed to hear that."

"You know I'm always here for you," I nudged her playfully. "Let the good stuff happen. You've been smiling non-stop. It's clear you're happy."

She rolled her eyes, but her grin betrayed her. "I really am happy."

"See? He checks all your boxes. You've won."

She laughed, almost choking. "I wouldn't say I've won."

"You deserve him," I said, leaning back. "I'm happy for you. Just don't overthink it."

She looked at me, her expression softening. "Thanks. I needed to hear that."

"Just let yourself enjoy it," I smiled.

"Will do."

After more chatting and laughing, Azzaria stood. "Alright, I should go. Early day tomorrow."

I walked her to the door. "Thanks again for the cake."

"Anytime. We'll catch up soon," she hugged me before grabbing her purse.

"Before you go..." I paused. "Have you ever googled Dillon?"

Her eyebrows shot up, and she let out a knowing laugh. "I did, and I still get notifications whenever his name pops up. It's a mix of rumors, half-truths, and tabloid nonsense. Makes you wonder what's real, especially with all the women who want him."

I nodded, strangely comforted by her honesty. "How do you separate who someone is from what the internet says?"

She leaned against the doorframe, arms loosely crossed. "I want to ask why you're asking, but I know you'll tell me when you're ready." A sigh escaped her lips before she continued, "Anyway, that's the thing—online, you find everything and nothing at the same time. People like Dillon have layers, and sometimes you wonder if you'll ever see what's beneath all the noise. It's not about trusting what I read—anyone can post anything. It's about trusting how he makes me feel, how he treats me. That's the real stuff."

I let her words settle, then nodded. "Alright. Thanks for answering."

"Anytime," she whispered before slipping out the door.

Once I finished cleaning up, I glanced at the clock. Time to leave for my appointment with Dr. Green.

The waiting room was quiet, soft music humming in the background. After checking in, I pulled out my phone and texted Mikkel.

Me
Just got to my appointment..

His reply was instant.

S
Let me know when you're home.

A few minutes later, Dr. Green appeared in the doorway, her smile warm and familiar. "Good evening! Come on in."

I followed her inside, sinking into my usual spot on the couch as she settled across from me, notepad in hand.

"So," she said, meeting my gaze. "How have you been since our last session?"

I took a deep breath and dived into the latest updates: my growing relationship with Mikkel, small victories at work, and the ongoing challenges of settling into my new apartment.

"Sometimes I feel guilty," I admitted, my voice barely above a whisper. "Happy but guilty."

Dr. Green's expression remained gentle as she prompted, "Guilty about what?"

"I've already... moved on?" The words tumbled out faster than I intended. "It feels weird to be this okay so soon, but it also feels good because of Mikkel."

She nodded in understanding. "It's natural to feel conflicted after a breakup, especially if you're moving on faster than you expected. Tell me more about what you're feeling."

I sighed, trying to make sense of the emotions swirling inside me. "I thought I'd be devastated, but I haven't shed a tear. And then Mikkel came along, making me feel things I've never felt before. It happened so fast. I keep thinking I should be sad longer, that I should be mourning, but a stronger part of me feels like I don't deserve to put myself through that."

Dr. Green leaned forward slightly, her gaze warm and reassuring. "Everyone processes breakups differently, and there's no right or wrong way to heal. The pain you went through before was already part of your 'mourning period,' and now that you're past it, it's not as heavy as you thought it would be. That doesn't mean your past relationship didn't matter—it just means you're allowing yourself to let go. Even if you overthink things, you're choosing to move forward with Mikkel and the happiness he brings into your life."

I thought of him, and I started blushing like an idiot. "He's generous and attentive. It's so easy with him, like I've known him forever, even though it's only been a short time. I get butterflies just thinking about him, when I'm with him, even when my phone lights up with his name."

She jotted something down, then met my gaze. "He's bringing something positive into your life. Moving on doesn't mean forgetting or erasing what you had with Joshua. It just means you're stepping into a new chapter."

Some of the anxiousness inside me eased. "I guess I just needed to hear that."

Dr. Green smiled. "You deserve happiness, Abigail. Joshua made his choice. And for the first time in years, you're making yours—you're choosing yourself, choosing joy. That's not something to feel guilty about."

I took a deep breath, letting her words sink in. "Thank you. I really needed that reminder."

She nodded. "Is there anything else on your mind?" She glanced at her notes before looking back at me. "How's work at *Book Culture*? And how are you adjusting to being away from your family?"

"Work's been great. I've already gotten positive feedback from customers and my manager. It's nice to feel appreciated, like I'm actually making a difference."

Her smile warmed. "That's wonderful. It sounds like you're finding fulfillment there."

I nodded. "Yeah, it's been a pleasant surprise. As for being away from my family, I miss them, of course, but I feel like it was time for me to step out on my own. Some days, the distance hits harder than others, but I'm managing."

Her gaze softened. "I'm really proud of the balance you're finding. And when those tough moments come, how are you coping with them?"

I shrugged lightly. "It's not overwhelming, nothing that stops me from going about my day. Some days are easier, but I'm adjusting."

Dr. Green leaned in just slightly. "Change can be overwhelming, but you've been handling it well. Give yourself permission to adjust at your own pace."

"You're right," I admitted, inhaling deeply. "I need to be more patient with myself."

"Exactly," she said. "You're juggling a lot—a new city, new job, new home, a new relationship. It's okay to take things one step at a time. It's normal to feel a mix of emotions right now."

I exhaled slowly, the weight on my chest feeling a little lighter. "Thanks, Dr. Green. This really helps."

She smiled. "That's what I'm here for. You're doing great, Abigail. Just keep taking it day by day."

CHAPTER TWENTY-ONE

Mikkel

"True love begins when nothing is looked for in return."
~ Antoine de Saint-Exupéry

She asked me what my favorite color was, and I froze. No one had ever asked me that before. It wasn't something I'd thought about, so I said white—simple, easy, the first thing that came to mind.

I had always worn white, surrounded myself with it. White felt safe. White felt like control.

But later, I realized my favorite color was yellow—not just because it was one of hers, but because it reminded me of her.

When I looked at her, I saw yellow—soft, warm, and impossibly beautiful. The kind of yellow that felt like the first touch of sunlight after the longest night. The kind that melted away the cold and whispered promises of something better. Yellow wasn't just a color. It was how she made everything brighter.

How she made me feel alive.

Before her, my life had been routine. Predictable. Monotonous. Then, everything changed. I didn't just see her—*I felt her*. Like sunlight breaking through a sky I hadn't even realized was gray. And she wasn't just a fleeting brightness. She was a constant light.

The next morning, soft sunlight streamed through my curtains, pulling me from sleep. I rubbed my eyes, reached for my phone, and dialed Abigail's number. My heart fluttered with every ring until her face appeared on the screen, her radiant smile and messy hair making the morning feel even warmer.

"Hey," she greeted, her voice soft, wrapping around me like warmth itself.

"Hey," I echoed, smiling back. *God, she was beautiful.* "I hope I didn't wake you."

"No, not at all," she assured me, her eyes sparkling. "I was just organizing some things."

"What are you doing today?"

Her lips parted slightly, hesitating before she spoke. "Actually, I was going to ask if you wanted to come over and spend the day with me." She exhaled softly, almost nervous. "I could use a break from organizing, and… it'd be nice to see you."

I didn't hesitate. "I'd love that."

Her brows knit together slightly. "Only if you're not… busy. I don't want to interrupt your day or anything."

I shook my head, smiling. "I'm never too busy for you."

A soft blush crept across her cheeks, her smile turning shy. "Okay, then. I'll see you soon?"

"Soon," I promised, already itching to be with her.

"Tell me you've got good news," Arnoldo said the moment I stepped into the glass-walled conference room at Reyes & Associates, the sprawling headquarters of the country's top law firm. He leaned back in his chair, a smirk playing on his face.

I dropped my bag on the table. "You know I don't show up empty-handed."

He arched an eyebrow, tapping a pen against the stack of documents in front of him. "That expansion of yours is ambitious, but if anyone can handle it, it's you."

"And that's why I'm here." I sank into the chair across from him. "I need the final bid airtight. No surprises, no loose ends."

He chuckled, shaking his head. "You always bring me the fun ones, don't you?"

"Wouldn't want you getting bored, Reyes."

When it came to anything legal, Arnoldo was the only one I trusted—he was the best in the business. We dove straight into the meeting, and as always, he was thorough, challenging every assumption and making sure we covered all the bases.

Two hours later, we'd addressed every concern and finalized the contracts, confirming the expansion was set in motion.

I stood up and stretched, letting out a long breath. "Alright, everything good?"

"We're good," Arnoldo said, leaning back in his chair. "Everything's set. Nice work, *amigo.*[1]"

I grabbed my laptop and slung my bag over my shoulder, ready to head out. Arnoldo glanced at me, amusement flickering in his eyes.

"By the way," he said, pointing at me, "what's with the casual look today? Showing off your tattoos?"

I glanced down at my outfit—definitely more laid-back than usual. I hadn't thought much of it, but it was clearly different from my usual business attire.

"I'm heading to Abigail's place," I said, shrugging.

---

1 *friend*

His eyebrows shot up. "Am I supposed to know who that is?"

I smirked. "The woman I've been seeing."

Arnoldo leaned forward, mock offense written all over his face. "Why am I *always* the last to find out?"

I chuckled, shaking my head. "A little dramatic, aren't you, Reyes?"

"Dramatic? Offended? Same thing!"

I rolled my eyes. "*Dramático.*[2]"

"So, what's she like? Are you happy?"

"I don't think I've ever been happier," I replied, the thought of her bringing an automatic smile to my face. "She's funny, smart, and possibly the most gorgeous woman I've ever laid eyes on."

"You've got it bad," Arnoldo teased, standing up to stretch. "But hey, as long as you're happy. Don't want you getting hurt."

"Yeah, yeah," I laughed. "Thank you, Reyes."

I didn't think he'd actually come.

Sure, I'd thrown the idea out there earlier during our FaceTime call—half-joking, half-testing the waters—but I hadn't expected him to show up in the middle of the week.

But here he was.

Mikkel stood at my door, holding a bouquet of primroses, a shopping bag, a white box, and a black leather bag slung over his shoulder. His gaze was steady, like he'd been waiting for this moment—*for me.*

"Hey, Red." His voice was smooth, deep, like he was drinking me in.

"Hey," I murmured, my breath catching as my eyes roamed over him.

He looked unfairly good, the kind of good that made the room feel too warm, *too small.* But it wasn't just his looks—it was the way he stood there, like he'd drop anything to be here.

---

2 *Dramatic*

“You look beautiful,” he said, his tone thick with something that made my stomach dip.

I should’ve answered immediately, but his eyes—heated, unflinching, like he wanted to memorize me—made my thoughts scatter.

“Thank you,” I finally managed, stepping back to let him in.

As he passed, the crisp scent of citrus, linen, and Mikkel enveloped me. The moment settled—heavy, certain.

I watched as he pulled out the flowers, moving with determination. He emptied the vase, rinsed it, filled it with fresh water, added flower food, and swirled it before carefully arranging the blooms.

My chest tightened. Not just at the sight of him standing in my kitchen like he belonged, but at the way he did it—with intention, with care, like keeping my flowers alive was just another way to show he was paying attention.

“You’ve done this before,” I said, my voice quieter than before.

“Can’t let your flowers die too soon.” He adjusted a stem, his focus unwavering. “And no, but I got directions from the florist.”

Something warm and sharp curled in my chest. He’d gone out of his way for this. *For me.*

The Songs For You playlist played softly in the background, and my mind flickered to the Lana show I’d missed out on. Disappointment stirred, but I forced it down.

“You okay?” Mikkel’s voice was gentle, but his gaze was searching, like he already knew the answer.

I swallowed. “Yeah.”

He didn’t look convinced. But after a beat, he turned to the flowers, his expression softening as he took them in.

Then, finally, he looked back at me. “Now they’re perfect.”

My chest tightened, and I had to look away before my smile gave too much away. “Thank you.”

Mikkel’s gaze held me, unwavering, as if engraving this moment into memory. “The pleasure is always mine.”

Before I could respond, he reached for the white box, holding it out like a promise. "For you."

My fingers brushed his as I took it, a small touch, barely anything, but somehow, too much.

"What's this?"

"Open it."

Inside was a rich chocolate cake, perfectly frosted, decadent. A masterpiece of indulgence.

"This looks amazing," I murmured, already imagining the taste, the way it would melt on my tongue.

"I stopped by the bakery and picked it up for you," he said, watching me carefully. "Figured you might need a little something sweet."

I shook my head, trying—and failing—not to be affected. "You're ridiculous."

He smirked, slow and deliberate. That dangerous kind of smirk.

"Cuando se trata de ti."[3]

I didn't know what he meant, but the quiet certainty in his voice sent warmth curling low in my stomach.

Note to self: download Duolingo. *Immediately.*

Before I could dwell on it, he reached for the shopping bag. "And this," he lifted it slightly, "is for your locks."

"My locks?"

"You mentioned a while back that you were considering installing a deadbolt, so I thought I'd take care of it for you."

I stared at him, words failing me for the second time today.

He remembered.

Not just in passing. Not just as an afterthought. He'd heard me. And then he did something about it.

"You didn't have to do that," I said softly.

His steady gaze held mine. "I wanted to."

The lump in my throat returned, thick and persistent. *How was I supposed to fight against this?*

---

3 *When it comes to you.*

Desperate for something—*anything*—to steady myself, I gestured toward the last bag still sitting on the counter. "And that one?"

Mikkel's lips curved into something slower, deeper.

"That," he said, his voice rich with meaning, "is for later."

I narrowed my eyes, trying to ignore the way anticipation curled through me.

"Mysterious," I teased.

He smirked, low and knowing. "Very."

I shook my head, trying not to grin as I took a bite of the cake. It was rich and decadent—almost too much, but exactly what I needed.

Mikkel just watched me, slow and intent, as if memorizing me—like this moment meant more than I could yet grasp.

That thought made my stomach dip.

I cleared my throat. "So? First time at my apartment. What's the verdict?"

His gaze flickered around before settling back on me. "Feels like you."

Simple. Certain. No part of me would survive this fall, and right now? I wasn't sure I wanted to.

Somehow, we ended up on the couch, his arm draped loosely over the back, *Beauty and the Beast* playing on the screen.

I wasn't sure how this would go. Mikkel didn't strike me as someone who watched Disney movies, but he looked comfortable, relaxed in a way that made it too easy to imagine this happening again.

For a while, I stayed stiff, my mind stuck on everything about today—how he showed up, how easily he fit into my space, how he always did these things that made me feel like I mattered without having to ask.

Finally, I let myself lean into him, just slightly.

His arm lowered from the back of the couch, brushing my shoulder as he shifted closer. But just before he touched me, he hesitated.

"Can I?"

The question sent a shiver through me, not because I doubted him, but because he asked.

"You don't have to ask."

"Yes, I do," he murmured. "You deserve to feel safe, Red. I never want to assume that."

My throat tightened. I gave a small nod.

His expression softened, and when he pulled me in, it was natural—like he'd been waiting for this, like it was always meant to be.

We got through *Beauty and the Beast* and transitioned into *The Enchanted Christmas*. During *Belle's Magical World*, he leaned over slightly and whispered, "You think she ever got scared or second-guessed herself?"

I paused, considering. "Probably, but she pushed through it anyway. I think that's what makes her brave, not that she's fearless, but that she acts even when she's scared."

He nodded, a thoughtful expression crossing his face. "I like that. It's real."

As we started the live-action adaptation, I relaxed completely against him, my head resting on his chest while his hand gently held my thigh. He rubbed slow, soothing circles into my leg, his touch light but grounding.

"What makes *Beauty and the Beast* stand out to you?"

I smiled, leaning back into him. "Because it's about seeing past what's on the surface, and it reminds me that good things can come from unexpected places."

He hummed in agreement, his fingers brushing lightly against my arm. "I like that. It's fitting."

"For what?"

"For you," he said with a certainty that always seemed to leave me speechless.

I grinned, tucking my head into his shoulder. "I thought you didn't like movies."

His lips twitched into a soft smile. "I don't."

"Then wh—"

"You like them," he interrupted gently. "And I like you—everything you do interests me. So here I am."

The simplicity of his words made my heart somersault, and I smiled so hard my cheeks hurt.

As the final movie played, I savored the rare comfort of leaning into someone who made me feel seen, safe, and cared for.

"I could never do this with anyone else," I murmured, almost to myself. "People always made me feel stupid for still liking these movies and everything."

"You *won't* have to do it with anyone else, Red."

I sighed contentedly as he pressed a kiss to the top of my head, holding me just a little tighter.

The frightening chime of his phone alarm broke our comfort as the credits rolled on. I blinked up at Mikkel, still comfortably tucked into his side, and frowned.

"Does that mean you have to go?" I asked, not quite ready to part with him, but fully understanding how much it took for him to leave work and spend an unplanned day with me.

He shook his head, a small, secretive smile curving his lips. "Nope."

"Then what—"

"It means you have to get ready."

I blinked at him, suddenly wide awake. "Ready for what?"

Mikkel grabbed the bag he'd called "for later" and handed it to me silently, watching me with an unreadable expression.

I opened it carefully, my breath stalling as I pulled out the items: a white eyelet lace corset-style top with delicate red ribbon accents, a tiny bow at the neckline. A red leather mini-skirt. Matching knee-high boots.

My mouth dropped open. "Mikkel…" I traced the fabric with my fingers, heart hammering. "Are you kidding me right now? This is… this is gorgeous."

His lips quirked, eyes dark with something warm. "I'm glad you approve."

"Approve?" I looked up at him, clutching the outfit to my chest. "This is everything."

His voice was impossibly casual, like he hadn't just made my whole week. "I was hoping it'd be." Then, even softer, "The corset has breast support. And the inside is lined with cotton so it won't mark your skin."

I blinked. *He'd thought of that?*

I swallowed, staring at him, at this man who noticed *everything* without me having to say a word.

"Wait—where are we going?"

Mikkel tsked, shaking his head. "Too many questions, *amor*.[4]" His hand cradled my face, thumb brushing my cheek. "Just get dressed."

I narrowed my eyes at him, but I was smiling. Beaming. "What about you?"

His smirk deepened. "Go get dressed."

I glanced down at the outfit again, running my fingers over the fabric. It was so perfect it almost felt unreal. And he'd known my size. *What the hell?*

I looked up at him, chest tightening. "Thank you," I whispered. "I mean it, Mikkel. Thank you."

He leaned forward, resting his elbows on his knees, his face suddenly so close. "You don't have to thank me for knowing what you'd love." His voice was quiet, intent. "I just pay attention."

Something thick rose in my throat. No one had ever done this—cared like this. I nodded, biting my lip to steady the emotions rushing in.

"I'll go get ready."

I stood, clutching the outfit like it was my most precious possession. My mind raced—he knew my style, my taste, the exact thing that would make my heart leap. And he didn't just know; *he acted on it.*

Once in my room, I quickly got ready—shower, hair, makeup—and slipped into the outfit, smoothing the corset top over my skin. The mini skirt fit like a dream, and the boots were the perfect finishing touch.

I turned in the mirror, admiring the look, and for a few seconds, just stood there, savoring how good it felt to be seen like this and how great I looked.

---

4 *Love*

I stepped out, smoothing my skirt, and spotted him by the window. His white open-collared shirt revealed a bit of his skin, and his dark jeans fit perfectly.

When he turned, his eyes widened, and a stunned, almost helpless look crossed his face as he took me in from head to toe.

"You're…" He paused, clearing his throat as he tried to find the words. "Wow. You're beautiful. No—*gorgeous.* Stunning. Just…wow. *Eres tan jodidamente hermosa.*"[5]

I bit my lip, smiling despite not knowing what that meant. "You're making me blush, Mikkel."

"Good," he said quickly, his voice slightly breathless. He took a step closer, his eyes locked on mine. "You deserve to know how *incredible* you look."

"Thank you." The warmth spread from my chest to my cheeks. "Sorry if I took so long. This was unexpected."

"*Never* apologize for that," he said firmly. "I'd wait forever if it meant seeing you."

His words sent a chill through me, but before I could respond, he added, "Leave your wallet, by the way."

I blinked at him, confused. "Why?"

He gave me a look, the kind that left no room for argument. "You don't need to bring any money; you're out with me."

My lips twitched, but I relented, setting it on the counter. "Okay."

He grinned, offering his arm. "Shall we?"

As we walked to his car, his hand lightly on my lower back, I tried to guess where he might be taking me. He hadn't given me any hints, well, one, but that was impossible at this point. My curiosity gnawed at me, but I held back from bombarding him with questions.

The city lights blurred past as we drove, the hum of the engine soothing. It wasn't until we pulled into the parking lot that my suspicions kicked into overdrive. My lungs stilled when I read the sign.

---

5 *You are so fucking beautiful*

"No fucking way," I blurted, turning to him.

He raised an eyebrow, feigning innocence. "Hm?"

I gestured wildly at the venue. "The outfit. The venue. Mikkel, are we going to see Lana?"

He smirked, pulling two VIP tickets from the glove compartment. "We're going to see Lana."

I gawked at him, my pulse racing. My eyes darted between the tickets and his face, trying to process what was happening. "I'm going to have a heart attack. You…this…oh my gosh!"

He reached over, taking my hand and squeezing it gently. "Breathe, Red. Let's go. We've got floor seats."

Floor seats. I was going to melt.

He climbed out first, opening my door with a steady hand, and we walked toward the entrance. Grinning, I followed him through the crowd, his hand firmly on my waist, guiding me. When we reached our seats, I nearly teared up—front and center, the best view in the house.

"Mikkel," I breathed, turning to him. The words I wanted to say eluded me, so I just stared, hoping he'd understand what I couldn't express.

He smiled, his expression softer now, and leaned in close enough that I could feel his breath against my ear. "Anything for you."

The concert started with an explosion of lights and sound, and the crowd erupted in cheers. From the first note, I was completely swept up in it, singing along with the songs I'd memorized years ago.

Mikkel didn't jump and shout, but I could tell he was enjoying it in his own way. His eyes never left me for long, and whenever I glanced at him, he'd smile—a real, genuine smile that made my heart ache in the best way.

At one point, I joined a group of strangers singing along to "Born to Die," swaying with them as if we'd known each other forever. Mikkel captured it all, his phone held steady as he took videos and pictures of me.

When I returned to him, breathless and exhilarated, he wrapped an arm around me and leaned in close. "You're having fun?"

"More than fun," I replied, my head resting against his shoulder. "This is perfect."

All night, he spoiled me, making sure I had anything I wanted—a drink, a snack, a souvenir. By the time the concert ended and we stepped outside, I was still on a high, practically floating.

I turned to him, my smile so wide it hurt. "This was the best night of my life."

"Seeing you happy is worth everything, Red."

His words struck deep, warmth blooming in my chest. I looked away, blinking fast. How did he always know what to say—make me feel treasured?

We walked on, his hand steady in mine. I glanced at him, amazed by his calm after everything tonight—the outfit, the venue, the energy. Anyone else would've been overwhelmed, but not Mikkel. He stood beside me, unwavering, as if nothing could change the way he saw me.

I still couldn't believe he'd let me wear this outfit, let alone that he was the one who bought it—looking ready for the spotlight instead of the crowd. Joshua would've lost it—accusations, threats, making me feel ashamed, like my body wasn't mine to dress. But Mikkel? He hadn't even flinched. He just looked at me like I was the only thing that mattered. *Like I was meant to be seen.*

Before I knew it, I stopped in my tracks again, and when he turned to me, confusion flashing in his eyes, I didn't even think. I kissed him.

It wasn't planned or even logical. It was instinctual, like something I'd been holding back for too long. The second our lips met, the world blurred—just him, just this.

He didn't hesitate. His free hand came up to cradle my face, his touch gentle but sure, and kissed me back like he'd been waiting, like he already knew exactly how to meet me in this moment. His lips were soft and warm against mine, his thumb brushing lightly over my cheek, and the way he kissed me—it wasn't rushed or demanding. It was deep, steady, unshakable.

Like he wanted me to feel every second of it.

Like he needed me to know this was real.

And I felt it.

I felt it in the way my heart pounded, in the way my body melted into his, in the way every inch of me screamed that this—*this*—was different. Because for the first time, a kiss wasn't about proving something or seeking reassurance. It was about being wanted. About being chosen.

When we finally pulled apart, I was breathless, my heart a wild, unsteady thing. His gaze locked onto mine, dark and searching, filled with something unspoken—something I felt all the way to my toes.

"I've been wanting to do that for a long time." His voice was low and steady, but the emotion in it made my knees weak. "And it was even better than I imagined."

My chest tightened at his words, my breath catching as I smiled softly and whispered, "Me too."

His hand stayed on my face for a moment longer, his thumb tracing an invisible pattern on my skin, like he wasn't ready to let go just yet. Then he leaned in and pressed a kiss to my forehead—tender, lingering. *Like a promise.*

"Let's get you home, *amor*," he murmured, his voice warm, sending a flutter through my stomach.

His hand found mine again, steady and sure, and I knew tonight would stay with me. Not because of the concert or the crowd.

Because of him.

Because of *this*.

The car hummed through the city, New York's lights casting a golden glow over everything. I leaned against the window, my lips still tingling from the kiss, sneaking a glance at him.

Mikkel's expression was calm, eyes steady on the road, but the slight curve of his lips told me he was holding onto something—something just for himself.

The sudden glow of a drive-thru sign snapped me from my thoughts.

"Hungry?" he asked, already pulling in.

I blinked at him. "You think I have room after all the popcorn and nachos?"

He smirked, parking as the line inched forward. "This is for later, when you wake up starving at two a.m."

Warmth spread through my chest. I shook my head, smiling as he ordered a barbecue shrimp sandwich and fries. When I shot him a curious look, he winked.

When we reached my apartment, he parked, grabbed the food, and followed me to the elevator without question.

"I'll wait until you're settled," he said, voice firm.

I didn't argue. My mind was a tangled mess of thoughts, but my body felt calm.

Inside, I moved through my bedtime routine, but the moment I stepped back into the room, my breath caught.

Mikkel stood near the door, hands in his pockets, but there was nothing casual about the way he watched me. His gaze lingered—heavy, knowing.

"So," I started, crossing my arms with a playful tilt of my head. "What did it feel like?"

His brow furrowed. "What?"

"The kiss."

For a beat, he didn't answer. His eyes traced my face, slow and deliberate, like he was memorizing every detail. Then, stepping closer, he reached up, adjusting my bonnet with careful fingers. His thumb grazed my bottom lip.

"It felt like stepping outside on the first warm day after winter." His voice was quiet, certain. "Like everything softens, everything melts, and for a second… the world feels perfect."

My heart stuttered. His fingers brushed my cheek, and before I could speak, he closed the distance between us.

"And now," he murmured, lips curving, "I'm going to kiss you goodnight, and every single day and night after this."

He leaned in slowly, giving me space to pull away. *I didn't.*

The kiss was deeper than the first—deliberate, unhurried, felt. His lips molded to mine with a certainty that sent a shiver down my spine.

When he pulled back, he rested his forehead against mine, breath warm against my lips.

"Goodnight, Red."

I opened my eyes and found his waiting for me. "Goodnight, Mikkel."

With that, he turned and walked out, leaving me standing there, heart full, lips aching for more.

I lingered by the door, fingertips resting on the knob, replaying every second.

Then, the moment his footsteps faded, I collapsed onto the couch, limbs flailing as I let out a silent scream.

"Oh my god." I slapped my hands over my face, legs kicking at the cushions. "Did that just happen?"

I barely knew how to process it—the concert, the kiss, *him fixing my bonnet.* The way he'd looked at me. The way he'd felt.

Rolling onto my back, I let out a breathless laugh. "This is real, right?" I whispered, half-expecting the walls to answer.

Instead, excitement pulsed through me, lighting up every nerve. My hands tangled in my hair as I grinned at the ceiling.

"What the hell, Abigail?"

But deep down, I already knew that this was only the beginning.

WARNING

This chapter contains mild mentions of sensitive topics. Please check the content warnings for potential triggers. Your well-being matters, so take care while reading.

CHAPTER TWENTY TWO

Abigail-Ann

"To love is to recognize yourself in another."
- Eckhart Tolle

After rescheduling our Coney Island date to cover an extra shift, I thought the night was lost. But Mikkel had other plans.

He showed up after my shift, grinning like he'd been waiting for this all day, and brought me to the High Line. Under the hum of the city, it felt like we existed in our own little world. The scent of burgers drifted in the air as we settled onto the grass, our food between us. The sky wasn't a perfect, cinematic expanse of stars, but it didn't have to be.

It was ours.

Lying back, he pulled me close, his arm settling around my shoulders like it belonged there. With effortless precision, he adjusted the telescope, his voice low and sure as he traced constellations above us. I wasn't looking at the stars, though.

I was looking at him.

At the quiet way he saw me.

At the way he felt like certainty in a world where nothing had ever been guaranteed.

At the way he made me feel safe. Cherished. Happy.

And then there was the way he kissed me.

Not just a kiss—something deeper. Something that made my breath catch and my body hum. His lips pressed against mine with a slow, aching intensity, like he was memorizing me. Like he wanted me to feel what he couldn't put into words.

For so long, I thought intimacy and sex were inseparable. That touch had to come with expectation. But with Mikkel, it was different.

When he reached for my hand, he didn't take it—he brushed his fingers against mine, waiting. When I curled my fingers around his, he traced slow, lazy circles on my skin. And I realized then—intimacy wasn't just about passion.

It was this. The quiet moments. The way he paid attention, how he never asked for more than I was ready to give. His touch spoke its own language—one I was only just beginning to understand.

And maybe, just maybe, I wanted to learn.

In the days that followed, we fell into an easy, intoxicating rhythm of closeness. Every moment with him felt like slipping into something warm and familiar, like my heart had known him long before my mind had caught up.

Then, one afternoon, before heading to an interview, he came over to install the extra locks on my door—something he insisted on doing himself.

I sat nearby, watching him work. His brows furrowed in focus, his hands sure and steady. Shirtless.

And utterly, devastatingly distracting.

Because somewhere along the way, without meaning to, I had fallen into something deeper than I ever expected.

And God, I was in trouble.

"Enjoying the view?" His voice cut through my thoughts, teasing and low, and I felt my face heat as his lips curved into a smirk.

"Just making sure you're doing it right."

He chuckled, standing to test the lock. "Am I doing it right?"

I nodded absentmindedly. "You're doing it perfectly."

I bit my lip, caught between a sharp reply and the flutter in my stomach. Tattoos had never tempted me before, but on him, they were dangerous, begging to be traced with my fingers. Or my lips. God help me.

Days of staying in, organizing, and Facetiming him soon turned into cozy nights on the couch—movies playing softly, his arm draped over my shoulders, our legs tangled like perfect puzzle pieces. He'd steal featherlight kisses, each touch igniting a slow-burning fire. He knew my quirks—showing up with barbecue Lay's, Chipotle, or chocolate cake—and cherished even the smallest gestures, like my hand on his back, drawing a contented sigh as the world faded away.

Lost in the comfort of those memories, I barely registered the time. A refreshing shower later, I slipped into my favorite flowy sundress and headed downstairs where he was waiting for me.

I was breathless as his cologne hit me first, my gaze drifting over his linen white shirt and matching pants, the erudite charm of his glasses adding to his rugged appeal.

"Hey," I greeted, warmth flooding me at the sight of him.

"Morning, Red," he rumbled, his deep voice sending shivers down my spine. "Ready to go?"

I nodded, sliding into the car as nerves fluttered in my stomach.

"You excited?" He shot me a teasing grin.

"I am!" I squealed. "I've never been to Coney Island."

He chuckled, shaking his head. "You'll never want to leave once you're there."

The drive was full of laughter and easy conversation, our excitement building with each passing mile. As we arrived, the buzz of carnival rides and the salty ocean breeze wrapped around us. Colorful banners fluttered overhead, and the sweet scent of cotton candy and popcorn filled the air, instantly reminding me of Pier 39.

"These lights are beautiful," I murmured, eyes wide with wonder.

When I turned to him, I caught him staring—not at the lights, but at me. My breath hitched, warmth rushing to my cheeks.

"Yeah," he said, voice quieter now. "Beautiful."

Our first stop was the Wonder Wheel, its towering frame glowing against the night sky.

"Are you ready for this?" he asked, flashing a grin as we climbed into one of the swinging gondolas.

"As ready as I'll ever be," I said, trying to sound brave, though my stomach was already fluttering.

The wheel lifted us higher, the boardwalk stretching beneath us like a sea of neon stars. The city skyline glittered in the distance, and for a moment, everything felt weightless.

"Look at that view," I murmured, nodding toward the horizon.

He hummed, but when I turned, his gaze wasn't on the skyline—it was on me.

"Mine's better."

"Oh yeah?" I arched my brow. "What's yours?"

His lips curved, eyes steady. "You."

Warmth bloomed in my chest, stealing my breath as the world shrank, dimming the carnival lights and crashing waves.

Next was the roller coaster, its neon-lit tracks twisting wildly against the sky.

"Are you sure about this one?" he asked.

"No," I admitted. "But we do it for the experience."

The second we dropped, my scream tangled with his laughter, adrenaline thrumming through my veins. By the time we stumbled off, breathless and exhilarated, I couldn't stop grinning.

We wandered through the carnival, our laughter mingling with the excited shouts around us. Every time I glanced at him, he wasn't just watching me—he was memorizing me, like he didn't want to forget a single second.

"This is amazing!" I said, spinning in place when we reached the carousel, its golden lights flickering beneath the moonlight.

"It's even better with you," he murmured, squeezing my hand.

We followed the scent of buttery popcorn and sweet funnel cakes, indulging in every bite. I licked powdered sugar off my fingers and sighed, blissful.

"This is so good. I feel like a kid again."

"That's the magic of America's Playground," he said, amusement dancing in his honey-brown eyes. "It brings out the inner child in everyone."

The night pulled us forward, until we ended up on the beach, the waves stretching dark and endless ahead of us. He pulled me close, his arm warm around my shoulders, my head resting against his chest.

I should've been overthinking—dissecting every touch, every look, every word—but I wasn't. Not when I could feel the steady rhythm of his heartbeat beneath my cheek.

I lifted my gaze, meeting his. And just like that, all the noise in my head stopped.

Some nights fade into memory. Others settle into your bones, unforgettable.

This was one of them.

"Today was perfect," I whispered, eyes closed, soaking in the feeling.

"Everyday with you normally is." His lips brushed the top of my head.

The night had fully settled around us now, the stars flickering to life above the water. The waves rolled in steady, rhythmic pulses, a calming backdrop to the quiet between us.

"You come here a lot?" I asked, tracing slow circles on my thigh.

He hesitated. "Not as much as I used to," he admitted. "Work keeps me busy. But back in university… yeah. I was here all the time."

I turned to him, curiosity tugging at my chest. "Why?"

His gaze drifted toward the horizon, his voice quieter now. "It was the only place that felt still."

Something in the way he said it made me pause. "You needed stillness?"

He exhaled, rubbing a hand over his jaw. "Yeah. College was… hard. Not just the workload. But—" He hesitated, as if debating whether to say more. Then, finally, he did. "Moving here was a lot. I was a kid, barely spoke English, and suddenly I had to learn fast. By the time I got to college, I had the language down, but the heavy accent, the cultural gaps… they didn't just go away." He let out a small, humorless laugh. "You think you're doing fine until someone laughs or mocks you when you mispronounce something. Or acts surprised when you're good at something. You start second-guessing yourself. Wondering if you belong."

A pang hit my chest, sharp and deep. I knew that feeling well—the exhaustion of constantly proving yourself, of knowing people had already decided who you were before you even opened your mouth.

"I get it," I murmured. "That feeling of walking into a room and knowing they've already made up their minds. Of having to fight to be seen before you even speak."

His head turned slightly, his gaze locking onto mine. And for a moment, neither of us spoke.

Then, finally, he gave a small nod. "Yeah." His voice was quieter this time. "Exactly that."

I reached for his hand without thinking, threading my fingers through his. "You never had to prove anything, Mikkel."

His thumb brushed over my knuckles, slow and deliberate. "That's what my parents used to say. And my friends. They were the ones who kept me from losing myself and constantly defended me." He paused, then glanced at me, something unreadable in his expression. "I don't talk about this with people."

I squeezed his hand. "I know."

His lips parted slightly, as if he hadn't expected that answer—as if he was still getting used to the fact that I saw him, really saw him, and wasn't looking away.

"But with you," he murmured after a beat, "it doesn't feel hard."

Heat stirred in my chest, something deep and real. This was trust. Maybe something even bigger than that.

A sudden streak of light caught my eye, and I looked up just in time to see a shooting star cut across the sky.

"Make a wish," he whispered, his lips brushing my ear.

I turned toward him instead. "I don't need to."

His brows lifted slightly, like he was about to argue, but before he could, I just smiled. Then, closing my eyes anyway, I made a wish—one that had nothing to do with the stars and everything to do with the man beside me.

I wished this feeling would never, *ever* end.

CHAPTER TWENTY-THREE

Mikkel

"Love is a fire. But whether it is going to warm your hearth or burn down your house, you can never tell."
~ Joan Crawford

Not every man got a chance like this—a chance with a woman who felt like a miracle from God made just for him.

Seeing her felt like stepping into a daydream, my heart practically sprouting yellow hearts above my head like some cosmic confirmation. She was it. The kind of woman who made me want to be better, who had me pining after her before I even knew her name. And that smile? It was blinding. Like catching the first sunrise after a lifetime of darkness. It wrecked me.

I wasn't one to talk about the past. But with her, it just spilled out. It felt right. And when she reached for my hand—when she looked at me like I was worth seeing—I knew.

She wasn't just a sign. She was the whole damn universe aligning.

I had plans. Big ones. Dates that would make her laugh until she forgot the world. Because if anyone deserved happiness in abundance, it was her. And if I had any say in it, she was going to get it.

That woman—that brilliant, breathtaking force of nature?

She was Abigail-Ann Asher. *My Red.*

And whatever came next, I'd make damn sure she never had a reason to let go.

Yet here I was, in a city that wasn't home, counting down the hours until I could get back to her.

As the car rolled up to the glass high-rise, I exhaled, restlessness settling deep in my chest. Chicago was fine—great, even—but home was wherever she was. And I needed to be there.

The buzz around the Elite Rides grand opening was palpable. The venue was polished, our branding bold and impossible to miss. Inside, the energy matched the chaos outside—everything falling into place. Or so I thought.

I stood at the entrance, frustration simmering as I took in the final touches. Staff moved swiftly, managing last-minute details while the first set of guests trickled in. Beside me, Morison straightened his tie, his sharp gaze catching the same imperfections I did.

"Everything looks good, sir?" he asked, eyeing me knowingly.

"Not yet," I muttered. "The display needs adjusting, the banner is crooked, and the lighting's too harsh."

He raised an eyebrow. "I'll handle it." He gave me a slight smile. "You won't stop until it's perfect, huh?"

I glanced at him, jaw tight. "Not until it's exactly how I envisioned it."

With the last few tweaks in place, the atmosphere shifted, settling into something that finally felt right.

"Everything's been adjusted, sir," Morison said confidently. "Media's all set in the back, and the investors are making their way in."

Sapphire joined us, clipboard in hand. "We've also got a lineup of local influencers covering the event, and the turnout's already looking solid. It's going to be a great day."

As they spoke, my phone buzzed in my hand with a text from Abigail lighting up the screen.

Red
Good luck today. I know it's going to be amazing
♥

Me
Thanks, Red. You get off work late tonight, right?

Red
Yeah, I'm there from open to close.

Me
Have you eaten?

Red
Not yet. I really want Chipotle.

Me
Then I'll have someone deliver it to you.

Red
I was gonna get it later...

Me
Don't worry about that, mi amor.[1] I'll handle it.

Red
Thank you ♥

Red
How's Chicago?

Me
Productive. I just really miss you.

Red
I miss you, too. Hopefully, you'll be back soon.

"Sir," Morison called, pulling my attention away from my phone. "The cars are arriving."

I nodded. "Perfect. Also, have someone deliver Chipotle and a bouquet of primroses to Book Culture. No later than half an hour from now."

He grabbed his phone. "The same order as last time? To Abigail?"

"Yes."

Morison gave a quick nod. "And it's all taken care of, sir. The delivery is on its way."

Turning back to my phone, I sent one last text.

Me
Sorry about that, Red. I have to go but I'll call you later.

I slipped my phone into my pocket, a flicker of a smile tugging at my lips. Outside, sleek black cars pulled up in perfect sync, their drivers stepping out in polished uniforms to open doors for their passengers. Effortless luxury. Seamless efficiency. *This* was the image we wanted to project.

"We're not just launching," I said, adjusting my cufflinks. "We're making a statement. Elite Rides is here to stay."

Morison checked his watch. "Thirty minutes until the speeches. Media talking points covered, sir?"

"Of course." I didn't need a reminder; I'd been preparing for this moment long before today.

The clock ticked down, and I took a breath, letting the anticipation settle. This was more than expansion—it was proof of what we'd built. Proof that we weren't just another name in the industry; we were the future of mobility.

When the time came, I stepped to the podium, and the crowd hushed. "Welcome, everyone, to the launch of Elite Rides in Chicago. This city has always been known for innovation, and today, we bring a new era of luxury transportation to your streets."

Applause erupted. I continued, laying out our mission, the tech behind our service, and the high standards we upheld. I highlighted our partnerships, our drivers' elite training, and the seamless experience that set us apart.

After the speeches, we worked the room. Sapphire handled investors, Morison engaged with the media, and I made sure to be everywhere, shaking hands, answering questions, and solidifying connections.

Sapphire smirked as she approached. "Did you catch that reporter's eye? She seemed very interested in our tech features."

I let out a short laugh. "Good. Let's keep the momentum going."

As the evening wore on, I slipped away for a few minutes to check in on Abigail before returning to the mix. That's when Damon Ashford, one of the most skeptical investors, approached me.

"I'll admit, Suarez, I had my doubts. Big ones." He gestured to the crowd, his smirk just this side of impressed. "But after seeing all this? Let's just say, I wouldn't bet against you. This kind of vision would do well in Seattle."

"This is just the beginning," I said, matching his energy. "Good. Let's keep them talking."

Sapphire joined us, eyes sharp with satisfaction. "We've already had new investors express interest."

Ashford nodded, his skepticism fading. "Now *that's* the kind of talk I want to hear. Looking forward to more business with you, Suarez."

The night ended with a toast—glasses raised, deals secured, the promise of something bigger taking root.

Then we were off, rushing to catch a flight to Seattle for an acquisition meeting before heading home. Exhaustion clung to me like a second skin, but there was no time to dwell on it. By the time we landed in New York, I'd texted Abigail, stolen three hours of sleep, and thrown myself right back into the grind. No rest for the relentless.

"Good morning, everyone," I said, stepping into my office. My team straightened as I walked in, their attention snapping to me. "Sapphire, do we have the final itinerary for the Dupont event tonight?"

"Yes, it's all set," she replied, handing me a neatly organized folder. "Drivers are briefed, and the cars are ready to go."

"Excellent." I flipped through the documents. "David, any updates on the maintenance checks for the fleet?"

"Just finished up. All vehicles are in top shape."

"Good. We have a new client meeting at three. Let's make sure everything is seamless."

My phone buzzed, Abigail's name flashing across the screen. My chest warmed instantly. "Excuse me for a moment." Stepping into my office, I shut the door behind me and answered.

"Hey, Red." My voice softened automatically. "Are you okay?"

"I'm good." She sounded gentle, but there was something underneath—something quieter, harder to read.

"Miss me?"

"I do." There was a pause.

I exhaled, leaning against my desk. "I'm sorry for the lack of communication today. I got in late this morning, and I'm at the office now. Things have been hectic with the expansion. I've got a client meeting soon, then I need to sign off on some paperwork with Sapphire."

"Sapphire?" Her tone shifted. It wasn't obvious—just a small flicker, like a note played off-key.

I frowned slightly. "She's the operations manager."

"Right," she murmured. A little cooler now. Not cold, but careful.

"What's wrong?"

Silence. Not long, but just enough. And when she finally spoke, her voice was quieter, hesitant.

"It's nothing." Too quick.

I stayed quiet, waiting her out.

She sighed. "It's just… I'm not a fan of hearing about other women." Her words were soft but certain. "I've been through some things, and it's hard not to feel a little uneasy when I hear that."

"I get it, Red," I murmured, my voice steady. "But listen to me, there's no one else. There won't be. You're it."

A beat passed. Then, finally, "Okay," she whispered.

"What time are you off today?"

"Eight."

"You've been there since seven," I pointed out, a frown tugging at my brow.

"Yeah, but it's fine. I don't mind. The library's a great fit for me, and everyone's really nice."

"I'm glad," I said, a smile tugging at my lips. "Just promise me you won't overwork yourself."

The irony wasn't lost on me. *Hypocrite.*

A knock at my door pulled me back. Sapphire stepped in, signaling that the clients were ready.

"The clients are here. I'll see you later, *amor*."[1]

"Later," she whispered.

The call ended, but the weight of her voice stayed with me. Later. Too far away.

Sapphire ushered the clients into my office, and I greeted them with a welcoming smile, instantly switching gears to professionalism.

"Good afternoon, Mr. and Mrs. Astar. It's a pleasure to meet you both," I said, motioning for them to sit.

Alexandria and Edmund Astar were powerhouses in East Coast real estate, owning several high-end properties across the globe. Everyone wanted to work with them, but only a select few made the cut. Today, I was one of them.

"Likewise, Mr. Suarez," Edmund responded, his voice carrying authority.

"We've heard excellent things about your services from Dr. Ronan Romano and our lawyer, Mr. Arnoldo Reyes," Alexandria added, her tone poised and assured.

"I appreciate their recommendation," I replied, making a mental note to thank Ronan and Arnoldo later.

They wasted no time outlining the specifics of a private driver contract for their daughters, detailing their expectations with clarity.

"Their schedules can be unpredictable, so flexibility is key," Edmund explained. "We also value discretion and professionalism above all else."

"I understand," I nodded. "We pride ourselves on both, ensuring privacy and providing top-tier service."

"We'd also prefer someone well-versed in the city's layout, especially for last-minute changes," Alexandria added.

---

1 *love*

Edmund met my gaze. "We've done our research, Mr. Suarez. With the praise your company has received, we're certain you're the only one we want to work with. We'd like to know if you'll take us on as clients."

The decision was easy. "I'll personally oversee the selection of a driver who meets your full requirements once they're officially drafted," I assured them. "We're honored to have the opportunity to serve your family."

"It's our pleasure, Mr. Suarez." Edmund stood, his handshake firm, decisive—an unspoken acknowledgment that this deal was worth both our time.

As they left my office, I turned to Sapphire with a satisfied grin. "That went well. Looks like we've landed another valuable client."

Sapphire nodded, her tone equally pleased. "Absolutely, Mr. Suarez. The Astar family is a major addition. I'll start on the paperwork and follow up with them to finalize the details."

"Perfect," I replied, leaning back in my chair. "Keep me updated. I want everything seamless—no room for errors."

Sapphire gave a sharp nod. "Of course."

As she exited the office, I swiveled my chair toward the window, gazing at the cityscape beyond. Another win. Another step toward making Elite Rides unstoppable.

Today was a disaster in slow motion.

Thirteen meetings. Interviews. Two photo shoots. Endless back-and-forth emails. By now, I was running on fumes and a whiskey buzz that was starting to backfire. I rubbed a hand down my face, willing the irritation away as Cataleya Nguyen pushed *another* question across the table.

"Mr. Suarez," she began, her voice calm but pointed, "with expansion into more cities, how will you preserve Elite Rides' exclusivity and premium appeal? Scaling up risks diluting the brand."

It was a fair concern, but my patience was wearing thin. I leaned back, adjusting my cufflinks—a subtle tell when I was keeping my temper in check.

"Our reputation is non-negotiable," I said evenly. "We're synchronizing driver training, customer perks, and app updates across markets to maintain consistency. Expansion isn't a risk, it's an opportunity, and we'll surpass expectations."

She studied me briefly, her brow furrowing before nodding in acceptance. The tension in my shoulders eased slightly as the discussion moved on to less critical topics.

The rest of the day unfolded in a blur: an interview with a tech magazine on our algorithm, followed by a development team meeting about a minor fare calculation bug.

By three, I'd managed to scarf down half a sandwich between phone calls, one with our marketing director, who needed approval for an upcoming ad campaign, and another with our lawyers about new regulations for transport services outside of the United States.

The first photo shoot of the day came after that, where I stood in front of a white backdrop while some overenthusiastic photographer barked orders at me like I was a damn mannequin.

"Chin up, Mr. Suarez. You look powerful but not very approachable," the photographer called out, adjusting the angle of the camera.

Approachable? I was one more instruction away from losing it.

I forced a tight smile, holding the pose for another shot. As the photographer leaned in to adjust the lighting, I leveled him with a sharp look. "Watch it. I don't have endless patience today."

The thought of the gym was almost laughable at that point. My workout gear sat in my car, mocking me. I'd promised myself I'd make it, even if only for thirty minutes. But by the time I considered it, another meeting was waiting, where someone on the board would ask the same question a thousand different ways, only to get the same answer.

The meeting dragged on as expected, and focus became harder as I wrapped up my last point. Glancing at the clock, I saw it was twelve minutes to eight.

The rest of the room started packing up their notes, murmuring polite goodbyes, but I stayed seated for a moment longer. I needed to breathe, to let the silence settle before heading back into the chaos.

My phone buzzed in my pocket, and I pulled it out, scrolling through emails. Another client issue, another marketing request, another update from the tech team. It felt endless, and the day still wasn't over.

Then I saw her name pop up, and *fuck*, I hadn't spoken to Abigail much today. Guilt settled in my chest as I opened her text.

Red
I hope your day is going okay.

Thanks for lunch, by the way!!

Me
You're always welcome. As for work, it's exhausting. How's your day going?

Red
Too busy, but we close soon.

Me
I can only imagine. We haven't seen each other much lately.

I'll come see you after I leave my office tonight.

Red
I'll come to you instead. I know how exhausted you are.

Me
Are you sure? It's no problem to drive to you.

It never is.

Red
I'm very sure. Text me your address.

Me
Okay, I'll see you later.

Red
Good.

Let me know when you're done.

Me
I will.

The longing of missing her sharpened as I set my phone down. A quick text thread wasn't enough, not when hearing her voice could've been the one thing to salvage this day. But for now, it was enough to keep me going.

There was a knock at the door, and Morison poked his head in. "The next photographers are waiting for your headshots, and *The New York Times* is asking for an extra five minutes on the follow-up interview about the expansion. Should I push them?"

"No," I muttered, standing. "Let's get it over with because I won't be in office tomorrow."

By the time I finished with the pictures, the interview, and wrapped up in my office, it was past nine—one of my longest days in a while. Days like these always took me back to the first eighteen months of Elite Rides, when I practically lived at the office, chasing deals and managing setbacks.

I sank into the seat, exhaling as the door shut. Silence, at last. Fifteen hours of chaos behind me. I checked my phone—Abigail's name lit up the screen.

Red
I'm twenty minutes away from your building.

Me
I can't wait to see you.

I shut off my phone, navigating the quiet streets with her on my mind—grateful for someone who cared enough to stay. At the penthouse, I dropped my keys and headed for a shower, but exhaustion clung to me.

Pulling on sweatpants, I collapsed onto the couch, my head sinking into the cushion. My body felt like lead—aching feet, a throbbing head, and muscles too tired to move.

The soft buzz of my phone broke through the haze of exhaustion. It was the front desk.

"Mr. Suarez, there's a Ms. Abigail-Ann Asher here to see you?"

"Send her up, and make it a standing order. Thank you." I hung up, relief crashing over me. Abigail was here. She didn't know it, but she was the only part of today worth staying awake for.

The elevator chimed, and I opened the door to find her standing there with determination in her eyes.

"You didn't have to come all this way," I murmured, leaning against the doorframe. "But I'm glad you did."

"And you didn't have to work yourself to exhaustion." She stepped inside, her gaze sweeping over me. "But I'm glad I'm here too."

A breathy chuckle escaped me.

"Come on." She slid her hand into mine, tugging me toward the living room.

"I'd give you the full tour, but…" I gestured vaguely, too drained to finish the sentence.

She waved it off. "Not why I'm here."

When we stepped into the living room, she stopped, taking in the white-on-white aesthetic. "You're officially the cleanest person I know."

I frowned. "Hm?"

"Your whole house is white. It's beautiful. Untouched."

A soft laugh rumbled from my chest, the first genuine one all day. "I'm hardly here enough to make a mess."

She arched her brow but didn't press. Instead, she turned to me and said, "Sit."

I obeyed, sinking into the couch as she settled beside me, cupping my face. Her thumb brushed over my cheek before she kissed me—soft, slow, calming the restless energy in my chest.

"I need another one," I whispered.

She chuckled, leaning in again, her fingers threading through my hair. "Better?"

I shook my head, shameless. "Not even close."

Her laugh filled the room—sweet, bright. As she started to pull away, I caught her cheek, my grip gentle but firm. "I think I need ten more just to make sure I'm fully recovered."

Was I desperate for her? No. I was beyond desperate. I was ruined, consumed, completely hers. Ten kisses wouldn't be enough. A hundred wouldn't either. I'd spend forever chasing her, holding onto every second she gave me, and still, I'd need more. Always more. Always her.

"Recovered from what?"

"Barely seeing you, Red."

She rolled her eyes but stayed, pressing a kiss to my temple, resting a hand on my chest. Then her fingers stilled. Her gaze lingered, brows furrowing.

I brushed my fingers over her cheek. "*Amor*?[2] What's wrong?"

She swallowed. "Your necklace… there's a silver pendant with an 'A'."

Glancing down, I lifted it slightly, smirking. "Yeah, there is."

Her lips parted. "How long have you had it?"

"A little over two weeks."

She exhaled. "Oh my gosh…"

I tucked a curl behind her ear, my voice softening. "You're with me, so you should be with me, even when you're not next to me." I pressed a kiss to her forehead. "You own me, Red. It's only fair I wear something to prove it."

Her fingers traced the pendant, her touch reverent. "There are stones…"

"Aquamarine," I murmured. "Your birthstone."

Her eyes shimmered with something I couldn't name. "Mikkel…"

I lifted my wrist, showing her the matching bracelet wrapped around it. "And this," I added, tilting my wrist so the 'A' charm caught the light. "Got it the same day."

Her fingers ghosted over the charm like she wasn't sure it was real. "You… I…" She swallowed. "You really wear these every day?"

"Every damn day." I caught her hand, pressing a kiss to her palm. "Because I'm yours."

She let out a shaky breath, her touch lingering on the necklace, the bracelet, as if memorizing them, as if trying to convince herself they were real.

I kissed her forehead again, pulling her closer, her warmth sinking into me. My eyes grew heavy, and with her in my arms, the world outside ceased to exist.

---

2 *Love*

My eyes snapped open, heart pounding from a restless sleep. That was the most amount of rest I've gotten in the past month and fuck, it felt good. The watch on my wrist read one in the morning, and my body ached, the exhaustion still clinging to me. I shifted, realizing I was no longer curled up in Abigail's arms but alone on my sofa with a blanket draped over me. A soft breath escaped me as I looked around, noticing her bag resting on the coffee table.

She was still here. *Thank God.*

I called her name softly, but when no response came, I groggily got up, rubbing my eyes. As I stepped toward the kitchen, I saw her standing by the sink, clearing dishes. I blinked, confused. Did I leave dishes out? And wait—what was that smell?

"Hey," I said, walking in.

She looked up with a small smile. "You're awake. Hey."

I dropped into a seat at the kitchen island, still shaking off sleep. "What are you doing?"

She turned, holding a mug and a bowl. "I made pasta." She set them down in front of me. "And ginger tea. It helps with exhaustion."

Warmth spread through my chest. Gratitude. Guilt. Something deeper. "I'm sorry for falling asleep on you earlier. I know you have work tomorrow and—"

She silenced me with a kiss. "My shift isn't until midday." She pulled back, her gaze steady. "You've been running yourself into the ground. You needed the rest."

I exhaled, my shoulders loosening. "Thank you. You didn't have to do this."

"I wanted to." Her voice was soft but certain. "Now eat."

I let her words settle, still amazed at how she always knew exactly what I needed. I took a bite, the rich, comforting taste sinking into me. "This is really good." I glanced at her. "Is that whiskey I taste?"

She smiled, leaning against the counter. "Just a little for flavor."

I took another bite, studying her. *Does she even realize what she's doing to me?* "Te aprecio, nena."[3]

She hesitated, then said, almost shyly, "Since I know you'll be working from home tomorrow, I prepped some meals for you." A pause. "Shrimp, steak, and chicken with fried rice and a side salad. They're in the fridge. And there's a smoothie and breakfast burritos, too. So you can grab them whenever you're hungry."

I stilled, staring at her. "*¿Qué?*"[4]

She shifted under my gaze. "I'm sorry if I o—"

"No." I cut her off before she could finish. "Don't apologize. I've just… never had anyone do this for me."

Something flickered in her eyes before she stepped closer, her fingers brushing mine. "I just want to make tomorrow easier."

The knot in my chest unraveled.

I swallowed hard. "I don't know how to thank you for this."

She tilted her head, like the thought hadn't even crossed her mind. "You don't have to thank me." Then, with a small, teasing smile, she kissed my cheek. "It's just cooking for the guy I really like."

I held her gaze, heart pounding. "The guy you really like?"

She rolled her eyes, but there was laughter in them. "Yes, Mikkel. The guy I really like."

It wasn't just the food. It was her. The way she made me feel like I mattered.

I took another bite of the pasta, letting the comforting taste wash over me as the exhaustion quietly crept back in.

"Eat, get some rest, and you'll feel better tomorrow."

I nodded, but sleep felt elusive with the warmth of her care and support settling in my chest.

When Abigail stood to gather her things, a quiet ache settled in my chest. I didn't want her to go.

---

3 *I appreciate you, baby*

4 *What*

"I should get going," she whispered, reluctance threading her voice like it did my thoughts.

I walked her downstairs, my mind heavy. At the door, she paused, offering a soft smile. "Goodnight, Mikkel."

My chest tightened. "Goodnight, *cariño*."[5]

She hesitated. "I would've stayed, but I don't have anything…"

Caught between wanting her close and respecting boundaries, I replied, "It's fine," though it didn't feel right.

She smiled faintly, reading me too well. "I'll see you tomorrow."

Before she left, I brushed a curl behind her ear, pulled her close, and kissed her—slow and unhurried, carrying everything I'd been holding back.

She kissed me back just as softly, her hands resting on my chest.

When we finally pulled apart, she was breathless, lips warm against mine. "I think I'm the one who needs ten more of those, now."

A soft laugh escaped me. "In that case…"

I kissed her again, a lingering touch, then pulled away. "Let me know when you get home."

"I will." Her gaze lingered before she slipped into the night.

Back on the couch, phone in hand, I waited. The moment her message came through, relief settled over me, and finally, I let sleep take me.

---

5 *sweetheart*

WARNING

The following chapter contains heavy mentions of mental health/physical health issues. Please refer to the content warning list to be reminded of any potential triggers. Your well-being is important to me, so please take care of yourself while reading.

CHAPTER TWENTY-FOUR

Abigail-Ann

"There is no remedy for love but to love more."
~ Henry David Thoreau

"What would you do if I was standing outside your window with a boombox on top of my head?" Mikkel's voice crackled through the phone, and his question sparked a deep, unexpected, and genuine laugh from me.

I missed him more than words could express. His name and face were everywhere in the media, and I found myself hooked on his interviews, hanging on every word. But with him bouncing between New York, Seattle and Chicago for weeks, we hadn't seen much of each other outside of FaceTime.

To fill the time, aside from work and therapy, I'd been having Netflix parties with my sister and using Duolingo every day. My goal? To understand Mikkel better without needing to run to Google translate.

Progress was slow, and the owl was relentless, but I was determined.

Snapping back to the present, I realized I was smiling. "I'd think you were in one of those late-eighties rom-coms," I managed to respond.

"Go look through your window."

I jumped up from the sofa, disbelief rushing through me. "Are you serious?"

He chuckled softly. "Get up and see, Red."

Without another word, I crossed the room, my pulse quickening with every step. I hesitated for just a moment before opening the window and there he was with that brilliant smile, a large bouquet of primroses and those glasses that never failed to make my heart flutter.

"There's no boombox," he said, his eyes twinkling with that familiar spark. "But I'm hoping this bouquet works."

Happiness, joy, elation—none of them felt big enough to capture the emotions rushing through me. From the moment our paths crossed, he had made me feel a little less broken and a lot more loved.

"You are something else," I whispered, pressing the phone to my face.

He shook his head, that playful grin still in place. "You gonna keep me hanging down here?"

"I'll be down in a second." I grabbed my coat as if my life depended on it and rushed downstairs.

When I finally reached him, I teased, "What are you doing here, Mikkel Suarez?"

His eyes locked onto mine, and the world around us faded. Just us.

"Just trying to make you smile, Red."

"Mission accomplished," I whispered as he handed me the flowers.

Mikkel's voice dropped, warm and sure. "I thought I'd come see my love."

His love?

I stepped closer, the space between us shrinking with every heartbeat. "Your love?"

He didn't hesitate. Strong arms wrapped around my waist, pulling me in, his familiar scent settling over me like warmth on a cold night. "Yes."

His lips brushed my ear, voice low and certain. "*Mi amor.*[1]"

"I like the sound of that." My voice barely carried over the thudding of my heart.

"*Y me gustas,*[2] so we're even," he said, a playful smile tugging at his lips.

Y me gustas. And I like you.

This man. This man. He was one of a kind. The kind you cherish. The kind you protect.

I glanced down, suddenly realizing I was still in my sleepwear, and a wave of dread washed over me.

Fuck.

I'd forgotten to change.

Heat crept up my neck. "I—I should go change," I mumbled, taking a step back. But before I could move, his fingers curled around my wrist, gentle yet firm.

"Change? Why?" His brow furrowed, gaze sweeping over me like he couldn't understand why I'd even suggest it.

"I'm… underdressed." The words felt small.

His head tilted, slow, assessing. "Red, it's nighttime. You're in pajamas. You're not underdressed."

A sigh slipped out before I could stop it. Joshua's voice echoed in my head, old wounds stirring.

Cover up.

You're embarrassing.

You look desperate.

I swallowed. "I couldn't be out showing this much skin with m—"

Mikkel kissed me.

Hard. With a hunger that made it feel like I was the air he needed to breathe.

Like he needed me to understand something words couldn't explain.

Like he wanted to erase every cruel whisper in my head.

---

1 *My love*

2 *And I like you.*

"You're perfect," he murmured against my lips, his voice steady, unshakable. "There's nothing wrong with showing skin, *amor*.[3]"

I wanted to believe him. But Joshua's voice still clung to me like smoke.

"Hey." Mikkel's fingers found my chin, tilting my face until our eyes met. His gaze, dark and unwavering, held me in place. "Your past doesn't define you, neither do the words of anyone from it."

I opened my mouth, but nothing came out.

He didn't push. He just saw me.

Then, softer this time, he said, "Let's go."

"Where?"

"You'll see." A ghost of a smile played on his lips.

Before I could overthink or protest, he led me to the car, opening the door like always. I slid into the seat, the city lights blurring past in soft streaks. The low hum of the engine, the familiar playlist—*Songs for You*—playing in the background.

The drive felt like a dream, suspended between reality and something more.

When the car finally stopped, I stepped out, and my breath hitched.

Beneath my feet, soft sand. Before me, the ocean stretched into the night, waves shimmering under the moonlight. It was quiet, peaceful, nearly deserted—except for a couple walking hand in hand far down the shore.

I exhaled slowly, my voice barely above a whisper.

"We're at the beach."

He nodded, a soft smile playing on his lips. "Night beach. Number six on the bucket list."

My eyes glistened as I looked around, overwhelmed by the beauty, the gesture—how he always remembered.

"This is perfect," I whispered, more to myself than to Mikkel.

He took my hand, his thumb tracing slow circles on the back of it. "Let's find a spot."

We settled into a sheltered nook near the dunes, hidden by tall grasses. Mikkel spread a blanket, and we lay down, backs flat, legs stretched.

3 *love*

The salty air was refreshing as I leaned into him, resting my head on his shoulder. His warmth, the soft blanket, the cool breeze—it all felt like a dream. The waves lulled me, but then a memory surfaced, sharp and unwanted, shattering the peace.

I was standing in front of the mirror, adjusting the straps of a dress I'd picked for a night out with Joshua. A deep shade of yellow, flattering against my skin. I felt beautiful in it.

Until he stepped into the room.

His eyes raked over me, his expression darkening. "What the hell are you wearing?"

I froze, fingers fumbling with the hem. "It's just a dress."

"Just a dress?" he scoffed. "Are you trying to embarrass me, or do you like when men stare at you?"

The words hit like a slap, stealing the air from my lungs. Shame burned through me. I wanted to defend myself, to say I'd worn it for him, but the words tangled in my throat.

"You're not going out like that," he said, voice hard. "Change."

So I had. And I'd done it every time after, until I no longer recognized myself in the mirror. Until I believed that no matter what I wore, I'd never be good enough—for him, or anyone.

A shaky breath left me as I forced the memory back into the depths where it belonged.

"Hey." Mikkel's voice pulled me back. "Where did you go just now?"

I blinked, refocusing on him. "Just… thinking about something."

His gaze sharpened. "Joshua?"

I nodded.

Mikkel exhaled, his grip on my hand tightening—not enough to hurt, but enough that I felt it. His frustration. His helplessness. His need to fix what he couldn't.

"I wish I could take away all the pain he caused you," he murmured, his thumb brushing over my knuckles. "But I need you to know that you never have to feel like that again. You never have to change who you are, Red. You're more than enough."

Tears welled, but this time, they weren't from hurt or shame.

He leaned in, pressing his forehead to mine, voice soft but unwavering. "I won't tell you to forget the past because that's not how this works. But I will tell you that history will never repeat itself."

I let his words settle over me.

"He always made me feel small," I admitted, my voice barely above a whisper. "He'd say someone with my body type shouldn't wear certain things. That I was begging for attention."

Mikkel stilled, disbelief flashing across his face. *"Your body type?"*

I nodded, that familiar knot tightening in my stomach.

His fingers dug into my waist, gentle but firm, as his expression darkened. "You've got to be kidding me." His voice was low, rough with conviction. "Your body type?" He scoffed. "People pay millions for what you have, and don't even get me started on your thighs—because I'd bury myself there if I could."

A breath caught in my throat, heat unfurling in my chest. The way he said it—like it was a fact, like he'd thought about it—made my pulse stutter.

"And if you're talking about belly fat," he continued, voice dropping to a husky whisper, "I'll be the first to tell you that it's fucking sexy."

His grip tightened slightly, his eyes burning with sincerity. "And those aren't even the most attractive things about you. Because nothing comes close to your mind, your heart, your strength, your intelligence. You're incredible, Red. Every. Single. Part. Of. You. "

I swallowed hard.

And for the first time, I didn't just hear the words—*I felt them.* Deep in my bones. Settling into the spaces Joshua had hollowed out.

My chest ached, my heart swelling as no one had ever spoken to me with such reverence and raw honesty, making me feel truly deserving of love and respect.

"Mikkel," I whispered, his name the only thing I could choke out past the tight knot in my throat. "I always felt like I needed to cover up."

The fierce edge in his expression softened into something impossibly tender. "You don't have to if you don't want to." His thumb traced my cheek, the touch grounding. "But just know, you never need to hide from me. Ever. You should wear whatever you want."

I shook my head, struggling to believe this was real. "It really doesn't bother you?" The words felt small, fragile, compared to how much this insecurity had consumed me.

"Why would it?" His brows pulled together like the question itself made no sense. "I know I'm dating a *ridiculously* attractive woman, and it's my job to protect you. Men will look whether you're in pants or shorts."

I blinked, still caught between disbelief and something dangerously close to hope.

"Clothes don't invite torment, *amor. Men do.*" His voice darkened, edged with quiet fury. "It's uncontrollable, disgusting men who take and take without consequence."

I opened my mouth to respond, but before I could say anything, he continued, "Plus, a man knows better than to touch what's mine. He'd lose his hands before he even tried."

A slow heat unfurled inside me, the way it always did when he said things like that—not suffocating, not controlling, just making me feel safe. Cherished. Wanted.

"I guess I'm insecure," I admitted, the words slipping out like a confession.

Mikkel exhaled sharply, shaking his head. "*He* was insecure. And because he knew you were better than him—way out of his league in every way—he made you doubt yourself. There's a big difference between a man and a boy, Red."

The weight in my chest grew heavier. I knew what I had to say next, but the words felt like stones in my throat.

"I—" My breath caught. "I was cheated on. Repeatedly."

Mikkel's whole body stilled. His eyes sharpened, disbelief and fury flickering in them. "What?"

I forced myself to meet his gaze. "Joshua," I whispered, and just saying his name made my chest tighten. "He cheated on me with someone I thought was a friend. Gianna."

Mikkel's grip on my hand tightened, his thumb brushing over my knuckles in slow, reassuring circles.

"I didn't see it coming," I admitted. "Or maybe I did. Maybe I ignored the signs, thinking if I just tried harder, gave him more, it would get better. But it never did. He was with her for months before I found out. Then came the drinking. The gaslighting. The fights."

Mikkel's jaw ticked. "*Ese pedazo de mierda*,"[4] he muttered, his voice low and dangerous. "You didn't deserve that."

I swallowed hard. "I thought I was enough for him." My voice broke, quieter now. "But clearly, I wasn't."

Mikkel cupped my face in both hands, holding me there, forcing me to look at him. "Abigail." His voice was steady, but it vibrated with something deeper. "*He wasn't enough for you.* Do you hear me?" His grip tightened just slightly, not enough to hurt, just enough to make sure I understood. "You. Are. Enough. You always have been."

A tear slipped down my cheek, but for the first time, it didn't feel like weakness. "Thank you," I whispered.

Something inside me cracked open. I had never told anyone before. Saying it out loud felt… freeing.

Mikkel watched me carefully. "Is there anything else you want to talk about?"

I hesitated, but the weight in my chest had lifted. "Another night." I exhaled slowly, nodding to myself. "Let's talk about you."

His lips curved slightly. "What do you want to know?"

I studied him, wanting to uncover him the way he had uncovered me. "What do you want to tell me?"

He shrugged, a thoughtful expression crossing his face. "I had a huge insecurity about my glasses growing up."

"Your glasses?" I echoed, surprised. "Why?"

---

4 *That piece of shit*

"I felt out of place," he admitted, his voice tinged with old wounds. "Imagine being the only one who couldn't speak English, in a country that wasn't home, wearing thick, nerdy glasses."

"I'm sorry," I said, my heart aching.

"Eventually, I grew into them. I remember leaving them at home one day, thinking I'd be fine. But, I couldn't see shit, and my dad had to rush to bring them to me."

The thought of a little Mikkel stubbornly refusing glasses, but realizing he needed them made me smile.

"You're picturing it, aren't you?"

"Maybe," I admitted with a laugh.

He leaned closer, tucking a curl behind my ear. "Of course you are."

His gaze lingered on me, his eyes soft but searching, as though there was something else he wanted to say but couldn't bring himself to.

"What is it?" I asked, tilting my head.

"It's nothing." He leaned back slightly, his hand brushing against the back of his neck, a small tell I'd learned to pick up on.

I reached out, gently touching his arm. "Tell me."

His lips pressed into a thin line before he exhaled. "I don't… It's not something I talk about often," he admitted, his voice steady but tinged with raw honesty that made my chest tighten. "I've mentioned it a few times, but never in depth. I've always been quiet. As a kid, I barely spoke—partly because of the language barrier, but mostly because that's just who I was. My parents worried, thought I was shy, but I just didn't know how to express myself."

He dragged a hand down his thigh, pausing as if searching for the right words. "That silence turned into frustration—frustration with myself when I couldn't get things right, when I felt like I was failing, when things slipped out of my control. Frustration when I couldn't be perfect. It wasn't anyone's fault. My parents worked hard and did their best for us. But as the oldest, carrying the weight of responsibility and the pressure to be perfect, it just kept building."

I nodded, staying quiet so he could continue.

"It's better now. I've learned to channel it into work, into structure," he said, his gaze dropping to our hands, his thumb gliding over mine. "But some days, the smallest thing can snap me back into that kid who didn't know how to let it out."

My mind wandered, unbidden memories of Joshua's anger flashing behind my eyes like fragments of a bad dream. The way his temper had made everything fragile—plates shattered against walls, words that cut too deep, doors slammed so hard they rattled the windows and came off their hinges. His rage had been wild, destructive, leaving me to pick up the pieces, both physical and emotional.

A voice in my head reminded me that Mikkel *wasn't* Joshua, and I clung to it, desperate to believe it because I didn't want to ruin this—ruin us. Even in his quiet admission, there was no threat in his tone, no undercurrent of danger. Just a man trying to share a part of himself he wasn't proud of.

His fingers squeezed mine, pulling me out of the past. "Red?"

I blinked, focusing back on him. "I'm here."

"You're thinking hard about something."

I shook my head with a small smile. "Just listening."

His lips curved, a flicker of relief in his expression. He studied me for a moment before I broke the silence. "You've never been angry with me," I said, the realization surprising even myself.

He chuckled softly, his thumb brushing over the back of my hand. "You're my calm in the storm, Abigail. I could never be angry at you."

My heart squeezed at his words, at the way he said them like they were the simplest truth in the world.

Before I could reply, he stood and offered his hand. "Now, how about a walk along the shore?"

I smiled and rose from the blanket. "I'd like that."

"This place…" I trailed off, searching for the right words. "It's like the world has slowed down just for us."

I turned to him, the moonlight casting shadows that made him even more striking.

"What are you thinking about?" he asked softly.

"That I've never felt more alive than I do right now."

He leaned down, kissing my forehead gently, and I closed my eyes, savoring the moment.

"Me too, baby," he murmured against my skin.

Baby.

My heart fluttered at the endearment. I tilted my head to look up at him, searching his eyes for any hint of hesitation. But all I found was a depth that made me feel as if I was the only person in his world. The thought felt fragile, almost too good to hold onto.

"I've never been called that before," I began, my voice barely above a whisper. "Not like this. Not outside of sex… "

He smiled, a slow, lazy grin that sent a wave of flutters through my body. "Then it's about time, don't you think?"

I laughed softly as he cupped my cheeks. "Maybe it is."

His phone buzzed incessantly on the blanket, slicing through the tender moment. With a reluctant sigh, he reached for it, his brows knitting together as he glanced at the screen.

"Give me a second," he whispered before answering.

I watched him shift seamlessly into business mode. "No, Morison, we don't respond directly. Release the prepared statement and keep an eye on the engagement. Anything concerning, flag it for me."

The conversation was brief but efficient, and as he hung up, I found myself thinking about the carefully curated image he projected to the world. Everything about him seemed so controlled, so polished.

"You know," I said after a moment, my voice tentative, "I've noticed that you have a very quiet media presence. There's so much about you out there, but somehow, it feels like there's nothing at all."

Mikkel's eyes narrowed slightly.

"I may have Googled you," I admitted sheepishly before he could respond. "It's not every day a man like you enters my life."

He chuckled, the sound warming my cheeks. "I'd hope it's not every day, and I can't blame you for being curious." He leaned in, pressing a soft kiss to my temple. "I'm big on privacy. I try to avoid the media at all costs."

I nodded. "I was just curious, no big deal."

Mikkel took my hand, his touch grounding. "Privacy doesn't mean I want to keep you at arm's length."

"I didn't think you were hiding me."

"I know the thought might have crossed your mind, so let me make it clear, I'd never hide you. I understand you want to take things slow, and I won't push you if you're not ready. Whenever you need reassurance, I'm here. *Siempre*.[5]"

"Thank you," I whispered, my heart lighter.

He smiled, brushing his thumb across my knuckles. "You don't have to thank me. I want you to feel safe with me."

I kissed him, grounding myself in the comfort of our connection—it was exactly where I needed to be.

---

5 *Always*

CHAPTER TWENTY-FIVE

Abigail-Ann

"The heart has its reasons which reason knows nothing of."
— Blaise Pascal

Azzaria stormed into my apartment at the crack of dawn armed with her homemade chocolate cake I should've known was a bribe disguised as breakfast. Before I could even finish a slice, she dragged me out of bed with no mercy. Apparently, we had to decorate Dillon's office for his thirty-third birthday, and absolutely *nothing* was going to stop her.

I yawned, trying to rub the sleep from my eyes. "Azzaria, what happened to 'I'm never getting feelings for anyone ever again'?"

Her lips twitched, fighting a smile. "That was before Dillon. Plus, I've got a whole strategy planned out." She shoved a folder at me, which I stared at like it was a bomb.

If I had known all it took to break her out of her 'I hate love' phase was an internship, I would've encouraged her to do it months ago.

After two hours of hanging banners and rearranging furniture, I regretted giving in to the cake. She'd turned into a tyrant, barking orders like a drill sergeant and obsessing over every detail. Amid the chaos, my thoughts kept drifting to Mikkel—his anger, his perfectionism, and how it had shaped him. I knew about his perfectionism; he'd run himself ragged with work, losing his mind if even a comma or semicolon was out of place, or how I'd overhear him on the phone trying to fix everything. But the anger? I never would've guessed it. Everyone has flaws, though, right? I wanted to understand more, but I wouldn't push him. All I could hope was that I'd never be on the receiving end of his wrath.

The sound of Azzaria's voice broke through my thoughts. "Help me fix this corner?" she asked, her brow furrowed as she glared at the sad cluster of crimson and black balloons floating in the corner.

"Yeah, sure," I said, straightening up from where I was kneeling on the floor. "Just as soon as I finish this slice of cake."

Azzaria gave me a look. "You're such a sucker for chocolate cake. But fine, keep eating. The faster we finish, the sooner you can take a nap."

I smiled, taking another bite. "The cake was clearly a trap."

She grinned. "A well-designed one. You'll thank me later."

After a few minutes of watching her put up streamers and dealing with the balloons, I couldn't resist teasing her. "Are you sure you're excited enough?"

She paused mid-task, glancing at me with wide eyes. "What do you mean?"

"You're hanging those banners like your life depends on it."

Her lips tightened. "It has to be perfect because he deserves it."

I leaned against the wall. "Well, if that's not love, I don't know what is."

She blinked, as if my words took a moment to sink in, then her face softened. "Do you really think so?"

I walked over to her, resting a hand on her shoulder. "I really do."

Azzaria didn't respond immediately. Instead, she looked over at the decorated office, her gaze lingering on the balloons, the streamers, and the table set with lemon flavored pastries she baked for him. Then, in a quieter voice, she said, "I just want him to know I care. I'm not good at showing that. But I want him to see it. To feel it."

My heart softened at her vulnerability. Azzaria was always so guarded, never letting anyone in too close. It was nice to see this side of her—the side that cared deeply, even if she didn't always know how to express it.

"This is perfect," I assured her. "He's going to see how much you care, even if it's through all this craziness."

"Thanks, Abi," she said softly. "You always know what to say."

I gave her a small grin. "That's what best friends are for. Now let me get these balloons fixed before Dillon thinks we've turned his office into a circus."

I carefully adjusted the balloons, aligning them just right. Each knot seemed to demand a little more attention, and I smiled as I straightened the strands.

"Okay, *maybe* I enjoy this a little," I admitted, pausing to admire my work.

She raised an eyebrow and grinned. "I knew it."

"I'm going to the bathroom," I said quickly, needing a moment away from the festivities. "I'll be back."

As I walked down the corridor after leaving the office, someone had suddenly pulled me into a corner.

"Holy–" I started to exclaim, ready to unleash a string of colorful language until I realized who it was.

"You scared me," I said softly, looking up into Mikkel's eyes.

"*Lo siento,*[1] baby," he murmured, his voice like velvet as he brushed a stray curl of hair from my face.

"Speaking Spanish to me will *never* get old."

"You like it, huh?"

1 *I'm sorry*

"I *really really* do," I admitted, unable to tear my gaze away from him, utterly entranced.

"In that case," he said, leaning, his gaze locked with mine. "*Hablaré español más a menudo, entonces.*[2]" Our lips met in a passionate kiss, and I melted into him, lost in the moment.

I was overcome by a rush of emotions—a sense of longing, of desire, of sheer bliss. It was as if every nerve in my body was alight with sensation, every touch sending waves of pleasure through me.

Breaking away from the kiss, he looked at me, his eyes sparkling with desire.

"Your lips are so soft," he murmured, his voice thick with longing.

"Do you plan to woo me every single day?"

"What kind of man would I be if I didn't?"

His gaze lingered briefly before he stepped back. "There's a gala later, and I want to take you."

"A gala?"

"It's Dillon's birthday tradition."

I hesitated, chewing on my bottom lip. "I'd love to go, but I don't have anything suitable to wear. Wouldn't it be…weird?"

"You'd be my date," he said, his voice steady.

I sighed, the weight of my thoughts pressing down on me.

"Are you sure?" I lowered my voice, unsure.

He studied my face for a moment before his expression softened. "I'm very sure."

"I just don't feel like I belong there... or that it's my scene." I paused, my mind racing. Would I be pretty enough? Would I even fit in with the other p—"

"Red." His voice cut through the chaos of my thoughts. "You belong there. Never doubt that. There's no one else I'd rather have with me. *Ever.*"

"I know it sounds stupid," I muttered, feeling the ridiculousness of it, even as I said the words.

---

2 *I'll speak Spanish more often, then*

"It's not stupid," he said, his voice soft but understanding. "I understand self-doubt." He reached for my hand, giving it a reassuring squeeze. "We'll figure it out because I want you there with me. But if you're not up to it, I won't press it. Okay?"

I nodded, the tightness in my chest easing slightly. "Okay. But even so, I have no gala attire."

He smiled. "It's nothing to take you shopping, or even bring the shopping to you."

I chuckled as the tension in my shoulders slowly disappeared. "Flattery—"

"Will get me everywhere?" he finished, his tone playful.

"Exactly," I confirmed, leaning in for another kiss.

The second we pulled away, three messages from Azzaria popped up, asking if I was good. I glanced up at Mikkel.

"I've been summoned," I said, showing him the message. "But can I let you know about the gala later?"

"I have a meeting soon." He nodded, then bent down to kiss my cheek. "And of course, don't feel pressured to say yes. Your comfort matters above all."

I smiled, and we walked out together. He walked me to the office door before heading off to his meeting.

"I'm here! Happy birthday, Dil—"

I never expected to walk in and find my best friend kissing her man, yet here I was, witnessing it.

"Heard of knocking?" Dillon's voice cut through the air, sharp and a bit grumpy. The man who'd swept Azzaria off her feet stood before me. His sharp three-piece suit, commanding presence, and powerful words spoke of his success, but it was his love for Azzy that truly defined him.

"*She* knew I was coming. I need to gouge my eyes out after seeing that." I pretended to gag. "Are you brooding because I'm her favorite?"

"Says who?" Dillon challenged.

"Her," I shot back without missing a beat. "You don't stand a chance against me, Xander."

"*Abigail*," Azzaria warned playfully, a hint of amusement in her voice.

"Sorry," I muttered, though my mischievous grin betrayed any hint of sincerity. "As much as I'd love to stay, I have work. Happy Birthday, Dillon, and bye Azzy. *I love you, Precious*."

I threw in those words just to piss him off.

"Crossing a line there, Abigail," Dillon admonished.

"Maybe," I replied, my tone unapologetic.

"Your first interaction and this is how it's going? *Great*," Azzaria remarked sarcastically, breaking the tension with her light-hearted remark.

"It's not our first," both Dillon and I chimed in simultaneously.

"I mean the first where I'm present, and I hope you guys won't be doing this every damn time," Azzaria added firmly.

"Boo hoo," I retorted with a playful roll of my eyes, blowing a kiss to Azzaria. "I seriously have to go. Bye, Azzy. Don't miss me too much."

"She won't," Dillon shouted after me, his tone tinged with sarcasm, eliciting a chuckle from me as I made my exit.

The worst part of my brain was that it never stopped. My entire shift was consumed by thoughts of the gala—every detail spinning in my head. Would I even fit in? I could barely picture myself in a room full of polished strangers. It wasn't about the dress—I could easily buy one—but the thought of being there, out of place, felt overwhelming. What if I wasn't graceful or confident enough?

Then I thought about Mikkel. He wanted me there. His words echoed in my head—steady, certain. *You belong there. Never doubt that.*

I opened my phone with the hopes of telling Mikkel I'd go with him but a call from Azzaria lit up the screen.

"Hey, what's up?" I answered the phone, greeting Azzaria as I dropped into the sofa, exhausted from my morning shift.

"I need you to meet me at the residency in like fifteen minutes. There's a gala tonight."

I sighed in disbelief. *How fitting that she asked that exact question at this exact moment?*

"But I don't have anything to wear to a gala," I protested.

"Don't stress about it. Just be there," Azzaria insisted before ending the call. "I'll explain everything once I see you."

I showered quickly, gathered my things, and rushed over to Azzaria's place. The moment I stepped inside, I froze. The scene before me looked like something straight out of a movie. Racks of stunning dresses lined the walls, an enticing spread of food covered the centre table, and the whole setup carried just enough flair to feel cinematic. This definitely had Dillon Xander written all over it.

A woman with a polite smile approached me. "Good afternoon. I'm Melinda, and you must be Ms. Abigail-Ann?"

"Abigail's fine, and yes, that's me," I said with a nod.

I considered texting Mikkel to say I'd be at the gala but decided against it. Surprising him would be more fun—besides, he thought I was home sleeping.

"Do I even have to ask?" I teased when Azzaria walked in a few minutes later, looking every bit as shocked as I was.

She laughed, catching my meaning immediately. "Dillon's a bit *extreme*, but his heart's in the right place."

"He's also completely in love with you," I said, giving her a pointed look. "And you deserve that kind of devotion."

Her smile softened, and for a moment, I thought she might cry. Instead, she turned her attention to the racks of dresses, expertly browsing through them while I started on my makeup.

The next hour flew by in a blur of brushes, palettes, and last-minute touch-ups. By the time I slipped into my dress, Azzaria was trying to settle on a hairstyle.

"You look *hot*," she said a little later, her voice full of approval. "The girls are sitting just right in that dress."

I smoothed the fabric over my hips, grinning at my reflection. The dress hugged me in all the right places and perfectly matched my fresh nail set.

Mikkel's gonna love this.

"Marlon's waiting downstairs in a silver BMW with 'X's on the license plate to take you to the gala."

"Did you just say he has 'X' on the plate?" I chuckled nervously.

She laughed. "Yep."

"The things rich men do," I joked in return.

"Imagine when you meet the rest of the group later tonight," she teased.

After giving her a quick kiss on the cheek, I grabbed my purse and headed downstairs.

Sure enough, parked on the curb was the silver BMW with 'X's on the plate.

Well, shit.

Here's to my first gala.

CHAPTER TWENTY-SIX

Mikkel

"Love takes off masks that we fear we cannot live without and know we cannot live within."
- James Baldwin

I hadn't heard much from Abigail since this morning, and it had been eating at me all day. The silence gnawed at the edges of my thoughts, a constant reminder of the unease I couldn't shake. I kept wondering if I'd pressured her into coming or, worse, if the invitation had scared her off completely.

Even before that, the last few days had been restless. I couldn't stop replaying what I'd told her at the beach, questioning whether it changed how she saw me or if it would put a strain on our relationship.

I'd texted her seven times already, but there was no response—a silence that wasn't like her. I almost asked Azzaria if she'd heard from her, but she and Dillon were preoccupied in the backseat, lost in their own world. Interrupting them didn't feel like an option.

The gala was in full swing when I arrived in an all-white Brioni tuxedo, paired with a black bow tie and polished leather shoes. I moved through the crowd, shaking hands with donors and posing for photos under the blinding flash of cameras. I'd forgotten how much I hated all of this—the forced smiles, the empty pleasantries. My thoughts were miles away, glancing at my phone for a reply from Abigail that never came.

Finally breaking free of the small talk and photo ops, I decided to leave. A Chipotle bowl, flowers, and chocolate cake might cheer her up, or at least give me a reason to check on her.

As my hand reached for the door, I spotted her, and every coherent thought vanished. The air thickened, and I couldn't breathe. She was pure elegance, *a force of nature*, seizing every part of my mind. Nothing else mattered—she consumed me completely.

The deep green dress she wore hugged her like it was made just for her, and I couldn't tear my eyes away. It was as if the color had been chosen to make her skin glow, and every step she took left me in awe. Her collarbones were exposed, and the neckline framed her so perfectly, offering just enough of a glimpse to make my heart race.

But it wasn't just the dress. It was *her*, the way her green eyes sparkled with excitement, as if daring me to get lost in them. She was a goddess, and I was just a man lucky enough to breathe the same air as her. I felt like the world stopped spinning the moment our eyes met. And her hair, styled in an updo with loose strands softly framing her face was nothing short of perfect.

She looked like a poem the universe wrote to keep me alive.

Our eyes locked, and I immediately closed the distance between us, drawn to her like a magnet.

"Your beauty is unrivaled, baby," I whispered, my hand gently cupping her cheek, careful not to ruin her flawless makeup.

"And you're incredibly handsome," she replied softly. "I thought I'd surprise you."

"Thank you, Red," I said, warmth spreading at her surprise. "I started to worry when you weren't responding, but consider me surprised."

She smiled, eyes softening as she rested a hand over mine. "I didn't mean to worry you," she murmured, her voice a soothing melody. "I kept going back and forth, then Azzaria called with a plan, and… here I am."

Her gaze flickered to my neck, and her smile deepened. "You really do wear it all the time."

I shifted my collar, giving her a better view of the chain, then held up my wrist to show her the bracelet. "Of course I do, baby."

Her fingers brushed over the fine silver, a quiet reverence in her touch, before her eyes lifted back to mine.

"I can't get over how amazing you look. This dress, your face, your hair, your body…" I trailed off, unable to contain my admiration as my hand instinctively found her hips, drawing her closer.

"Don't move your hands," she whispered, her breath hot against my ear as she leaned into me. "I like them right there."

Fuck.

I kissed her, our lips colliding in a fiery embrace. Hands roamed, bodies pressing together as she tangled her fingers in my hair, pulling me closer. The taste of her was intoxicating, each kiss deeper than the last. She melted into me, perfectly in sync, until footsteps broke the spell. Reluctantly, I pulled away, struggling to ground myself.

"Mikkel Suarez," a familiar voice broke through the haze of desire, and I turned to see Alex standing there in his burgundy tuxedo, a sheepish grin on his face.

Frustration flickered, but I quickly composed myself, though the warmth of the kiss remained on my lips.

"Alexander Williams," I replied, my voice slightly strained as I tore my gaze away from Abigail's and turned to face him.

"You gonna introduce me, Suarez?" He asked, walking closer to us.

"Alex, this is Abigail. Abigail, this is Alex," I introduced, trying to maintain a composed demeanor.

"Ah!" he remarked, his eyes lighting up. "The famous Abigail I hear so much about."

"It's nice to meet you," she chimed in, her cheeks flushed with color as she attempted to regain her composure.

"You've got my brother in a tailspin," Alex remarked with a chuckle, his eyes twinkling with amusement. "I'd say you added color to his rather bland world, but I'm not a poet, I'm a pilot." He turned to me. "I came to check on you since I heard you were taking a breather about thirty minutes ago."

"I'm good."

"Oh, I can definitely see that," Alex said with a knowing grin. "Let's get inside. Dillon's going to speak soon."

With a resigned sigh, I reluctantly tore myself away from Abigail.

"You okay, *mi amor*?[1]" I asked, and she nodded, leaning in to kiss me again.

"I'll see you inside," she said, and I watched as she swayed her hips while walking ahead of us.

Alex's unrestrained curiosity couldn't be ignored. "You two f–"

"No," I replied, trying to deflect his probing. "And *never* ask me that again."

"You could've fooled me," Alex joked, his tone lighthearted.

"Whatever."

We made our way to the table, and I quickly scanned the room. Everyone from our group was present, except Dillon and Azzaria. Before I could ask where they were, Ronan leaned in, his voice low and casual. "They just stepped out to meet donors and Azzaria told us to keep an eye on her friend, Abigail."

I leaned closer to Ronan. "Can I talk to you for a second?"

He raised an eyebrow, but followed me without question as I stepped away from the group.

"What's up?" He crossed his arms, his usual cool and collected demeanor in place.

I hesitated for a beat, running a hand down my face. "What do you know about anxiety?"

---

1 *my love*

He blinked, caught off guard. "I have some knowledge, but it's not my area of expertise. I can get in touch with one of my psychiatrists if you need it."

"Please do," I said, my tone sharper than I intended. I softened it with a sigh. "Ask them if they can recommend any resources or books about dealing with anxiety and self-image."

Ronan studied me for a moment, before sipping whatever was in his glass. "You really like her, huh?"

"I do," I admitted without hesitation. "But I don't know much about mental health, Ro. I don't know how to help her, how to… *be there* the way she needs me to be. I've tried the blogs, but they don't give me enough information."

Ronan's smirk faded, replaced by something softer, more genuine. "I'll make sure you get what you need," he promised. "She's lucky to have you, you know."

"You know I don't believe in luck," I said, shaking my head. "But, I'm the lucky one."

Ronan gave me a knowing look and nodded. "I'll reach out to them tonight."

"Thank you." I nodded, then turned my focus to Abigail, unable to think of anything else. I watched her pace, agitated but laughing. Her glass was nearly empty—third one already—as she sipped, her gaze darting around like she was fleeing something.

Before I could make my way over to her, Arnoldo slid up beside me with a drink, likely gin, in hand. "I see you've got your eyes on your redhead."

"She's far too beautiful for me to look away, Reyes."

"I just got saved from the worst night of my life."

I raised an eyebrow. "*¿Por qué?*[2]"

He smirked. "Maybe age is catching up to me, but when Dillon called while I was with two blondes, I was relieved for the excuse to leave."

My brow furrowed. "*You* turned down sleeping with someone?"

---

2 *Why*

He nodded, his tone serious now. "Yeah."

I stared at him, trying to wrap my head around it. "*You?* Turned down two blondes?"

Arnoldo chuckled softly, the edge of disbelief still evident in my voice. "Yeah, man."

I raised an eyebrow, the surprise still lingering in my voice. "Rough day, Reyes?"

He took another sip of his drink, his expression turning a bit more serious. "You have no idea. Is your sister here?"

I looked at him, confused. "No. Why?"

He sighed, a hint of something unreadable in his gaze. "Just curious. Thought I saw someone else here who might have been her."

My brow furrowed slightly, but before I could respond, my attention was already pulled back to Abigail.

"Excuse me," I muttered, turning away, trying to push aside the odd feeling creeping up on me.

She was standing by a booth, looking slightly distracted. I stepped closer, my voice low and concerned. "You okay, *amor*?[3]"

"Mikkel." She glanced up, her face brightening with a smile. "I'm okay, just looking at the different displays."

I stepped closer, my eyes narrowing slightly as I noticed how measured and unsteady her voice sounded. "Are you nervous?"

She hesitated, then answered with a smile that didn't quite reach her eyes. "Why would I be?"

I raised an eyebrow, glancing at her empty glass. "Because that's your fourth glass of champagne in twenty-eight minutes."

Her gaze flickered to me, surprise flashing across her face. "You've been watching me?"

She grabbed another glass from a passing waiter and took a gulp.

"It's hard to look at anyone else when you're here," I murmured, my voice low but firm. "But don't change the topic."

Stepping closer, I found her hand, pressing a kiss to her forehead. She swallowed the rest of the champagne, and I took the glass, setting it on a

---

3 *love*

nearby table. "I'll be by your side all night. And trust me, no one in this room even comes close to your level."

She held my gaze, and for a moment, I saw her walls crack just a little. "I needed to hear that."

Before I could say another word, Lewis Baker—one of Dillon's old partners—appeared, sliding into her space with that same cocky attitude I'd seen too many times before. His eyes dragged over her in a way that made my skin crawl.

"You look like you could use a drink, or maybe some company," he said, clearly trying his luck.

My hand went straight to her hip, pulling her against me in one smooth motion. "Wrong woman, Baker," I said, my voice cold as I stared him down.

"Oh, uh, didn't know she was taken," he stammered before retreating.

"How's your wife?"

He shifted uncomfortably, eyes darting between me and Abigail, his earlier bravado gone. "She's good," he muttered, rubbing the back of his neck. "Really good."

I didn't blink, my gaze still locked on him. "Glad to hear it."

He cleared his throat, taking a small step backward.

"Anyway, I, uh… I should probably get back." He chuckled nervously, looking for a way out. "Nice to see you, Mr. Suarez." His voice cracked slightly as he nodded, turning on his heel.

I watched him walk away, his pace quickening like he couldn't leave fast enough.

Once he was out of sight, I turned to Abigail, half expecting her to scold me for being so possessive. Instead, she looked up at me with a soft glint in her eyes.

"You know," she said slowly, her voice dropping to a sultry tone, "your whole possessive thing is hot."

I blinked, not expecting that response. "Yeah?"

She grinned, stepping closer so that her body was flush against mine. "Totally."

I tightened my grip on her waist, pulling her closer. "Good to know, *mi amor.*[4]"

She smiled up at me, but then her eyes drifted toward the displays. "I want to go see those," she said, her voice soft but insistent, pointing toward the art pieces and sculpture garden nearby.

I nodded, guiding her toward the displays, taking in the luxury around us—priceless paintings hanging on the walls, limited-edition jewelry catching the light, and a collection of haute couture gowns on mannequins.

However, I had to pull away briefly for photos with the guys. Abigail chose to stay behind, not comfortable with the attention. When I returned, I saw her with yet another glass of champagne.

Sighing, I tried to take it from her, but she pulled it away, flashing me a defiant look. "I'm fine, Mikkel."

As if on cue, Ronan showed up with a fresh bottle of champagne, and I almost snapped at him. I suppressed it, offering Abigail water with each glass she drank, but it barely helped.

By the time Azzaria stepped up, she asked, "Has she been at it all night?"

"From the moment Ronan brought the bottle over."

"Stay with her till I'm back, please?" Azzaria asked. "I need to change these heels."

"The car's parked around the back and the doorman has the key."

"Thanks, Mikkel."

Abigail, now clearly feeling the effects of the alcohol, leaned in closer, her words slurring slightly.

"You're a *really* great guy," she murmured, her gaze unsteady as she searched my eyes.

"Thanks, Red."

"I m-mean it," she insisted, her voice softer now. "You make me feel good about myself."

Warmth spread through me at her words, unexpected but hitting

---

4 *my love*

deep.

"Hey, you know what?" she slurred, swirling the last remnants of her drink in her glass, watching the liquid slosh lazily.

"What, baby?"

"I think… I think you're like… like a puzzle." She nodded emphatically, as if she had just unraveled some profound truth. "One of those really hard ones with a thousand pieces."

I chuckled. "And what kind of puzzle are you?"

"I'm… I'm one of the simple ones."

"Nope." I shook my head, studying her. "You're more like a painting. One of those abstract ones that catches your eye, and you can't stop thinking about it—you don't want to stop thinking about it."

Her brows furrowed. "That sounds complicated."

"You're worth it."

Her laughter faded, replaced by something quieter, more contemplative. "You mean that?"

I swallowed hard, nodding. "I mean it."

A beat of silence passed before she whispered, "Do I really make you see color?"

The question made me pause. Then it hit me—Alex's words from earlier, about how I was bland before her.

Brushing a loose curl from her face, I murmured, "You are the color, Red."

Her breath hitched, and her eyes widened slightly, like she hadn't expected me to say something like that. But it was the truth. From the moment she walked into my life, everything was brighter, bolder—*alive.*

She blinked, searching my face, her heartbeat quickening against me. Then, looking down at her hands, she blurted, "I'm a chronic overthinker. I over analyze every look, every word, everything. My brain doesn't know how to shut up sometimes, and it's exhausting."

I shifted closer, my voice steady. "Let me silence the voices, then."

She froze, eyes wide, like I'd just spoken a language she didn't understand.

"What?"

"I mean it." I smiled a little, softening my tone. "If your mind won't stop running, I'll quiet it. I'll be there to make sure you feel peace, even if just for a moment."

Heat rushed to her face. "T-that's not how it works, Mikkel."

"Why not?" I reached for her hand, my thumb brushing over her skin. "You tell me what's going on in your head, and I'll take it from there. Every worry, every fear, everything."

She gulped the remaining alcohol, her eyes glassy with tears. "I always thought I was too… intense for anyone to want to stay."

The words hit hard. I squeezed her hands, lacing our fingers together. "They were too dull for you."

A hesitant smile curved her lips, but uncertainty lingered. "Sometimes I feel like I'm too much… or that I burn too brightly."

"You were, and still are, more than enough. And even if you do burn brightly—that's okay, too." My forehead rested against hers. "I'd rather drown in your light than live in the dark without you."

She inhaled sharply, her fingers tightening around mine. Her lips parted like she wanted to say something, but no words came.

Instead, she reached for the champagne bottle.

I caught her wrist gently, my fingers brushing her pulse. It was quick, fluttering—whether from the alcohol or something else, I wasn't sure.

"That's enough for tonight, baby." My voice was low, coaxing. "Let's get you home."

Abigail pouted. "Bu–"

"You've had enough." I stood, pulling her up with me. "Come on."

She nodded, a sleepy smile playing on her lips as she leaned into me for support. After retrieving the keys from the valet, I helped Abigail into the car, where she quickly drifted off to sleep.

By the time we reached her apartment, she stirred just enough to show her ID before we headed upstairs, but it wasn't long before her head lolled against my shoulder again.

I pressed a kiss to her temple. *God, she had no idea what she did to me.*

Fumbling through her purse, I finally found the swipe card and keys buried beneath lipstick tubes and crumpled receipts. With a sigh of relief, I unlocked the door and guided her inside, steadying her as she stumbled slightly.

“Thanks,” she mumbled, voice thick with sleep.

“Let’s get you to bed, Red.”

She sank on the edge of the mattress, heavy-lidded but still holding on.

“I saw something beautiful at the gala,” she murmured.

I crouched beside her. “Yeah? What was it?”

Her lips curled into the softest smile. “A necklace. Gold, with these tiny diamonds. It caught the light… like it was glowing.”

“Whe—”

She yawned, her lashes fluttering shut. “It was so pretty…” The words faded as sleep pulled her under.

“Red?” I called out but it made no sense, she was out like a light.

Carefully, I helped her lie down, gently removed her makeup and dress, then tucked her under a soft blanket. One by one, I pulled the pins from her hair, watching her curls tumble free. I let my fingers glide through them—slow and reverent—massaging her scalp before slipping on her silk bonnet.

By the time I returned with water and Tylenol, she was still fast asleep.

I kissed her forehead, savoring her peaceful expression, before slipping out to meet a visibly irritated Dillon at the gala.

“What happened?” I asked.

“Nothing, just… tired.”

“You sure?”

“I’m sure. Let’s go.”

I wanted to push, but the look in his eyes told me everything. Whatever it was, it had to do with Azzaria.

The car ride was quiet until he finally glanced at me.

"So, you and Abigail…?" His eyebrow lifted slightly, curiosity flickering in his gaze.

I nodded. "Yeah, but I haven't officially asked her to be my girlfriend yet. I'm working on the details."

Dillon smirked. "Happy for you, Suarez. Though I'm offended I wasn't the first to know."

I laughed. "That's exactly what Arnoldo said."

"Of course he did." He chuckled, shaking his head. Then his expression softened. "Happiness looks good on you."

I swallowed hard. "Thanks, brother." I met his gaze, my voice quieter. "It looks good on you, too."

He sighed, and for the first time tonight, his shoulders didn't look so tense.

When we reached his building, I helped him out of the car, then headed home, already reaching for my phone.

Me
I'll come see you in the morning.

I stared at the message for a second before locking my phone.

Morning couldn't come fast enough.

CHAPTER TWENTY-SEVEN

Abigail-Ann

"In the end, we discover that to love and let go can be the same thing."
– Jack Kornfield

I groaned as sunlight streamed through the gaps in the blinds, stabbing my eyes the moment I dared to open them. My head throbbed—a blunt reminder of last night's one-too-many drinks. A muffled knock sounded at the door, pulling me from bed.

I shuffled to the door and caught a glimpse of myself in the mirror: a disheveled mess in a pair of shorts and a bra, my hair sticking out in all directions. I grimaced, but opened the door anyway.

"Good morning," Mikkel greeted me, an energetic smile on his face. He held up a brown paper bag, a bouquet of primroses, and a bottle of something that looked suspiciously like an energy drink. "Thought you might need these."

"Thank you." I stepped aside to let him in, my brain too foggy to muster a proper greeting. "What's in the bag?"

"Breakfast," he said, setting the bag on the kitchen counter. "Bagels, cream cheese, some fruit, a couple of those hangover cure shots from the convenience store, flowers and something we'll look at later."

Something we'll look at later? I didn't question it, but I made a mental note to ask him about it.

"You're a lifesaver," I mumbled, already tearing into a bagel. "These are perfect."

He watched me with amusement as I took my first bite. "You drank too much."

"Yeah," I said, my mouth full.

"Next time," he said, his tone turning serious, "let's find other ways to sublimate."

"Right, and thank you. I woke up tucked into bed, makeup off, and out of that dress, so thank you."

"You're always welcome," he replied.

"I'm gonna shower," I said, finishing my bagel.

"Take your time," he replied.

After a quick shower, I threw on some shorts and a top. I headed into the living room and settled on the sofa next to him.

"I haven't taken you out in a bit," Mikkel mused, biting into a bagel. "And I haven't planned anything either."

"Things are good how they are," I said softly.

It was still hard to believe I deserved more than what I was used to. The shift—from being lusted to being truly loved—felt almost too big to grasp.

He sighed, leaning in. His voice was quiet, but it hit deep. "I hate that he made you think that's all you deserve." His fingers brushed mine, deliberate. "But I'll always chase you like I never had you, because that's the love you deserve. One that never gets complacent. One that's always reaching, always wanting more."

I swallowed. "Chase me?"

His lips curved slightly as he lifted my hand, pressing a slow kiss to my knuckles. "I'll never stop trying to win your heart, baby. I'll always want to impress you, make you smile, surprise you. You deserve more than something easy or expected." His thumb traced slow circles on my wrist. "You're worth the effort. You're worth the chase."

My heart wasn't just fluttering. It was in freefall.

"You make me speechless, Mikkel," I whispered.

And for the first time, I thought… Maybe I wanted to be chased.

Then I blinked, remembering. "What was it you said we'd look at later?"

"Right." He reached for the bag beside him, unzipping it with a smooth flick. My breath caught as he pulled out the gold necklace I'd admired last night, the diamonds catching the light. Then came the matching bracelets, each one glimmering like scattered stars.

"M-Mikkel," I stammered, jaw slack. *"You got me this?"*

"You mentioned it last night," he said simply. "So I got it this morning."

My mind reeled. I barely even remember mentioning it.

"You just… went and got it?" My voice was barely above a whisper.

"Yeah," he said, watching me closely. "I thought it'd make you happy."

Emotion swelled in my chest, so fast, *so intense,* that I launched myself into his lap, arms winding around his neck.

"This is… Mikkel, what? This was expensive. The tag said thirty thousand dollars."

"Sixty-five," he corrected with a shrug, hand resting on my thigh.

I jerked back, stunned. "Sixty-five thousand dollars?"

His gaze held steady. "It's not expensive."

Not expensive.

Was he just casually dropping nearly a hundred grand on jewelry?

I blinked at him, my thoughts a tangled mess—until his hand covered mine, grounding me instantly.

I rolled my eyes, nudging his shoulder. "That's not the point, Mr. Suarez."

He laughed, rich and effortless, clearly mirroring his bank account. "The point is, you saw it, you liked it… so now it's yours."

I had expensive things, sure. But nothing from someone I was with.

My parents? Of course.

My sister? Definitely.

A man? Never.

"Mikkel, you didn't have to do this."

"I wanted to," he murmured, his eyes glinting with quiet determination. "And I'm not going to apologize for spoiling you."

Emotion swelled in my chest. Thank you didn't feel like enough, so instead, I leaned in and kissed him.

When I pulled back, breathless, I whispered, "Thank you. For this. For everything."

He smiled, brushing a strand of hair from my face before pulling me close again. And just like that, the morning melted into easy laughter and quiet moments of comfort. We curled up on the couch, scrolling through movie options until we settled on a lineup of cheesy classics—starting with *Clueless*, then *Legally Blonde*, and finally wrapping up with The *Holiday Calendar.*

Mikkel turned to me with a knowing look. "Since Friday's your day off, I was thinking of taking you on a date."

I arched a brow, intrigued. "Back to this conversation again? What kind of date?"

He smirked, leaning back into the cushions. "That's a surprise. But I'm picking you up on Friday."

I laughed, shaking my head. "You *know* I hate surprises."

"All the more reason it's going to be perfect."

The conversation drifted into a comfortable silence as the credits rolled. Mikkel's hand rested on the arm of the couch, his lips curved into a faint smile—but I didn't miss the flicker of weariness in his eyes, the quiet frustration lingering beneath the surface.

I tilted my head, studying him for a moment. "Hey," I said gently, my voice cutting through the quiet. "What's wrong?"

He paused for a beat, his smirk faltering just slightly before it returned. "Just tired," he muttered, glancing away for a moment.

I raised an eyebrow, watching him more closely. "You work too hard, Mikkel."

He shrugged, his posture slumping just enough to show the weight of the words. "It's what I do."

I let out a quiet sigh, my gaze softening as I reached over and placed a hand on his arm. "I just hope you know you're doing great," I said sincerely. "All of this... you're amazing."

His smile widened, a rare vulnerability slipping into his voice. "Thank you, Red."

I stared at him for a moment, a thought forming in my mind which caused my eyes to light up. "I have an idea."

He raised an eyebrow, looking intrigued. "Tell me."

Without warning, I grabbed his hand and tugged him up from the couch. "Come with me," I said, guiding him toward the bathroom. "Let me cut your hair."

Mikkel blinked, surprise and amusement flashing across his face. "You want to cut my hair?"

I nodded, grinning. "Trust me."

He laughed softly, shaking his head. "I trust you."

A few minutes later, I was standing behind him, my fingers working with careful precision as I trimmed the ends of his dark hair. The sound of scissors snipping and his occasional low chuckles filled the air, making the room feel cozy in its own way.

When I was halfway through, I stepped back, admiring my handiwork. "See," I said, brushing my hands together in satisfaction.

He turned his head, running a hand through his hair and giving me a grin. "I never doubted you, Red."

I beamed. "Let me finish up."

By the time I finished trimming his hair, a comfortable silence settled between us. The simple act of doing something just for him felt intimate. His neatly styled hair and relaxed jaw made him look effortlessly sexy—so much so, it stole my breath for a moment. Stepping back, I smiled, marveling at how the small change softened his stress, even if only for a brief moment.

"All done," I said, gently tapping his shoulder.

He turned to face me, running his fingers through his freshly cut hair. A lazy smile spread across his face.

"*Muchas gracias, mi amor,*[1]" he said, his voice soft. "I needed that."

Before I could respond, he glanced at his watch, his expression shifting. "It's almost time for your shift, and I have a call."

I nodded. "I'll get ready for work."

As he stepped into the next room, his voice turning all business, I tidied up—putting away the scissors, sweeping up the hair—then took a quick shower. After changing into a simple shirt and gathering my curls into a puff, I found Mikkel still on his call, pacing the living room, his focus elsewhere.

Grabbing my bag, I waited near the door, not wanting to interrupt. The moment he hung up, his gaze lifted, softening as it landed on me. "Ready?"

I nodded, slipping on my coat as we headed out.

The city hummed with life, downtown traffic crawling as we drove. I settled into my seat, absently tapping my fingers against my lap. Then, without warning, Mikkel pulled off to the side of the road.

I glanced at him in confusion.

"I'm buying you lunch," he said with a grin, nodding toward the familiar Chipotle sign.

I beamed, warmth blooming in my chest at the small gesture. "You're the best."

A moment later, he handed me the warm bowl, and my smile deepened.

"Thank you," I murmured, taking a bite as he refocused on the road.

As we neared the bookstore, he slowed to the curb. His fingers brushed against mine before he leaned in, pressing a soft, lingering kiss to my lips. Brief but grounding, it settled something deep inside me.

"Take care of yourself, please," I whispered, my hand still resting on his.

---

1 *Thank you so much, my love*

His thumb traced gentle circles over my knuckles before he kissed me again—this time slower, more tender. "I'll be fine. Just call me when you're done so I can come get you."

With a small nod, I stepped out of the car, my heart full. "I will. Have a good day."

Even as I walked to the entrance, his gaze remained—steady, unwavering. A sense of comfort settled over me, wrapping around me as I started my shift.

CHAPTER TWENTY-EIGHT

Mikkel

"If I had a flower for every time I thought of you...I could walk through my garden forever."
~ Alfred Tennyson

My control was slipping. Maybe it was the long hours at the office or the constant demands coming at me from every direction, but everything felt wrong. The tension in my neck and the pounding in my head weighed heavier than usual, as if my body was rebelling against the pressure I refused to let up. I'd dealt with worse before, but this time, everything was stacking up—one thing after another—until I was teetering on the edge of snapping.

I tried to push through, focusing on the presentation in front of me. I meticulously adjusted every slide and fine-tuned every number, but even the smallest imperfection—a bracket out of place or a line slightly misaligned—set my teeth on edge. My fingers tapped against the desk, my irritation building with each futile attempt to regain control.

The expansion of Elite Rides was everything to me. Chicago was a success, but I needed that same outcome in every other state. Every detail had to be flawless—meetings, investor calls, follow-ups, and endless back-and-forth with my team. It all demanded perfection. And the more I pushed for it, the more it seemed to slip through my fingers.

Oddly enough, the best part of my week was the haircut Abigail gave me. It might sound ridiculous, but when her fingers brushed through my hair, her touch careful and deliberate, it soothed me in a way nothing else could. For a moment, I felt calm, the chaos and the crushing need for perfection fading into the background.

That calm vanished the moment I answered the phone. First, Arnoldo launched into a rant about zoning laws. Then, my mother called, dragging me into petty arguments with her and Emilia—like I wasn't busy enough already.

This morning, though, I found some peace. I attended a seminar on women's health, *The Healing Path: Navigating Endometriosis and Chronic Pain*. The women eyed me curiously, likely because I was the only man in attendance. One even recognized me and asked for a photo, which I agreed to with a smile. At the end of the session, I wrote a check for the awareness fund, hoping to contribute however I could.

But despite the calm of the morning, as I sat in the car parked outside Abigail's therapist's office, that restless energy clung to me like a second skin. No matter how much I tried to push it down, it wouldn't leave.

The sound of the door opening snapped me out of my thoughts. She slid into the seat, and before she could even settle, I leaned in, cupping her cheek as I pressed a deep, slow kiss to her lips.

"Hey, baby," I murmured, my voice softer than the tension curling in my chest. "How was the session?"

"It was good," she said, smiling up at me. That smile eased the tight coil of unease just a little.

I reached for the bag beside me, handing her lunch, watching the way her eyes lit up. *That helped too.*

"You're definitely a mind reader," she said, her voice light. "I was starving."

I let her eat as we drove in silence, but I felt her eyes on me as we came to a stop.

"You're tense," she said after a while, her voice gentle.

"Just a tiring day," I muttered, trying to hold back the frustration.

"Mikkel." Her fingers brushed my jaw before cupping my cheek. I leaned into her touch instinctively. "You've been like this for a while."

"I'm fine," I said, my voice quieter. "Just a bit off today."

She sighed but didn't push. "Do you want to talk about it?"

"Maybe later."

She studied me before pressing a soft kiss to my lips. "I'll hold you to it."

I chased her lips again, but she pulled away with a small smile, grabbing her bag. "Pick me up at the salon later. My nails need a refill, and I'm getting bohemian knotless braids."

My lips twitched. "How much?"

"It's fine."

I pulled out a thousand in cash, tucked it into her purse, and kissed her palm before she could argue. "It's not a discussion, *mi amor*[1]. I like knowing you're taken care of."

She shook her head but smiled, brushing her lips over mine. "I know you do. Thank you."

"Always," I whispered. "Can't wait to see you later."

She stepped out of the car, flashing one last smile before disappearing into the bookstore. As I watched her go, a tight knot formed in my chest. I needed to clear my head. Without thinking, I drove straight to Lucio's house; he was the one person I could talk to.

A few minutes later, I pulled into his driveway. Sugar, his fluffy gray kitten, greeted me with a soft meow, brushing against my legs. I scratched behind her ears, then followed Lucio into the sitting room. Tall, lean, and with piercing blue eyes that seemed to see everything, he studied me silently as if he already knew why I was here.

---

1 *my love*

"Drink?" Lucio asked, his deep voice warm.

I shook my head. "I'm good."

He nodded and gestured for me to take a seat. We both sank into the adjacent arm chairs and I noticed his wife wasn't here.

"So, where's Marina?" I asked, trying to break the silence.

"She's on a trip in Italy."

I raised an eyebrow. "I'm surprised you're not with her."

He laughed, taking a sip of his drink. "My jet's flying me out there tomorrow. I get physically ill being away from my wife."

I chuckled, but it didn't quite reach my eyes. "I know the feeling."

Lucio looked at me and the smile slowly faded from his face. "You look like you're about to explode, *hermano*,[2]" he said, leaning back into the cushions.

I exhaled, rubbing my hand over my face. "I feel my grip on my anger slipping."

Lucio chuckled softly. "Well, God had to give you the anger as a flaw or you'd be way too perfect, Suarez."

I let out a short laugh, the tension in my shoulders easing just a little. "*Vete a la mierda.*[3]" I paused, taking a deep breath. "Speaking of perfection, the constant need for it is just as overwhelming as it is frustrating."

Lucio raised an eyebrow, his blue eyes narrowing slightly. "Who's holding you to that need?"

I leaned back, folding my arms. "I'm holding myself to it. It's just who I am."

Lucio tilted his head, studying me. "There's something else bothering you. I've known you for a decade, and this side of you has always been there. It's the one thing you've never really liked about yourself. So…"

I sighed, feeling the weight of his words, but I wasn't sure I was ready to say it out loud. But I needed to get it off my chest.

---

2 *brother*

3 *Fuck off*

"I told Abigail about it," I said quietly, looking down at my hands. "I opened up about it a while ago, and I just feel different. It feels like maybe she's scared, but I don't know for sure. She doesn't show it, but I know how much she can get lost in her head, and I don't want her to feel like I'll snap at her."

Lucio was silent for a moment, his eyes softening. "You think she's scared? No. You are, Mikkel."

I looked up at him, confused. "What?"

"You're just like me, Suarez," Lucio said, his voice matter-of-fact. "We're not talkers. We don't open up unless it's *absolutely* necessary. We stay out of the media, not by chance but because it's a preference. And when Abigail came into your life, you wanted to make it perfect for her because of whatever you know she's been through. You think sharing your vulnerabilities will make you less of a man in her eyes, but it won't."

I sat there, stunned by how well he read me, how he could peel back the layers I'd always worked on suppressing. I didn't realize how much I was holding back until he put it into words.

I didn't even notice that Sugar had curled up in my lap until I felt her claws pressing into my thigh.

"You're scared of letting her see you like this," he continued. "And that's why you're holding on to the anger, because it's easier than showing her your weaknesses."

I didn't have a response. He was right, and that truth hit me harder than I expected.

He leaned back in his chair, his drink in hand, and a satisfied look on his face . "You've gotta let go of the idea that you need to be perfect for her. She's with you because she wants to be, not because you've built some illusion around yourself. You're allowed to have flaws, Mikkel."

The weight in my chest started to lift, the tension in my shoulders easing as I let out a slow breath. Sugar stretched in my lap, her fluffy tail swishing lazily.

I gave Lucio a dry look, shaking my head. "You should add therapist to your portfolio. All this wisdom, and I didn't even have to book an appointment."

He smirked, tipping his glass toward me. "Therapy's too much work. I'll stick to reading you like a book for free. Besides, I prefer my current job—drinking expensive scotch and being right."

I laughed, the sound feeling lighter than it had all day. "You're a real pain, you know that?"

"And yet we're best friends."

"Yet we are." I stood up, gently moving Sugar off my lap and giving her one last pat. "I'm heading out. Thanks for the session, Lucio."

He chuckled, standing as well. "That's what brothers are for, Suarez. Anytime."

I gave him a firm handshake, the tension in my chest completely gone. "Appreciate it, man."

"Anytime. Tell your love I said hello, and that she's a saint for putting up with you."

I laughed again as I made my way to the door. "I'll let her know. Try not to scare Marina with all this wisdom when you get to Italy."

Lucio waved me off with a grin. "She'll just tell me I'm full of it, like always."

I left Lucio's house feeling lighter, his words still echoing in my mind. The weight that had been pressing on me seemed to lift as I stepped out into the fresh air. Instead of going straight home, I decided to stop by my office to catch up on work. The quiet atmosphere helped me focus as I cleared emails, reviewed contracts, polished proposals, and tied up loose ends.

When I finally wrapped up, I grabbed some Chinese takeout for dinner before driving to pick her up from the salon.

WARNING

The following chapter contains heavy mentions of mental health/physical health issues. Please refer to the content warning list to be reminded of any potential triggers. Your well-being is important to me, so please take care of yourself while reading.

CHAPTER TWENTY-NINE

Abigail-Ann

"Romance is the glamour which turns the dust of everyday life into a golden haze."
~ Elinor Glyn

I woke up with a start, the pillow beneath me slightly damp from where my cheek had pressed into it. Disoriented, I blinked at the faint glow of the bedside lamp. My bed? The last thing I remembered was collapsing on the couch, utterly drained.

Mikkel must've carried me here.

I groaned and buried my face into the pillow. *Three hours.* That was all the time I had left before my shift, and the exhaustion still clung to me. I'd never imagined working in a bookstore could be this draining. The constant movement, the barrage of questions from customers, and the endless shelving was physically and mentally taxing. But at least it didn't give me much time to sit and think.

Dragging myself out of bed, I stumbled into the bathroom. The hot shower was supposed to wash away the tension, but the gnawing unease I'd carried all day remained.

After wrapping myself in my robe, I stepped into the hallway. That's when I heard a loud, sharp noise, like something being slammed.

I froze.

The sound came again, muffled but unmistakable, followed by Mikkel's voice. But this voice wasn't the calm, warm tone I knew. It was sharp, cold, and filled with a fury that made my stomach twist.

I inched closer, my feet almost hesitant as I approached the living room.

"Are you even listening to me?" Mikkel's tone cut like a blade, sharp and venomous. "I gave you a fucking deadline. I handed you everything you needed on a silver platter. What part of this did you not understand?"

His voice boomed through the room, the kind of anger that didn't just fill the space—*it smothered it.*

"*Esto es jodidamente inaceptable!*"[1] he roared, slamming his palm on the countertop, the sound reverberated like a warning shot. "Don't come to me with bullshit excuses when your incompetence is the reason we're in this mess."

My heart pounded as the tension in the air thickened, suffocating me where I stood.

"No!" he barked, the word like a gunshot. "Fix it. I don't give a fuck how you do it, but this better be resolved by sundown. If it's not, someone's losing more than just their job. Do you understand me?"

His face was hard, his eyes blazing with fury as he paced the room, his phone pressed to his ear. His shoulders were tense, and his free hand moved wildly, as if he couldn't contain the rage that poured out of him. This wasn't just frustration; it was a warning of the man he could become when things spiraled out of control.

I couldn't breathe.

---

1 *This is fucking unacceptable!*

My chest tightened as his voice hit me like a tidal wave. I gripped the edge of the wall, my knees shaking.

And then, just like that, I was back there.

Joshua.

"Are you stupid, Abigail? How many times do I have to tell you?" His voice echoed in my mind, searing and cruel. I remembered standing in the kitchen, feeling small as he towered over me, his rage consuming every inch of the space. Plates shattered against the floor, one after the other, his fury growing with every crash. I couldn't move, couldn't speak, couldn't breathe.

The sound of his anger blended with Mikkel's voice, and for a second, I couldn't tell where one ended and the other began.

No. No. This isn't Joshua. This isn't the same.

I forced myself to blink, to pull myself back to the present. But the fear lingered, curling around my ribs like a vise.

Mikkel's voice was still sharp, cutting through the room like a blade. "I don't give a fuck about anyone's excuses. Get it fixed." He slammed his hand down on the counter, the sound making me jump.

I stepped forward without realizing it, the soft pad of my feet on the floor catching his attention. His head snapped up, and for a second, his face was unrecognizable—his jaw clenched, his eyes stormy, and his entire body radiating fury.

But then he saw me.

His expression softened slightly, but the anger didn't entirely leave his features. He exhaled harshly, running a hand over his face.

"Fuck," he muttered, his voice lower now but still rough. He looked at me again, his eyes searching mine. "Baby."

The word was soft, but it didn't ease the tension in my chest. I couldn't move, couldn't respond, as his earlier anger still lingered in the air like smoke after a fire.

Mikkel stepped closer, his hands raised slightly as if to calm me, but it only made my chest tighten further.

"*Amor*,"[2] he started, his voice softer now, the edge of anger gone.

"Don't," I managed to say, stepping back.

His eyes widened, and he stopped in his tracks. "Abigail…"

"Don't," I repeated, barely above a whisper, backing further into the bedroom. The door felt like salvation, and I reached for it, closing it firmly behind me.

I slumped against the door, the wood cool against my back as my legs gave out and I slid to the floor.

The tears came before I could stop them. My hands pressed to my face, trying to muffle the sobs that wracked my body. My mind raced, faster than I could catch up to it.

I'd known. From the moment he told me about how his anger sometimes got the better of him, I'd known it was there. A part of him. But I'd never witnessed it. Never thought I would have to.

And seeing it now, seeing *him* like that… It was a shock I hadn't been ready for.

A muffled knock sounded against the door, followed by his voice, low and filled with guilt.

"Baby, I'm so sorry."

I didn't respond, my throat too tight to form words.

"I—I didn't mean for you to hear me like that," he continued, his voice cracking slightly. "It's work. Things went wrong, and I let it get the best of me."

He paused, and I heard him exhale heavily. "I should've handled it differently. I know I scared you. I saw it in your eyes. Abigail, please…" His voice softened even more, almost pleading. "Please don't shut me out, *mi amor*."[3]

The words spilled out, tumbling over each other like he was desperate for me to hear him.

"I never wanted you to see that side of me. God, the last thing I ever want is for you to feel unsafe with me. You're everything to me, baby. *Please*."

---

2 *Love*

3 *my love*

I didn't move. My hands rested in my lap, trembling as I tried to sort through the rush of emotions. This wouldn't change how I felt about him. I knew that much. But I needed time—just a moment to sit, *to think*, to let myself breathe again.

After what felt like an eternity, I glanced at the clock. My three hours were almost up. Work beckoned, demanding my attention.

Reluctantly, I forced myself to my feet, wiping at my face and willing the tears to stop. I got dressed quickly, pulling my braids into a high ponytail. When I reached for the door, it felt heavier than usual, like it was carrying the weight of the day.

But what stopped me in my tracks was Mikkel.

"You're still here," I said softly, almost to myself.

He stood in the living room, his tall frame tense, and his eyes… They were red. His expression was panicked, vulnerable, like he'd been crying.

I didn't know what was worse—seeing him angry or seeing him like this.

"I couldn't leave," he said quickly. "I couldn't leave knowing you were upset, knowing I scared you. I—I can't lose you. I need you to know how sorry I am. For everything. For all of it."

I opened my mouth, but he kept going, his words spilling out faster than I could process them.

"And I have to take you to work. I wouldn't be able to—"

"Okay," I said, cutting him off, unsure of what else to say. My voice sounded foreign, flat, but it was all I could manage.

He followed me to the door, his presence quiet but heavy. As I reached for my bag, he spoke again, his tone hesitant.

"Abigail, I know this probably reminded y—"

I froze. The air around me felt thick again, suffocating. "Don't finish that sentence," I said, my voice sharper now. I turned to him, my eyes meeting his. "Let's just go."

The words hung between us, heavy and unspoken. He nodded, stepping aside to let me pass.

As we stepped outside into the cool afternoon air, I felt the weight of the moment—his apology, his panic, the lingering tension—and wondered if I'd ever be able to forget the look on his face.

The drive to work felt different today. Mikkel sat in the driver's seat, his hesitation palpable. His hand twitched by his side, like he wanted to reach out but wasn't sure how, or if I'd even let him. For the first time, we drove in complete silence, the absence of our usual playlist making the quiet almost deafening.

I kept my eyes fixed on the road, watching the city blur past. I felt his gaze on me—brief glances from the corner of my eye—but I couldn't bring myself to meet them. Not yet. My thoughts were too tangled, my emotions too raw.

The silence stretched all the way to Book Culture. When the car finally rolled to a stop at the curb, we both moved to speak, but the words faltered and died before they could form.

For now, I had to go to work, even if I had no idea what came next.

The day was slow, or maybe it just felt that way because my mind refused to stop spinning. Every time I passed a mirror or glanced at a reflection in the glass doors, I found myself pausing, as if I could see something in my own eyes that wasn't quite right.

Mikkel's messages popped up, one after another, each one seemingly more apologetic than the last. *Baby, I'm sorry... I'm sorry I made you feel unsafe... Please talk to me.*

I didn't know how to respond. I wanted to, I really did, but I couldn't bring myself to type out the words. *What could I say that wouldn't sound like a lie?*

I was almost halfway through checking the stock when a coworker popped their head around the corner.

"Hey, Abigail. Someone's outside to see you."

I set the clipboard down and raised an eyebrow. A visitor? I hadn't been expecting anyone. Frowning, I followed her out, scanning the area.

Then I spotted a man in a dark suit, standing by a black car—far too formal for a casual visit.

"Ms. Abigail?" he asked, his voice polite but firm.

I blinked, taken off guard. "Yeah?"

He extended a small bag and a bouquet of flowers, a slight smile on his lips. The moment I saw the arrangement—primroses and yellow roses arranged together beautifully—I knew this was from Mikkel.

"Mr. Suarez sent me to give these to you."

"Thanks," I replied, taking the items from him. He gave me a slight nod before turning back to the car, leaving me standing there, thoughts swirling in chaos.

I took a deep breath, pushing the tension aside as I returned to finish my shift. The store was quieter now, and thankfully, someone had come in an hour earlier to cover for me. Relieved, I grabbed my bag and the flowers, heading for the door, eager to finally go home.

But as I stepped onto the curb, my gaze landed on a black Bentley parked a few feet away, one of Mikkel's license plates unmistakable. My steps faltered, unease prickling at the back of my neck. I froze, staring at the car, and then the door opened. A man stepped out.

"Ms. Abigail?" he asked respectfully.

I nodded. "Yes?"

"Mr. Suarez sent me to get you. He's at a meeting in Jersey City, so he won't be able to get you tonight."

"Alright, then."

As I slid into the car and dialed my sister's number, the call rang a few times before she picked up. Aurora's voice came through just as I lifted the screen, seeking a moment of solitude to catch my breath.

"What happened?" Aurora asked immediately, always sensing when something was wrong, even before I could find the words.

"I need to talk. Are you free?" I asked, my fingers gripping the phone a little too tightly.

"I'm free."

I took a deep breath, trying to steady my racing thoughts. "Something happened today… and I don't know how to feel."

I exhaled slowly, gathering my thoughts. "He got so angry, Aurora. I've never seen him like that before. He was on a work call, and it was like… like he wasn't even himself. It scared me. I just… I'm so anxious, and it brought back all these memories of how Joshua used to get…"

I stopped, letting out a shaky breath. "It felt too familiar... like I was right back in that dark place. I... I felt like I was suffocating."

There was a pause before Aurora spoke, her tone calm but steady. "I'm listening, Abi. Keep going."

I took another breath, trying to hold myself together. "I don't want to push him away, but I thought we were dif—"

Aurora interrupted gently, "You *are* different. Mikkel's anger wasn't directed at you. I know it might feel that way right now, but you need to remember that."

I swallowed hard, trying to hold back the tears that were threatening to spill.

"It's okay to be scared and shaken," Aurora's voice was warm with understanding. "But think about everything he's done for you, how he makes you feel safe and loved. I know this has shaken you, I can feel it through the phone. It's terrifying, but don't let this one moment make you forget the good. Ask yourself, is this a dealbreaker? Can you still be with him knowing he has this side?"

Her words cut through my anxiety, and I felt a tear slip down my cheek.

Aurora softened her voice. "I know you're scared, but I don't think leaving is what you want. I believe you two can work through this, but it only works if you talk. Communicate. Everything will be okay."

"I'm not…" I whispered. "I'm just scared. I'm overthinking, and my thoughts are a mess."

"That's okay," Aurora said gently. "You're allowed to feel overwhelmed. This situation triggered something for you, and no one can invalidate that. But this is just one of those things in relationships. It's how you move forward that matters. Talk to him when you're ready. Be honest with him. And don't push yourself away."

"I just…" I sniffled, wiping my eyes. "I feel like a mess."

"Take your time," she said softly. "Don't rush. You don't have to have it all figured out right now. Handle it when you're ready. Together."

"Thank you," I whispered, feeling lighter. "I needed to hear that."

"I'm always here, Abi. You know that."

"I know," I said, steadier now, as I realized we had arrived at my building.

"Call me if you need anything. Anytime," she added.

"I will," I promised, heading for my apartment, until I was stopped in my tracks.

Mikkel was at my door. *Wasn't he to be in Jersey City?*

"What are you doing here?"

He looked at me with wide, almost frantic eyes, his words tumbling out in a rush, as if they were fighting to escape before he lost his nerve. "I… I couldn't just go home and know you're in this state." He swallowed hard, his voice trembling slightly. "I don't want you to hate me. I just… I couldn't leave you like this."

His words hit me as his mask of control slipped, leaving me struggling to process the flood of emotions.

I stepped forward, slowly, and whispered, "I could never hate you, Mikkel."

His face seemed to ease at my words, but he still looked like he wasn't sure what to do with himself. "Can I come in?" he asked, his voice much quieter now, almost hesitant.

I nodded. "Yeah." I stepped aside, allowing him in.

He took the flowers from me gently, placing them in the vase with a tenderness only he could possess.

"I need tonight to breathe," I said, my voice quieter now. "To think."

His eyes softened as he turned toward me, and I could see how badly he wanted to say something, but instead, he just nodded. "Of course." He ran a hand through his hair. "I know it doesn't feel like it, but you're always safe with me. Today, I lost it. I should've been more mindful, and for that, I'm sorry, mi reina. I d—"

Mi reina. My queen.

Oh Mikkel.

I cut him off before he could say anything else. "I know."

His gaze softened, his lips forming a small, apologetic smile. I closed my eyes for a moment, trying to steady myself.

Before I could move, anxiety hit me like a wave. My chest tightened, and I turned toward my room, desperate for space to breathe.

I didn't want to seem weak, but once I reached my bed, I broke down. Sobs wracked my body as everything—my past, the fear, the confusion—came crashing down. My heart ached for him, for us, but I didn't know how to fix it.

Eventually, the tears slowed, but my mind raced. I clung to the thought that Mikkel was not my past, reminding myself over and over, or my fears would consume everything good we had.

WARNING

The following chapter contains heavy mentions of mental health/physical health issues. Please refer to the content warning list to be reminded of any potential triggers. Your well-being is important to me, so please take care of yourself while reading.

CHAPTER THIRTY

Abigail-Ann

"If you live to be a hundred, I want to live to be a hundred minus one day so I never have to live without you."
~ A. A. Milne

I woke to the quiet sound of my own breath, tangled in the remnants of a dream I couldn't quite grasp. But something felt different. A shift in the air. A weight I couldn't name.

I sat up slowly, exhaling as I swung my legs over the bed. When I opened my bedroom door, my breath caught.

Mikkel.

He was slumped against the wall outside my door, fast asleep. His head tilted awkwardly to the side, his breathing uneven. The tension in his face hadn't faded—not even in sleep. His glasses lay discarded beside him, and a furrow still creased his brow, as if whatever plagued him hadn't let go, even now.

A sharp ache bloomed in my chest.

Before I knew it, I was kneeling beside him, fingers brushing the edge of his glasses as I picked them up.

"Hey," I whispered. Just a breath, but it was enough.

His lashes fluttered, eyes squinting slightly as he stirred. "Sorry," he mumbled, voice hoarse with sleep.

"You don't have to apologize," I murmured, gently sliding his glasses back onto his face.

His exhale was sharp, almost like relief. He rubbed a hand over his jaw, still groggy. "I'm not trying to crowd you," he said, voice low. "I just—" He hesitated, swallowing thickly. "I couldn't… I didn't want to be away from you. I needed you to know… the anger wasn't at you."

Something inside me cracked. "I know," I whispered. "But it scared me. It brought me back to a place I never wanted to revisit."

His gaze softened as he reached for me, fingers barely grazing mine. Without thinking, I sat beside him, but the moment I did, he pulled his shirt over his head and laid it on the cold floor beneath me.

My throat tightened.

"You *never* have to explain," he murmured. His voice was so soft, so careful. "I should've *known* better. I should've *been* better. But I'll make it up to you, baby."

He didn't ask for forgiveness. Didn't rush me. He just waited, his fingers tracing the back of my hand in light, rhythmic strokes.

"I trust you," I whispered, the words fragile. Like glass.

His breath hitched, but his expression remained steady. "But you don't feel safe," he whispered. "I can see it in the way you're sitting and how far away from me you are."

My chest tightened. I wanted to deny it, to reach for him first, to tell him he was wrong. But I couldn't.

He exhaled, leaning in just slightly, his breath warm against my skin. And then, before his lips could reach mine, he whispered something in Spanish—soft, reverent, almost like a prayer.

"What?"

His throat bobbed, his voice barely above a breath. "It means, sometimes I forget to breathe when I'm near you."

A tear slipped down my cheek before I could stop it. I turned away quickly, but he was already reaching for me, his thumb sweeping it away with infinite care.

"I can't promise I'll always be perfect." His voice was thick with quiet devotion. "But I will always be here with you."

CHAPTER THIRTY-ONE

Mikkel

"I will never stop trying. Because when you find the one… you never give up."
~ ***Crazy, Stupid, Love***

I couldn't breathe without her.

Not really. Not fully.

The space between us had become suffocating, a weight pressing down on my chest, making every breath feel shallow.

I was just miserable.

I spent the entire night staring at the ceiling, chasing sleep that never came. Every time I closed my eyes, I saw her—the way she looked at me before everything shifted. Before the distance.

And I was drowning without her.

I tried to function. To go through the motions. But I felt like a ghost in my own life. I sat through meetings, nodding at the right times, signing contracts, pretending to care. But nothing registered. The numbers, the projections, the deals—none of it meant anything when she wasn't near.

I gripped my pen so tightly I thought it might snap. My investors assumed I was lost in thought, but my mind was stuck on her.

Was she okay?

Was she eating?

Was her anxiety high?

I caught myself checking my phone too often, hoping for a message, a sign—anything that meant she was still thinking about me. But my screen stayed blank.

Nights were the worst.

Some nights, I paced in front of her door, forcing myself not to knock. Other nights, I gave in to the ache and let myself stay close—curled up outside her door, just to feel near her. Even if she didn't know. Even if she wouldn't open it.

The floor was uncomfortable. The air was cold. But it didn't matter. Nothing mattered if I couldn't have her warmth.

And when the morning came, I'd slip away, leaving a quiet offering behind—a cup of coffee, fresh flowers in her favorite vase, breakfast on the table. Small things. Little pieces of me. The only way I knew how to say, I'm still here. I'll always be here.

The worst part was knowing she wasn't angry. She wasn't punishing me. She just… needed space. And I had to give it to her.

But I didn't know how to exist in that space.

She was my air. My center. My home.

And without her?

I was nothing more than a man desperately wanting her forgiveness.

A man barely breathing in a world without her.

WARNING

The following chapter contains heavy mentions of mental health/physical health issues. Please refer to the content warning list to be reminded of any potential triggers. Your well-being is important to me, so please take care of yourself while reading.

CHAPTER THIRTY-TWO

Abigail-Ann

"I've tried so many times to think of a new way to say it, and it's still I love you."
~ Zelda Fitzgerald

The weeks blurred—*work, therapy, home, repeat.* Some mornings, just getting up felt like a battle. The weight of everything sat heavy on my chest, my body trembling as I walked toward the door. Then came the pain—sharp, persistent. My endometriosis flared again, each cramp stealing my breath, draining my energy. The exhaustion, the discomfort, the tangled mess in my head—it all made everything harder.

But therapy helped. *Slowly.*

"You're holding yourself to a past that isn't yours anymore," Dr. Green had said, voice gentle but firm. "His anger isn't what hurt you. It's the echo of what came before."

I stared at my hands, gripping them tight in my lap.

"How do I… move on?"

"By reminding yourself that you are safe. By letting yourself see him for who he is, not who your fear says he might become."

And he was there. *Always.*

Mornings, parked on the curb, silent but steady. No words, just the soft click of the car door as he drove me to work. Even when I knew he should've been in a meeting. Even when he should've been running his empire. He still chose to be here.

One afternoon, I walked into the bookstore and found him waiting—a slice of chocolate cake and a Chipotle bowl on the table. No expectations. Just a quiet offering of comfort.

The next morning, I woke up aching, body heavy with pain. But on the kitchen table, a bouquet of primroses waited for me, along with a note:

You're gonna be okay, baby.

I stared at it for minutes, my vision blurring, my fingers tracing the ink like it could hold me together.

After work, he showed up with barbecue ribs, sat beside me, and held my hand. Didn't fill the silence with words. Didn't need to.

Some nights, when I couldn't sleep, I'd hear faint rustling outside my bedroom door. I never opened it, but I knew he was there. Close enough to catch me if I shattered, far enough to let me come back to him on my own.

And then, one night, I stepped out of the bookstore, drained and distant. And there he was—hoodie, street light glowing behind him, a smoothie in his hand.

Before I could say a word, his fingers softly brushed mine.

"Take all the time you need," he murmured. "I'm not going anywhere."

And I believed him.

He never went anywhere.

When I was too exhausted to make dinner, food appeared—my favorites, still warm. When my body ached too much to move, the heating pad was already plugged in. When my anxiety crept in, my phone would vibrate:

Breathe, baby.

I'm here with you.

I've got you.

He should've been at board meetings, press conferences, expanding his empire. Instead, he was outside my door. Choosing me.

We sat together, talking about nothing while *Beauty and the Beast* played in the background. And as the weeks passed, the safety I thought I'd lost slowly returned.

One night, I finally reached for his hand first.

His breath hitched, just slightly, before his fingers closed around mine.

His voice was quiet, reverent. "I missed you, *mi reina.*[1]"

I didn't have the words yet, but I squeezed his hand.

And for now, that was enough.

Little by little, I let myself trust again.

Little by little, I came back to him.

After countless back-and-forths, moments of doubt, and waves of hesitation, I found myself standing outside Mikkel's office.

No plan. No rehearsed speech.

Just my pulse pounding in my ears and my fingers trembling at my sides.

I almost turned back. Almost let the fear win.

But Dr. Green's words surfaced in my mind.

"Fear is a habit, Abigail. So is self-protection. But love? Love is a choice. A scary one, sometimes. But if you want to heal, you have to let yourself choose it."

I took a breath. Then another.

And I stepped forward.

---

1 *my queen*

The door was slightly ajar, voices drifting from inside. Before I could second-guess myself, I pushed it open and walked in.

Mikkel, mid-sentence, froze.

His entire body went still.

"Gentlemen, meeting's over," he said immediately, voice sharp, commanding—final.

No hesitation. No second glances.

The men filed out silently, but Mikkel's eyes never left me. Wide with surprise. Shadowed with confusion.

"What ar—?"

I didn't let him finish.

I crossed the room, closed the space between us, and kissed him.

Raw. Desperate. Passionate.

The world blurred, leaving only his sharp inhale, the heat of his hands near my waist, and the unspoken words heavy between us.

When I pulled away, I rested my forehead against his.

"I was a mess," I whispered, my voice steadier than I expected. "The past bled into the present, and it scared me. But none of that matters now." I swallowed. "I'm here. I'm safe with you."

His breath caught—just slightly. His hands flexed at his sides like he wanted to reach for me but didn't know if he should.

Dr. Green's voice echoed again. "You've been wired to expect disappointment. To prepare for abandonment. But Abigail, you have to let yourself believe in the love that stays."

"But," I continued softly, "you have to control the anger. You have to try. I know it's not easy. I know you've never had to."

His eyes darkened—not with defensiveness, but with something heavier.

I let my hands trail down his chest, grounding both of us. "I have my anxiety, Mikkel. You have your anger. But we can help each other. Let me help you the way you've helped me."

His gaze dropped. "I don't know how."

The admission was barely above a whisper.

"I don't snap often," he muttered, voice tight. "I don't—I don't lose it like that. But that day… it just happened." He exhaled, his hands raking through his hair. "And I lost you."

I reached up, cupping his cheek, urging him to look at me. "Then let me be your calm until you find it."

His exhale was slow.

Dr. Green's words resurfaced: "Healing isn't about erasing the hard parts of yourself. It's about learning to hold them with gentleness."

I took a careful breath. "When you feel it building, don't shut me out. Don't let it fester until it explodes. Talk to me. Even if it's hard. Even if you don't have the words. Let me be the one you lean on the way I always lean on you."

Mikkel's jaw clenched. "I don't want you to see me like that."

I smiled—soft, knowing. "Mikkel, I already have."

His breath hitched.

I let my hands settle over his chest, feeling the way his heart pounded beneath my palms. "You don't have to be perfect. You don't have to always be in control. But when it feels like too much, focus on something you love. Something that keeps you grounded."

His stare held mine, unreadable. Then, slowly, he nodded. "I'll do better. I promise, baby."

A pause. Then, softer, "I swear it."

Mikkel rested his forehead against mine, hesitation replaced by intent.

Then, after a long pause, he whispered, *"Gracias por volver a mí."*

I swallowed hard, blinking up at him. "You're gonna have to translate that, Mr. Suarez."

A small, almost shy smile flickered across his lips. "Thank you for coming back to me."

Emotion swelled in my chest. I kissed him again, slower this time. *Softer.*

When I pulled back, I whispered, "I couldn't stay away."

Mikkel cupped my face, his thumb tracing my cheek as if memorizing the feel of me choosing him.

Then, finally—his voice barely above a breath:

"I'll never scare you like that again."

I didn't answer with words.

I stayed close enough to hear his unsteady breath, letting his promise sink in.

CHAPTER THIRTY-THREE

Mikkel

"Love is not about how much you say 'I love you,' but how much you prove that it's true."
~ *Unknown*

I had never been the kind of man to let anger rule me—after all, it was the part of myself I hated most. Control was second nature. I knew how to hold my temper, keep my voice even, and make decisions without hesitation.

But that day, I slipped.

And what made it worse? I slipped in front of Abigail.

For the first time in my life, I understood what true fear felt like.

She had come back, but the weight of that night still lingered between us. The anger I'd let loose had shaken her. It had shaken us.

Even now, as I sat on the ivory couch in my living room, the weight of my mistake settled deep in my chest. I had scared the woman I loved, and no amount of distance or silence could change that.

I wouldn't let that happen again.

Lately, the weight of her workload and stress had only made things worse, leaving her with debilitating headaches. She never said it outright, but I saw the toll it took—the way her shoulders tensed at sudden sounds, the slight tremor in her fingers when she thought I wasn't looking.

But she had been fighting.

She'd been going to therapy more, pacing herself, listening to her body. Facing everything head-on. And as much as she worked on herself, I knew I had to work on me too.

Dr. Green's words echoed in my mind from a session Abigail had shared with me:

"You don't have to carry everything alone, Abigail. Healing doesn't mean doing it in isolation. It means allowing yourself to be supported, to be loved through it."

She let me in, leaned on me. And I had to do the same.

I had to do the work.

It wasn't just about managing the rage when it hit—it was about catching it before it came. Learning the patterns. The way my jaw locked first, then my fists curled, then the heat crawled up my neck, suffocating me.

So, I put things in place.

The stress balls sat in my desk drawer, one in my car, another by my nightstand. I kept them close, forcing my fingers to squeeze, to move, to focus on anything but the building fire inside me.

And when the tension still refused to leave? When I could feel it rattling in my bones, demanding to be let out?

I wrote.

Not business strategies. Not notes for the company. Just thoughts. The things I couldn't always say aloud, the feelings I didn't know how to name, love letters to Abigail. Some nights, my pen tore through the paper, my handwriting nearly unreadable, but it was out of me.

And it helped.

Ronan kept his word about reaching out to psychiatrists and returned with books from a limited-edition store in Italy, all highly recommended for managing emotions and anxiety. They had also suggested weighted blankets, so I bought them in twenty different colors—every shade that had been listed as soothing, hoping one might bring her comfort.

Now, holding titles like *The Gifts of Imperfection* by Brené Brown, *Feeling Good: The New Mood Therapy* by David D. Burns, *Burnout* by Amelia and Emily Nagoski, and *Self-Compassion* by Kristin Neff, I felt hopeful.

These books weren't just for her. They were for us. For me to understand her better. For her to find comfort and tools to help herself.

I spent my free time annotating them, learning how to highlight key passages and leave sticky notes with reminders. Next to a section about intrusive thoughts, I wrote, *"Is this fear talking or truth?"* Beside an excerpt about self-worth, I left a note: *"You are brave, capable, and deserving."*

It wasn't just about the books. It was about proving that she didn't have to fight this alone.

The journey hadn't been easy. There had been tough conversations, uncomfortable silences, nights where she curled into herself before slowly relaxing against me. But I had been ready to face it all with her, willing to carry the weight when she wasn't ready to.

Because a life without Abigail-Ann Asher?

That wasn't a life at all.

I exhaled, rolling the stress ball in my palm, letting the tension ease from my chest. Small habits—steady breaths, a loosened jaw, walking away—kept me in control. The rage didn't own me; I owned it. And I intended to keep it that way.

The clack of keys beside me barely registered.

"I can't believe you've been seeing my client this whole time," Emilia said, her voice slicing through my thoughts.

I looked up to find my sister typing away on her laptop, looking far too pleased with herself.

It wasn't often she *willingly* dropped by, but she'd had a client nearby and used it as an excuse to visit. The best part? Today didn't feel strained at all. In fact, she'd been unusually extroverted—new, but much appreciated.

"Right," I admitted, rubbing the back of my neck. That was another shocker—finding out they knew each other all along.

She tilted her head, curiosity gleaming in her eyes. "After a decade of no love, how'd you end up here?"

I chuckled softly. "She's my blessing from God, *hermanita.*[1]"

Her expression softened. "Is it official?"

"Not yet, but I've got a date planned." Technically, our date should've happened weeks ago, but with everything going on, it had to be postponed. I wanted to make sure she felt secure, that this was the right time for both of us.

Emilia grinned. "I'm happy for you."

"Thanks, Em."

My phone buzzed, the alarm flashing: **Meeting in 30 minutes.** I sighed, slipping it into my pocket and standing.

"I've got a meeting soon," I said, grabbing my jacket.

"Elijah and I will head out then," she said.

"No, stay the night," I replied.

She hesitated. "Are you sure? I don't want to disrupt anything."

"Emilia, you're not a random person—you're my sister. Of course, I'm sure."

She smiled. "Okay, but don't be surprised if I eat all your food."

I laughed softly. "Fair warning, but kiss my nephew for me."

Grabbing my keys, I felt a flicker of gratitude. We didn't always get along, but moments like this reminded me that we could.

I switched gears as I headed to my office, my mind shifting toward business. The Astar contract was still on pause, the family overseas in Germany leaving the deal in limbo. I couldn't afford to let things stagnate, though, so strategizing with my team was necessary.

A request from the Milton Group sat on my desk, but since it wasn't a priority, I let Morison set it aside.

---

1 *little sister*

After wrapping up, I stopped by Book Culture. The usually quiet bookstore buzzed with activity. I walked in, juggling a sandwich, a slice of cake, and a bouquet of primroses.

Then I saw her.

She stood by the shelves, helping a customer, her braids catching the light as she nodded—effortless, captivating, the kind of beauty that turned heads and stopped hearts.

When she turned and saw me, her eyes widened in surprise.

"What are you doing here?" she asked, walking over, still stunned.

I grinned, pulling her in for a kiss. "I brought these for you." I held up the goodies. "I missed you."

Her expression softened, and she smiled. "You spoil me."

"As any man would do for his lady."

She shook her head. "I think you're just obsessed with me, Mr. Suarez."

"That I am," I agreed.

"How's your day?" I asked, glancing around at the busy room.

"Exhausting," she admitted with a sigh. "How was your meeting?"

I shrugged. "Still at a standstill, so we're waiting for updates. But we've got a plan to move forward once they're back."

She nodded, a glimmer of understanding in her eyes. "Azzaria's sleeping over tonight, by the way."

"I remember," I said with a grin. "Call me if you need anything."

"Okay," she said softly, her eyes shining as I leaned in for another kiss.

"Goodbye, *mi reina*,"[2] I murmured.

She smiled, watching as I turned and headed out, my heart lighter than it had been all day.

After the gym, I felt alive in a way I hadn't in weeks. My muscles burned with that good soreness, my mind clearer than it had been in weeks. Getting back into the rhythm of lifting weights and focusing on each

---

2 *my queen*

rep had grounded me. It wasn't just about staying in shape; it was about shutting out the noise, regaining control. And after months of being pulled in a thousand different directions, tonight, I found that balance again.

And it felt damn good.

On the drive back, my phone wouldn't stop buzzing. The group chat was on fire—as usual. These guys never knew when to quit. At a red light, I glanced at the screen, smirking as I read through the chaos.

Dill
Suarez, your woman stole mine tonight.

Me
Sucks for you.

Reyes
God, I hate lovesick men.

Luc
I'm in Greece with my wife. Life's good, gentlemen.

Ro
and I'm at my hospital.

Reyes and 4 others
As usual.

Alex
i'm nailing this whole dad thing. y'all should really try it.

I huffed out a laugh, shaking my head. *Same shit, different day*—someone whining, someone bragging, and Arnoldo pretending he didn't care.

Reyes
Can we talk about how soft you all sound?

Me
Careful, hermano. You might be next.

Ro
i agree, Reyes.

Dill
Says the guy pining for five years.

Ro
Says the guy who fell for his intern.

Luc
Arnoldo probably googles "how to not catch feelings."

Reyes
I hate you all.

The banter was endless, but I wouldn't change a thing.

Then my eyes flicked to the takeout bag on the passenger seat, and just like that, my focus shifted. Dinner for Abigail, and by extension, Azzaria, was just a cover.

The truth? I couldn't spend another second away from her.

The drive to her apartment felt like a blur, my mind already racing ahead to the moment I'd see her. By the time I reached her door and knocked, I was already smiling.

Gone.

She stood there in a pair of shorts and a loose tank that clung to her chest, her hair piled into a top bun, skin glowing under the dim light.

I swallowed hard, my brain short-circuiting.

Fuck.

I should say something.

I really should.

But all rational thought had left the building.

"Hey," she murmured, her voice wrapping around me like a warm blanket.

"Hey."

I stepped inside, letting the door swing shut behind me. The second it clicked into place, I pulled her in, capturing her lips in a deep kiss. Soft. Warm.

She sighed against me, her fingers curling into my shirt like she needed to anchor herself.

When I finally pulled back, I brushed my knuckles against her cheek, taking my time. "You're so fucking beautiful."

She blushed, and I smiled, ready to say something else—until she caught me staring.

"You're staring," she said, a playful glint in her eyes.

I blinked, grinning. "There's a lot to look at, baby."

She shook her head, biting back a smile, but just as I leaned in again, footsteps sounded from the hallway. Azzaria.

"Alright, lover boy." Her voice cut through the moment, arms crossed, an unimpressed look on her face. "Let's set something straight. Don't break her heart."

I turned to face her, standing my ground. "I would never."

Azzaria didn't say anything right away. She just studied me, tilting her head slightly like she was weighing something.

Finally, she exhaled sharply and nodded. "Good. I'd hate to come after you."

I smirked. "I believe you."

Abigail laughed, and the tension melted into something lighter. The three of us talked for a while, easy conversation filling the space. It felt like home.

Eventually, I knew I had to leave—to get back to my sister and let her enjoy her girls' night—even though every part of me wanted to stay.

Abigail walked me to the door, slipping her hand into mine. "Thanks for dinner."

"Any excuse to see you." I smiled, leaning in for another kiss. This time, I took it slow, savoring the feel of her lips. She melted into me, parting just enough for me to deepen it, pouring a silent promise into every lingering second.

When I finally pulled away, I cupped her face, my thumb tracing the curve of her cheek. "I'll see you tomorrow, baby."

She nodded, but her grip on my hand tightened slightly. Then, in a whisper, "When you kiss me like this… I don't want you to leave."

A slow breath left me, my thumb now grazing her lower lip. "I don't want to either."

The air between us grew heavy, thick with something unspoken, the moment stretching taut. If I kissed her again, I wouldn't be able to walk away.

But I forced myself to step back. "Goodnight."

She held my gaze for a beat longer before offering a soft smile. And as I finally turned to leave, I swore I could still feel the warmth of her touch lingering in my palm.

When I got home, Emilia was curled up on the couch with Elijah, trying to settle him down. He squirmed in her arms, still fighting sleep, but her touch was gentle, practiced. She looked up as I walked in, her expression unreadable.

"You're back earlier than I thought," she said, adjusting Elijah slightly.

I shrugged, tossing my keys onto the counter. "You okay?"

She sighed, sinking deeper into the cushions. For a second, I thought she wasn't going to answer. Then, finally— "I'm tired. It's not easy doing all this alone."

Her voice was flat, but the words seemed to cost her something.

I watched her, noticing the tension in her shoulders, the way she kept her gaze on Elijah. "Emilia, you—"

Her laugh was dry, humorless. "I know what you're going to say, and I appreciate it, but I don't… I don't think you really get it." She swallowed hard, her jaw tightening. "It's triggering to have someone promise you everything and then disappear. To watch them ignore their own son."

I frowned. This was the first time she'd ever said something like this out loud.

"You think I don't understand because I haven't been through it," I said carefully, "but that doesn't mean I'm not here for you."

Emilia looked at me then, like she was trying to decide if she believed that. Finally, her voice softened. *"Te lo agradezco."*[3]

We sat in silence for a while, the air heavy with everything left unsaid. I watched as she carefully laid Elijah down, her touch gentle and precise. She looked exhausted.

Then, to my surprise, she scooted closer to me. And before I could react, she wrapped her arms around me.

---

3 *I appreciate it*

I froze for a second, caught off guard. Emilia wasn't the type to do this. She wasn't the type to cry, or hug, or lean on anyone. But tonight, she did.

And it meant everything.

"I thought you hated hugs," I teased, my voice quieter now.

She muttered something against my shoulder, her voice muffled. "*Cállate.*[4] I need it."

I smiled slightly, holding on a little longer than I usually would. *"Te amo, Em.*[5]"

For a second, she didn't say anything. Then, just as quietly, *"Te quiero también, hermano.*[6]*"*

Her voice was soft, barely above a whisper, but it hit harder than anything else she could've said.

I tightened my arms around her, letting her know without words that I wasn't going anywhere. She felt safe enough to open up tonight, and that meant everything.

I'd always be here for her. *Always.*

---

4 *Be quiet*

5 *I love you, Em*

6 *I love you too, brother*

CHAPTER THIRTY-FOUR

Abigail-Ann

"Love is not something you find; love is something that finds you."
~ Loretta Young

I knew something was up the second I stepped into the lobby.

It was a feeling, a shift in the air—like the moment before a first kiss, electric and waiting to spark.

Then I saw Mikkel.

He stood by the curb, all sharp lines and confidence, the city's glow catching the silver chain around his neck and wrist. His car door was open, but he wasn't in a hurry. No, he was standing there like he had all the time in the world—like I was the only thing worth waiting for.

And in his arms?

A bouquet so massive it could have been used as a weapon.

My breath stalled. *What the hell?*

This wasn't just a bouquet. This was a statement. A ridiculous, oversized, unhinged arrangement of yellow primroses, ivory garden roses, and soft sprigs of baby's breath—all tied together with silk ribbon that probably cost more than my rent.

People were staring. A couple walking past did a double take.

One thing about Mikkel Suarez? Subtlety was not in his vocabulary.

His lips curled into that slow, knowing smile as I reached him. "Took you long enough, *amorcita.*[1]"

I folded my arms, fighting a grin. "Did you rob a florist?"

Mikkel chuckled, shifting the bouquet under one arm just to free a hand for my waist. "What? Too much?"

"You're out of control." I shook my head, reaching for the flowers. They were heavy. Like, genuinely heavy.

Mikkel bent down slightly, pressing a lingering kiss to my cheek. The scent of his cologne mixed with the blooms, all rich spice and warmth, curling around me like something dangerous.

"I—" My voice faltered as I traced my fingers over the delicate petals, the sheer excess of it all hitting me in the chest.

My heart flipped. *God, he was thoughtful.*

"They're beautiful," I whispered, breathing them in.

"So are you."

I swallowed. *Hard.*

This man. *This man.*

We slid into the car, and before I could even reach for my seatbelt, his hand was already on my thigh, warm and possessive.

I bit my lip, grabbing my phone to snap a quick photo of the bouquet now taking up half the damn backseat.

When I glanced up, sunlight poured through the windshield, casting his sharp features in a golden glow. Our eyes met, something slow and intense passing between us.

Then, I saw the bracelet on his wrist, the silver charm dangling with my initials.

---

1 *little love*

Damn him.

I knew it was there, but it still sent a thrill through me every time.

"You know," I said casually, shifting so his grip on my thigh tightened, "I keep forgetting you're much older than me, Mr. Suarez."

His fingers flexed. "I'm pretty sure I asked you this before, but does that ever bother you, Ms. Asher?"

Bother me? Never.

I shook my head. "No way. You're my sexy, patient, and ambitious man."

His honey-brown eyes flickered with something dangerous. "And you're my beautiful, compassionate, and remarkable woman."

The words sank into me, hot and sweet. I was blushing, I knew it.

Then his hand slid further up my thigh. Too slow. Too deliberate.

I exhaled shakily. "I love the way your hands feel on me."

Mikkel smirked, his fingers tracing lazy circles against my skin. "I don't think it feels as good as the way your skin does against my palm."

Jesus.

"You always know what to say," I muttered, pressing my thighs together.

He grinned, shifting gears without a word. He *knew* exactly what he was doing to me.

Desperate for a distraction, I cleared my throat. "So, where are we going?"

He chuckled. "It's a surprise, but I promise you'll love it."

A surprise. *Of course.*

With a sigh, I leaned back, surrendering myself to whatever he had planned.

The city faded behind us, the skyline softening into quiet calm. I traced patterns on his forearm, the scent of my bouquet and his cologne lingering in the car. Every so often, his thumb brushed absentmindedly over my knee, and each time, my breath hitched just a little.

Eventually, the car slowed, the sound of waves filling the space between us. I blinked, taking in the familiar setting as we pulled into Pier 84.

The docks lay ahead, water reflecting the sunset's last hues. Boats bobbed in the distance, salt and warmth in the air. Mikkel's hand found mine as we strolled, his thumb tracing slow, steady circles over my skin.

And then I saw it.

Twinkling lights hung above, casting a soft amber glow over the setup—a beautifully arranged table, candles flickering, the scent of lasagna, warm bread, and herbs filling the air.

I blinked.

What the fuck?

The small details captured me—pictures strung above, each a snapshot of our time together. Moments of joy, laughter, and adventure, frozen in time. Aquarium dates, Coney Island at sunset, Dillon's gala, lazy days tangled in sheets, FaceTime photos, the beach, the High Line, the Lana concert.

Every single one taken by him. A collection of us.

My throat tightened. "Mikkel," I whispered, barely audible.

The moment wrapped around me like a warm embrace, and then—soft guitar chords filled the air.

"Can I Be Him" by James Arthur.

The song drifted through the night, mingling with the flickering candlelight and settling deep in my bones. My pulse thrummed as I turned to him, only to find his gaze already on me.

Adoring. Unwavering. Like I was the only thing that mattered.

"I can't believe you went to all this trouble," I murmured, my heart a restless flutter.

His lips curled, that dimple peeking through. "It's never trouble to do anything for you."

His fingers brushed against mine before he pulled out my chair with an easy, effortless grace. A gentleman. My Hispanic gentleman.

"Let's sit."

Dinner was lasagna, barbecue ribs, and fried rice. A strange mix, yes but it was so me. Comforting, rich, indulgent. Every so often, he reached for my hand between bites, his thumb stroking slow, absentminded circles over my skin.

"I wanted tonight to be special," he said, his voice low, his eyes locked onto mine. That look—the one that made my stomach somersault.

I swallowed. "It already is."

He smirked. "I've been planning something."

My pulse jumped. "What is it?"

Mikkel leaned in, his scent—a mix of spice and warmth—sending a shiver down my spine. "I've hidden clues around here. Each one leads to a surprise."

Intrigued, I grinned. "Like a scavenger hunt?"

"Something like that." He tapped my nose. "And knowing you, I bet you're dying to solve it."

He wasn't wrong.

I followed his lead, my heart racing with each clue, anticipation growing with every discovery. He used Lana Del Rey song titles—mostly from my favorite album, *Born to Die*—to reveal the first letter of each word. It was perfect, and I was overwhelmed in the best way.

Without You
If You Lie Down With Me
Lolita
Lucky Ones
Yayo
Off to the Races
Ultimate
Born to Die
Elements of Life
Million Dollar Man
Young and Beautiful
Gods & Monsters
Interlude
Radio
Love
Freak
Ride

In My Feelings
Endless Summer
National Anthem
Dark Paradise

By the time I pieced it together, I went still. The letters formed something I wasn't expecting.

Will you be my girlfriend?

The world tilted.

Tears shimmered in my eyes as I turned to him, my heart crashing into my ribs. He planned all of this. He did all of this.

For me.

"Yes," I whispered, barely audible over the soft lilt of the music.

Mikkel exhaled sharply, like he had been holding his breath. Then, in one fluid motion, he pulled me into his arms, crushing me against his chest.

"You've just made me the happiest man alive, Red," he murmured against my hair. His voice was thick, almost disbelieving.

I closed my eyes, sinking into him, *into us.*

Then he pulled back, reaching into his pocket. "Do you know the song Sad Eyes by James Arthur?"

I shook my head, still breathless. "Barely. Why?"

He handed me something.

A letter.

Handwritten.

My fingers trembled as I took it, heart pounding in my ears.

Mikkel didn't just tell me how he felt.

He wrote it down.

And somehow, that meant everything.

Dear Abigail-Ann (My Red),

For someone who always finds the right words, putting my feelings on paper wasn't easy. But I needed to write this, so when I'm not with you, you'll have a piece of me to hold onto.

Every moment with you is a gift, and I find myself constantly thinking about the way you've touched my life. You remind me of the song Sad Eyes by James Arthur because it captures the beautiful complexity I see in you. I see and know how heavy life has been for you at times. You've endured so much, and it breaks me to know how deeply you've been hurt. I know the scars of your past linger, and I don't just want to kiss them—I want to help you heal them.

I can't promise perfection, but I can promise you this—I will always strive to be the man you deserve.

I want to be the person who dries your sad eyes. I want to share in your laughter, your joy, and even your tears. You deserve so much happiness, and I want to be a part of that—supporting you, encouraging you, proving to you that there is always light, even after the darkest of nights.

Me haces sentir como si estuviera en un sueño, mi amor. Cuando dices que estás aquí conmigo, todo lo malo se desvanece, como si tu sola presencia iluminara hasta la noche más oscura. La ansiedad se aleja, y en tu abrazo encuentro paz. Nunca imaginé que podría sentir algo tan profundo. La vida se vuelve más hermosa, más luminosa, desde que te tengo a ti. Tus ojos verdes, tan intensos, me envuelven por completo. Cuando me miras, el mundo entero desaparece, y solo existimos tú y yo.

Forever Yours,

Mikkel S.

The letter trembled in my hands, my vision blurred with tears. A sob broke free from my chest, raw and unrestrained. I pressed a palm to my lips, overwhelmed by the weight of his words, the depth of what he saw in me—*what he wanted for me.*

Mikkel made me feel things I had spent years yearning for. He didn't just love me—*he saw me.* The little girl inside me, the one who had begged for scraps of affection. The woman I was now, unsure how to accept it. He made space for both, holding them with devotion.

Through my tears, I smiled.

"I don't have the words to describe how happy I am." My voice trembled, thick with emotion.

Mikkel exhaled softly, his grip tightening around my hand. "I know you've been through certain things in the past," he murmured, "but I promise you, I'll make this worth your while."

I took a deep breath, slipping the letter carefully into my purse, as if safeguarding a sacred piece of him.

"I'm sorry I made you cry," he whispered, his thumb brushing a stray tear from my cheek.

I let out a watery laugh. "Of all the tears I've shed in my lifetime, these are worth it. Mikkel, tonight. You… everything you've done. The bouquet. The pictures. The song titles. The letter. I've never… I can't put it into words. You make my heart and soul happy."

His expression softened, the corners of his mouth lifting in a slow, adoring smile. "I'm glad I could, *mi reina.*[2]" He paused, leaning in to press a lingering kiss to my forehead.

"And before I forget," he continued, reaching for the back of the letter, "I translated the Spanish for you."

His voice was soft as he read aloud:

"You make me feel like I'm in a dream, my love. When you say you're here with me, everything bad fades away, as if your presence alone brightens even the darkest moments. Anxiety recedes, and in your embrace, I find

---

2 *my queen*

peace. I never imagined I could feel something so profound. Life becomes more beautiful, more luminous, since I have you. Your green eyes, so intense, envelop me completely. When you look at me, the whole world disappears, and only you and I exist."

My breath hitched as his words sank into my skin, deeper than ink, deeper than memory.

I reached for him, cupping his face, and pressed a kiss to his lips—soft, slow, lingering. He exhaled into it, his hands cradling my waist as he pulled me closer.

When I pulled back, I searched his face, my heart pounding with certainty. "I never thought I could feel like this, but with you, everything feels right."

His fingers brushed a loose curl from my cheek, his gaze warm, reverent. "You're my dream, Red."

The weight of his words lingered between us, heavy with unspoken desire. My pulse thrummed as I took in the way his eyes darkened, the way his fingers flexed slightly where they rested against my hip.

"I want you," I whispered.

His brows furrowed slightly, as if deciphering my meaning.

I tilted my chin up, my gaze steady. "You heard me."

Something flickered in his eyes—understanding, hunger, restraint fraying. The air grew thick, charged.

He brushed his lips over mine, a whisper of tenderness before urgency took hold. His hands roamed, tracing every curve as if memorizing me.

Fingers grazing my thigh, he pressed gently, drawing a soft moan he silenced with another kiss—pulling me closer, unwilling to let even a breath of space remain.

And I didn't want there to be.

"Please," I whispered, my voice barely audible but filled with longing.

"The first time I get to fuck you won't be here," he whispered.

I couldn't convey my words and most importantly, I've never seen this side of Mikkel, and fuck, I was loving it.

The quiet ones always have the dirtiest mouths.

Thank God.

"Mikkel," I whispered, my voice trembling with anticipation.

"I'll make you cum tonight, but I'll never fuck you for anyone to see," he murmured, his eyes smoldering with a mix of possessiveness and desire.

"Why?"

"Because you deserve to be explored, and savored. There's nothing quick or easy about you, *mi amor*."

He slid his hand up to my sopping-wet thong and rubbed his fingers over the drenched fabric, his touch electrifying.

"This wet for me, baby?" he whispered, a devilish grin spreading across his face.

I couldn't form the words to answer.

If he kept talking to me like that, I was gonna cum right now all over his fingers.

"Talk to me," he whispered, kissing my neck. "Use your words, *amor*."

"Y-Yes," I stammered. "F-For you."

Without another word, he twisted my panties in his hand and ripped it.

"Mikkel," I panted, my eyes wide with surprise.

"*Tu coño está tan mojado*,[3]" he said, a wicked smile playing on his lips.

"I don't even want to know what that means," I breathed, shivering with anticipation.

"Your pussy is so wet," he whispered. "That's what it means."

With his other hand, he freed my breasts from the dress, taking my nipple into his mouth. As he rubbed between my lips, feeling the wetness there, he moaned again and nipped lightly at my nipple, sending jolts of pleasure through my body.

"Fuck," I whispered. "*Please.*"

I moved my hand to his crotch, which felt too big to even comprehend, and wait, was that a piercing?

Did he have a fucking Jacob's ladder?

---

3 *Your pussy is so wet*

Mikkel groaned momentarily as I started rubbing his crotch, looking for the zipper to free it.

"Next time." He swatted my hand. "It's your night, *mi amor*.[4]"

I couldn't even muster the words to argue with him. I conceded, and he continued moving his finger over and around my pussy and rubbed his thumb over my clit, making me shudder.

"So fucking warm," he whispered into my ear, and I whimpered against his mouth. "So fucking tight."

"Mikkel," I squealed, as he inserted two fingers inside of me.

I rocked against his fingers, a third slipping in as I trembled, holding back to savor the moment.

"Cum for me," he whispered, and that was it. All restraint I had was gone and there I was, falling onto him, a shaking, wet mess. "Cum for me, baby."

Thinking he was done, he pulled his fingers from my pussy and tasted it. "About to be my favorite flavor."

"I n-need a minute." My breathing faltered, and I was shocked out of my mind. "That was…I've never come that hard in my life."

"Your ex is pathetic," Mikkel spat, his voice low. "With pussy that addicting and a personality that great, I'd never let you leave my bed."

I felt my cheeks heat up instantly. He was always like this—so sure, so bold—and no matter how much I tried to brush it off, his words always hit me deep.

"Never letting me leave your bed, huh?"

His eyes locked on mine, and I could feel the heat building between us. It was magnetic, the kind of tension that stole your breath without warning.

"*Exactamente*.[5]" His voice was deeper now, more dangerous. My heart started to race when his hand slid around my waist, pulling me just close enough for his breath to tickle my lips. "I can't imagine how good your

---

4 *my love*

5 *Exactly*

pussy will grip my cock, especially after the way it gripped my fingers," he whispered, eyes never leaving mine.

I swallowed hard and subsequently cleared my throat. "Mikkel," I managed to say.

He gave me that smirk—the one that always made my stomach flip. "I suppose that's how you'll say or rather, scream my name," he murmured, and before I could even think of a response, his lips brushed against mine.

It was soft at first, a tease, but the impact hit me like a wave. When he pulled back, his fingers were still tracing lazy circles against my skin, like he knew exactly what he was doing to me.

I felt like I was starving, and only he could satisfy my hunger.

I chuckled, my voice steady, though my heart was anything but. "You're always so sure of yourself, aren't you?"

He leaned in again, this time close enough for his lips to graze my ear. "When it comes to you?" His voice dropped to a whisper that set every nerve in my body on edge. "Always."

My body was still throbbing, pulsing with the very thought of him.

The mouth on this man was fucking unreal. He carried on as if he hadn't just fingered me to *two* orgasms, tasted his fingers, and whispered the filthiest words I'd ever heard—all in one breath, without missing a beat.

After the picnic and my failed attempts at coherent conversation, we strolled hand in hand through moonlit streets. By the fountain, he kissed me—long and promising—then drove me home in comfortable silence.

At my door, he cradled my face, kissed me again, and left me utterly breathless.

"Goodnight, *mi amor*,[6]" he whispered, his forehead resting against mine.

"Goodnight, baby," I murmured, my heart swelling. "I can't wait for more days with you."

---

6 *my love*

"Soon," he promised, stepping back and handing me a bag. "But first, a gift, and there's a box waiting inside for you."

Another gift? I needed to hide his credit cards.

I took the bag, noticing the unexpected weight. "What's inside?"

He smirked, stealing another quick kiss. "You'll see."

Curiosity bubbled up, but I let him go, watching as he walked to the elevator. With a deep breath, I stepped inside, shutting the door behind me. I barely made it to the sofa before collapsing onto it, hugging the pillow he'd given me as a giddy little squeal escaped.

"He used Lana song titles," I whispered to myself, clutching the pillow tighter.

Then my eyes landed on the massive box sitting in the middle of my living room.

How the hell had he even gotten that up here?

I scrambled to the kitchen for scissors, heart pounding with anticipation. When I opened it, I froze.

Weighted blankets.

He bought me *twenty* fucking weighted blankets.

Lifting the first one out, a small note fluttered to the floor. I bent down to pick it up, hands trembling slightly.

> Weighted blankets help with anxiety (so I read), and I hope these help you.
>
> I got different colors (twenty to be exact), so if one gets dirty, you'll always have another. They're also pre-washed and range from 15-20 pounds.
>
> ~Tu novio.

My throat tightened. I squeezed the blanket to my chest, its weight comforting me in ways he already knew I needed.

Swallowing hard, I grabbed the bag he'd given me earlier—and *what the fuck?*

---

7 *Tu novio - your boyfriend*

Inside were self-help books, each one meticulously tabbed, notes peeking from the pages. I stared in disbelief before pulling out another note resting on top of the stack. His familiar scrawl made my chest ache.

My handwriting is awful, I know, but I made notes and annotations just for you. At the front of each book, there's a sheet with the sections I picked out. These helped me, and they're still helping me help you. I hope they help you help yourself.

~Tu novio.

Don't cry. Don't cry. Don't fucking cry.

It was pointless. I sobbed.

A choked sound left me as I opened the first book. His handwriting was everywhere—small notes in the margins, underlined passages, carefully highlighted sentences.

He read them. He read them for me.

And he hadn't just read them—he had taken the time to pick out things he thought would help. *How to breathe through anxiety. How to be kinder to myself. How to embrace my body as it is.*

The thoughtfulness of it overwhelmed me. The weight of his care settled over me as surely as the blanket I still clutched. He wasn't just loving me—he was helping me love myself.

A fresh wave of tears threatened to spill over. Sniffling, I reached for my phone with shaky fingers and typed out a message.

Me

I know you're probably driving, but I couldn't wait to say thank you. The blankets are amazing. I'm going through the books now, and I can't even begin to explain how much this means to me. You're amazing.

I set my phone down, hugging the books to my chest, breathing in deep. He understood me in ways I hadn't even thought possible.

Moments later, my screen lit up.

S
I'm glad you love them, mi amor. Sleep well, beautiful.

I smiled, wiping at my damp cheeks. *I would.*

CHAPTER THIRTY-FIVE

Abigail-Ann

"The strongest love is the love that can demonstrate its fragility."
~ Paulo Coelho

I spent the day wrapped in Mikkel's arms, falling harder for him with each passing moment. Every night, I thanked God for bringing him into my life.

"Mikkel?" I called, stepping into the hallway.

"Living room," his voice drew me in.

I found him lounging on the sofa, a lazy smile spreading across his face as he saw me. Without hesitation, I curled into his lap, sighing as his fingers drifted through my hair in slow, soothing strokes.

"This might be the softest sofa I've ever sat on," I murmured, melting into him.

He chuckled, the sound deep and warm. "I'll take that as a compliment."

"You should. This feels like luxury," I teased, shifting slightly so I could look up at him.

His lips curved into a smirk. "It is luxury."

Before I could respond, his lips captured mine, stealing the breath from my lungs. His hand slid to my waist, fingers pressing lightly, drawing me even closer. The world outside this moment blurred, my senses drowning in the way he kissed me with the kind of hunger that made me forget everything else.

I traced my fingers along the sharp line of his jaw, deepening the kiss, my body pressing against his. Heat unfurled between us like a slow-burning flame, steady and consuming. Just as my hands slipped beneath my sweater, his phone buzzed on the table.

Mikkel groaned against my lips, resting his forehead against mine. "Terrible timing."

"Terrible," I agreed breathlessly, unable to hold back a small laugh.

Annoyance flickered across his face as he checked the caller ID. With a sigh, he pressed the speakerphone.

"Ronan," Mikkel said, his voice edged with impatience. "There better be a damn good reason for this call."

"Very hostile," Ronan's voice crackled through the speaker. "What are you doing?"

"My girlfriend."

"Ah, so everyone's just in love. I wonder if it's the season," Ronan muttered, sarcasm thick in his voice. "Tell her I say hello."

Mikkel rolled his eyes, clearly unamused. "Did you need something?"

Ronan's tone shifted, turning grave. "I have a message from Dillon. Something's happened to Azzaria, and he can't get to her friend—which I'm guessing is who you're *doing*—so he said to call you."

The warmth in my body vanished. My skin went cold. My stomach twisted painfully.

"I was with her this morning," I blurted, my voice unsteady. "What happened?"

Ronan cleared his throat. "She ran into her ex, but Dillon stopped it before things escalated. They're headed to his penthouse."

Azzaria's ex. Matthew.

I shot up from Mikkel's lap, my breath coming in sharp, shallow pulls. "Mikkel…"

He was already moving, his eyes dark with concern as he caught my waist, steadying me. "I know, let's go."

The thought of her in distress, of Matthew anywhere near her, tore through me with a ferocity that left me shaking.

We waited in Dillon's study, the silence stretching, thick and suffocating. Panic clawed up my throat, my breath slow but heavy. Every second that passed only fed the gnawing dread in my chest.

Mikkel sat beside me, his warmth a tether. He massaged my palm, then pressed into my neck, each stroke unraveling tension. His touch grounded me just enough to keep me from spiraling.

The room was filled with faces I barely knew but had heard plenty about. Ronan and Lucio, identical in appearance but sharp in contrast—one with an easy smirk, the other with an intensity that spoke volumes. And then there was Arnoldo. Unlike the others, he didn't try to blend into the weight of the moment.

"So you got one best friend and Azzaria got the other?" His voice cut through the silence, careless, almost amused.

Mikkel's response was instant, his tone sharp enough to slice. "Time and fucking place, Reyes."

Arnoldo smirked, unbothered. "Ah, he speaks." He stretched, arms draping over the back of the chair. "I'd argue my question lightened the mood."

"You're an asshole," Ronan muttered, shaking his head.

Arnoldo shrugged. "I'm blunt."

Lucio exhaled, pinching the bridge of his nose. "Ignore him," he told me. "He was born without a filter."

Arnoldo only winked.

I barely processed their exchange before my focus snapped back to the one thing that mattered. "Where's Dillon?" I asked, my voice strained with urgency.

"No cl—" Ronan began, but the door swung open before he could finish.

Dillon stood in the frame, his expression drawn tight, a bottle of scotch clenched in his fist. The tension rolled off him in waves, dark and volatile.

"Where is she?" The words left my lips in a rush, my pulse pounding. "Is she okay? Did he do anything to her?"

Dillon's gaze swept over us, his jaw ticking before he exhaled sharply. "She's sleeping." His grip tightened around the bottle. "Don't go to her." The last part came out a low warning, rough with frustration.

Mikkel's head lifted, his gaze hardening.

"Xander." His voice was quiet but carried the kind of authority that sent a ripple through the room. "Watch your tone when you're speaking to her."

I *shouldn't* have found that hot.

Not the time, Abigail. I needed a cold shower. No, a damn ice bath.

Dillon exhaled, some of the tension in his shoulders easing. "I'm sorry," he muttered, dragging a hand through his hair. "I'm just… pissed."

I nodded. "I get it, but she's my best friend before she's your girlfriend. Don't forget that."

Dillon's expression softened with understanding, but frustration still simmered beneath the surface. "I know. I just—" He broke off, shaking his head.

"She's strong," I said. "Give her time and space, and she'll be okay."

"I hope so." His tone darkened. "Or Matthew's a dead man."

Lucio sipped his drink, gaze drifting to the window. Then he smirked, his voice smooth yet dark. "Matthew's a dead man either way, Xander."

Dillon stared at the bottle in his hand for a long moment before murmuring, "You're right." He turned toward the window, his voice dipping lower. "I need some air. You can all see yourselves out whenever."

Wordless, we slipped out, leaving Dillon with his thoughts. The night's weight hung heavy as we strode down the hall, footsteps hushed against the hardwood.

Mikkel reached for my hand, his fingers warm as they laced with mine. "What do you want to do?" he asked, his voice soft. "A drive? A *Beauty and the Beast* marathon with Chipotle?"

I smiled, warmth spreading through me at how well he knew me. But tonight, I wanted something different—something long overdue.

I squeezed his hand, looking up at him. "I just want to spend the night with you," I whispered. "Naked. In your bed."

A slow, wicked grin spread across Mikkel's face, his dark eyes heating instantly. "Naked?" His thumb traced over my knuckles, deliberate and teasing.

Heat crawled up my neck, but I held his gaze. "Yes."

He chuckled, tugging me closer. "Then let's go."

Twenty-five minutes later, we were back at the penthouse. I reached for my phone, intending to check on Azzy, but before I could dial, it rang.

Relief swept through me when I heard her voice.

"Hey," she said, still a little shaky but stronger than before. "I know you're worried, but I'm better now."

I exhaled, tension easing from my shoulders. "I'm relieved to hear that. You're safe now, I promise." My voice softened. "Call me if you need anything, okay? I'll see you tomorrow."

"I will. See you tomorrow, Abi."

As I hung up, I let out a breath I hadn't realized I was holding. The worry still lingered, but knowing Azzy was safe helped.

Mikkel watched me carefully. "Is she okay?" Concern creased his brow, his head tilting slightly.

"She's shaken up, but she'll be fine," I assured him. "I'll see her first thing tomorrow."

Mikkel's gaze lingered on me, searching. "Are you feeling better, Red?"

I met his eyes and, for the first time tonight, I really meant it.

"I am."

Abigail disappeared into the bathroom for a moment, stepping out in one of my T-shirts and a pair of underpants, a sight that hit me like a slow-burning flame, leaving my chest tight and my thoughts scattered. She climbed into bed, curling up against me, her body molding to mine like she belonged there—because she did.

Her fingers traced idle patterns across my chest, lingering over the inked lines of my tattoos. Each stroke sent sparks racing down my spine, and I clenched my jaw, barely holding back the groan clawing its way up my throat.

"I still can't get over how hot these are," she murmured, voice soft but full of admiration. "I see them every day, but I never get used to it."

A low chuckle rumbled from my chest, but I was barely listening—too focused on the way her touch felt like a brand. "Yeah?"

She hummed in response, then pressed her palm flat against my chest, right over my racing heart. Her fingers flexed, like she was trying to hold it, to keep it for herself. Maybe she didn't realize she already owned it.

Then, she looked up at me. And fuck, I was gone.

The way her green eyes darkened, pupils swallowing the color whole. The way her lips parted slightly, like she was on the verge of asking me for something. And God help me, I'd give her anything.

Her fingers skimmed lower, a teasing path down my stomach, and I sucked in a sharp breath. She knew exactly what she was doing—driving me to the edge, watching me crumble for her.

I caught her wrist, bringing her hand to my lips. "Baby," I murmured, my voice rough, desperate.

She arched a brow, amused. "Yes?"

I kissed the inside of her wrist, then her palm, lingering, letting her feel how badly I needed this—*needed her.* "Let me have you," I whispered. "Please, baby."

She didn't answer.

Just watched me.

I swallowed hard, my pulse pounding in my ears. I leaned in, pressing my lips to the corner of her mouth, barely there. "A kiss," I begged, my voice raw. "Give me something, *amor*."

Still, nothing.

My fingers traced her jaw, my lips hovering over hers, breathing her in, drowning in her. "Anything," I whispered. "Please."

Her nails scraped against my scalp, slow, teasing, like she was savoring my suffering. Like she wanted to see how far I'd go for her.

And fuck, I'd go anywhere.

I let out a shaky breath, my forehead pressing against hers. "I need you," I confessed, voice thick with longing. "I need you so fucking bad."

A slow exhale left her lips, warm against mine. Her fingers tightened in my hair, tugging me closer. Then, finally—finally—her mouth brushed mine, the softest, sweetest torment.

I groaned, gripping her waist, barely holding myself back. "More," I pleaded. "*Please*. I'll do anything."

She let me suffer a second longer, her lips barely moving, teasing, taunting. Then, in a whisper so quiet it almost wasn't there, "Then take me."

That was all I needed.

I claimed her mouth in a kiss that left me shattered, lost, drowning in her. My hands roamed, greedy, desperate, like I could somehow pull her closer, make her a permanent part of me.

I'd begged for her. And now, she was mine.

My pulse raced, but I found my hands steady as I reached out to run my fingertips down one of her breasts, pinching her nipple sporadically.

Her words struck something deep inside, igniting a primal hunger I couldn't ignore.

I leaned in closer, my voice low and commanding. "Take off your clothes and lie down on the side of the bed."

She hesitated, then met my gaze—curious, dark. One brow arched, no fear, only anticipation.

"I'll be right back." I rushed to the closet for my suspenders, unhooking them from a pair of pants. When I returned, she was already lying there, waiting. I crossed the room, my focus locked on her.

"Slide closer." My voice came out rough, unrecognizable. "Legs bent, heels on the edge."

She obeyed, lifting her legs, and my mouth watered as my gaze locked between her thighs.

I ran my hand up her foot, over her leg, gripping her knee to spread her wider. With a firm pull, I wrapped a suspender around her leg, securing her ankle to her thigh. "Is that too tight?"

"No," she whispered, her attention glued to my face. "It's perfect."

Within a few seconds, I tied the other leg in the same bent angle. "Keep your legs spread, arms overhead."

"Mmm," she mumbled.

Kneeling before her, I took a deep breath, memorizing every inch of her—spread open, *mine*. I ran a blunt fingertip through her wetness, claiming her with a single touch.

"This goes without saying." My voice was low and full of intent. "But let me make it clear." My finger trailed up her slit, drawing a soft gasp from her lips. "This."

My other hand moved to pinch her nipple gently, her body responding to my touch with a subtle arch. "This." Finally, I slid a finger into her mouth, her lips parting to take it, her eyes locked on mine. "And this," I whispered. "It's all mine."

"All yours," she whispered, her words coming out in breaths.

"All mine," I replied without hesitation, my grip on her hip tightening. "Every inch of you belongs to me, just like every piece of me belongs to you."

Needing to finally have a taste, I leaned in and traced the slits with my tongue. Satisfaction coursed through me, and I licked up to her clit, pressing my finger in as far as it would go. I kept going, each movement deliberate, watching as she trembled beneath me. The sight of her shaking, the mix of surrender and desire in her eyes, fueled something darker inside me.

"M-Mikkel," she moaned. *"Holy fuck!"*

Wrapping one arm around her leg and placing my hand on her stomach, I held her still beneath my exploration—nibbling downward, sucking her pussy lips into my mouth.

"Oh." She groaned, her hips lifting once more as she was getting closer.

I bit down on the hard nub, and she jolted with a sharp inhale.

"Let go, baby," I whispered, and she obeyed, letting out a scream that echoed in the room.

I looked up at her, realizing her body was still shuddering, her expression lost in a haze of sensation. She tried to speak, but the words faltered on her lips.

"I know, *mi amor,*[1]" I whispered, my voice low and reassuring. "I know."

Removing the suspenders and tossing them aside, I stood between her spread, trembling thighs. Her chest heaved, eyes half-lidded, hair tangled, arms overhead and shaking like her legs.

My cock bobbed mere inches away from the mystery I had contemplated and dreamed of for weeks.

"I- bu-" she stuttered, her eyes glancing at my hard pierced cock.

I gently brushed my hand against her face, my thumb grazing her cheek. "Words, *amor.*"

"I—well..." She paused, biting her lip, clearly struggling to find them.

"Use your words," I coaxed softly, my thumb tracing small circles on her clit, and she whimpered.

"I- um. Y-you..." She swallowed, her eyes widened as she looked down, then back at me, whispering in disbelief, "You are huge... and it's p-pierced."

For a moment, she just stared, her mouth slightly open. Then, to my surprise, a pleased grin broke out across her face, her eyes lighting up as she flung her head back. *"That's so hot."*

I raised an eyebrow, amused by the sudden shift. "Yeah?"

---

1 *my love*

I chuckled and reached my hand down to stroke her clit.

"Is it gonna fit?" she whispered.

"We'll make it fit, baby," I replied.

"I need you," she whispered, her gaze flirting over my upper body.

I let out a low chuckle, pulling back slightly. "Let me go get a condom."

Her hand shot out, gripping my wrist firmly, her eyes dark with need. "Fuck the condom," she demanded, her voice breathless but sure. "Please."

I froze for a second, searching her eyes. "Are you sure?" I asked again, my tone serious even though the desire in me was building by the millisecond.

She didn't hesitate. "No barriers," she whispered, her gaze locked on mine, filled with longing. "I want to feel all of you. *Please*, I'm sure."

Her words sent a shock of electricity through me. My breath hitched and my heart pounded as I stared at her, unable to tear my eyes away. "You have no idea what you do to me."

She bit her lip, eyes burning with hunger.

"Sh-show me," she begged, her voice soft but demanding, her fingers tightening around my wrist.

A low groan escaped my throat, and every ounce of restraint I had was gone.

Grasping her knees and pressing them wide again, I stepped closer, dropping my attention to the small distance closing between our bodies.

I waited for the span of three heartbeats. Waited for the voice to tell me to stop, but only her *"please"* rang in my ears.

The head of my cock brushed against her wetness, my pre-cum adding to the slickness easing my way in as I pressed forward, inch by slow inch, teeth grit to keep from exploding.

"Mikkel," she gasped, clinging to the sheets, her body twisting and turning.

Tight. Hot. Wet.

"Dios mío…[2]" I groaned. This was *nothing,* and I mean *nothing*, I could ever have imagined. *It was a hundred fucking times better.*

---

2 *My god*

Seated deep inside of her, I held still and inhaled a deep breath.

I could stay here forever.

"Fuck!" she squealed, as she fidgeted beneath me. "I n-need a s-s-second."

"You good, baby?" I asked. "Let me know when you want me to move."

I stayed there for about a minute, maybe a minute and thirty seconds, before she exhaled and nodded. "M-move."

I slowly pushed in deeper, eliciting a gasp from her and with each push, a gasp followed until her greedy cunt took all my cock.

"Look at your wet pussy taking all my cock," I groaned. "You take me so well, baby."

She moaned in response, the sound echoing through the room.

"Mikkel," she whispered and fuck, there was nothing I loved more than hearing my name on her lips.

I pulled back, savoring every sensation of her body gripping me, flutters hitting my chest, my heartbeat pounding in my ears, and a weakness in my knees. My attention was glued to her pussy as I withdrew to the tip, making sure the ring on my piercing gently, but effectively rubbed against her clit.

Then, I thrust back in, faster than before.

"*Mierda*,[3]" I grunted as she tightened around me, the sensation enough to drive me crazy. "This is what you wanted?"

She nodded, her eyes fluttering closed as her breath came in shallow gasps.

I cupped her face with my free hand, tilting her head so she couldn't look away. "I asked if this is what you wanted?"

She trembled beneath me, a low groan escaping. "Y-yes," she gasped, thick with need.

Propping herself up on her elbows, she looked down between us, her gaze locked on where we were aligned.

"So g-g-good," she stammered.

---

3 *Fuck*

I pulled out and thrust deep, our combined moans edging me toward losing the self-control I held onto with a loosening grip. Slamming into her over and over again, I lost my focus to the tightness gripping me—*how perfect she felt*—how I wanted to see my cum leaking from her.

"So tight," I groaned, words pouring from me unheeded.

She gasped and lay back again, arms overhead and grasping at the bed linens.

My body took over, and I abandoned my desire, grunting and cursing as my balls slapped against her ass. I gripped her knees tight, my fingers digging into her as she reached between her legs, her finger flicking her clit back and forth.

I stopped her with a low growl. "Move your hand."

She looked at me, confused. "What?"

"Move your hand, *mi reina.*[4]"

She looked at me for a second longer, then slowly shifted it. I watched, a satisfied smirk tugging at my lips. "*Buena chica.*[5] Now come for me."

Her body clamped around me like a vice and she cried out my name again, her back arching off the bed and her hair splattering all over the pillow.

"Are you okay?" I breathed as I felt my orgasm nearing.

She nodded. "Cum inside of me."

"Are you—"

"I'm sure," she repeated.

Primal. Overwhelmed with desire. Burning hot.

That was how she made me feel.

It was intense. Too much. Too damn perfect.

Before I could ask again if she was sure, she repeated, "Cum inside of me."

Without even a second to spare, my orgasm ripped up through my legs, into my spine, and rushed from my balls. I spurted deep inside of her

---

4 *my queen*

5 *Good girl*

twice and forced myself to pull out, needing to mark her—see my cum on her. Another two spurts shot over her clit and lips as a strangled groan escaped me, tremors ripping through my body.

Her legs once again shuddered in my hold as her pussy contracted, dripping my cum from her.

This was living.

This was satisfaction.

I lay on my back, the soft sheets tangled around our legs, my chest rising and falling as I caught my breath.

Turning my head to the side, I found her eyes in the dim light.

She smiled, a slow, satisfied curve of her lips. "T-That was everything," she said, her fingers tracing random patterns on my chest.

I reached up to brush a braid from her face, tucking it behind her ear. "I don't think I'll ever be able to not fuck you." I paused, trying to catch my breath. "You're perfect, *mi amor*."

Her smile widened, and she nestled closer, her warmth seeping into my skin. "Thank you." Her breath was a soft caress against my neck. "I've never felt so much pleasure or comfort during sex. I came like three times."

"Five," I corrected. "Once on my fingers, once on my tongue and three times on my cock, baby. We'll double the digits next time."

"Oh gosh," she whispered, her cheeks flushing. "I'm in a daze."

We lay there for a moment, my arm wrapped around her as I pulled her closer and after a few minutes, I shifted slightly, planting a gentle kiss on her forehead before slipping out of bed. "Stay right there," I whispered. "I'll get you some stuff, then clean you up."

Her laugh was light, almost teasing. "You spoil me," she said, watching me as I moved across the room.

I threw a grin over my shoulder. "You deserve it, *cariño*,[6]" I replied, disappearing into the kitchen.

I returned with water, Lay's, and berries, setting them down before climbing into bed. She took the glass, eyes locked on mine as she sipped.

---

6 *sweetheart*

"You know," she said after a moment, placing the glass on the bedside table, "I can't move my legs. They're sore."

I sat up, slid my hands beneath her, and lifted her into my arms. Her legs instinctively wrapped around my waist as she mumbled a sleepy protest, "What are you doing?"

"A warm water bath," I replied, heading toward the bathroom.

"Let me walk," she insisted. "I'm heavy."

"You're my warm-up weight," I teased, earning a soft laugh from her as I stepped into the bathroom.

The tub quickly filled with warm water as I added bath salts, then gently lowered her in. She sighed, leaning back against the edge, letting the water soothe her aches.

I knelt beside her, hands working over her shoulders and arms, then down to her thighs, legs and back. She groaned softly, her eyes fluttering shut.

"How aren't you worn out?"

"I am," I admitted, leaning in to press a kiss to her damp forehead. "But I have to make sure you're okay first."

"Come inside with me," she murmured, her tired smile dissolving my resistance.

I stepped into the tub, the warm water wrapping around us as she nestled into my chest.

Her fingers traced my arm as she tilted her head, meeting my gaze. "Promise me something."

"Hm?"

"Promise me you'll never leave."

Her words hit deep, and I cupped her face, brushing my thumb over her cheek. "They'd have to kill me to keep me away from you."

PART 2

This part depicts events occurring TEN WEEKS LATER, following the epilogue of *After Hours,* book one of the series, to maintain consistency with the timelines and avoid repetition of events.

CHAPTER THIRTY-SIX

Abigail-Ann

"The strongest love is the love that can demonstrate its fragility."
~ Paulo Coelho

The past ten weeks have been… Well, let's get to the rundown. Work, home and therapy remained the usual routine, and I was happy with it. I graduated, thankfully. Top of my program with a 3.9 GPA. That moment had been surreal, made even better because my boyfriend, my mother, and my sister were in the audience. Dad couldn't make it—he was performing open-heart surgery on a patient, but I knew he was proud.

Before that joy came sorrow. Aunty Leann's sudden passing hit hard, leaving a deep void. During that difficult time, I was there for Azzy—late-night calls, getting her new books, constant company, and little notes to remind her she was loved and never alone. Then, as if fate decided it was time for brighter days, Dillon proposed, and not long after, they shared the wonderful news that she was pregnant with twins. Seeing her face light up as she shared her happiness was everything.

As for me, I had finished my apprenticeship applications, though I hadn't had much time to think about them. Mikkel had us everywhere, celebrating my graduation and his ongoing expansions. Elephants in Thailand, the pyramids in Giza, snorkeling in Tobago Cays, The Pitons in Saint Lucia, hiking the Blue Mountains in Jamaica, and visiting Hoyo Azul in the Dominican Republic. We'd had sex on more surfaces than I could count, and I wasn't even sorry about it.

The Dominican Republic had been a welcome escape from the city and the highlight of our trip. Mikkel flew us out on his jet, casually remarking, "The best place to experience a farmers' market is in the Caribbean." *And, of course, he was right.*

Sunny's Green Haven was breathtaking. Vibrant flowers, sweet fruits, and fresh herbs perfumed the air. Stalls overflowed with homemade jams, handcrafted jewelry, warm baked goods, and irresistible local cheeses. I checked off both *explore a farmers' market* and *visit somewhere new* from my bucket list, and under the golden Caribbean sun, it was unforgettable.

We briefly met Mikkel's cousins, but their backhanded comments rubbed me the wrong way. I almost snapped, but Mikkel suggested we leave.

And Mikkel... oh, Mikkel. He had been—*and still is*—the best person in my life. *The love of my life.* He cared about me in ways that constantly left me speechless. He talked me through everything, no matter how small or big it had felt to me. Flowers? Always. Chocolate cake and Chipotle whenever I wanted? Of course. Nothing ever stopped him from making sure I had my heart's desires.

Beyond that, he was actively working on himself, making a real effort to manage his anger. I recognized the tells—the tight set of his jaw, the slight twitch of his fingers—but he handled them differently now. He squeezed his stress ball, wrote (which was surprisingly wholesome to see), confided in me instead of bottling things up, and stepped away when work became overwhelming. It wasn't easy, but he was trying. And that? Meant everything.

He made it easy for me to be a woman. I never had to pick up the pieces if I couldn't because he was always there with his arms open. I didn't have to prove myself or mask my strength with softness. I never had to beg to be loved wholly, and I never noticed who didn't clap because his applause always drowned out everyone else's.

When he looked at me, it was as if he saw every part of me without hesitation. He never once asked me to be anything other than who I was, which made me feel more like a woman than anything else ever had.

One night, when my anxiety had me feeling so weak I couldn't stand without thinking I might fall, he held me close and sang every song from Lana's *Born to Die* album. The circumstances were far from perfect—he'd just returned from his Singapore work trip, and I felt guilty for dragging him into my chaos. But his voice, filled with heart and love, made everything feel like it was exactly what I needed.

Adjusting to his prominence came with its challenges. I never imagined I'd walk through Times Square and see Mikkel's face towering above, the headline bold: *Elite Rides Expands—Meet the Man Behind the Multi-Billion Dollar Empire.*

I let it sink in—the weight of his success, the eyes drawn to him. Pride swelled in my chest, and that night, we celebrated in every way possible.

My mom, however, found it hilarious, joking, "You're dating the Dominican Denzel Washington!"

She adored Mikkel. Every FaceTime felt like a chat between old friends—she'd ask about him, how he was doing, and when he'd visit. Honestly, I think she loved him more than me, and I was perfectly fine with that. Seeing her welcome him so warmly made me happy.

As for his parents, I had a few nerve-wracking FaceTimes with them. We hadn't met in person yet, but their happiness for him put me at ease. His mom even sent me the sweetest daily Spanish prayers, which I started saving.

Oh, and speaking of Spanish, I'd been using Duolingo more often. At this point, I was basically fluent or at least that's what the green bird kept telling me. Sometimes I'd thought it was just trying to get me to level up faster to escape my endless attempts at pronunciation. But hey, if it didn't, I'd just blame it on the bird, right?

It had been a whirlwind—a chaotic, messy, beautiful whirlwind. And I wouldn't change a thing.

I took a deep breath and stepped out of the salon, feeling like a brand-new woman. After ten long hours, my 30-inch boho faux locs were finally done, and I couldn't be happier with how they turned out. Mikkel had stayed with me for the first five hours before leaving for a meeting, but as expected, his pristine white Range Rover was parked at the curb, gleaming under the streetlights. Technically, it was mine—a graduation gift from him—but I rarely drove it. Being his passenger princess was just too tempting.

I slid into the car, barely settling before he pulled me close for a kiss—warm, full of love, making everything else fade away.

When he pulled back, he looked at me in awe, his eyes wide. "You look absolutely breathtaking," he gushed, his voice full of admiration. "I mean, seriously, this is… wow. You've always been beautiful, but this?" He shook his head, his smile growing. "*Me estás matando*, Red.[1]"

"You always know just what to say," I said in response, and he just kissed me.

Before I could even say I was hungry, he handed me a Chipotle bowl with chips and queso—like he'd read my mind. Then, to my surprise, he pulled out a box of cookies in different flavors for us to try. We sat in the car, tasting and laughing at our favorites, until we hit a flavor so bad that neither of us could stomach it.

"Some things we can definitely live without," he grimaced.

I playfully slapped his hand. *"Mikkel."*

"Am I wrong?"

"Nope."

"I've had better things in my mouth," he added, his tone teasing.

"Interesting. Like what?" I challenged, arching an eyebrow.

"Your pussy," he said without hesitation.

---

1 *You're killing me, Red*

I couldn't believe he just said that. *"Mikkel Suarez."*

He chuckled softly. "It's true."

I tried to keep my composure, but the way he looked at me made it impossible not to blush. "You're dirty."

"A luxury reserved just for you, *mi reina.*[2]"

I caught Mikkel's gaze as he looked at me, his eyes softer than usual, filled with a tenderness that made my heart flutter.

"You've got that look," I said, teasing but with a hint of curiosity.

He stared, drinking me in, then slowly reached over, two fingers guiding my face closer.

"I'm just admiring how your beautiful soul shines through you, making you glow with happiness, baby."

The words lingered, sinking in as he kissed me—soft and fleeting. I sat there, thoughts swirling. It was the most beautiful thing I'd ever heard.

He wasn't finished, though. His voice was a little hushed as he spoke again.

"Seeing you like this is a reward for living, a reason for breathing. It's inexplicable, but it's everything. And it's something I'd die for, because it just makes the world make sense."

I blinked, overwhelmed by him. "I'm so glad I'm here with you."

He leaned in and kissed me softly. "*Eres mi todo.*[3] Always will be."

His phone then buzzed on the dashboard, vibrating incessantly, and he groaned as he reached for it, glancing at the screen.

"It's my Mamá,[4]" he said, his expression softening as he swiped to answer the FaceTime.

"Mi hijo, ¿cómo estás?[5]" Her voice was warm and her smile evident even through the screen.

"I'm good, Mamá. How are you and Papa?"

---

2 *my queen*

3 *You are my everything*

4 *Mom*

5 *My son, how are you?*

"We're fine, busy as usual. And Abigail? How is she?"

Mikkel turned the phone toward me, his hand resting on my thigh. "She's right here."

"Hi, Mrs. Suarez." I waved awkwardly, smiling as her face lit up.

"Abigail, it's so nice to see you! *Estás radiante,*[6]" she said warmly.

I laughed softly. "Thank you. It's nice to see you, too."

She looked back at Mikkel. "We're coming to New York at the end of month."

Oh.

He blinked, caught off guard. "Actually?"

"Yes," she confirmed. "Once we book the flight, I'll send you and Emmy the details."

"Don't book a flight, I'll have the jet ready instead," he promised, running a hand through his hair.

"Lovely. We'll see you both soon. *Nos vemos pronto.*"[7]

"Goodnight," I managed, my smile polite as the call ended.

As soon as the screen went dark, the realization of her announcement settled over me.

They're coming at the end of this month.

"Are you okay?" His voice was gentle as he rubbed my thigh.

"Meeting your parents in person for the first time." I exhaled, twisting my fingers nervously. "It's a big deal."

He shifted closer, his warmth steadying me. "You've talked to them before and they already love you."

"It's different now," I admitted. "What if I s—"

He cut me off, his hand tilting my chin, so I could look into his eyes. "They're going to love you, Abigail," he assured me. "And if they don't, you're mine, not theirs."

A small laugh escaped me despite my nerves. "That's not how it works, Mikkel."

---

6 *You are glowing*

7 *See you both soon*

"It is for me." His smile was so confident, so sure, I felt a little steadier. "I'm always going to be sure of you, Red. *Siempre*."[8]

I nodded, leaning into him. "Okay."

---

8 *Always*

WARNING

The following chapter contains heavy mentions of mental health/physical health issues. Please refer to the content warning list to be reminded of any potential triggers. Your well-being is important to me, so please take care of yourself while reading.

CHAPTER THIRTY-SEVEN

Abigail-Ann

"There is no charm equal to tenderness of heart."
~ Jane Austen

The night I met Joshua's parents, I was seventeen and stupidly in love. I thought it mattered that he picked me up from classes every day, that he held my hand in the halls, that he called me 'his girl' like the title meant something.

But then I walked into their house.

His mother barely looked up from her phone before her eyes landed on my hair, her lips twisting in disapproval. "Red hair. So bright and untamed. It's not dyed, is it?"

"It is dyed, ma'am," I said, my voice small, shoulders shrinking under her stare.

Joshua had smiled nervously beside me, like he wasn't sure if he should laugh or agree. His father was worse—his sharp glance slid down to the floral sundress I'd picked out because Joshua loved it.

"Girls these days don't believe in modesty, do they?" he said.

My face burned as his mom chimed in, "It's a bit much, isn't it? Showing that much skin. Not exactly ladylike."

I shot a glance at Joshua, hoping he'd say something. Hoping he'd defend me. But all he did was shrug. "I told her it might be too short."

The room felt like it was spinning.

"She's got potential, though," his mom said, like I was some kind of project she could fix. "Maybe tone down the bold choices. The hair, the clothes. It's a bit distracting."

I bit my tongue so hard I tasted blood. They didn't know who I was. They didn't want to know.

And neither did Joshua, apparently.

That night, I cried into my pillow while Joshua's silence echoed louder than their words ever could.

I blinked away the memory, my eyes fixed on the neutral walls of Dr. Green's office. The soft tick of a clock somewhere behind me, and the perfectly arranged couch I was perched on felt too perfect, *too quiet.*

"I don't know why meeting Mikkel's parents freaks me out," I blurted. My hands twisted in my lap as I avoided Dr. Green's gaze. "I've talked to them on the phone a few times, and they seem great."

"But?" she asked gently, her pen poised over her notebook.

I let out a shaky breath. "I'm terrified."

The words felt too loud in the quiet room.

Dr. Green didn't rush me or fill the silence, which only made my chest tighten even more.

"It's just…I've been here before," I finally admitted. "Meeting the parents, hoping they'll like me, only to feel like I'm not good enough. Like I'll never be good enough. And what if…" I trail off, unable to finish the thought.

"Things go the way it did with Joshua?"

I flinched, even though I brought it up. "Yeah."

"Abigail." Dr. Green's voice was gentle but firm. "You've shared a lot about your relationship with Joshua—how it shaped the way you see yourself and still influences your expectations. And we've also talked about Mikkel. From everything you've told me, he's shown you, through his actions, that he's different in many ways."

I nodded because she was right. I *knew* she was right. Mikkel wasn't Joshua. But sometimes, my past felt too heavy to shake.

"What if I'm just too much for them?" I whispered.

She leaned forward slightly, her eyes kind. "What if you aren't?"

"I don't know," I whispered. "It feels like I've always been too much. Too loud, too bold, too me. I'm scared they'll see it the same way… and that it'll matter."

Dr. Green tilted her head slightly. "Do you think Mikkel would let anyone else's opinions about you dictate how he feels?"

"No," I admitted, though the word came out hesitant. "But—"

"But you've been deeply hurt before, and that hurt is causing your anxiety and self-doubt to overshadow everything?"

I nodded, the lump in my throat too big to speak.

She sat her pen down. "The past has a way of whispering lies about the present. Meeting Mikkel's parents will be a new experience, one that doesn't have to look anything like your past. And if there's anything you need, you know you're not alone in facing it. You've got Mikkel now."

Her words comforted me, even though fear still lingered beneath the surface.

We wrapped up the session with a grounding exercise—simple, practical, and exactly what I needed. She encouraged me to keep reading my self-help books and practicing grounding techniques whenever anxiety crept in. By the time I left her office, I felt a little lighter as I headed to work.

If nothing else, I was grateful for the store's quiet. A few patrons browsed, soft music played, and there was no chaos. I busied myself at the circulation desk, scanning returns and restocking carts—routine work that let my thoughts slow down.

My phone rang midway through my shift, and when I saw Mikkel's name, I glanced at my coworker, who gave me a knowing smile and waved me off.

"Hey, *hermosa*,[1]" he greeted, his voice warm despite the bustle I could hear in the background. "The conference is dragging a bit, but I'm just checking in."

"I'm okay," I said, smiling. He'd been texting me throughout the day—little summaries of his meetings, random observations, and even a photo of the Hartford skyline from the venue. "How's everything going?"

"Productive but boring. Wish I was with you, though." His voice softened on the last part, and I felt a warmth bloom in my chest.

"I wish I was with you too."

He sighed. "I have to oversee a pitch in five minutes. I'll call again later, okay?"

"Okay."

The call brought me peace. While restocking, I spotted a romance novel Azzy mentioned, grabbed the series, and bought them with my discount before my shift ended.

Me

I hope your pitch went well.

Always proud of you, handsome ❤

"Abi!" Azzy greeted me with her usual warmth when she opened the door, her hand resting protectively on her small bump.

"Hey," I grinned as I held up the books. "I brought you something."

Her eyes lit up as she took them from me. "You are my soulmate. Thank you."

---

1 *Beautiful*

"You're welcome." I nudged her playfully. "How's the wedding planning going?"

She groaned dramatically, letting her head fall back against the cushions. "Exciting but stressful. Dillon's been helping too, but there's just so much to do."

I chuckled. "You're doing great, Azzy. Everything will work out."

"Thank you." Her eyes softened as she looked at me. "I always thought I'd be doing this with my mom by my side. It's just… hard without her, sometimes."

"I can't imagine how much you miss her, but what I do know is that she's watching over you every step of the way."

Azzy nodded, blinking back tears. "I just miss her, that's all. Anyway…"

"How are you and Dillon handling the pregnancy?" I asked, changing the subject gently.

She chuckled. "Dillon's at a whole different level of excitement and protectiveness. He's been unstoppable. He upgraded our mattress and pillows to ones he found to be better for pregnant women and won't let me lift a finger, which I'm perfectly fine with."

"I'm glad you have him. I've never seen you happier."

She nodded, her eyes soft. "I've never seen me happier either, but enough about me. How are you? How's everything with Mikkel?"

"It's good," I said quickly, then sighed. "I'm nervous about meeting his parents. You know how that went the last time."

Azzy frowned, reaching over to squeeze my hand. "It's understandable to feel this way, because no matter what happens, the past will resurface. I know you're in your head, thinking you're a bad person for letting this affect you, even though you've moved on. But no matter how much time has passed, certain events will trigger emotions and thoughts, pulling you back to that moment, even if just for a second. Just take it one step at a time. You'll get through this, and if you need me, I'm here."

I let out a quiet laugh, shaking my head. "You really do know me so well."

Azzy smiled, then moved to pull me into a tight hug. "Almost two decades of friendship, Abi. We're basically married."

I was truly blessed to have a best friend like her. Even if we didn't talk every day or got caught up in our own lives, we were always there for each other when it mattered most, and our bond never changed.

We talked a bit longer, but I could feel my anxiety starting to creep up again. "I'm gonna head out," I said with a sigh. "I'm really tired."

Her face softened, and she wrapped me in a tight hug. "Take care, Abi. You know I'm always here for you."

"Thanks, Azzy," I whispered, returning the hug. "I'm here for you, too."

With a final wave, I headed home. A quick shower did little to wash away the lingering unease, so I grabbed *The Gifts of Imperfection* and my peach weighted blanket before settling into bed. As I flipped through the pages, I marveled at the notes Mikkel had left in the margins.

It still amazed me how far he'd gone to support my mental health—twenty weighted blankets, a mood-switch octopus, and fully annotated self-help books.

I skimmed a page where he had written: *You're enough just as you are. You don't need to prove anything to anyone.*

Another note read: *You are not a failure because you struggle. You are a success because you keep going.*

My phone buzzed with a FaceTime call from Mikkel.

Perfect timing.

"Hey," he said, his voice soothing. "Someone's coming in the next hour to bring dinner for you."

I just realized I hadn't eaten all day. "Thank you for always thinking of me."

"You never have to thank me for that," he replied, adjusting his glasses. "What's wrong?"

"Hm?"

"You're wrapped in your weighted blanket which means you're anxious," he pointed out. "What's wrong, *amor*? Was it something that happened in therapy?"

I sighed. "I feel like I'm suffocating."

"We'll work through this together," he said gently. "Put your feet flat on the floor and take a deep breath with me." I did as he suggested, closing my eyes and breathing in time with him.

"Good, keep going," he encouraged as we continued for about seven minutes, but the feeling never left, if anything, it got worse.

I let out a shaky breath. "I don't know, Mikkel. I just… feel off."

He listened patiently, his tone calm. "That's okay. It's okay to feel off because you're human. It also doesn't make you any less of a person. What's going through your mind, Red?"

I hesitated, not wanting to burden him. "Just the usual stuff. Old habits, old fears."

"I understand," he said softly. "But remember, we're breaking those old patterns together. You're not and you never were defined by them, baby."

I took a deep breath, feeling his words settle over me.

"I'm right here with you, helping you through it, Red."

My eyes burned with unshed tears. "Thank you for always being here."

"*Siempre*,[2]" he replied, his voice reassuring. "I'm here to remind you that you're enough, that you're not defined by your past, and you're stronger than you think."

"I was reading the book you gave me…" I trailed off, unsure of what I wanted to say or where I was going with it. All I knew was that having him here—making his presence known despite being hours away—meant everything to me.

"Which one of them?"

"*The Gifts of Imperfection.*"

"There's a section about embracing imperfections and accepting who you are instead of striving for perfection. It's fitting." His voice softened. "You're perfect as you are, flaws and all, Red."

His assistant's voice broke in from the background. "Mr. Suarez, they're starti-"

---

2 *Always*

Mikkel looked around, then said, "I'm busy. All the mingling has to wait until I'm done. Understood?"

"Yes, sir," I heard Morison say before I heard the door shut.

"Mikkel—" I started.

"No," he interrupted. "You need me. I'm hours away, and if I have to miss a few minutes of the conference to make sure you feel even one percent better, then so be it. You *always* come first."

We stayed on the phone for a while longer, Mikkel helping me through the unease by talking about the book, doing more grounding techniques, and reassuring me that it's okay not to have everything figured out.

"Text me or call me if you need anything at all," he insisted.

I smiled, feeling grateful. "Thank you for tonight."

"Everything for you, *amor*,[3]" he replied softly. "*Always*."

Switching the phone off, I settled in to watch *Say Anything* until dinner came, which was Chinese, and sleep called to me before it took over.

---

3 love

CHAPTER THIRTY-EIGHT

Mikkel

"Love is not only something you feel, it is something you do."
~ David Wilkerson

Here's the latest report, sir," Sapphire said, sliding a thick folder across my desk.

I exhaled, rubbing a hand over my face. Exhaustion clung to me after back-to-back flights to Chicago, Seattle, Miami and Connecticut. But more than the travel, what really got to me was being away from Abigail, especially when I knew she needed me. Her anxiety had been high, and I wasn't there to hold her, to ground her.

Shaking off the frustration, I flipped through the pages, scanning figures, deadlines, and client updates. Everything looked in order, until I reached the section marked *Seattle Acquisition.*

"The Seattle acquisition is becoming a bit tricky," she continued, tapping the folder lightly with her pen. "There are some unexpected complications with local zoning laws. We might face delays."

My grip tightened on the edge of the desk, the words causing a knot to form in my stomach. Seattle. Of all the damn things to go wrong.

I wasn't sure if it was the sound of her voice or the way the report laid out the issue so simply, but I felt my blood pressure rise. I was already aware of the stakes here—Seattle was crucial for our expansion, and delays would push everything back by months, maybe even years. I took a deep breath, resisting the urge to snap.

I reached into the drawer to pull out my stress ball. Squeezing it tight, I repeated the words in my head like a mantra: *There's nothing to explode over. I'll fix it.*

I let out a slow breath, focusing on my palm against the squishy rubber.

In. Out. In. Out.

I could feel the tension leaving my body, the anger starting to fade. Slowly, the fiery storm in my chest turned to something more manageable. I could think. I could act.

"Alright." I met Sapphire's gaze again. "Let's break this down."

She nodded, and I motioned toward the door. "Call Antonio in—we'll need his expertise for this meeting."

He handled acquisitions and zoning, expertly navigating the red tape that could make or break a deal.

As she stepped out to get him, I refocused on the papers in front of me. Another problem, another challenge. *Fuck me.*

When they returned, we dove into the details. With both of their expertise combined, we made steady progress. Each issue we tackled brought us closer to a solution. No rushing, no rash decisions—just methodical work. Slowly but surely, the problem took shape into something solvable.

By the end of the three-hour meeting, Antonio left, and what once seemed like an obstacle was now just a minor task. I leaned back, letting the satisfaction settle—until a knock at the door pulled me from my thoughts.

Morison peeked in. "Mr. Suarez, someone's here to see you."

Before I could ask who, the door swung open, and Abigail walked in, arms full with a bag and a wide smile. Her locs looked richer, deepened in color like fire-kissed mahogany, and damn, she looked amazing.

Gah, my girlfriend is beautiful. Too beautiful. Every time I see her, it hits me like the first time—like I've been starving for her, and now she's finally within reach.

I cleared my throat, trying—and failing—to regain my composure as Sapphire stood up to leave.

"Sapphire," I began, "this is my—"

"Future wife."

Abigail stepped forward and finished my sentence as if she already knew—like our future was certain, like there was no other path but us.

And God help me, I think my brain just stopped working.

The idea of someone else having my last name never intrigued me until I met her.

Sapphire's brows lifted in pleasant surprise, glancing between us. "Very nice to meet you. I'm the operations manager."

"It's nice to meet you too," Abigail responded with a friendly nod, completely unfazed.

Sapphire noted briskly, "I'll have Morison prepare the final document, sir," before turning on her heel and exiting the office.

As soon as the door clicked shut, Abigail turned to me, eyes sparkling. "Hey," she greeted, walking further inside and placing the bag on my desk. "I missed you."

A grin broke across my face as I stood up, my entire body humming with warmth. I moved around my desk, closing the space between us. "Hello, future wife," I drawled.

She melted into my arms before pulling away slightly, eyes bright. "I brought something for you."

With a concentrated look, she dug into the bag and pulled out three containers of food, carefully placing them on the desk.

"What's all this?" I asked, brow lifting.

"Lunch." A shy smile graced her lips, soft and so damn sweet. "I cooked for you."

My heart slammed against my ribs, warmth blooming through my chest. My Red—*my heart*—had cooked for me.

I reached for the containers, lifting them close, and the second the rich, familiar scents hit me, something deep in me tightened. It smelled like home.

"Wait." My eyes widened in surprise, recognition washing over me. "Is this Sancocho, tostones, and Pollo Guisado?"

She nodded enthusiastically, her smile stretching wide, pleased. Proud. "Yes, but the taste may vary. I used recipes I found from *Allrecipes*."

I set the containers down, cupped her face, and kissed her—slow and deep—pulling her close. She did this for me. Thought of me. Went out of her way to make something she knew would mean the world to me.

I pulled back just enough to whisper, "I really appreciate this. You're amazing, and you put so much thought into it."

Her fingers curled against my chest. "I hope you like it," she murmured, voice soft, almost uncertain. But this wasn't just about the food. It was the effort, the love she poured into it. The fact that she made Dominican dishes for me meant everything. I knew from watching my mother prepare them just how much work, patience, and care went into each one.

"You have no idea how much you've brightened my day, Red."

I pulled out the nearest chair and sat down, already digging in. The sancocho was perfectly tender, the flavors deep and rich. It had a kick, spicier than I was used to, but it still tasted like home. The tostones were crisped to perfection, and the pollo guisado? Unreal.

I took another bite, closing my eyes briefly, savoring every bit. Then I glanced up at her, a teasing smirk curling at my lips.

"What do I have to do to get a plate of these per day?"

Excitement beamed across her face. "Exist."

I'm doomed.

I reached out, running my hand through her hair, then stilled. "You changed the color?"

A small, knowing smile tugged at her lips. "I mixed the copper platinum with burgundy. Didn't think you'd notice."

I let out a slow breath, my eyes dragging over her, drinking her in. "I noticed the second you walked in." My voice dropped, rougher now. "I always notice you."

Her blush deepened, her fingers twitching at her side like she wanted to reach for me. Like she was holding herself back. And fuck, that made me want her more.

"How's work?" she asked, her voice softer now, like she felt it too.

I told her about the acquisition, about how close I'd come to losing my patience, about the hours of negotiations that had me this close to snapping. And she just listened—eyes locked on mine, soaking up every word.

When I finished, she reached up, brushing her fingers along my jaw, her touch featherlight. "I'm proud of you, Mikkel," she whispered. "Not just for what you're doing, but for how you're handling things."

Something in me broke.

I swallowed, my throat tight, my chest burning with something I couldn't name—something too big, too consuming. I needed her closer, needed to feel her against me.

I cradled her face in my hands, letting my thumbs trace the curve of her jaw, my forehead pressing against hers. "You make me want to be better," I admitted, my voice raw. "You make me—" I exhaled sharply, shaking my head. Fuck. "You have no idea what you do to me, Red."

Her breath hitched, fingers tightening around my wrist. She didn't answer with words, but the way she melted into my touch said it all.

Smiling, heart full, I kissed her forehead, grateful for the calm she brought to my chaos. After a little more conversation, I took her to her nail appointment, hoping to beat traffic and make it back for my budget meeting.

I wiped the sweat from my forehead and set the dumbbell back on the rack. The gym was quieter than usual, the hum of treadmills and clinking weights forming a steady rhythm. I took a deep breath, savoring the brief pause before my next set.

The budget meeting went smoothly. The Astar's contract was on track, Chicago's expansion was progressing, and Miami's was underway. Seattle's acquisition was being redrafted, while we explored transport markets in Africa and Europe. Client satisfaction remained high, though supply chain delays continued to slow our fleet. To counter this, we were actively streamlining operations and securing alternative suppliers.

As I caught my breath, my phone buzzed in my pocket. It was Abigail.

"*Amor*?[1]" I greeted, glancing at the gym clock. She was probably just about done with her nails..

"Mikkel Suarez, you are *truly* something else."

"What happened?"

She chuckled softly. "I went to pay for my nails, but Kody told me you'd already covered this set and the future ones."

"I don't see the need for you to spend your own money when I exist."

Her laugh was sweet, like the gentle clink of a champagne glass. "You know you spoil me?"

"I'm very aware, and besides, you're too beautiful to be spending your money," I said, leaning back on the treadmill. "Send me a picture so I can see how they look?"

"I will," she promised.

I nodded, checking the time. "I'll come see you after my workout."

"Alright, baby."

Just as I hung up and reached for my water bottle, the gym door swung open, and in walked Arnoldo with a stupid smirk plastered on his face.

"You're here, *cabrón*,[2]" I called out, a grin spreading across my face.

Arnoldo rolled his eyes at my comment and made his way over, cutting through the rows of equipment like a knife through butter.

---

1 *Love?*

2 *asshole*

"Never thought I'd see you here, being in love and all," he joked, giving my shoulder a friendly thump.

"You can try it out sometime?" I urged. "Being in love, I mean."

His expressions fell and all of a sudden, nothing was funny.

"What's the plan today?" he asked, ignoring my questions while flexing his arms.

"Arm day," I replied with a mock grimace.

He groaned dramatically. "Torture as always."

I shrugged, trying to hide my smirk. "Get to work, Reyes."

He grabbed dumbbells and started his warm-up. "What are we wearing to Dillon's wedding?"

"You mean the wedding that is almost a year away?"

"Yes, Suarez, *that* wedding."

"Azzaria has very strict dress codes but aren't we groomsmen?" I replied, slightly bemused. "I'd assume it's a tux."

¿Quién será el padrino?[3]

"No idea, Reyes. I doubt there will be a best man, but I heard Bryce wants the role since he's known Dillon the longest."

Arnoldo hissed, nearly tipping over the loose gear. "Dillon's a better man than me. Bryce would've found out I was getting married from a tabloid."

"Let's switch topics before you turn as red as a tomato, Reyes."

We pushed through our workout in uncomfortable silence, focusing on sets and reps. By the time we finished, my muscles were burning, but I knew I'd accomplished something.

As we packed up and headed for the door, Arnoldo broke the silence. "Same time next week?"

"We'll see."

He clapped me on the back. "Alright, man, I'm gonna grab a smoothie. *¿Vienes?*"[4]

---

3 *Who will be the best man?*

4 *Coming?*

"*Sí.*"[5]

We took the elevator to the café. I grabbed a green smoothie for myself, a berry smoothie for Abigail, and Arnoldo grabbed a triple-nut protein shake.

As we walked out, I noticed Arnoldo had been unusually quiet—he was never like this. "You've been off today. *¿Estás bien?*"[6]

He took a slow sip of his shake. "A lot on my mind. Nothing to worry about."

I raised an eyebrow. "That doesn't sound like nothing."

He shrugged, glancing away. "Nothing a good night's rest can't fix."

I didn't press him further, just gave him a nod. "If you need to talk, I'm here."

He let out a soft sigh, then gave me a half-smile. "I know, man. Appreciate it."

After a brief silence, I got in the car, stopped by the florist for fresh flowers, and headed to Abigail's apartment. Her smile lifted my spirits the moment she opened the door, but the shadow in her eyes hit me hard.

"These are for you, baby." I handed her the smoothie and the flowers.

"Thank you," she murmured, placing them on the counter. "The flowers are beautiful."

I caught a glimpse of her nails as she reached for the smoothie. Gently, I took her free hand in mine. "French tips with diamonds?" I smirked. "They're beautiful."

Her cheeks warmed as she smiled. "You really notice everything."

"Hard not to when it's you," I said, brushing a kiss over her knuckles.

I kicked off my shoes and settled on the couch. "Bedroom," she said, and I got up to follow, closing the door behind us.

She collapsed onto the bed, her hair fanning out across the sheets, and her white tank top rode up slightly, revealing her perfectly striped stomach.

"What's wrong?"

Releasing a heavy sigh, she muttered, "I just feel bleh."

---

5 *Yes.*

6 *Are you okay?*

"Anything happened after you left my office?" I prodded gently.

Shaking her head, she replied, "No."

Moving to the bottom of the bed, I began massaging her feet, hoping to alleviate some of her tension.

"Anything bothering you?" I pressed softly.

She sighed again, a mixture of frustration and resignation evident in the sound.

"You know you can talk to me about anything, right?" I reassured her, my fingers gently kneading her tired muscles.

She nodded, her eyes meeting mine with a hint of vulnerability. "I know," she whispered. "That foot rub also feels so good."

Feeling her tension beneath my fingertips, I gently squeezed her leg. "Is it about my parents coming to visit?"

Her eyes widened in surprise as if I'd just unraveled her innermost thoughts. "How did you know?"

"Because I know you, Red." I traced circles on her sole with my thumb. "Because I see you."

"I'm just so anxious," she whispered. "We've spoken over the phone, but meeting in person is different. What if the—"

"Hey," I interrupted gently, tilting her chin up to meet my gaze. "You're amazing, and my parents will adore you. And even if they don't, it won't change how I feel about you."

"But what if they think I'm too young or—"

I cupped her face, wiping away a tear. "What we have is real, *mi reina*,[7]" I said softly. "That's what matters."

She took a shaky breath, her eyes clouded with worry. "But what if I'm not…"

I could feel her insecurities, the way they clung to her like a shadow, and it broke my heart to see her doubt herself this way. "You're *more than* good enough," I reassured her. "You don't need to prove anything, especially to my parents."

"I just don't want to let you down."

---

7 *my queen*

I shook my head, caressing her cheek. "You could *never* disappoint me. I see how hard this is, but you're perfect as you are. You bring more happiness into my life than I ever imagined."

She blinked back tears, her vulnerability clear.

I pulled her close, feeling her tremble. "There's nothing to mess up, baby. Even if things don't go perfectly, it won't change us. I'm here, and I'm not leaving. We'll face it together, like we always do."

She clung to me, her grip tight as if she was afraid to let go. "Thank you for always getting me out of my head. I don't know what I'd do without you."

"You'll never have to find out." I pressed a kiss to the top of her head. "Because I'm right here with you."

She nodded against my chest, her breathing gradually slowing. "Okay."

"No 'what ifs,'" I stated firmly, wiping away her tears with my thumb. "*Tú y yo, contra el mundo.*[8]"

Her lips trembled as she searched my eyes, seeking reassurance. "Against everything."

I pressed my lips to hers in a tender kiss, pouring all the love and devotion I felt for her into that single moment.

"You're my love, Red," I whispered against her lips. "And I'll always be here with you no matter what."

---

8 *You and me against the world*

WARNING

The following chapter contains heavy mentions of mental health/physical health issues. Please refer to the content warning list to be reminded of any potential triggers. Your well-being is important to me, so please take care of yourself while reading.

CHAPTER THIRTY-NINE

Abigail-Ann

"Being deeply loved by someone gives you strength, while loving someone deeply gives you courage."
~ Lao Tzu

The only thing I hated more than having anxiety was how crippling and debilitating it was.

A tear slipped down my cheek, soaking into the pillow beneath me. I didn't bother wiping it away.

It was just me and the silence. Me and the thoughts that wouldn't stop clawing at me.

I couldn't take it anymore.

The storm in my head was too loud, my chest too tight, and I felt like I was drowning. My pulse hammered in my ears, so fast it felt impossible to catch up.

I turned toward Mikkel, my voice barely a whisper. "Mikkel."

He didn't stir. I swallowed hard, my heart racing, and shook his arm lightly. "Mikkel," I tried again, a little louder this time, my voice breaking.

His brow furrowed as he shifted, still half in a deep sleep.

"I can't breathe," I said, my words spilling out. "I can't—Mikkel, I can't stop thinking—"

His eyes snapped open, and he jolted upright like I'd pulled him from the depths of a dream. "Red?" he said, his voice low and rough with sleep as he reached for his glasses on the nightstand. He shoved them on quickly, blinking at me in the dim light. "What's wrong, baby?"

Tears burned my eyes as I struggled to get the words out. "I can't," I choked, my voice shaking. "I can't… I can't breathe."

"I'm here with you." His voice softened into something calm and steady. He moved closer to me, careful but determined. "Let's do this together, okay? Can you trust me for a minute?"

I nodded weakly, my breath still shallow, my hands gripping the blanket tightly.

"Alright," he said gently. "We're going to try something. Follow my lead, *mi amor.*[1]"

He rubbed his hands along mine, grounding me for just a second before he spoke again. "Tell me three things you can see."

I blinked at him, my mind still racing.

"Three things," he said softly. "Anything. Just look around and tell me."

My eyes darted across the room. "The… the lamp. Your glasses. The pillows."

"Good," he said, his voice a soothing balm. "Tell me three things you can hear."

"Your breathing," I whispered. "The ceiling fan. And…" I hesitated, closing my eyes. "Your voice."

Mikkel nodded, brushing a thumb over the back of my hand. "Perfect. Now move three body parts. Can you do that for me?"

---

1 *my love*

I swallowed and nodded, flexing my fingers, rolling my shoulders, and wiggling my toes beneath the blanket.

"You're doing so well, Red." Relief softened his face. "Can you breathe with me now? In for four, hold for four, out for four."

I matched his pace as he counted, his tone calm. My chest was still tight, but breathing came easier. I clung to his hand, grounding myself.

When the worst of the storm passed, my breath steadied, and exhaustion settled in, my shoulders sinking with relief.

"Feeling better?" Mikkel asked softly, brushing the back of his fingers against my cheek.

I nodded, unable to say much more than, "A little."

"Do you want to go sit by the window?" he offered. "Get some air?"

I shook my head immediately. "I just want to stay here."

"Okay," he said quickly. "That's okay."

He sat up against the headboard, pulled me close, and pressed a lingering kiss to my head as he spoke. "I'm right here with you, and we'll do whatever you need."

I closed my eyes, focusing on the sound of his heartbeat beneath my ear, but Mikkel wasn't done yet. He rubbed circles into my back, whispering soft reassurances: *I was safe, it would pass, and he wasn't going anywhere.*

When that didn't fully calm me, he gently placed my hand on his chest. "Feel that? I'm breathing with you, baby. We'll take it one breath at a time."

When my shoulders tensed again, he murmured, "Wanna hear a story? Something to distract you?"

I nodded faintly against him.

He started sharing memories from his childhood in the Dominican Republic—climbing mango trees with Emilia and sneaking bites of *habichuelas guisadas* or *buñuelos* when their parents weren't looking.

"Did you get caught?"

He chuckled, the sound vibrating through me. "Never. We played it cool, but deep down, we thought they knew."

The storm hadn't disappeared completely, but Mikkel held me steady as the waves crashed. He didn't let me drown. He *never* let me drown.

As I finally started to drift off, Mikkel pressed another kiss to my hair and whispered, "I'm proud of you, baby. *So proud.* You're gonna be okay." We stayed there for a moment longer, just breathing together, until my eyelids grew heavy.

The next morning, I checked the clock and saw it was past twelve. I hadn't realized I'd slept so late. Panic crept in, but then I remembered it was my day off. I relaxed back into the pillow, letting the tension melt away. That's when I noticed a note on the nightstand.

I had to leave early for a meeting. Call me when you're awake.

Love, Mikkel.

I called, but he said he'd call back soon since his meeting wasn't over yet. After a deep breath, I got up, brushed my teeth, prayed, and threw on one of his shirts before heading to the kitchen for leftovers.

I cleared the counters—tossing the wilted flowers and putting away the dishes. Whenever anxiety crept in, I used the *four-four-four* breathing method Mikkel showed me, and it worked wonders.

By the time I was done, my head felt clearer, and the knot in my chest had loosened. I called my family to catch up, then spent twenty minutes on Duolingo, though I was pretty sure the bird was judging me.

When the session ended, I checked my phone and saw new messages from Mikkel.

S
Hey baby. The meeting just ended.

How are you feeling?

Me
So much better. I can't thank you enough for all you do.

S
You never have to thank me. I'm always here.

I'm picking you up at five.

Me
I know better than to ask where we're going, so I'll see you then.

S
Good girl. ♥

God, what am I gonna do with this man?

Five o'clock came, and I knew it was Mikkel when I heard the knock at the door.

I sauntered over in black boyfriend jeans and a yellow crop top with HOT stitched across the center.

I swung the door open, and there he was. His cologne wrapped around me like a slow embrace. Honey-brown eyes behind black glasses, perfectly straight white teeth, and lips that made my knees weak.

He held a bouquet of the most stunning yellow and white primroses, a thoughtful gesture that never failed to touch my heart.

"Gonna let me in, Red?"

I blinked, realizing I'd been standing there, staring.

I stepped aside quickly. "Sorry… I spaced."

He handed me the flowers, his fingers brushing mine, and warmth spread through my chest.

"Thank you," I murmured. "The last set you got me wilted, so I threw them out today."

"I know," he said casually.

"How?"

"Every time I buy you flowers, I keep a few at home to know when to replace yours."

My breath hitched.

He wasn't just giving me flowers—he was keeping track, making sure I always had fresh ones. The ones in his kitchen weren't just decoration. *They were for me.*

I stared at him, my heart pressing against my ribs. "You… do that for me?"

He shrugged, a hint of pink dusting his cheeks. "Flowers make you happy, and your happiness matters to me."

I reached up, cupping his face, struggling to find the words. But what could I even say? How could I possibly articulate the way he made me feel?

His hands slid to my waist, pulling me closer, his voice husky. "Todo para ti, *nena.*[2]"

Then he kissed me. And God, *God*, did he kiss me.

It wasn't rushed, wasn't desperate—it was slow, deep, devastating. Like he was trying to say everything without words. Like he needed me to feel it, to understand what I meant to him.

My fingers tangled in his curls, knees weak as his lips brushed mine again and again. When he pulled away, breath unsteady, his grip remained firm.

"And your outfit?" he whispered. "*It's hot.* You're gorgeous."

A slow smile curled my lips. "Wait till you see what's under it."

His jaw tensed. "What's under it?"

"Nothing," I whispered, turning away to gather my hair into a bun.

A sharp inhale. A groan. A second of silence.

Then his hand was around my throat, firm but careful, tilting my head back until my lips were inches from his.

I gasped, fingers gripping his wrist. His eyes darkened, molten with heat.

"You say things like that," he rasped, "and expect me to walk away?"

His thumb brushed over my pulse, feeling how erratic it had become, how much I wanted this.

Then he kissed me again—harder, deeper. Like he needed to. Like he was two seconds from losing control.

---

2 *Everything for you, baby*

I whimpered against his lips, my fingers tightening around his wrist, and his hold flexed, just for a second, before he groaned and let me go, stepping back like it physically pained him.

"Let's go before I forget where I'm supposed to be taking you." His voice was rough, strained.

Smirking, I grabbed my bag.

By six, we were out the door, and by seven, we arrived at our date spot. Mikkel stepped away for a moment, stirring my curiosity.

When he returned, he opened my car door, his jaw still tight. "Come on."

Intrigue buzzed through me as I followed him inside, then stopped short.

A pottery studio.

"I thought we could take a class tonight."

My jaw dropped.

Romantic. Thoughtful. Perfect.

And this man? He was going to ruin me.

"You are incredible," I gasped, touched by his thoughtfulness.

He nodded, his smile widening. "Number eight on your bucket list."

A delighted laugh bubbled out of me as I threw my arms around him, overcome with gratitude and something even deeper—something I wasn't quite ready to name.

The instructor greeted us with a warm smile, her apron speckled with colorful splotches of clay. "Welcome! I'm Sierra, and I'll be guiding your lesson tonight."

Mikkel and I exchanged excited glances as she led us to our designated pottery wheels. The studio was bathed in soft light, the steady hum of spinning wheels and the faint, earthy aroma of clay surrounding us.

"First things first," Sierra began, her voice animated. "Let's get our hands dirty! Grab a block of clay and start centering it on the wheel."

Mikkel flashed me a wicked grin. "You ready to get your hands dirty, Red?"

I chuckled, catching his teasing tone. "In more ways than one."

Sierra laughed. "That's the spirit! Pottery is all about letting go and embracing the imperfections."

Mikkel's attempt at shaping a bowl turned into something resembling a lopsided muffin.

"I may have created a new art form," he mused. "Good thing business is my strong suit."

Sierra winked at him, which made something tighten in my stomach. I brushed it off, not wanting to ruin the moment over something so insignificant.

"Picasso had his blue period," she said, "so I wouldn't worry too much."

The class wrapped up with Sierra guiding us through the final steps of finishing and glazing our pieces. By the end of the night, we each had something to take home—mine was a bowl, his… a *very* abstract vase.

"Thank you both for coming," she said warmly as we gathered our work.

"Thank you for having us!" I exclaimed, my heart still buzzing from the experience.

With our pottery "masterpieces" packed up, we walked to the car, and Mikkel turned to me with a grin.

"Did you have fun?"

A mini squeal slipped out before I could stop it. "I loved it! I can't wait for our next art class." I paused, catching my breath. "Thank God it was just us three; I'd have been nervous with others."

He smirked. "Figured. That's why I rented the whole studio."

My steps faltered. "You *what*?"

Mikkel chuckled, lacing his fingers through mine. "I wanted tonight to be perfect for you, Red."

A flurry of nerves swarmed me.

Still riding the high of his thoughtfulness, we stopped at a nearby Shake Shack for burgers and milkshakes, replaying the best parts of the night.

Then, just as I was about to take another sip of my shake, Mikkel spoke.

"Also," he said, his voice steady, "I've never met the instructor before."

I blinked. "Huh?"

"Arnoldo recommended the studio," he explained. "I secured the space, but that's the first time I've ever seen her."

I frowned slightly, confused. "I'm… not following."

His honey-brown eyes flicked to mine. "When she winked at me, your grip tightened on the wheel, and you rolled your eyes."

My breath hitched. "You saw that?"

His lips curled at the corner. "While you were looking at the wheel, I was looking at *you*." His voice dropped, deep and deliberate. "*I'm always looking at you.* But I wanted to address it because I know you'll let it eat at you, and I don't want that to happen."

I swallowed, my throat suddenly tight. "Mikkel…"

He reached across the table, tucking a loc behind my ear, his fingers lingering against my skin.

"You don't have to say anything, baby." His voice softened. "I just need you to feel secure."

The way he knew me, how he anticipated the things I wouldn't even voice, left me undone.

I leaned in, pressing a soft kiss to his lips, letting it linger.

"You're everything to me, Mikkel."

His thumb brushed over my cheek, catching a tear I hadn't realized had fallen. His eyes never left mine, his expression raw, *unguarded.*

"You're my infinity."

Mikkel had made himself comfortable on my couch, lounging back in just his boxers like he belonged here, like he knew exactly what he was doing to me.

Cocky. Relaxed. Looking every bit the man who owned the moment.

But I wasn't going to let him have the upper hand tonight.

I changed into pajama shorts and a sports bra before coming back, watching his gaze drag down my body, slow and heated.

I settled beside him, fingers dancing over his arm, tracing the ink curling over his muscles. Barely touching. Just enough to tease.

"I'm amazed every time I see them," I murmured, dragging my nails lightly along his bicep.

Mikkel's fingers flexed on his thigh, his breathing slowing. "They all mean something. A time, a place…a decision."

My hand trailed lower, skimming the deep ridges of his stomach, stopping just before his waistband. I glanced up, watching the way his jaw clenched, the muscle there ticking.

"And this one?" I whispered, dragging my fingertips over a design near his ribs.

His abs tensed under my touch, his voice rough. "That's a story for another time."

A slow smile curved my lips.

I wasn't looking for stories tonight.

I let my fingers wander lower, dragging along the deep ridges of his stomach. Barely brushing the band of his boxers.

His breath hitched.

I smirked, then slid off the couch and settled onto my knees between his legs.

Mikkel's entire body went rigid.

His hands fisted at his sides, his jaw clenching so hard a vein popped in his neck.

"Red," he rasped, his voice already wrecked.

I ignored him, pressing my lips against the outline of his cock—barely touching, just enough to tease—then pulling back like nothing happened.

A full-body shudder wracked through him. His abs clenched, his thighs tensed so hard they trembled.

"Oh," I cooed, tilting my head up at him, "you liked that?"

His fingers flexed, fighting the urge to grab me, to force me closer. To make me stop teasing and just fucking touch him.

"Baby," he groaned, his voice low and strained, like he was physically in pain. "*Please.*"

I pouted. "Please what?"

Mikkel's thighs twitched, his cock throbbing visibly through his boxers, and I could hear the breath he sucked in through his teeth.

"Take it out," he groaned out, his hips lifting slightly, chasing the ghost of my touch.

I giggled.

His hands twitched violently, his control hanging by a thread. "Abigail," he warned, his voice breaking.

I let my fingers dance along the waistband of his boxers, *slow, lazy, maddening*, watching as his entire body locked up.

"I don't know," I teased, my lips ghosting over him again, the heat of my breath making his cock jump. "You're being very impatient, Mikkel."

His head dropped back against the couch, muscles pulled so tight he looked like he might snap.

"*Mierda*,[3]" he gritted, his fingers digging into his thighs so hard his knuckles went white.

Then, soft, desperate, ruined. "Baby. Please."

My stomach fluttered, because fuck, I loved seeing him like this—wrecked, desperate just for me.

I ran my tongue along the thick outline of him again—slow, deliberate, just the barest pressure—and his full-body jolted.

"Ah, fuck," he whimpered, his breath stuttering out.

His hips lifted, involuntary, desperate, chasing the heat of my mouth.

I pulled back again.

And he groaned, loud, tortured, head falling forward as he throbbed visibly in his boxers, body coiled tight, aching.

I traced him so softly it was barely a touch, just the tips of my nails dragging over the swollen length of him, and his entire body shuddered.

"You're shaking," I whispered, my voice sweet, taunting.

Mikkel let out a strangled, wrecked groan, thighs tensing around me, chest rising and falling like he just ran a fucking marathon.

"Red," he panted, his voice so hoarse it barely made a sound.

---

3 *Fuck*

Then, half Spanish, half broken breath. "*Por favor, mi amor. No puedo más.*"[4]

My smirk deepened, thrill rushing through me, because finally, *finally* I had him where I wanted him.

"Yeah?" I mused, trailing my tongue along his waistband, feeling his cock twitch violently beneath me.

His whole body twitched.

"Yeah," he choked, wrecked beyond recognition, trembling under my hands.

I hooked my fingers under the band of his boxers.

Mikkel held his breath, his entire body going still, bracing for it.

Then, finally, I pulled them down—slow, torturous, letting him feel every single second of relief creeping in.

And when my mouth finally touched him, Mikkel let out a guttural, broken groan. His head snapped forward, fingers tangling in my hair like he never intended to let me go."How'd you get it?" My fingers traced over the piercing, feeling his body tense beneath my touch.

Mikkel's breathing hitched. "I don't really wanna talk about that when you're…" He paused. "Fuck, baby."

"When?" I squeezed harder, my hand moving with deliberate slowness. I wanted to hear him say it.

He exhaled. *"Abigail."*

"Use your words, love," I teased as I stroked from the base of his shaft to the head, letting my thumb tease the piercing again, watching his eyes darken with lust. "When I'm doing what?"

"Baby," he whispered, his voice breathless. "When you're about to suck my cock."

"See? Wasn't that easy?" My closed lips experienced the heat that was radiating from his cock, the wetness from the tip, and the pulsing from the head. I parted my lips and felt the perfect sensation of his tip slipping between them.

The metal felt so good, *so different*, on my tongue.

---

4 *Please, my love. I can't do it anymore*

"*Joder*, Red[5]," he moaned and grabbed a fist full of my hair, "keep sucking my cock like that, *mi reina.*[6]"

His praises only pushed me further and I kept gliding my tongue over the head. I traced the ridge with my tongue, sucking easily on the head, while still jerking his dick with my hand.

Continuing for a moment, I let my lips follow my hands until reaching the base, releasing it as I focused on sucking harder before pulling away.

I dragged my tongue along the underside of his cock, and then massaged the head, hard, causing him to let out a groan of pleasure.

"Fuck," he muttered and tightened his fist. "I love feeling my cock down your throat, baby."

I pushed my head forward a couple of times and grinded his cock into my throat. As I snuck my tongue out, licking his balls, I heard him scream a trail of curse words and let out a very audible moan.

His sounds of pleasure, combined with the fact that sucking him off turned me on more than almost anything else, made me start to squirm. Unable to resist, I snuck a hand into my shorts, and feeling the immense wetness and heat, I was compelled to give my pussy a long stroke.

I settled into an easy routine, sucking in quickly and deeply, each time deepthroating him, as I stroked my clit and so my orgasm washed me.

He gently pushed me off, firm enough to take control but careful not to hurt me. Taking my hand, he led me to the bedroom, undressing me until only my bra remained. Lying down, he motioned for me to straddle his face, then guided me back down, silently instructing me to continue.

I submitted, happily, and started to ease back into the blowjob, but the second his tongue connected with my pussy, it was over. My thoughts vaporized. I got closer to gagging on each stroke, somehow seeming to take his cock deeper.

"Spin around," he commanded and I took his cock from my mouth, turning around to straddle him.

---

5 *Fuck, Red*

6 *my queen*

Before speaking, his hands explored me, tracing every inch. He kissed, caressed, and marked my skin, his grip firm, his touch possessive. I was lost in him—*lost in bliss.*

"Ride me, baby," he rasped, "I wanna feel your tight, wet cunt on my cock."

His accent was ten times stronger than normal and that alone was bound to make me cum again. With weakened knees, I slowly lifted my body, as he aligned himself with my entrance and I slid down on his cock, feeling fuller than the last time we fucked.

"Oh fuck," I whispered.

Slowly, I started grinding my pussy down on his dick, getting deeper as he unfastened my bra and tossed it to the side of the room.

"Te gusta cuando mi polla está dentro de ti, ¿verdad?[7]" he groaned.

"Huh?" I asked, breathlessly.

"You like when my cock is deep inside you, don't you?"

I chuckled, fixing my angle and leaning over his mouth for him to bite my nipples while I rode him. He placed one hand on my other breast, while his other hand squeezed and caressed my ass before spanking me, urging me to ride him faster. I lifted myself until only the pierced head remained inside me, then came down hard, feeling him fill me completely as I moved against him.

"Do that again," he instructed, pinching my nipple and slapping my ass.

Without wasting any time I continued riding until both of our bodies got tossed up into strong, intense orgasms. My orgasm was so strong, that I plopped right beside him, trying, *and failing*, to catch my breath.

"It was a dare," he whispered in between breaths.

"What?"

He brought my hand down to his cock. "The piercing."

"Who dared you?"

"Arnoldo," he responded. "Almost six years ago."

---

7 *You like when my cock is deep inside you, don't you?*

"That's intense," I responded, which came out as more of a question.

"I got my payback," he said and nuzzled into my neck. "Are you okay?"

"Better than ever, baby."

Pulling me into a hug, he mumbled, *"Eres asombrosa, mi dulce mujer.*[8]*"*

My mind was too scrambled to process his words, but by the time he finished caressing me, planting soft kisses, and whispering sweet nothings, I drifted off to sleep.

---

8 *You are amazing, my sweet woman*

CHAPTER FORTY

Abigail-Ann

"The very essence of romance is uncertainty."
~ Oscar Wilde

The moment we stepped into The Shops & Restaurants at Hudson Yard*s*, I exhaled.

"Mikkel, you *really* didn't have to do this," I muttered, my voice soft but insistent.

He shot me a look that was part amusement, part determination. "I insist, *amor*. Besides, we're already here." His hand, warm and steady, slipped into mine, and with that simple gesture, any argument I had left dissolved.

I glanced at my outfit: white sneakers, dark skinny jeans, and a yellow sweater—casual yet cute. Meanwhile, Mikkel looked like he'd just stepped out of a goddamn *GQ* spread. A white turtleneck stretched over his broad shoulders, tucked into dark gray jeans that sat on his hips like they'd been tailored just for him. *He was the only man who could make a turtleneck look devastatingly sexy.*

We barely made it past the first few stores before the press swarmed us—flashes, voices, questions flying in rapid succession. About him. About his company. About me.

Mikkel barely flinched. His grip on my hand tightened, thumb brushing over my skin in quiet reassurance as we moved through them, his presence a shield against the chaos.

Soon, we entered Tory Burch, and it was far more beautiful than the ones I've been to. The bags and shoes were displayed like art pieces, but the price tags made me hesitate. Mikkel moved through the store with ease, while I stayed behind, running my fingers over a pair of slippers here and there but never committing to anything.

I wasn't used to *taking*. To being given without strings attached. It felt too indulgent, too much.

We moved from Dior to Fendi, then Sephora, Rudsak, Stuart Weitzman, and Kate Spade, the pattern repeating each time. Whenever he caught my eye, I offered a small smile and shook my head, silently telling him I didn't need anything. The clothes, the shoes, the bags, the makeup—everything was gorgeous, but I couldn't bring myself to say, *Yes, I want this.*

Then we stepped into Piaget.

The jeweler's face practically lit up when he saw Mikkel. "Mr. Suarez," he greeted, beaming. "I didn't know you were coming. You didn't make an appointment."

Mikkel flashed his charming smile. "It wasn't planned, Ross. I just decided to take my love shopping today."

His words made my heart melt, but I still felt uneasy. My fingers tightened around his arm as I glanced around, trying to ground myself.

"Right this way," Ross announced, guiding us to a gleaming glass case. With a practiced hand, he slid it open, revealing a delicate diamond-encrusted rose gold bracelet that glittered like stars and a bold, masculine watch with a black band. Both were breathtaking.

"Mikkel…" I whispered, lightly tugging his sleeve.

His eyes softened, and without hesitation, he picked up the bracelet. "Try it on, baby." His voice was low but insistent. "It'll look beautiful on you."

I opened my mouth to protest, but he was already slipping it onto my wrist. It felt cool and surprisingly light against my skin, and I couldn't get over the way the diamonds caught the store's light in ways I hadn't thought possible.

"Do you like it?"

"I don't need it."

He chuckled, slipping his other hand around my waist. "I asked if you liked it."

I nodded, unable to form the words.

He leaned in, his breath warm against my ear. "It's settled then."

My heart fluttered at his words and I nodded once more. "Alright."

He picked up the watch we viewed earlier. "And I'll take this one for myself."

Ross beamed. "An excellent selection, Mr. Suarez."

"Mikkel Sua–" I began, but he silenced me with a swift kiss.

"Let me take care of you," he whispered, leaving no room for argument.

Then the jeweler typed in the total—*$150,589.25*—and I damn near stopped breathing.

My stomach churned at the number, but Mikkel handed over his card without hesitation, completely unfazed. Within moments, Ross had the items neatly boxed in green velvet and passed them to him.

"It's always a pleasure, Mr. Suarez," Ross said and then turned to me, "Very lovely to meet you, *bellissima*[1]."

"Likewise," I whispered, offering a smile though I was in a bit of shock.

Mikkel smiled. "Take care, Ross."

With the bags in hand, we stepped back onto the bustling walkway. The luxury of it all still clung to me as we strolled through a few more

---

1 *beautiful*

stores, each one filled with beautiful things I admired but had no intention of getting. Then, as we reached Coach, a black wristlet in the display window made me pause.

"You like it?" Mikkel's voice came from behind me.

I bit my lip and nodded, my fingers grazing the smooth leather. "I want it."

"Then it's yours, baby."

Mikkel flashed that heart–melting smile and handed it to the sales associate. "We'll take this."

"Just the wristlet, or the set with the matching handbag and crossbody?"

I froze, caught off guard. "The set?" I glanced at Mikkel.

He nodded slightly, his gaze unwavering. "The set," he confirmed, his tone leaving no room for debate.

I opened my mouth to protest, but the look in his eyes silenced me. There was no arguing when he was this determined to spoil me.

The associate smiled. "Will that be all, Mr. Suarez?"

"Yes," Mikkel replied smoothly, pulling out his card.

"Your total is three thousand dollars," the associate said, typing on the register.

Three *thousand* dollars for the set and almost sixty *thousand* dollars for the bracelet.

This was making me lightheaded.

"*Mi amor*." He turned to face me with warm eyes. "Get out of your head, you're worth it."

I bit the inside of my cheek at his words. *Worth*. I didn't know how to respond. Doubt crept in as past memories resurfaced. I'd spent so long convincing myself I didn't deserve even the smallest gestures of kindness that now, receiving so much generosity, felt jarring. Not because of him, but because of me—*because of my past.*

As we stepped out of the store, I glanced at the bags in his hand, emotions swirling within me.

"That's all you wanted?" Mikkel asked, his voice light but edged with concern.

I nodded, meeting his gaze. "This is more than enough."

He studied me for a moment, head tilting slightly. "Are you sure? I haven't seen you pick much."

"I don't need much," I admitted with a soft smile. "Besides, what about you? You haven't bought anything except the watch."

"Today isn't about me." His chuckle was warm as he rested a hand against the small of my back, guiding me toward the next set of stores. "It's about you."

I sighed, rolling my eyes playfully. "You are something else, Mr. Suarez."

"I'm fine being anything as long as it's with you, Ms. Asher."

Smiling, I kissed him softly before we wandered toward Mercado Little Spain. The air was thick with the aroma of grilled meat and spices, wrapping around us like a warm embrace. After ordering loaded barbecue chicken tacos for myself and birria tacos for Mikkel, we settled at a small window table.

Just as I was about to take a bite, his phone buzzed, stealing his attention.

"Who is it?" I asked, my curiosity piqued.

"Morison," he replied, glancing at the screen.

My brow furrowed slightly. "Everything okay at the office?"

He nodded, but I could see the wheels turning in his head.

"He just reminded me about the big meeting we have later," he said before taking a bite of his taco, his expression contemplative.

"The investors, right?"

"No, the Seattle acquisition." He waved it off like it was nothing, but I caught the underlying tension in his voice. "We're closing the deal today."

A proud smile tugged at my lips. "I'm proud of you. You're doing amazing, and I know the meeting will go great. Just promise me you won't overwork yourself."

His gaze softened as he reached over, placing his hand over mine. "Thank you, *mi amor,* and I won't. I have it under control."

After we finished eating, he took my hand, guiding me through the bustling food court and out to the car. The ride back was quiet, comfortable in a way that needed no words. Before I knew it, we were outside my apartment, and a wave of disappointment settled over me. I wished we could spend the rest of the day curled up on the sofa, lost in each other, but responsibility called.

"I'll see you later?"

"Of course. I'll be back after the meeting," he assured me, running a hand through my hair. His gaze held a promise, one that sent butterflies fluttering in my stomach.

"Drive safe and have a good meeting."

"Always." He leaned down, pressing a lingering kiss to my lips before pulling away and heading to his car.

I sighed, stepping inside and plopping onto the sofa. My gaze drifted to the shopping bags beside me, but instead of unpacking them, I got up to start laundry, Lana playing softly in the background. I thought about texting him but didn't want to disturb him. As the day stretched on, exhaustion crept in, and before I knew it, I was curled up on the sofa, drifting into sleep.

A sudden knock at the door startled me awake. I blinked, disoriented, the apartment now bathed in the dim hues of evening.

Fuck, it was almost seven p.m.

Rubbing my eyes, I got up, wondering if I'd imagined it. But as I opened the door, my heart warmed instantly.

Mikkel stood there, looking as handsome as ever, his hair slightly tousled as if he'd come straight from his meeting. In his hands were several shopping bags, leaving me both intrigued and confused.

"Why do you have so many bags?" I asked, still feeling disoriented from sleep.

"I went back to the mall after my meeting."

I looked up sharply at him. "Why?"

He shifted the bags to one arm and reached out, his palm cupping my cheek. "To get everything you touched or intensely stared at earlier."

I stood there for a moment, dumbfounded. "Y-you actually went back?"

"I did." His expression was so damn sincere it made my chest ache. He placed the bags on the coffee table then turned back to me. "I saw how much you liked them, and I couldn't leave them behind. I know it's hard for you to say 'yes' to things, and I *never* want you to feel like you can't have what you want."

My heart raced as I grabbed a bag and pulled it open, only to gasp at the sight of the stunning black Dior tote from their newest line, emblazoned with *MISS DIOR.*

I barely had time to process it before Mikkel stepped closer. "If you want something, it's yours. I'll always make it happen."

I swallowed, struggling to find my voice. "I don't want to be the kind of person who just takes from you, though."

He shook his head, and closed the space between us, his hand finding my waist. His voice dropped lower, rich with certainty. "Do you know what turns me on?" His fingers traced a slow path down my arm, his touch light but commanding. "Seeing you happy. Watching your eyes light up when you find something you love. Knowing that my money is being spent on you."

A shiver ran down my spine, not just from his words but the way he said them—like this was fact, undeniable, irrefutable.

"Thanks for always getting me out of my head," I whispered.

His lips brushed my forehead. "You never have to thank me."

I exhaled, my heart lighter now. "I can't believe you bought everything I touched."

His smirk was nothing short of devastating. "I doubt I missed a thing, but let's check."

I grabbed the tote bag again, marveling at its beauty.

"Saw you eyeing this and thought it'd go perfectly with your red leather dress," he murmured, watching me with quiet satisfaction.

"What leather dress?"

"The mini one, with the splits at the side."

My head jerked up. *How the hell did he remember that?*

Before I could question it, he handed me another bag and I pulled out a fine silver bracelet from Cartier, adorned with tiny charms—a flower, an airplane, a heart, a book, a tassel, and the letter A.

A lump formed in my throat. "Mikkel, this is beautiful."

"I want you to think of where you are in life every time you wear it," he said, his voice gentler now. "And how much you've grown from everything you've been through."

Words fell short, so I kissed him, pouring all my love and gratitude into it.

Among the other surprises were a Fendi bag, a Kate Spade wristlet, a Rudsak jacket, Stuart Weitzman heels, Fenty and Huda Beauty lip products, and Lululemon leggings.

He was right; this was everything I touched or looked at today. Hell, it was everything I wanted but would never ask for.

He couldn't possibly get any dreamier.

I looked up at him, and he brushed his thumb across my lips.

"The way your eyes widened when you saw these, and the faint smile that followed, told me you wanted them," he said. "I can't wait to see how amazing you'll look in them."

I swallowed hard, overwhelmed. "I don't do half as much for you. I– I just don't."

His gaze softened, and he took my hands in his, his grip firm. "You don't have to earn your place in my life, *mi reina*.[2]" His voice was absolute. "You already have it."

My tears were threatening to spill over. "Thank you for everything."

Mikkel's thumb moved gently across my cheek, his expression soft, unreadable.

And then, just as I was about to ask what was on his mind, he spoke, his voice quieter now. More certain.

"I know this might be random, but… would you move in with me?" He exhaled, his gaze never leaving mine. "Not now. But eventually."

---

2 *my queen*

The question stopped me in my tracks, my mind scrambling to process his words. Move in? With him?

I hesitated—not from doubt, but because this was monumental. Living together meant more than sharing space; it meant intertwining lives.

"Would you really want to live with me?"

His gaze held steady, dark and resolute. "Nothing compares to waking up beside you every morning and coming home to you every night."

"I would," I admitted softly, then bit my lip. "But if we were to move in, we'd need to split responsibilities."

His head tilted slightly, brow furrowing in confusion. "Split responsibilities?"

"What are your thoughts on fifty-fifty?" I asked, my nerves buzzing beneath my skin.

For a moment, he looked at me—assessing, considering. Then his lips curved into a slow, knowing smirk.

"The only fifty-fifty I'm interested in is giving you my last name one day very soon…" He leaned in, his breath warm against my ear. "And hearing you scream my first when you're coming all over my cock, fingers, or tongue."

Heat *flashed* through me, stealing the air from my lungs. My face burned, and I looked away, struggling to compose myself.

"I'm *serious*, Mikkel," I murmured, though I couldn't stop the small, betraying smile that tugged at my lips.

"So am I." His tone was softer now but no less intent, no less real.

I swallowed against the sudden sting of tears, overwhelmed by the depth of his love and devotion. He wasn't just saying what I wanted to hear—he meant it. *Every word.*

"Let's talk about it later," I finally said, my voice wavering but steady enough to let him know I wasn't brushing him off.

His expression didn't change. If anything, it softened even more. "Of course, *mi amor.*[3] Whenever you're ready."

---

3 *my love*

Because Mikkel wasn't just patient.

He knew how to love me in a way I was still learning to accept.

I sat at my vanity, finally taking a break after three hours of unpacking which had somehow turned into a full closet reorganization. When I grew too tired, Mikkel had stepped in, folding and hanging the rest of my clothes without hesitation.

"Baby," he called from the closet. "Do you want the jeans on hangers too?"

I laughed, still in disbelief. "No, just fold them."

"Okay."

His voice was so casual, as if him stepping in to do this for me was the most natural thing in the world. I exhaled, turning my attention back to the lip products—lipsticks, glosses, lip liners—unpacking them one by one. My fingers brushed over the sleek tubes, pausing.

I *hated* swatching shades on my skin.

I swiped a soft mauve across my hand, regretting it immediately as it clung like a stubborn stain.

Before I could spiral, warm hands grounded me. I met Mikkel's steady gaze in the mirror, my racing thoughts slowing.

"What's wrong?"

I bit my lip, hesitating before sighing. "I'm gonna need to get testers at Ulta tomorrow."

His brow lifted slightly, a knowing smile tugging at his lips. "You don't need to do that."

Confused, I turned to him. "You know I hate swatching on my skin."

His arms slid around my waist, fingers grazing my hips as he leaned in. "Use something else."

"Like what?"

The slow smile that curved his lips sent a flutter through my chest. He took the tube from my fingers, his touch lingering before he tapped his cheek with two fingers.

"Me."

I blinked at him, expecting a teasing smirk, but he was completely serious.

"Right here, *mi reina.*[4]"

I let out a startled laugh. "Are you serious?"

He nodded, unfazed. "Since you don't like swatching on your skin, use my face."

"But the kiss marks, Mikkel."

His fingers tucked a curl behind my ear, his voice steady. "You're just testing the pigment, *correcto*?[5]"

"Yes, but—"

"Exactly. So use my face."

I stared at him, completely thrown. "People would see you walking around with ki—"

"Let them."

My breath hitched. He said it so simply like it was the most obvious thing in the world. But the weight of those words slammed into me. He *wanted* them to see.

To be loved was to be loved out loud.

My heart squeezed as I stared up at him. "You're serious."

His expression softened, his voice a deep, steady rumble as he cupped my chin. "I don't care who sees it. The whole universe knows I'm yours, Abigail."

Something in my chest cracked wide open.

"If you say so," I murmured, trying to hold back the emotion swelling in my throat.

---

4 *my love*

5 *right?*

I reached for a deep red lipstick, twisting it up before pressing my lips to his cheek. The creamy pigment transferred easily, staining his warm skin. His breath ghosted against my neck, making me linger a second longer than necessary.

When I pulled back, I half expected him to tease me. But instead, his fingers brushed over the mark, his tone dropping into a husky rasp.

"You missed a spot."

Before I could process that, his hand cupped my face, pulling me in until our lips met in a kiss that was slow and deliberate.

When he finally pulled away, his grin was downright mischievous. "Let's see how the other shades look."

I laughed, shaking my head. "I don't think I'll ever get used to you."

His nose brushed against mine, his breath warm as he murmured, "We have all the time in the world. And I don't look too bad, I love my lipstick-testing side."

I rolled my eyes. "You don't have a lipstick-testing side."

He smirked, rubbing a finger over the kiss mark. "I do now, *mi reina.*"

"Mikkel…." My voice wavered, the overwhelming tenderness creeping in before I could stop it.

He shrugged, as if he wasn't completely wrecking me. "If it means letting you test all those colors, plus more, then I'm happy to have that side."

I exhaled a soft, breathy laugh. "You're unbelievable."

His hands tightened around my waist, his lips grazing my temple as he whispered, "And completely yours."

CHAPTER FORTY-ONE

Abigail-Ann

"Love brings to life what is dead around us."
~ Franz Rosenzweig

I stood in the kitchen, fingers brushing the counter as I stared at the bubbling pot. The scent of sancocho filled the air but did little to calm me. My thoughts raced, stomach tight with nerves.

The week had blurred by—late nights at the bookstore, an aching back, pounding headaches, and mounting anxiety. Last night was the worst. I'd spiraled into a breakdown, biting my nails to the quick. When Mikkel came home, he didn't hesitate. He left and returned with a Sephora bag, determined to fix them. His large hands moved gently as he followed YouTube tutorials like a pro. With every quiet reassurance, he steadied my chaos. I felt ridiculous, helpless to stop my body from shutting down.

Now, the anxiety only deepened. Mikkel's parents were coming today, and the thought twisted my stomach. Memories of Joshua's parents' critiques—about my hair, body, skin tone, and clothes—rushed back. Their judgment had left scars, and those old insecurities resurfaced, suffocating me.

A sharp beep jolted me. The timer. *Right. I was cooking.*

The stove was a flurry of activity. One pot bubbled with *La Bandera*, another simmered with *pollo guisado*, and at the center was the *sancocho*. A cooling dish of *habichuelas con dulce* waited for finishing touches. It was ambitious, maybe too ambitious, but I wanted to recreate a taste of home for Mikkel and his family. Or at least something close.

The kitchen was a war zone. Chopped vegetables were scattered across the counter like casualties, and my phone was balanced precariously on a stack of napkins, playing a YouTube video. The bright-eyed woman in the tutorial had made it all look so easy, but I was sweating like I was on an episode of *Chopped*.

"Add the adobo," I muttered to myself, grabbing the container. My hands shook as I measured it out, and I ended up spilling some onto the counter. "Oh, crap…" I sighed, brushing it aside and turning back to stir the pot.

Cooking had seemed like such a great idea when I mentioned it to Mikkel earlier this week. But now, standing in the middle of this chaos, I wondered if I'd bitten off more than I could chew.

The scent of plantains frying in the pan beside me was mouthwatering, though. *At least the tostones were coming out fine.*

My gaze drifted to the clock. *They'll be here any minute.*

I quickly finished up and cleaned both the kitchen and myself before setting the table. Once the dishes were laid out, I stepped back, my heart swelling with pride.

Then as if they were timing me, I heard the elevator door open. *They're here.*

His mom's voice echoed through the penthouse before I saw her.

"Hijo![1]" she exclaimed. "Your home is gorgeous. It's so bright and elegant."

I moved quickly, smoothing my sweater as my hands trembled.

When I finally stepped into the living room, I saw them. His mother was stunning with long dark hair, honey-brown eyes, and a full figure that exuded warmth and elegance. Behind her stood his father, the spitting image of him: tall, broad-shouldered, with sharp features and those same light eyes.

Mikkel entered last, his eyes locking onto mine. A slow, proud smile spread as he crossed the room. "*Mi reina*,[2]" he murmured, leaning in to kiss my temple.

His mother's eyes lit up as she turned toward me, her warm smile melting some of the tension I'd been carrying. "And this must be the lovely Abigail."

"Yes, Mamá," Mikkel said, his voice filled with pride as he wrapped an arm around my waist. "*Esta es Abigail.*[3]"

I felt my cheeks heat as I nodded, stepping forward. "It's so nice to finally meet you, Mr. and Mrs. Suarez."

His mother clasped my hands, her smile widening. "We've heard so much about you, *mi querida*[4]. Thank you for going through all this trouble for us."

"It's no trouble at all," I said quickly, my voice soft. "I just wanted to make sure you felt at home."

His father stepped closer, his deep voice warm. "It already feels like home," he said, his eyes scanning the table filled with food. "We're grateful, and it's lovely to finally meet you, *nuera*.[5]"

Nuera? Apparently, Duolingo had missed that one.

---

1 *Son*

2 *My queen*

3 *This is Abigail*

4 *my dear*

5 *daughter-n-law*

"Also, call us Valeria and Manuel," she said gently. "We're family now, Abigail."

I nodded, their kindness easing my nerves despite expecting a more formal greeting.

"I'll let you guys settle in for a bit, and then we can eat," I suggested as I glanced over at the table.

"That sounds perfect, *cariño*,[6]" Valeria agreed, her smile never fading as she pulled me into a brief but warm hug. "*Gracias de nuevo.*[7]"

Mikkel nodded, slipping an arm around his mother's shoulder. "I'll show them to their room," he said, glancing back at me. "Be right back, baby."

When he returned moments later, he grounded me with a gentle touch, cupping my face and brushing his thumbs over my cheekbones. "You're thinking," he observed softly.

I sighed. "Well, yeah…"

He shook his head. "I know you feel like the walls are closing in, but I promise you everything will be fine."

I pouted, unable to hide my unease, and tipped up to kiss him softly. As I pulled away, he whispered, "It's all in your head, baby."

I rested my forehead against his, letting his words calm me. "I've got you, *amor*," he murmured, and the tension melted away. "*Te tengo.*[8]"

Valeria took a deep breath, her eyes lighting up with approval. "The food smells wonderful."

Manuel nodded with a soft smile, glancing at me. "*Parece delicioso.*[9]"

I smiled shyly, feeling a bit proud. "I hope you like it," I replied, trying not to let my nerves show.

---

6 *sweetheart*

7 *Thank you again*

8 *I've got you*

9 *Looks delicious*

Valeria's smile grew wider. "I'm sure we will."

As Mikkel took the serving utensils from me with a smile, he said, "Let me take care of this, baby," plating my food with practiced ease before handing it to me with a reassuring nod.

Manuel leaned forward with a broad smile. "I'm sure I've said it before, but we do appreciate you cooking for us, *nuera*.[10]"

I really needed to translate that word.

Valeria took a bite, her eyes lighting up with delight. She smiled at me. "I'd be happy to teach you more of our recipes before we leave, Abigail," she said warmly. "But it looks like you've already got the hang of it. *Está delicioso*.[11]"

"I'd love that," I replied sincerely, feeling my nerves ease. "Thank you."

Just then, the conversation shifted, and I noticed Valeria glance over at Mikkel with a sharp, almost knowing look.

"I remember seeing your graduation pictures, and they were beautiful, by the way. What's next for you in terms of your career now that you've gotten your degree?"

"I'm planning to start my real estate apprenticeship next year," I explained, "but until then, I'm working in a bookstore."

The moment I finished speaking, I felt a rush of insecurity. The smile on Valeria's face seemed genuine, but I couldn't shake the nagging fear that my answer wasn't enough.

I could see the slight shift in her expression as she processed my words. It wasn't a negative reaction, but I scrutinized every subtle nuance of her response, searching for any sign of judgment or disappointment.

What if my responses didn't meet their expectations?

What if they saw my job as a sign of indecision or lack of ambition?

The questions swirled in my mind, making it hard to focus on the conversation at hand.

Valeria's smile widened, and she *finally* responded with genuine interest. "That's wonderful, Abigail. It sounds like you're on a great path."

---

10 *daughter-in-law*

11 *This is delicious*

"Thank you." My voice steadied as I met her gaze. "I'm excited about the transition and looking forward to what's next."

Manuel nodded thoughtfully. "I admire your proactiveness in your decision to work straight out of school. I didn't have the willpower to do that," he joked, causing a laugh to ripple through the table. "Why real estate?"

My passion shone through my eyes. "I've always been drawn to spaces and how they reflect people's lives. Real estate felt like the perfect fit, with great potential for growth and investment."

Manuel smiled. "It's a noble pursuit, making people feel at home."

I smiled back, feeling the anxiety fade. "Everyone deserves a place where they feel safe and happy, and one day, I'll be the one helping them find it."

Valeria's eyes brightened. "How's working at the bookstore been?"

"It's been a new experience, but I've come to appreciate it. I meet all kinds of people and learn new things every day."

Mikkel squeezed my hand. "That's an understatement; she's been amazing."

I blushed at his praise. "I've really come to love it since I've moved here."

Valeria's gaze softened. "You lived in San Francisco before, ¿no?"

"I did, but I moved because I needed a fresh start."

She placed her hand over mine. "A change of scenery is always beneficial. I wish you all the best, *querida.*[12]"

I relaxed into the warmth of his parents' company. Their genuine curiosity and acceptance made me feel valued, and my earlier anxieties melted away, replaced by a sense of belonging and happiness.

As dinner came to an end, the chatter quieted, and I started cleaning up. But Mikkel quickly stopped me, rolling up his sleeves. "I'll do it," he said, and I let him. Grateful for the reprieve, I stepped outside for a breather.

---

12 *dear*

When I came back inside, feeling a bit more settled, I was about to head upstairs, but I paused at the wall, hearing Valeria say my name.

"Well, *hijo*[13], this makes me so happy to see you so smitten," she said, her voice full of affection. I heard Mikkel chuckle softly in response.

Valeria continued, "She's educated, headstrong, and don't get me started on how she looks at you, *mi hijo. Ella te ama.*[14]"

Mikkel's voice was tender when he replied, "*Yo también la amo.*"[15]

I love her too.

My heart skipped at hearing him say that.

Then Manuel spoke up. "She's a breath of fresh air," he said, before continuing in rapid Spanish, words I didn't fully catch.

Mikkel's voice came again, teasing but affectionate. "You called her *nuera*[16], *Papá*?"

Manuel chuckled, his voice warm. "I'm guessing within a year or so, we'll be getting a call about your proposal. So, she's my daughter-in-law... it's inevitable."

The words hit me like a sudden wave. It was one thing to feel the love, but hearing it aloud made it ten times more real.

I stood there for a moment, my thoughts swirling. When I decided I'd heard enough, I turned and made my way upstairs, my heart still racing.

I showered and slipped into bed, a contented smile on my lips. Meeting his parents had gone better than I expected, and his words still lingered, keeping me on a high. I relaxed into the quiet of the room, waiting for him to join me.

A moment later, he entered, his gaze fixed on mine as he crossed the room. I pulled him onto the bed, our lips meeting passionately. His shirt quickly came undone, and he paused, teasing, "You're in a really good mood."

---

13 son

14 She loves you

15 I love her too

16 daughter in law

I trailed slow kisses down his stomach, savoring the heat of his skin. Grabbing a scrunchie, I quickly secured my hair without breaking eye contact. Then, sinking to my knees, I met his gaze.

"Sit down," I murmured, my voice low and sure. "Let me show you just how good a mood I'm in."

His lips curled into a grin as he threw his head back. "I'm all yours, *amor.*[17]"

---

17 amor

CHAPTER FORTY-TWO

Abigail-Ann

"Love will find a way through paths where wolves fear to prey."
~ Lord Byron

The bed jolted beneath me, pulling me awake. My first thought was that there had been an earthquake. But as I blinked through the haze of sleep, I saw Mikkel beside me, twisting and turning as he sat up.

"Good morning, *amor*," he said with a sleepy grin, his voice warm but oddly insistent as he reached for his glasses. "I was just about to wake you."

I grabbed my phone from the nightstand, squinting at the screen to check the time. *Four in the morning.* "Why were you about to wake me?"

Mikkel's eyes sparkled with excitement and urgency. "We're going out."

Still groggy, I rubbed my eyes. *"At four am?"*

He gave me a mischievous smile. "Yes."

Despite the ungodly hour, I forced myself to sit up, the drowsiness making my movements sluggish. "Alright, alright," I muttered, pushing the covers off. "Let me get ready."

The cold morning breeze rushed through the bathroom window as I showered, making me shiver. Twenty-five minutes later, we were both ready; me in a black sweater dress with my hair in a ponytail and light makeup, and Mikkel in a white sweatshirt and dark jeans.

"All set?"

I nodded, spritzing a bit of perfume and slipping on my bracelets. "Let's go."

We made our way down the stairs, and the sight of Valeria around the kitchen island startled me. Apparently, we weren't the only ones awake at this hour.

"Good morning, Valeria!"

"Buenos días, *Mamá*,[1]" we both said in unison.

"*Buenos días!*[2]" She looked up from her book and smiled at us. "Where are you lovebirds off to so early?"

Mikkel responded smoothly, "*Campo de aviación.*[3]"

Duolingo did not teach me that. I'm officially revoking my subscription.

"*¡Eres tan romántico!*[4]" she exclaimed. "Have fun."

With a final nod from her, Mikkel and I left the penthouse. Sliding into the passenger seat, I asked, "Where exactly is out?"

He gave me a look that said, *You know what I'm going to say,* and I scoffed, rolling my eyes.

Nerves swirled in my stomach as I admired Mikkel's adventurous spirit. The changing scenery fueled my anticipation until we arrived at an airfield, where a multi-colored helicopter stood against the dark sky, sparking my excitement.

I turned to Mikkel, eyes wide. "What's… happening?"

---

1 *Good morning, Mom*

2 *Good morning*

3 *Airfield*

4 *You are so romantic*

His grin was infectious as he turned to face me. "Number one on your bucket list." Hiis voice brimmed with excitement. "You didn't think I'd forget about the list, did you?"

With trembling hands, and teary eyes, I reached for my phone and read aloud the item: *Helicopter ride BD.*

"We're going on a helicopter ride," I whispered, still in awe.

Mikkel leaned closer, his thumb gently brushing away the tears that had spilled onto my cheeks. "Right before dawn, baby."

I leaned into him, overwhelmed by his love and thoughtfulness. As we neared the waiting helicopter, the hum of the engines and the glow of zodiacal light surrounded us, creating a moment suspended in time.

Carlos from Manhattan Helicopter Tours greeted us as we boarded. Moments later, we were strapped in and the helicopter lifted off, the city below shrinking to a miniature version of itself.

"Are you okay?"

I turned to him, heart swelling. "I'm completely in awe. You always make my dreams come true."

He leaned in and kissed me passionately, igniting a fire deep within.

The first rays of sunlight painted the horizon in shades of pink and gold, and I marveled at the beauty. As the sun climbed higher, he snapped a picture of me against the sky.

"Now we can print this," he murmured, "and remember it was taken right before dawn."

A thousand thoughts swirled in my mind, but one stood clear—I never wanted to leave his side.

As the city lights sharpened during our descent, the thud of the landing gear grounded me. The moment we stepped off the plane, dewy morning air wrapped around us, and Mikkel's steady grip in my hand reminded me I was exactly where I belonged.

I turned to him, my voice soft. "With you, it's like everything I've ever hoped for."

His fingers tightened around mine. "I'll make sure you always feel that way."

"You already do."

Settling into the car, warmth bloomed in my chest. I snapped a picture—my hand resting on his cheek as he kissed me. With trembling fingers, I set it as my wallpaper, determined to hold onto the magic of this morning.

We stopped for breakfast at Balthazar, a cozy SoHo spot known for its French pastries and eggs Benedict. By the time we returned to the penthouse, exhaustion had settled deep in my bones.

Stepping inside, we were greeted with warm smiles from Valeria and Manuel. Mikkel, still carrying the faint trace of a smile, grabbed some cherries from the fridge before turning to his parents. "So, what's the plan for today?"

"Val and I have some business to handle, *hijo*,[5]" Manuel replied.

Mikkel raised an eyebrow. "That's why you came to New York? For business?"

Valeria smiled fondly. "Not exactly. We came because we missed you and Emilia, though she's out of town. And, of course, to meet Abigail."

I smiled, touched by her words. "That means a lot to hear. How long are you staying?"

"Five days. We'll have to head back to California after that, because there's always something waiting for us."

I nodded. "I can only imagine."

Valeria glanced at her phone, sighing softly. "Looks like our ride is downstairs, Manuel. *Vámonos!*[6]"

Manuel stood, smiling. "Always in a hurry, *mi vida*,[7]" he teased, his eyes filled with fondness as he turned to her.

Valeria walked over to Mikkel, placing a gentle kiss on his cheek.

"Have a good day, *mis amores*,[8]" she said, before turning to me and kissing my cheek as well.

Manuel followed suit. "We'll be back in a few hours."

---

5 *son*

6 *Let's go*

7 *my life*

8 *my loves*

As the door closed behind them, a soft thud echoed, but the love lingered. Heading upstairs, I sighed, the exhaustion fading when I turned to him.

"Can you clear your schedule for a week?"

Without hesitation, Mikkel took my hand, his expression serious. "I'll have it done tomorrow morning."

I smiled softly. "You didn't even ask why."

He shrugged with a grin. "I don't need to. You want me to clear my schedule? Done. No questions, no hesitation."

I chuckled, feeling a rush of affection for him. "I want you to meet my dad."

He paused, then nodded. "I'll arrange the details with my flight crew."

I grinned, knowing full well that whatever I needed, he would give it to me. "Next week. The Friday after your parents leave."

Mikkel laughed, his joy infectious. "It's a plan. But for now, let's sleep."

We woke to the glow of streetlights streaming through the windows. Stretching with a yawn, we shared a sleepy smile before slipping out of bed, showering, and heading downstairs.

"*Buenas Noches*,[9]" Valeria greeted us with a warm smile. "Did you *aves del amor* have a good rest?"

"Love birds," Mikkel whispered, "*Aves del amor* means lovebirds."

Pink stained my cheeks as I replied, "We did. Thank you."

Manuel looked up from the kitchen counter, his eyes perceptive. "I hope you're ready for game night. We brought a few special games from home to show you, *nuera*.[10]"

"Please tell me we have *Dominó*?" Mikkel asked, excitement spreading through his eyes.

"We do. Get ready to lose, *hijo*,[11]" his dad joked.

---

9 *Goodnight*

10 *daughter-in-law*

11 *son*

"In your dreams, *Papá*."

We moved onto the rooftop deck, where a large table was set up with various board games, cards, and dice. His parents explained the rules of each game with enthusiasm, their love for these traditions evident in every word. A spread of snacks covered one corner of the table, from bowls of chips to plates of cookies and sandwiches.

The first game we played was *Dominó*, a traditional Dominican game similar to dominoes, but with unique twists that made it faster-paced and more competitive. We paired off into teams: Valeria and I against Mikkel and Manuel. To our surprise, we won two consecutive rounds, which had me grinning ear to ear.

"Didn't expect that, did you?" I teased, feeling a small spark of pride.

But Mikkel just flashed me a confident grin. "Lady's luck, *mi reina*,[12]" he said with a playful smirk. "*Papá* and I are winning the next round."

Sure enough, they insisted on a best-of-five. We were determined, but they were relentless, with Manuel's sharp strategy and Mikkel's calculated moves. The next few rounds were a blur of fast plays and laughter, with every point feeling like a mini victory, even when it didn't go our way. In the end, they took the win, but it felt like we'd had our fair share of triumphs too.

Next, we played *La Vieja*, a variation of tic-tac-toe played on a large board with colorful pieces. The simplicity of the game belied its strategic depth, and I found myself deeply engrossed, trying to outwit Mikkel's father, who was a master at it. Seriously, the man never lost a game and if he did, he was determined to get the final win.

I could now see where Mikkel got his competitiveness from.

Finally, we gathered in the living room for *El Juego de la Silla*, a lively game of musical chairs that had us darting around, laughing breathlessly as we fought for the last seat. My breasts put me at a clear disadvantage, but the infectious joy kept us going. By the end, we were all panting, grinning, and completely spent.

I loved tonight and I loved bonding with his family.

---

12 my queen

CHAPTER FORTY-THREE

Mikkel

"A loving heart is the truest wisdom."
~ Charles Dickens

I woke to an empty bed and made my way downstairs, where I found my love and my mother making breakfast and baking Bizcocho dominicano—a fluffy cake with pineapple filling. My heart warmed at the sight, relieved that everything was falling into place as I had hoped. The thought that she could ever feel unloved pained me; I loved every part of her, even the parts she hated.

The day quickly picked up speed. I had three meetings—two went smoothly, but the last was a challenge, tangled in legal issues that needed to be resolved. Morison and Sapphire's trips to Miami and Seattle had been successful, and our expansions were progressing steadily.

I also had two virtual interviews—one with The New York Times about Elite Rides' expansion, which went well, and another with Good

Morning America, where Jasmine kept straying off-topic. Frustrated, I wrapped it up, got ready, and told everyone to do the same.

In between, I spent half an hour on the phone with Emilia, trying to convince her to join us. As expected, she found excuse after excuse. I let it go but warned her not to be surprised when Mamá and Papá showed up at her door before they left. She sighed but didn't argue.

Just as I set my phone down, another notification lit up my screen—this time from the group chat.

Dill
Gentlemen, we need to start with the measurements for your tuxedos.

Alex
no problem. who's doing the fitting?

Dill
We're getting them custom-made by Kiton.

Reyes
Why are we getting fitted this early?

Dill
When your pregnant fiancée tells you to get on it, you get on it.

Reyes
Men in love. Who's next so we can do that fitting too to save time?

Dill
Fuck off.

Reyes
No.

Me
Most likely me, and sure Dillon. Can we do it in about two weeks?

I sent the message without a second thought.

Reyes
As I said, men in love.

Alex
the day Arnoldo Reyes falls hopelessly in love will be a day to put down in history.

Ro
we can have it documented in Dillon's museum.

Reyes
Shouldn't you be on my side since you're just as out of love as I am, Ronan?

Ro
I am in love... She just isn't in love with me right now.

Alex
baby steps?

Ro
precisely.

Dill
I'll have the appointment made, then.

Luc
Reyes, go find love. Alex, how's our godson? Dillon, just let us know the date. Ronan has never been out of love. Mikkel, have a good week.

Reyes
The one time you choose to speak, it's against me.

Luc
Love you too, sweet face.

The conversation quickly turned into its usual chaos, an ongoing debate about who would make the best man. Lucio and Alex were more than happy to fan the flames, letting Arnoldo and Ronan go at it.

I shook my head, setting my phone aside. Same arguments, different day.

I turned off my phone just as Abigail stepped into the living room, my parents following behind her. The moment I saw her, my breath caught.

She wore a white sundress—simple, elegant, beautiful. The fabric hugged her perfectly, flowing like a sun-drenched painting.

I exhaled slowly, steadying myself.

"Wow," I said, my voice rougher than I intended. "You look incredible."

Her lips curled into a smile, her eyes bright with amusement. She knew *exactly* what she was doing to me. "Thank you."

I felt my parents' quiet scrutiny, their silent approval passing between them. I wasn't sure if they were more entertained by my reaction or by the way Abigail had effortlessly settled into our family dynamic.

Clearing my throat, I forced my focus back to the afternoon ahead. "Shall we?"

"Let's go," Mamá said, and we headed out toward Midtown Manhattan.

By the time we arrived at the Empire State Building, the sky had settled into an overcast gray, but nothing about the day felt dull. The city hummed with life, and Abigail stood in the middle of it all, her excitement shining through.

"It's bucket list day, *amor*," I whispered, wrapping my hand around her from behind.

Abigail spun around, her face lighting up before she kissed me quickly. "It feels so surreal to be here."

I held her close, letting my fingers settle at her hip. "This is just the beginning."

We moved inside, and I made sure everything was taken care of—the best tickets, the best view, everything. As we navigated through the crowd, my mom pulled Abigail aside for a moment. I watched them exchange a few words, their soft laughs blending with the noise of the bustling floor.

"It's beautiful, isn't it, *querida*?[1]" I overhead mom ask, her eyes searching Abigail's as she took in the view.

"Even more than I ever expected," Abigail replied, smiling back. "I'm just happy to be here with you, Mikkel, and Manuel."

---

1 dear

Mamá's expression softened, and she reached for Abigail's hand, squeezing it gently. "We'll have plenty of moments like this because we're *familia*[2] now."

My heart thumped at her words. I'd never doubted they'd get along, but seeing it unfold before me was a reward in itself.

We stepped out onto the observation deck, and I grinned at the awestruck looks on everyone's faces. The city stretched out before us, its pulse unmistakable in every corner.

"Now this is what I call a view," my dad commented as he admired the skyline.

I smiled, brushing a hand against Abigail's back. "*Es hermoso*, Papá.[3]"

As we wandered around the deck, snapping pictures, I noticed my parents busy with their cameras. I took the opportunity and pulled Abigail aside, pressing her lightly against the wall.

"You look amazing," I murmured, my voice lower than I intended.

Her breath hitched, a familiar reaction that only fueled the hunger building inside me.

"Are you obsessed with me, Mr. Suarez?" she asked, her eyes gleaming.

"That shouldn't even be a question." I leaned in, brushing my lips along her jawline. "You're all I think about, Red. Every damn second."

Her smile deepened as she kissed me again, slow and deliberate. "I feel it every day I'm with you."

And that—her knowing it, feeling it—was all I could ever ask for.

Before the moment could escalate, my mother's voice called out for us to take pictures. I exhaled, forcing myself to pull back. "We should join them."

We spent the rest of the time capturing moments with the skyline, then had lunch at the restaurant on the ground floor. The conversation was light, filled with laughter, mostly about the neighborhoods we'd seen earlier.

---

2 *family*

3 *It's beautiful, Dad*

"The views here are almost as good as the food," Abigail said, smiling across the table at me.

I held her gaze. "The views are incredible."

She shook her head, amusement flickering in her eyes. "You're looking at me."

I leaned in just enough for only her to hear. "And I have no plans to stop."

The Empire State Building exceeded my expectations, made unforgettable by exploring it with Mikkel and his parents. Valeria insisted on dozens of pictures, and while Mikkel groaned, he indulged her, his smile returning each time she teased, "One day, you'll be glad I made you do this, *hijo*.[4]"

Now, back in the bedroom, I was packing for our trip to San Francisco while Mikkel hadn't returned from his meeting. A soft knock at the door startled me. I turned to find Valeria standing in the doorway, a small box in her hands and a gentle smile on her face.

"Do you have a moment, *cariño*?[5]" she asked, stepping inside.

"Of course," I said, setting aside the neatly folded shirt in my hands.

She crossed the room, handing me the box.

"I meant to give you this earlier but it slipped my mind," she said. "It's something I made for you."

Surprised, I took the box, untied the ribbon, and revealed a stunning Larimar pendant on a silver chain. Its pale blue stone shimmered like sunlight on water, making my eyes water at the beauty.

"You made this?" I asked, my voice soft with awe.

She nodded, her smile widening. "Jewelry making is a hobby of mine. When Mikkel first mentioned you, I thought of Larimar because

---

4 *son*

5 *sweetheart*

he described you as the ocean: calm, strong, and beautiful in ways words can't capture. After seeing you on that video chat—and every call since—I understood exactly what he meant. Spending this week with you only confirmed it."

Tears pricked at the corners of my eyes as I ran my fingers over the pendant. "It's absolutely gorgeous," I whispered. "This means so much to me."

"It's my pleasure," she said warmly. "Truly."

She glanced at the open suitcases. "Do you need any help packing?"

"Oh, no, I couldn't—"

"Nonsense," she said, already reaching for a sweater to fold.

I laughed softly and nodded. "Thank you, Valeria."

As we worked together to organize my suitcase, I found myself speaking without thinking.

"I was so nervous to meet you in person," I admitted, keeping my gaze on the neatly folded jeans in my hands.

Valeria paused and looked at me, surprised. "Really? Why?"

"Well…" I hesitated, trying to find the right words. "I've been judged before. People assumed I wasn't good enough or that I didn't belong. I thought maybe you'd feel that no one could be good enough for Mikkel."

Her expression softened, and she set the sweater aside, giving me her full attention. "Oh, Abigail," she said gently. "I'm so sorry you've experienced that. People can be so cruel, and their judgments often say more about them than about you."

I nodded, swallowing the lump in my throat.

Valeria continued, "Mikkel's love life is none of mine or Manuel's business. I love my son dearly, but he's a grown man who makes his own decisions. My only concern is that he's truly happy and that he treats whoever he's with kindness, respect, and care."

Her words felt like rays of sunshine on a warm summer day, easing the knot of nerves in my chest.

"Thank you for saying that," I murmured. "I didn't realize how much I needed to hear it."

Valeria smiled, gently running a hand through her hair. "Abigail, you're a wonderful young woman. I'm so glad he found you because *mi hijo*[6] has never been happier or more at peace, and I have you to thank for that."

I hugged her impulsively, and she wrapped her arms around me without hesitation.

As we pulled apart, she rested a hand on mine. "And, *querida*[7], if you ever need anything, call me."

The sincerity in her voice nearly brought tears to my eyes again. "I will," I said softly. Valeria's acceptance and kindness were a gift as precious as the beautiful larimar necklace now resting on the dresser, waiting to be worn.

---

6 *my son*

7 *dear*

CHAPTER FORTY-FOUR

Abigail-Ann

"Love is an act of endless forgiveness, a tender look which becomes a habit."
~ Peter Ustinov

"You okay, Red?" Mikkel asked, his voice soft as it cut through the hum of the jet engines. His dark eyes searched mine, flickering with concern.

I nodded, though the tightness in my chest begged me to do otherwise.

But I wasn't. Not really.

I turned to the window, toying with my larimar necklace as I watched the endless sea of clouds below, with San Francisco waiting just beyond. I loved it there: the fog rolling over the Golden Gate, the hills alive with the rattle of cable cars, and my family. But love wasn't the issue. My past was. It lingered, tangled in every street, every corner, every faded memory that refused to stay buried.

"I'm fine. Just thinking," I replied, trying to sound nonchalant, though I wasn't sure I succeeded.

"Okay," he murmured, leaning in to place a tender kiss on my forehead before returning to his crossword puzzle.

The flight attendant's voice crackled over the speakers, announcing that we'd be landing in ten minutes. The flight had felt much quicker than usual, but maybe it was just the nerves messing with my sense of time. Almost immediately, a familiar tightness settled in my chest, making me fidget in my seat.

"What's wrong?" Mikkel asked, his concern deepening as he peered over at me.

"Nerves?" I said, though it came out as more of a question. He closed his book without hesitation, took my hands, and brushed his thumbs over my knuckles in a soothing rhythm.

I took a deep breath, my gaze dropping to our intertwined fingers. "Going back home can be tense. The last time I came back, it was a mess."

He tilted his head slightly, his eyes searching mine, trying to understand. "The airport debacle?"

I swallowed hard, the words lodging in my throat like they didn't want to be spoken. "Not just that," I admitted, my voice barely above a whisper. "It's everything. Being here… it's overwhelming."

Mikkel nodded, his expression turning serious, almost protective. "I'll be right there with you," he said, his voice steady with determination, his gaze unwavering. "Besides, he'd be a dead man if he even *thought* about messing with you."

The promise in his tone should have been comforting, and it was to some extent, but it only added to the knot of anxiety in my chest. That was another reason why I was on edge. The truth was, I knew I'd see Joshua or, at the very least, some unavoidable reminder of him.

And when that happened, no amount of stress balls or coping methods would be enough to hold back Mikkel's temper.

He was fierce, and while I loved that about him, it terrified me too. I didn't want this to escalate into something that would haunt us both.

The jet landed, jolting me from my spiraling thoughts. I turned to the window, expecting to see Welcome to San Francisco.

But something was off.

The landscape outside felt wrong—the muted skyline, the unfamiliar road signs.

I turned to Mikkel. "We're in Pennsylvania?" My brow furrowed as I searched his face for answers.

His response was maddeningly casual. "We rerouted for a bit."

"Rerouted? Why?"

His gaze held mine, warm and unreadable. "There's something we have to do first."

That was all he gave me. No further explanation, no hint. Just enough mystery to send my pulse skittering.

When we stepped off the jet, his voice cut through the hum of activity. "We'll be ready for takeoff in five hours," he told his crew.

A sleek black car waited for us. Mikkel led me inside, his touch as effortless as always, like it never wasn't second nature to have his hand on me.

Thirty minutes passed in silence, thick with my unanswered questions and his deliberate patience. I tried to map the roads; tried to predict where we were going. Nothing clicked.

Except for one thing—Mikkel Suarez loved keeping me on my toes. And I had never found anything sexier.

I pulled out my phone and texted Aurora.

Me
We're landing later than expected.

Aurora
Mikkel already told us.

Me
YOU KNEW?

Aurora
Go have fun, Abigail.

I scowled at the screen. *So everyone was in on this except me?*

Before I could even attempt to figure it out, Mikkel stepped out of the car and opened my door, hand extended.

"Is it on my bucket list?" I pressed, my mind racing.

His lips twitched. "See for yourself."

I turned, and my breath caught.

The world before me was alive.

A vast garden bloomed endlessly—roses, tulips, orchids entwined like a painting. The air brimmed with flowers and earth, birdsong threading the stillness.

My heart slammed against my ribs.

"Number ten from your list," Mikkel said softly.

Longwood Gardens.

A stunned laugh escaped me. I had dreamed of this place, scrolled through hundreds of photos online, and imagined what it would be like to stand here. But I never thought I'd actually come.

And yet, here I was.

"Oh my gosh! Mikkel!"

His response was effortless, steady. "Let's start exploring, Red."

I barely heard him. My feet carried me forward, drawn to a cluster of pink roses. Their petals curled like delicate whispers of magic, and without thinking, I reached out, brushing my fingers against the softness.

Mikkel didn't say a word. But when I turned, he was already watching me.

His gaze was heavy, reverent—like he'd been waiting for this moment.

"This is so beautiful." My voice came out breathless.

He stepped closer, his hand sliding around my waist, pulling me into him like it was instinct.

Then, his voice low and certain, he said, "Not even close to how beautiful you are."

Hand in hand, we wandered through the garden, every step deepening the magic. Vibrant flowers painted the landscape, birdsong wove through the air, and a peaceful silence wrapped around us. I forgot everything else—completely lost in this serene haven, with the man I love.

We passed a breathtaking bed of pink and white orchids, and I paused, taking it all in. Mikkel, always attuned to me, plucked one and gently tucked it behind my ear.

"Mikkel, I don't think you can do that," I said, smiling.

He chuckled softly. "I can do whatever I want." His gaze roamed my face before settling on my eyes. "Besides, it looks beautiful in your hair."

His quiet, sure tenderness tightened something in my chest. A tear slipped free.

Mikkel brushed it away with his thumb. Then, with that soft, knowing smile, he whispered, "Smile for me."

I smiled as he pulled out his phone, capturing the moment with a few clicks, each shot making my heart flutter.

"You're a work of art, *mi reina*," he murmured, still focused on the camera.

Warmth bloomed in me. I pulled him close, kissing him—soft, unhurried—a silent exchange beyond words.

When we finally pulled apart, I whispered, "That was perfect." Then, with my fingers laced through his, I led him forward, savoring the scenery, the unexpected adventure, him.

A few minutes later, a tour guide named Louis appeared, his friendly grin breaking the spell.

Curious, I fired off questions, eager to learn more.

Most unique plant here? Corpse flower.

How old is the garden? One hundred and eighteen years old.

Best time of year to visit? Spring and fall.

With each answer, my excitement grew, like the garden itself was unfolding as a living storybook.

Then, I spotted clusters of yellow primroses, glowing under the afternoon sun.

I gasped. "These are my favorite!"

Louis smiled knowingly, glancing at Mikkel. "We were informed. There's a set inside for you."

I turned to Mikkel, my vision blurring.

"Don't cry, *mi reina*," he said, his voice a quiet caress. "*Te adoro.*[1]"

I let out a teary giggle. "*Te adoro* too."

Louis explained that primroses typically didn't bloom this long, but the cool weather had extended their season. Even nature itself had conspired to make this moment last.

As the tour ended, my excitement didn't fade. I rambled on about the flowers, my words tumbling out in breathless awe, and Mikkel—*always listening*—watched me with quiet affection.

"And did you see those roses? And the peonies?" I gushed. "I didn't know they came in so many colors!"

Just as we prepared to leave, Louis returned with a small basket. From it, he pulled out a delicate, hand-knitted bouquet of primroses.

"These are for you," he said, handing it to me. "Ten primroses, just as Mr. Suarez requested."

I held the bouquet close, my heart nearly bursting. "Why ten?" I asked Mikkel softly.

His voice dropped, slow and deliberate. "Because 'visit a flower garden' was number ten on your bucket list. I first saw you on the tenth of March. Our first kiss was at ten p.m. on concert night. And not to mention—" his lips curved slightly, "you're a ten."

A shiver ran through me.

His words, his thoughtfulness, and the way his love showed in every detail—it was beautifully consuming.

"Oh, Mikkel," I whispered, my voice thick with emotion.

He pulled me into his arms, pressing a soft kiss to my forehead. "I know, baby. I know."

After thanking Louis and handing him a tip, Mikkel turned back to me, his gaze heavy with something deeper than love.

"You deserve the universe at your feet." His fingers brushed my cheek. "I had these flowers knitted for you, so they'll never wither."

Tears pooled in my eyes, but I smiled. "There aren't enough words in English or Spanish, to say how much you mean to me."

---

1 I adore you

Then, without hesitation, I closed the distance, kissing him softly.

Because this—this moment, this man—was everything.

Money did make the world go round. Three phone calls and a few thousand dollars later, we had the perfect day at Longwood Gardens. After the tour, we grabbed food to go and settled onto the jet.

Scrolling through the pictures of her, I found myself pausing on each one—her lost in nature, breathing in the scent of flowers, her smile radiating pure joy. Her beauty was almost too much to take in. The way she laughed, the way her eyes lit up at everything, completely captivated me. Every time I looked at her, I felt like the luckiest man alive, falling deeper with each glance. I didn't just see her; I felt her—in my heart, my soul, every part of me. It was overwhelming, like constantly rediscovering her, finding new ways to fall for her every single day.

Five hours later, the jet touched down at a private airfield in San Jose. As we descended the steps, Aurora stood by a black SUV, arms crossed, eyes scanning the runway.

When Abigail spotted her, she sprinted toward her, nearly knocking her over with a tight hug. Laughter and squeals filled the air as they clung to each other. Aurora's gaze flicked to me over Abigail's shoulder, her eyes assessing, before a smirk curved her lips.

"Finally decided to pay us a visit, huh, Mikkel?" she teased.

I chuckled, shaking her offered hand. "Good to see you again, Aurora."

We loaded the luggage and made our way to San Francisco. The drive passed in a comfortable mix of conversation and music, and the light mood continued with a few playful exchanges.

"Do you know how surreal this is?" Aurora asked, glancing at me through the rearview mirror as we drove. "You have a jet."

"I bought it recently."

"Why?" Her brow furrowed in confusion.

"Abigail has flight anxiety. I thought it was necessary."

Aurora paused, disbelief and curiosity in her eyes. "You bought a jet because my sister has flight anxiety?"

I shrugged. "Pretty much."

Abigail, a bit surprised, chimed in, "I didn't know that."

I smiled. "I didn't tell you, *mi reina*."

Aurora glanced at me sideways. "Do you have any friends? Asking for a friend…"

I laughed. "They're all taken or don't date."

"Well, there goes my luck."

Abigail's eyes widened as a thought hit her. "Is that why it's yellow?"

I nodded, a playful smile tugging at my lips. "Yes, *mi vida.*[2]"

Her face lit up with excitement. "You're insane."

I squeezed her hand gently. "You're worth it."

When we arrived at the Asher family home, I was struck by its beauty—modern architecture, large windows, and an expansive driveway. A lovely front garden softened the edges, and a koi pond near the entrance added a peaceful touch.

But the green Rolls Royce Black Badge in the driveway truly caught my eye. Gleaming in the sunlight, its smooth curves and black accents made it look dreamlike. Absolutely stunning.

Aurora led us inside, locking the door behind us. I scanned the cozy space, my attention drawn to the picture wall—dozens of photos of Abigail, her family, and their shared memories.

Aurora smiled at us. "Mom and Dad aren't home yet, so we have some time. Make yourselves comfy."

Abigail rolled her eyes. "Aurora, I live here."

Aurora shot back with a playful grin. "*Lived.* You moved out, remember?" They both laughed, the sound light and easy, before Aurora walked off.

---

2 *my life*

Abigail squeezed my hand and pulled me toward the stairs. "Let's go upstairs."

I followed her up, taking in every detail of the place she grew up in—each piece of her past adding layers to the woman I fell for. Her room was a perfect reflection of her: music posters, stacks of movies instead of a bookshelf, and fairy lights framing her vanity. A cozy yellow throw draped over an armchair made the space feel warm and inviting.

After we showered together, I noticed something was off. Abigail was moving slower than usual. When she collapsed onto the bed, rubbing her eyes, I could tell she wasn't feeling well. I knelt beside her, concern clear in my voice. "What's wrong, baby?"

"I just have a bad headache."

I quickly helped her get dressed, pulling her hair into a bonnet before kissing her forehead. "Get some rest, *amor*. You need it."

Her tired eyes met mine. "Aren't you tired?"

I smiled, brushing a strand of hair from her face. "I'm fine. Just make sure you sleep."

She curled up on the bed, her breathing evening out as she drifted off to sleep.

A knock at the door pulled my attention. "Abi, come help me chop these vegetables!" Aurora called.

I stood, glancing at Abigail before opening the door. "She's got a headache. I can help if you want."

Aurora hesitated. "That's fine—"

"I insist."

She sighed, then nodded. "Alright."

Downstairs, we fell into a rhythm, preparing chicken chow mein. After a while, Aurora glanced over and said, "Thanks for making my sister happy, by the way."

I set down the knife. "I was just her moral support. She did it all on her own."

Aurora's expression softened. "She's been through a lot, you know. Seeing her like this… she's found her spark again. And I know you had a part in that, so yeah, I have to thank you."

"It's my pleasure, Aurora," I said sincerely.

We continued cooking, the buzz of the kitchen filling the space until a voice rang through the house.

"Angel."

Aurora turned, smiling. "Mom, you're home!"

I looked up as Alicia entered, her brown curls streaked with gray bouncing around her shoulders. Her almond-shaped green eyes gleamed as she greeted us, warmth radiating from her presence.

But it was her husband who held my attention.

He stood a few inches shorter, salt-and-pepper hair neatly combed, sharp brown eyes assessing—no warmth, just quiet calculation, as if fitting me into an unfinished puzzle.

Before I could dwell on it, Alicia's familiar voice cut through the moment as she pulled me into a warm hug. "Mikkel! You get more handsome every time I see you."

"It's lovely to see you again, Alicia."

I turned to her husband next, extending my hand. "It's good to finally meet you, Mr. Asher."

He clasped it in a firm shake, his grip measured. "Daniel," he corrected, but his tone didn't hold the same ease as his wife's. "Likewise, Mikkel."

Aurora wiped her hands on a kitchen towel. "Abi's got a headache, so she's sleeping, but Mikkel was helping me with dinner."

Alicia shot me an approving look before turning to her daughter. "We can take it from here, angel."

Aurora hesitated for half a second before nodding. "Alright." She glanced at me briefly before disappearing down the hall.

That left just the three of us.

I shifted my stance. "Do you want me to check if Abigail's awake?"

Daniel shook his head. "No need." His voice was smooth but held an undercurrent of something firmer. "We want to talk to you."

Alicia smiled, but there was something knowing in her expression. Like she could already tell where this conversation was headed.

Daniel grabbed a bottle of water from the counter, twisting the cap off with slow precision. "How did you and Abigail meet?"

I met his gaze, unfazed. "At SFO. She was having a rough morning, so I went over to check on her. After that, we kept crossing paths in New York, and the rest is history."

His brow lifted slightly. "A rough morning?"

I nodded. "She was stressed. I could tell."

"And you decided to step in." His voice was even, but there was something in the way he said it—like he was trying to see if I'd slip, if I'd say the wrong thing.

"She looked like she needed a moment to breathe," I said simply. "So I gave her one."

Alicia hummed, her lips curving. "Sounds like fate."

Daniel didn't comment. He set the water down with deliberate care before leaning against the counter. "Abigail mentioned you own a luxury car service?"

"That's right. Elite Rides specializes in high-end transportation."

"Quite the venture. Didn't you just expand to Chicago?"

I inclined my head. "We did. The market was tough, but the expansion was worth it."

"Chicago isn't an easy city to break into," he mused. "What made you choose transportation? It's a competitive business."

"I've always been drawn to logistics and efficiency," I said. "But more than that, I saw an opportunity—people crave convenience, luxury, and security all in one package. So, I built an empire that delivers just that."

His expression didn't shift. If anything, his scrutiny sharpened. "Ambitious."

There was a weight to the word, something between respect and skepticism.

"What's next after Chicago?"

"Miami and Seattle," I replied. "Then working through the East Coast."

Daniel nodded slowly. "You have a solid plan." He tapped his fingers against the counter, his gaze holding steady. "That brings me to my next question. You're obviously busy; how do you balance all this with a relationship?"

I didn't hesitate. "Abigail is my priority. We understand each other's responsibilities, and we make it work. Communication is key, and no matter how demanding things get, I always make time for her."

His silence stretched for a beat too long. His stare didn't waver, didn't give anything away, but it was pressing in its own way. Searching.

Then, finally, he exhaled, nodding once. "That's what I wanted to hear."

The conversation shifted after that, easing into business, life, and family. But even as Alicia's warmth softened the moment, Daniel's presence remained like an unspoken test, each question measured, each response dissected.

"So, what do you do in your free time, Mikkel?" Alicia asked.

"Mainly the gym," I admitted. "It helps me reset."

Daniel nodded. "Balance is important. I've seen too many men lose themselves in their careers."

"My friends are my family, and Abigail is the most important part of my life."

His gaze lingered, thoughtful, but something about his posture shifted. It wasn't approval exactly, but it wasn't rejection either.

Alicia smiled. "You've built a great life, Mikkel, and we can see that reflected in Abigail."

I met her eyes, my voice sure. "She's everything to me, and she knows it."

She patted my arm before pressing a kiss to her husband's cheek. "I'm going to get some work done."

She left, and he didn't move right away. Instead, he exhaled, swirling the last of the water in his bottle before setting it on the counter with a soft clink. His gaze found mine again, this time less like a test and more like a warning.

"I've heard the praises my wife sings about you," he spoke evenly, his voice carrying an unmissable weight.

"And from this conversation, I can see why. You're a determined, level-headed man—ambitious but grounded. A man who knows what he wants."

A pause. A shift. And then—

"Abigail is my baby," he said, quieter now. "She's twenty-three, but she'll always be my little girl."

I nodded, understanding the unspoken meaning.

"She's far from home, and I want to thank you for making her happy."

"I wouldn't have it any other way. Mr. Asher."

"Daniel," he corrected, his voice deliberate. He held my gaze, his silence charged with something protective, personal.

"I know how badly she's been hurt," he finally said. "And I never want her to go through that again."

"You don't have to worry about that," I replied, my voice steady and certain. "I'd never let that happen."

For the first time, something flickered in his expression—reluctant but unmistakable. After a pause, he nodded. "Alright, Mikkel. I'm trusting you with her."

Without another word, he turned and walked out of the kitchen.

I took a deep breath and turned toward the stairs, but froze when I saw Abigail sitting on the steps, tears staining her cheeks.

Panic gripped my chest as I rushed to her side. "Baby, what's wrong?"

She sniffled, wiping her eyes. "I heard everything. The whole conversation with you and my parents." Her voice was shaky, but a hint of humor crept in. "Aurora and I were eavesdropping—well, mostly me. She said she was going to die from the cuteness and then left to probably annoy mom."

I chuckled, amused by how animated she sounded, mimicking her sister's dramatic flair.

She pulled me into a kiss, and I wrapped my arms around her. "You have no idea how happy hearing that made me. I know my dad can be intense, and you, as expected, handled it so well, but actually hearing it… everything just…" She paused, taking a deep breath, and I placed my hand on her thigh. "It just made me feel all warm inside, Mikkel."

I didn't respond—just kissed her forehead and held her tighter.

I pulled back slightly to look at her. "Are you feeling better?"

She shook her head. "I still have a headache."

"Maybe you need to eat," I suggested gently.

"Maybe."

We walked to the kitchen, and I admired her as she moved around.

Without even looking back, she said, "I can feel your gaze on me."

"Because I'm admiring you."

She turned, setting a plate in front of me before sitting down at the table.

"My hair's a mess, I'm in a worn-out sweatsuit because I'm cold, and my eyes are puffy."

"You just called yourself beautiful in three different ways."

She kissed me again, and we settled into a comfortable silence as we ate. Eventually, Aurora and her parents joined, and the conversation stayed light—full of laughter and casual chatter. I overheard a funny story from her dad about how, when Abigail was five, she'd tried to convince him she was a culinary genius, only to burn the toast.

As dinner came to an end, I started clearing the table, but Alicia stopped me.

"It's fine, Mikkel, I can handle it."

I shook my head. "It's the least I can do."

Alicia turned to Abigail, offering her a warm smile. "You're in good hands, baby."

Abigail smiled back, her eyes soft with reassurance. "I know I am."

WARNING

The following chapter contains heavy mentions of mental health/physical health issues. Please refer to the content warning list to be reminded of any potential triggers. Your well-being is important to me, so please take care of yourself while reading.

CHAPTER FORTY-FIVE

Mikkel

"Love is a friendship set to music."
~ Joseph Campbell

I woke up with a jolt, the warmth beside me gone. My arm instinctively reached out, but I grabbed nothing but the cold sheets. I frowned, pushing myself up. *Where is she?*

I blinked, my vision hazy. *My glasses.* Fumbling on the nightstand, I knocked over my phone before finally finding them and slipping them on.

"Abigail?" I called out, my voice sounding harsher than I intended.

Nothing.

A sudden quietness filled the air, eerie and unnerving. Then, faintly, I heard water running. *The shower.*

My heart rate picked up, and I threw the covers off, nearly tripping over my feet as I rushed toward the bathroom. The moment I stepped in, the mist hit me; warm and suffocating. Through the steam, I saw her, sitting on the floor of the shower with her knees drawn up to her chest, head down, and water pouring over her as if it was trying to wash everything away.

My heart lurched.

"*Amor?*[1]"

She didn't move, didn't even flinch and I felt a sinking pit in my stomach as I stepped closer. "Baby, what's wrong?"

She slowly lifted her head, the curls sticking to her face. Her eyes were red and filled with something I couldn't read.

Without hesitation, I opened the glass door, stepped into the shower fully clothed, and let the water soak through me. She blinked in surprise, her brows furrowing as if confused by my presence.

"W-what are you doing?"

I knelt down beside her. "Sitting with you."

For a moment, she just stared at me, like she wanted to argue but couldn't. Then something in her broke. She leaned in, burying her face in my chest, and sobbed—deep, gut-wrenching cries that shook her entire body.

I held her close, whispering soothing words that may not have even made sense. Each sob hit like a punch to my chest, and I wished I could carry the weight for her.

"I've got you, baby," I whispered, pressing a kiss to the top of her head. "I'm right here with you."

It took a while for her to calm down, her sobs fading into soft sniffles. As her breathing steadied, I reached up to turn off the water and pulled her closer.

Gently, I cupped her cheek, tilting her face to meet my gaze. "Talk to me, baby. What's going on?"

She shook her head, wiping at her eyes. "It's s-stupid," she muttered, her voice small.

I brushed away a tear with my thumb. "Your feelings are never stupid. Tell me."

---

1 *Love?*

Her lips trembled as she sucked in a breath. "My anxiety's just high all of a sudden," she whispered. "It feels like a weight on my chest, like I can't breathe. Like I'm losing control… or that someone's going to hurt me."

Her words cut through me. I saw the fear, the worry, the burden she carried.

I cupped her face, making sure she saw the conviction in my eyes. "No one's going to hurt you. That's a promise, *mi reina*."

She didn't speak, but something in her gaze flickered—trust, hesitant but there. I held her stare, waiting, letting her find comfort in my presence.

After a long moment, she sighed, leaning into me, her body easing just a little. When she was ready, I helped her out of the shower, dried her off slowly, then quickly dried myself.

She looked exhausted, worn down. I wanted to take it all away, to make it easier. And it fucking killed me that I couldn't.

"I'm going downstairs to get some things for you," I said, pulling on a sweatshirt.

"I can get it," she mumbled, wiping at her eyes.

I shook my head. "You stay here. Let me take care of you."

She hesitated, then nodded.

As I made my way downstairs, the weight in my chest refused to lift. Rounding the corner into the kitchen, I stopped short.

Alicia stood by the counter, a mug in her hands. At the sound of my footsteps, she turned.

"Mikkel?" she said, brows knitting together. "Is everything okay?"

I hesitated. "By any chance, do you have barbecue Lay's or cake?"

"Aurora had the last ones. Is Abigail okay?"

I ran a hand through my damp hair. "She's anxious, and those usually give her comfort."

She set down her mug, her face softening. "Oh, sweetheart. It's late, though—"

"I'll Uber if I need to," I cut in, more determined. "I need to get them for her."

She studied me, then handed me her car keys. "Take my car."

"Thank you."

She nodded. "Drive safe, Mikkel. Call if you need anything."

I gave her a small smile before heading out.

For thirty minutes, I scoured the city, frustration mounting with every closed sign, until I finally found an open store. Spotting a bag of Lay's and a small chocolate cake nearly made me sigh with relief.

An hour later, I pulled into the driveway, grabbed the snacks, and dropped Alicia's keys on the kitchen table before heading upstairs.

Abigail sat on the bed, knees to her chest, arms wrapped around them. She looked so small, so fragile. Her eyes widened when she saw me.

"Where did you go?" she asked, her voice soft, almost timid. "I went downsta—"

"I got you something," I said, cutting her off gently as I walked over. I held up the bag. "The closest stores didn't have the right flavor, so I kept looking."

Her eyes flicked between the bag, the cake, and me. "You... drove around for that?"

I nodded, sitting beside her. "I know they help calm you down." My heart pounded as I searched her face. "I'd do anything to make you feel better."

Her lips trembled. She stared at the chips in her lap before meeting my gaze, her glassy eyes making my chest tighten.

"Mikkel..."

I cupped her face, brushing my thumb across her cheek. "You matter to me, Red. More than I can put into words."

Her breath hitched. For a second, I thought she'd pull away, but instead, she leaned into my touch, eyes closing.

"I'm here," I whispered, pressing a kiss to her forehead. "Always."

She let out a shaky breath, her body relaxing. She wasn't okay yet, but she wasn't alone.

"You mean everything to me," she murmured.

I smiled softly, resting my forehead against hers. "Eres todo mi mundo."

The next morning, I woke to the smell of fresh coffee and instinctively reached for her, only to find empty space. Rubbing my eyes, I sat up and spotted her by the window, bathed in soft light, a cup in hand, lost in thought.

Running a hand through my hair to shake off the sleep, I paused as my phone buzzed with a reminder of our plans for the day.

My voice finally broke the quiet. "You're up early."

She turned at the sound of my voice, a faint smile playing on her lips as she made her way toward the bed. "I couldn't really sleep."

Seeing her so broken in the shower had gutted me, but now, watching her offer me a smile felt like a reward. I pulled her wrist, guiding her beside me. She melted into my arms with a soft laugh, her head resting on my chest.

"How are you feeling this morning?" I asked, my hand brushing through her locs as I tried to gauge her mood.

"Better." Her voice was soft, almost as if she were trying to convince herself more than me.

I pressed my lips to her head, holding her as she curled into me. After a moment, she whispered, "Thank you for last night. For everything."

"You never have to thank me," I whispered back. Then, shifting gears, I added, "We're going to Pier 39 today."

She pulled back, amused. "We're in my city, and somehow, you have the plan?"

I grinned. "I like keeping you on your toes."

She laughed softly, shaking her head. "I know you do."

I kissed her, pulling her closer.

"I'm ready!" she exclaimed, and I turned around, taking in her appearance. The high-waisted light blue jeans fit her perfectly, and the long-sleeved bodysuit gently followed the lines of her figure.

"You are…." I trailed off. There weren't enough words in the dictionary to describe how fucking ravishing my girlfriend was. "You are *divina*[2], truly."

She smiled, taking a few small strides over to me. "You make me feel like the prettiest woman in the world."

"Because no one can *ever* compare to you, Red."

She kissed me softly, whispering, "You have no idea how good you always make me feel."

Smiling, I pressed my lips to hers again. "Then let me keep showing you."

We took the private car I'd arranged to the pier, arriving in about twenty-five minutes, where the lively crowd and the mingling scents of saltwater and freshly baked churros heightened our excitement.

"Look at that!" She pointed to the towering rock-climbing wall that loomed over the pier.

"Race you to the top?" I suggested, already breaking into a run. "I may just win."

"You *will* win. These girls," she said, gesturing dramatically to her breasts, "cannot handle the hassle of running."

"Fair point," I noted with a chuckle. "But I'll give you a head start as an advantage, *amor*."

She laughed, her competitive spirit ignited. "You're on!"

With adrenaline rushing through us, we scrambled up the colorful handholds, the cheers of onlookers spurring us on. I never thought I'd be doing this, but it didn't matter. Not when her laughter rang out, not when every second with her felt like winning something I never even knew I needed.

---

2 *divine*

At the top, as she caught her breath, I reached for her, fingers tangling in her hair as I pulled her close. Every kiss felt like a promise of something more, and in that moment, nothing else existed except us.

When I finally pulled away, her eyes sparkled with surprise and delight. "What was that for?"

"A taste of victory."

"Consider me inspired," she teased, the playful glint in her eyes making my chest tighten.

"I felt like a kid again," she admitted as we made our way down. "Are we going back now?"

"Not yet," I said, taking her hand. "There's still so much to see."

We drifted toward an outdoor stage where acrobats performed daring feats, their graceful movements holding the crowd spellbound. Just beyond them, a street magician worked his illusions, drawing gasps and applause as objects vanished and reappeared in his hands.

Laughter bubbled between us as we stepped onto the musical stairs, each note adding to the playful energy of the moment. The city buzzed around us, but the world felt smaller—just the two of us moving through it.

As we wandered closer to the water, sailboats cut smoothly across the bay, the golden light reflecting off their sails. The sight pulled us in, leading us to a quiet bench overlooking the Golden Gate Bridge. A salty breeze wrapped around us, carrying the chatter of passersby, the distant clang of a buoy, and the rhythmic calls of seagulls overhead.

She squeezed my hand, her fingers threading through mine. "I don't know what I did to deserve someone like you," she whispered.

I pulled her close, my hand resting on her ass, and pressed a tender kiss to her forehead. "Deserving has nothing to do with it," I murmured, brushing my thumb over her hand. "In a lifetime of wrong and calculated turns, you're the one I never want to lose."

Her gaze softened, a quiet smile tugging at her lips as she met my eyes. We continued our walk, and she bumped into someone, quickly looking up with an automatic apology on her lips.

"Joshua," she uttered, her voice carrying a hint of surprise and uncertainty.

I paused, scanning the scrawny guy from head to toe with complete and unconcealable disgust.

His gaze rested on me, his already unpleasant features dulling. "And who's this? Your new fling?" he taunted, his voice dripping with contempt. "Are you sucking his bank accounts dry too?"

"Men with money don't worry about their bank accounts being dry," I replied, sarcasm edging my words. "But you don't strike me as wealthy, nor a man, so I shouldn't expect better."

As he struggled to muster a response, she leaned in to me. "He's my boyfriend."

"Your boyfriend in…" He paused, his eyes flicking over me, dissecting my clothes as if it were evidence of some grand deceit.

"Hermès," I finished, a smirk creeping across my face, relishing the shift in the atmosphere. "Mr. Dumas sent it to me himself. Nice, isn't it?"

His expression darkened, the taunt replaced by annoyance, his jaw tightening. He was gearing up to respond, but I realized we'd entertained this conversation long enough.

"Let's go, *mi reina*," I said, my voice steady and sure. "He's not worth it."

But then, his whispered insult or what I was assuming he thought was an insult, hit my ears. "*Coward.*"

My steps faltered as I turned to face him, my gaze sharp. "I don't argue with imbeciles," I stated evenly, my voice low and steady, refusing to let his provocation rattle me. "You let that remarkable woman—*no, that goddess*—slip through your fingers, and you think you're smart? Get a grip, *puta madre.*[3]"

"Gonna let him talk to me like that, Abi?" He smirked, his arrogance radiating from him like a noxious cloud.

---

3 *motherfucker*

She opened her mouth to respond, but I cut her off, my expression hardening. "I suggest you keep your distance from her."

"Or what?" He leaned forward, his bravado faltering.

I narrowed my eyes, letting a cold smile creep onto my lips. "That depends on how much you value your limbs."

"Is that a threat?"

"Oh, God no." I chuckled, shaking my head. "What kind of man do I look like? That's a *promise*, and I keep my promises."

His face paled, anger—or maybe sheer bewilderment—overtaking him as his jaw tightened. Ignoring him, I took her hand, her warmth grounding me as we walked away.

"I knew I'd run into him," she whispered, worry flickering in her eyes. "I just didn't ex—"

I silenced her with a kiss. "He wasn't worth a response, but I wasn't going to stand by in silence after everything he did to you."

She huffed a quiet laugh, shaking her head. "You make it sound so simple."

I squeezed her hand. "It is. He doesn't get to take up space in your life anymore."

She didn't say anything right away, just exhaled and let her fingers tighten around mine. Then, as if shaking off the last of the moment, she nudged me. "Come on. I want a churro."

A smirk tugged at my lips as I led her toward the stand. "One churro? I was thinking at least three."

CHAPTER FORTY-SIX

Abigail-Ann

"The best proof of love is trust."
~ Joyce Brothers

One minute, my mom was talking about spending the day in Chinatown—something about wanting to see the markets and try new foods. The next, Mikkel was telling them to get ready. By the time they were, a car was already waiting, and he'd arranged an entire tour.

Mom, Dad, and Aurora stood there, stunned, their jaws practically on the floor. I couldn't blame them. He had pulled it all together in less than an hour. But I wasn't surprised. I knew Mikkel all too well.

"You really didn't have to go through all this trouble," my mom said as we piled into the car.

Mikkel adjusted his glasses with an easy shrug. "It's no trouble at all, Alicia."

Her smile was warm, appreciative. "Still, we appreciate it."

The day unfolded in a blur of vibrant sights and rich aromas. We wandered through Chinatown, snapping pictures in front of colorful storefronts, tasting dumplings from a tiny, bustling shop, and exploring the markets. At one point, we stopped in an antique store, and as I admired a display of old teacups, I felt Mikkel's gaze settle on me.

He didn't even ask, just walked over and, without hesitation, bought the whole set, clearly catching the owner's eye. I stared at him with a knowing smile on my face. "Thank you."

He just smiled, handing me the bag with the teacups. "Always, baby."

We kept browsing, and when we talked with the couple behind the counter, Mikkel switched to Mandarin with ease. My mom's eyes widened, and my heart skipped a beat. I knew he spoke Mandarin, but I'd never actually heard him use it.

"I didn't know you speak Mandarin," my dad said, clearly impressed.

Mikkel flashed a grin. "I learned it a few years ago."

Aurora's eyes widened. "I definitely didn't see that coming."

We continued down alleyways with hanging lanterns, Mikkel joking with my dad and effortlessly charming everyone. My mom was drawn to a tea shop, where she and Mikkel spent an hour tasting blends and chatting with the owner. After a fun morning, we stopped for lunch at a cozy restaurant, enjoying baozi and spicy noodles, the kind of comfort food that made everything else fade away.

Afterward, we returned home, full and happy. Mikkel excused himself to take a work call, leaving me with my family in the kitchen.

"So, when's the wedding?" Aurora teased, leaning against the counter.

"Soon enough." I smiled, feeling content in this moment.

My dad nodded, looking pleased. "Well, I have to say I'm impressed."

Aurora raised an eyebrow, shocked. "Dad? Impressed? That's new."

I rolled my eyes. "That's Mikkel. He's just…"

I paused, trying to find the exact words to capture how great he is.

"In love with you?" Aurora finished for me.

My smile softened. "Yeah."

Aurora smirked. "I mean, you've got a guy who's willing to make a day in Chinatown happen for your family in under an hour. Can't argue with that."

"That's not even close to being the best part of him," I replied, my voice quieter.

A lull settled in, and I felt a sudden urge to escape for a moment. Without saying much, I quietly slipped away, making my way upstairs to my room.

Mikkel was on the bed, his brow furrowed, looking slightly irritated yet deep in thought. I walked over and, without hesitation, sat down on his lap.

"Everything okay at the office?"

He nodded, but his expression didn't change. "There's this company, Luxe Transports."

"A smaller transport company, right?"

"Yeah," he said, running a hand through his hair. "They want me to buy them out, but it's a bit sudden."

I thought for a moment. "Is it?"

He looked at me, confused.

"I don't think it's sudden. You're having back-to-back successful expansions on the first try, plus your Seattle acquisition is huge. Maybe they want to join the ever-winning side instead of competing."

He grabbed my thigh, his fingers sending a jolt of warmth through me, then flashed that grin.

Thank God I was seated because my feet went lifeless.

"That's one of the things I love about you, baby. You're so fucking smart." He leaned in closer, his breath warm against my skin.

I grinned. "I know."

The conversation faded as we lingered in the silence, but I soon stood up, a new idea sparking in my mind.

"I want to take you somewhere."

Mikkel raised an eyebrow. "Where?"

I smirked. "It's my turn to surprise you."

He chuckled, his eyes glinting. "Lead the way."

I handed him a pocket knife.

"We're gonna need this."

His brows raised in curiosity. "What kind of adventure are we in for?"

I just laughed, letting the mystery linger as I turned to lead him on.

I loved how the leaves turned warm shades of brown, and the crisp air carried just the right chill of autumn—a natural romance, even without a love story. What made it unforgettable was sharing it with my favorite person.

As we stepped into the park, a brisk autumn breeze greeted us, rustling the leaves and sending golden foliage swirling around our feet. I glanced at Mikkel, admiring how the amber sunlight illuminated his features, casting his strong jawline into sharp relief. He looked striking in a white sweater and jeans, perfectly layered for the San Francisco chill, his style blending with the vibrant park backdrop.

"Where exactly are we headed?" he asked as he gently squeezed my hand.

"We're almost there," I replied, a mischievous smile playing at my lips. "Just trust me."

"I trust you, Red."

We followed the winding path deeper into the park and the sounds of the city faded away, replaced by the gentle rustling of leaves and the occasional chirp of a bird.

"This place is beautiful," Mikkel remarked, his gaze sweeping over the tranquil surroundings.

"It's one of my favorite hidden gems." Nostalgia crept into my voice. "My family and I come here all the time."

I pointed out landmarks—a towering redwood, a babbling brook—until we reached a secluded clearing, where a stream trickled over smooth stones. His eyes widened in awe at the serene beauty, and I smiled.

I then led him to a tree, its bark carved with initials and symbols. "My family carved our initials here, and when my parents were busy, I'd come with Aurora."

He ran his fingers over the carvings, tracing the letters with a soft smile. "This is perfect."

Sharing this special place with Mikkel felt right, like I was giving him a piece of my past, a part of myself. I turned to him, finding his eyes already on me, filled with love and gratitude. That was the thing with Mikkel, no matter what I was looking at, he was always looking at me with an indescribable fire and an undisputed amount of passion.

"Thank you for sharing this with me." There was a tenderness in his tone that made my chest clench.

I stepped closer, wrapping my arms around him and inhaling his familiar scent. "I want us to carve our initials in the tree."

He placed a soft kiss on my lips. "Now I know why we needed a knife."

I chuckled, followed by a nod, and he grabbed it, glancing at me for approval. At my silent cue, he began carving.

When he finished, he turned to me, his eyes full of love. "Now we're a part of this place too, baby."

Tracing the freshly carved letters with my fingers, warmth bloomed in my chest. "It's perfect," I whispered, leaning in to kiss him, feeling whole in that moment.

Hand in hand, we strolled down the shaded path, the scent of pine and earth in the air. My heart felt lighter, and a smile tugged at my lips. The day was perfect.

Until it wasn't.

My steps faltered as I spotted Joshua's father, leaning against a red car. His sharp suit did little to mask the venom in his gaze. He wasn't just looking at me—he was dissecting me, the same way he used to, with judgment and disdain that suddenly felt heavier than ever.

Anxiety tightened my chest, crawling up my throat. Mikkel noticed immediately, his thumb brushing over the back of my hand as he murmured, "What's wrong, baby?"

I forced myself to look at him, pulling my hand free to straighten his collar nervously. "Don't get mad…"

His brows drew together, a mix of curiosity and concern shadowing his features.

I exhaled shakily, darting a glance toward the man who still hadn't stopped staring. "The man staring at me…" My voice cracked, my words coming out in a stutter. "It's… it's Joshua's father."

The shift in Mikkel was immediate. His hand flexed at his side, his jaw tightening like he was biting back a storm. "The one that told yo—"

"Yes."

His eyes blazed with an anger I hadn't seen before. "I'm going over there."

I quickly grabbed his arm. "Are you sure you want to do that?"

He turned to me, his expression softening just enough to remind me why I loved him so fiercely. "I'm sure. He raised the idiot who hurt you, played a part in it, and now he's staring you down like a fucking creep."

I hesitated, torn between stopping him and letting him fight the battle I never could. Finally, I exhaled. "Okay."

And just like that, Mikkel's grip tightened on my hand and he strode toward the man, every inch of him radiating the kind of power that made people think twice about crossing him. Joshua's father straightened at the sight of him, his smirk slipping into something more measured. *Did they know each other?*

"Mikkel Suarez," he greeted, his voice dripping with feigned cordiality. "This has to be some form of sign. I just re-sent a proposal to your company. I'm hoping we can—"

Mikkel chuckled, interrupting him. The sound was low and sharp, sending a chill through me. "What makes you think I'd ever work with you?"

His smile faltered, confusion flickering across his face. He glanced at me briefly before snapping his attention back to Mikkel. Recognition dawned in his eyes, but he acted as if I weren't there.

"I'm not—"

"*Cierra la puta boca,*[1]" Mikkel snapped, his voice cutting through the air like a blade. His expression hardened as he stepped closer, his frame towering over the man.

The man blinked, his mask slipping just enough to reveal the cracks.

"Your son," Mikkel continued, his voice calm but seething with rage, "humiliated her, treated her like nothing. You and your wife played a part in breaking her down, making her question her worth. And then you have the audacity to stare at her. Do you even realize the damage you've caused?"

"Mikkel, I—"

"It's *Mr. Suarez* when you address me." Mikkel's voice was sharp, cutting through the air like a blade. "Don't flatter yourself by thinking we're on the same level."

The man swallowed hard, his confidence wavering. "Mr. Suarez, I'm sure there's been some misunderstanding—"

Mikkel let out a bitter laugh. "Misunderstanding? No. I understand perfectly. You and your son are nothing but cowards—pathetic little men who thrive on tearing others down because it's the only way you can feel powerful."

My breath caught, tears stinging my eyes. His words—his unwavering defense—hit harder than I'd imagined. No one had ever stood up for me like this.

"Please," the man tried again, his tone shifting to desperation. "This doesn't have to affect the proposal—"

"There is no proposal." Mikkel's voice was ice. "I wouldn't let you within a mile of my company, let alone entertain doing business with you."

The man's face paled, his mouth opening and closing like he wanted to argue, but Mikkel had already made his judgment.

Without another word, Mikkel wrapped his arm around my waist, his grip firm, protective. As he led me away, the world blurred around us, but I didn't care. I clung to him, my heart pounding. For the first time, the battles I fought in my mind weren't mine to fight alone.

---

1 *Shut your fucking mouth.*

CHAPTER FORTY-SEVEN

Mikkel

"True love stories never have endings."
~ *Richard Bach*

As much as I wanted to stay a bit longer in San Francisco, work called.

But my mind wasn't entirely on business—not yet.

As soon as we boarded the jet from San Francisco, I called Arnoldo, my voice tight with anger. I briefly filled him in on Abigail's history with Joshua Milton and his father Joseph's vile role in enabling it. Arnoldo didn't need a second to read my tone.

"Find everything you can on them," I told him. "I want every crack, every weak spot."

By the time we were preparing to land, he'd delivered.

I'd wondered why his name sounded familiar—until Morison reminded me that Joseph Milton had sent a proposal months ago. At the time, we had filed it away, deeming it low priority.

Now it made sense. Milton was likely hoping Elite Rides' expansion could rescue his failing business. His finances were in shambles; the family company had been hemorrhaging money for years. A string of poor investments and questionable decisions had left them clinging to what little they had left. This proposal wasn't just business—it was a last-ditch effort to survive.

Perfect.

I rejected their bid before I even stepped off the jet. The email was short and to the point:

Joseph Milton's proposal has been denied. Elite Rides will not engage in business with individuals of such reprehensible character.

But I didn't stop there. I sent a detailed list of the Milton family's misdeeds to every major player in the industry, then had my friends do the same. The companies they relied on for contracts, the suppliers they depended on, the investors they begged for funding—every one of them now had a reason to blacklist the Miltons.

I wasn't just denying them business. I was erasing their legacy.

Arnoldo called again as the crew unpacked our luggage.

"It's done," he said, his tone steady. "The Milton company's assets have been bought. Employees are being generously compensated, and some skilled workers will join Elite Rides. The building will be demolished in two to three weeks."

"Thank you, Reyes."

Arnoldo hesitated. "I must admit, you don't usually do business this way, Suarez."

"When dealing with vultures, you treat them as vultures," I said. "You taught me that."

He chuckled. "I'm proud. I'll see you at the meeting later to finalize everything with the Miltons."

Their empire was crumbling, and I wouldn't lose a wink of sleep over it. Abigail deserved peace, and I'd make sure those who hurt her couldn't move forward—not while I had the power to stop them.

Once we were back, I made sure Abigail was home safe before heading to my meeting. My execs and legal team were already gathered in the conference room, waiting to discuss the acquisition proposal from Javier Cortez, CEO of Luxe Transports.

This wasn't a merger. It was a buyout.

We reviewed the financials, client base, risks, and rewards. Luxe Transports had a solid customer base, but their fleet needed upgrades. There were always risks—hidden liabilities, merging cultures—but the opportunity to strengthen Elite Rides and accelerate growth was undeniable. The pros far outweigh the cons, and as such we were moving forward with the acquisition.

As the meeting wrapped up, Arnoldo reminded me, "The bigger the acquisition, the bigger the eyes on you. Everyone's watching." His words echoed in my mind—this wasn't just a business decision; it was a statement.

Afterward, I had Morison schedule a meeting with Cortez to finalize the deal. Sitting at my desk, the pressure mounted, so I grabbed the stress ball and tossed it to release some tension. Feeling a little steadier, I returned to work, signing off on documents, catching up on missed files, and focusing on the next steps.

My phone buzzed with a message from the group chat.

Luc
ready to be uncles again?

Ro
HOLY SHIT! (I already knew

Dill
Marina's pregnant?

Luc
why else would I ask that question?

Dill
🙄 congratulations!

Me
I'm happy for you, brother.

Luc
thank you, man.

Reyes
Congrats, Luci. Name the kid Arnoldo Jr.

Alex
thank God someone's joining the dad club.

wishing you and Marina all the best, bro.

Luc
appreciate it, fratellos.[1]

Reyes
Drinks to celebrate?

Luc
I'm in Egypt.

Reyes
Egypt? What the fuck?

Luc
vacation days.

Dill
I should've retired that early too.

Luc
you should've. and yeah, Marina broke the news while we were in the middle of the desert.

The group chat exploded with arguments over who'd be the better uncle. Arnoldo claimed it was him, Dillon and Alex called it bullshit, and Ronan, as usual, declared himself the obvious choice. Lucio barely entertained them, definitely used to the chaos by now.

I smirked, leaning back and shaking my head. I was happy for Lucio—fatherhood was a big deal, and Marina would be an incredible mom. Once they got back from Egypt, I'd make sure to send them something meaningful.

Tuning out the chat, I refocused on work—finalizing the acquisition documents, reviewing logistics, and signing off on reports. I checked in with my team, ensuring smooth operations, then analyzed a fleet check report. Expansion meant nothing without a solid foundation.

I was just wrapping up when a familiar voice cut through the office.

"The only time I see you is in tabloids, Suarez."

I looked up, already knowing who it was. "Ronan Romano. To what do I owe this pleasure?"

"I missed my best friend."

I let out a laugh, rolling my eyes. "Love you too, sweet face."

He poured himself a drink before sinking into the chair before me. "I'm in the area with a developer surveying some buildings."

I raised a brow. "You're buying a building?"

"Thinking about it."

We went back and forth for a bit—him asking about my current projects, me prying into his real estate plans—until he finally headed out.

Not long after, I grabbed my keys, picked up dinner, and drove to Abigail's.

She was curled up on the couch, completely absorbed in *Anora*, barely glancing up as I set the food down. I leaned in, pressing a kiss to her lips. She hummed softly, her fingers brushing my jaw for a fleeting second before turning back to the screen.

We settled into a comfortable silence. I stretched out, resting my head between her thighs as she absentmindedly ran her fingers through my hair. Nothing in the world felt better than this—the drag of her nails against my scalp, the way her touch soothed something deep inside me. Every so often, her hand drifted to my face, fingertips brushing over my lips. I kissed them each time, and even without seeing her face, I knew she was smiling. I felt it in the way her body jerked slightly, and in the quiet happiness radiating off her.

For a while, there was nothing else. No meetings, no acquisitions, no weight of expectations. Just her, just us.

Then she shifted beneath me, sitting up with a sigh.

I groaned, tightening my hold around her waist. "Stay."

"I know," she said softly, pressing a quick kiss to my forehead. "But I need to take my hair down. I've had them in for too long."

I eased up, watching her carefully. "You okay?"

She nodded. "Yeah, just a slight headache."

I sat up straighter. "Show me what to do, and I'll help."

She stared at me, blinking, like she hadn't heard me right.

"I'm serious."

She exhaled a small laugh. "Alright then."

With an online tutorial playing in the background, we got to work on removing her boho locs. It was more challenging than I expected, but I stuck with it, carefully unraveling each one. At first, Abigail coached me through the process, her voice soft but steady. Eventually, though, she grew quiet, her head dipping forward.

When I glanced down, I realized she'd fallen asleep in my lap.

Her breathing was slow and even, exhaustion and her lingering headache finally catching up to her. I kept going, mindful not to tug too hard, working through each section with patience. When the last loc was gone, I reached for a wide-tooth comb and gently began detangling her curls.

I moved through her hair with slow, deliberate strokes, savoring the way each coil softened under my touch. The only sound in the room was the rhythm of her steady breaths. When I finished, I ran my fingers through her hair one last time, letting them linger before leaning back, content just to be here with her.

My gaze lingered on her peaceful face—beautiful, mine. I pressed a soft kiss to her temple. "Rest, *mi amor*."

WARNING

The following chapter contains heavy mentions of mental health/physical health issues. Please refer to the content warning list to be reminded of any potential triggers. Your well-being is important to me, so please take care of yourself while reading.

CHAPTER FORTY-EIGHT

Abigail-Ann

"We loved with a love that was more than love."
- Edgar Allan Poe

I'd mop the fucking ocean or count every grain of salt on this planet before I'd willingly sign up to have my period. But, of course, the one day I had to work for ten hours straight, my uterus decided to return from its months–long vacation in full force.

No warning. No slow build-up. Just pure, unrelenting agony.

The only thing keeping me from spiraling into full-blown misery was the beautiful bouquet Mikkel had left in the kitchen this morning. He didn't just buy fresh flowers—he also got a new vase, arranging them with the same care he always showed. As if that wasn't enough, he placed the knitted ones in a cute stand on my bedside table, no words, no fuss—just doing it like it was second nature.

Coffee with Azzaria had been a welcome distraction for a while, but it didn't last long. She had to rush off, something about Dillon and a flight they needed to catch.

Now, though, I was at work, and nausea hit me like a brick wall. I gritted my teeth, shelving books with robotic precision, nodding politely at the authors here for today's signing. They were nice enough, excited about their books and the readers trickling in, but I wasn't exactly in the mood to be chatty.

The minutes crawled by, stretching out into an eternity. I barely spoke unless necessary, keeping interactions short and efficient. Answering a patron's question. Directing an author to the right table. Sorting a never-ending pile of returns.

I didn't even take a lunch break. Not because I was too busy—though that was part of it—but because my stomach felt like it was waging a war against me, and food was the *last* thing on my mind.

By the time my shift ended, exhaustion clung to me like a second skin. I didn't think twice before booking an Uber, desperate to get home and unwind. The moment I stepped through the door, relief washed over me.

I headed straight for the shower, letting the hot water work out the tension in my muscles. By the time I emerged, wrapped in soft pajamas, I already felt a little lighter. With a cup of chamomile tea in hand, I curled up on the couch, pressing a heating pad to my stomach. The soothing warmth dulled the lingering ache, and for the first time all day, I let myself exhale.

The pain in my lower abdomen intensified, twisting into a relentless ache that made it hard to focus. I tried watching a romcom, but the words blurred and my head pounded even harder. The nausea returned, stronger than before, and I barely made it to the bathroom in time. I retched over the toilet, shaky and weak, then collapsed onto the floor, tears streaming down my face.

My body felt like it was turning against me, the physical pain merging with the weight of the day's exhaustion. I wanted to curl up and disappear, but all I could do was lie there, silent tears slipping down my cheeks.

My phone rang, startling me. I fumbled for it, hoping the sound wouldn't trigger another bout of nausea.

Seeing Mikkel's name on the screen, I swiped to answer, my voice trembling as I spoke, "H-Hello?"

"Baby." His voice was warm and comforting, a stark contrast to how I felt. "Wait, what's going on? Are you okay?"

His concern broke through the fog of pain, and I burst into tears again. "No, I'm not okay," I managed between sobs. "My period came, and the pain is unbearable. I was planning to wash my hair, but now I can't even move without feeling like I'm dying."

"Just hang on a bit more, okay?" he whispered. "I'm on my way."

His words were a remedy, soothing some of the chaos inside me. "Okay," I whispered, my voice barely audible.

I ended the call, dragged myself off the floor, and sank back onto the couch. Placing the heating pad on my stomach, I let its warmth soothe the ache. Exhaustion settled over me, and despite the lingering discomfort, my eyelids grew heavy.

I drifted in and out of a restless sleep, the pain still throbbing in waves through my body. Each movement felt like a Herculean effort, and I was barely aware of the passage of time when I heard a faint knock on my door.

Summoning what little strength I had, I shuffled to the door and pulled it open. Mikkel stood there, a box in his arms, his gaze sweeping over me with a mix of concern and determination.

Without a word, he stepped inside, set the box down on the table, and pulled me into a tight hug.

"I wasn't exactly sure what you needed, so I picked up a few things," he admitted softly. "Food since I wasn't sure if you'd eaten, along with cake, fruits, and Lay's just in case."

Don't cry. Don't cry. Don't cry.

I swallowed. "I don't know what to say…"

Mikkel pulled back slightly. "Did I get it wrong? I ca—"

"No," I interrupted quickly, shaking my head. "You're perfect. It's perfect. I'm just… grateful. More than I can say."

Relief softened his expression, and he pulled me into another hug, holding me gently against him. "I'm here now," he whispered into my hair.

I buried my face against his chest and for the first time all day, a flicker of peace settled over me.

He was here, and that was all that mattered.

Eventually, he helped me get comfortable on the couch, adjusting the heating pad just right. As I sank into the cushions, he unpacked the box, neatly arranging everything on the coffee table within easy reach. Then, he set the yellow and white roses in the new vase—no wonder he'd bought a bigger one.

"Thank you for being here," I whispered again, unable to stop the tears that slipped down my cheeks.

He kissed my forehead gently. "I'll always be here with you, Red."

"You really didn't have to do all this," I murmured, my voice still shaky with emotion.

His hand found mine. "I couldn't live with myself if I didn't."

I squeezed his hand gratefully, and we spent the next hour in comfortable silence, nibbling on snacks. He gave me soft belly rubs as we chatted quietly about inconsequential things. The painkillers began to take effect, dulling the sharp edges of the cramps, though my stomach continued to churn uncomfortably.

"I'm gonna go to bed," I admitted reluctantly. "My stomach's cramping again."

"Of course," he replied, moving to help me from the couch to the bedroom, where he gently tucked me under the covers with the heating pad.

"I'll clean up out there," Mikkel offered quietly, brushing a strand of hair from my face with a gentle touch.

"Thank you," I whispered, overcome once more by his kindness. "For everything."

He kissed my forehead tenderly. "That's what I'm here for, *mi reina.*"

Before meeting him, I thought to be loved was just being told you were loved. But to be loved is being seen. It's being heard. It's the way he listens to everything I say and understands what I haven't, how he remembers the smallest details about me—even the ones I tend to forget. Love is found in the silence between us, never empty but filled with understanding. It's knowing he'll show up when I need him, without me asking. It's the comfort of him making room for my flaws, fears, and dreams, never questioning it.

To be loved is knowing that even on my worst days, when I'm far from my best, I'm still worthy. It's the reassurance that my lowest moments don't define me, and in those times, I'm still cherished. Love isn't about perfection; it's the steady presence that reminds you, no matter what, you're enough.

To be loved, to feel love, is to experience it from Mikkel. Because in all my life, the purest, most gentle love I've ever known has come from him.

CHAPTER FORTY-NINE

Abigail-Ann

"If I had to choose between breathing or loving you, I would say 'I love you' with my last breath."
~ Shannon Dermott

I woke to the scent of something sweet and warm, my body still heavy with sleep. Blinking drowsily, I saw Mikkel walking in, a tray balanced in his hands. Before I could even attempt to sit up, he set the tray on the dresser and was at my side, his strong hands gently guiding me against the pillows.

"Good morning," I mumbled, my voice thick with sleep.

"Good morning, Red," he said as he settled at the edge of the bed, his fingers already finding my feet.

That was when I took him in—completely shirtless, tattoos on full display. It was something I'd seen a thousand times, but never got tired of it. I loved the way the ink wrapped around him, as if it was a part of him, just like the initials of my name engraved on the chain around his neck and wrists. Every time I saw them, it felt like a mark of something deeper between us.

Then, as if it was second nature, his hands moved from my feet to my lower abdomen, then to my back. The gentle pressure made my body melt.

I exhaled. "I'm feeling less nauseous today. And… thanks for making breakfast."

"My pleasure," he whispered before pressing a lingering kiss to my thigh.

I got up to brush my teeth, and when I returned, Mikkel was setting a tray on my lap. It was neatly arranged with a fruit smoothie, a fresh fruit bowl, French toast, and a bagel sandwich layered with egg, ham, and avocado. Beside it, a glass of water and a dose of Midol waited, his attention to detail as thoughtful as ever.

"I Googled what was best for cramps," he said casually, still rubbing slow, soothing circles into my foot. "Fruits and eggs came up a lot. But I know you don't like seeing papaya in your fruit salads, so I put in the smoothie instead."

A lump formed in my throat as warmth unfurled within me, moved by the depth of thoughtfulness behind it all. I didn't have the words to thank him, so I just kissed him. Slow and deep, hoping he could feel what I couldn't say.

When I pulled back, I exhaled. "I want to eat on the floor."

Without hesitation, he moved, settling onto the floor with me as if it was the most normal thing in the world. I took a bite of my bagel sandwich before glancing at him. "Are you gonna eat?"

"I already did."

Of course he did.

"By the way," he added, his voice even but firm, "I had Morison clear my schedule so we could stay in for a while. At least until you're feeling better."

I paused mid-bite. "You—"

"I know I didn't have to," he said before I could argue. "But I wanted to."

I swallowed, staring at him for a long moment before looking away, the weight of his gaze almost too much.

"What do you want to do today?" he asked after a beat.

I sighed. "I want to dye and wash my hair. I missed wash day, and it's driving me insane."

"Let me do it for you."

I blinked. "Wash my hair?"

"Yeah, and dye it."

I snorted. "Are you sure? My hair is thick, and the dye is—"

"No excuses," he cut in smoothly. "When you're done eating, I'll get it done for you."

Breakfast was *delicious*. Every bite of the bagel sandwich, the warm French toast, and the perfectly sweet fruit had me stuffed and satisfied. And Mikkel? Well, he made sure I didn't lift a finger the entire time. After I finished, he pulled me back onto the bed for another massage—this one even better than the first. His hands were magic, easing the last bits of tension from my body, making me forget about the lingering cramps altogether.

Eventually, I dragged myself into the bathroom, needing a moment to just sit and breathe before tackling the beast that was wash day. But to my absolute shock, Mikkel strolled in not even a minute later, his arms full of products—shampoo, conditioner, a hair mask, all sorts of oils, combs, and even the exact hair dye I used.

I blinked at him, my mouth parting. "Where did you get those?"

His lips tugged into a proud smile as he set everything on the counter. "When you called me yesterday, I did some runs. Ulta was one of them. The representative there gave me a *very* passionate lecture about how curly hair needs special care. And I know your hair is important to you, so I needed to make sure I got the right products."

I just *stared* at him, my brain short-circuiting.

What the fuck?

What the *actual* fuck?

"You went to Ulta?" My voice came out small, almost disbelieving.

"Of course," he said, looking entirely too pleased with himself. "Even that curly hair quiz they made me take was worth it."

My eyes widened. "*Oh my God.*"

And suddenly, I was sobbing.

I covered my mouth, shaking my head. "I can't believe you went shopping at Ulta."

He chuckled, brushing a stray tear from my cheek. "And I'd do it again."

I watched, speechless, as he rolled up his sleeves, slipped on gloves, and mixed the dye with precision. His hands moved with practiced ease, sectioning my hair effortlessly.

"You know what you're doing, huh?"

"Yeah. I have a sheet right here with steps from Aurora." He pointed to the laminated sheet I hadn't even realized was propped up in the shower. He called my sister? And wait, he fucking *laminated* it? "Then I watched about four YouTube videos for reinforcement."

I huffed a soft laugh, shaking my head. "You never fail to amaze me."

He bent down, pressing a kiss to my lips before murmuring, "Let's get started, Red."

And he did.

Mikkel worked methodically, ensuring the dye coated every strand. He even went over it twice, something I never had the patience for. When it was time to rinse, he guided me to the sink, his hands steady and sure.

Then came the real care.

He started with a pre-shampoo treatment, gently working it through my curls before detangling with slow, deliberate movements. Next came the shampoo—twice, to make sure the dye was completely out, he explained. His fingers massaged my scalp repeatedly, his touch firm but careful, lulling me into complete relaxation.

When he applied the hair mask, the scent of vanilla and honey filled the air, warm and familiar. He took his time, making sure every inch of my hair was coated before moving on to the conditioner with the same thoughtful attention.

"How does that feel? Am I doing it right?" he asked, his voice softer now.

I let out a slow breath, eyes closed. "You're doing it even better. And so much gentler."

His lips brushed the top of my head before he applied a rich moisturizer, his fingers gliding through my curls with unhurried care. I tilted my head, meeting his gaze as he continued, his touch both gentle and sure.

"You know," I murmured, "if you ever get tired of your billion-dollar company… you might have a future in this."

He smiled, amusement flickering in his eyes, before tucking a damp curl behind my ear. His knuckles brushed my cheek. "I'll keep that in mind, baby."

After helping me up from the shower bench, he stepped outside while I took a quick shower.

When I stepped out, steam curling around me, the soft hum of the heater was the first thing I noticed—a relief, given the cold outside. Then my eyes landed on the neatly folded clothes waiting for me, already picked out, as if he knew I'd be too tired to choose them myself.

Just then, he walked in from the living room, holding a hairdryer and a few other hair tools.

"You did *not* buy a four-hundred-dollar hair dryer!" I stared at him, half in disbelief and the other in amazement.

He chuckled softly, running a hand through his hair. "I wasn't paying attention to the price tag." His eyes met mine, amusement flickering. "The sales rep said it's best for your hair type, so I didn't hesitate. Also grabbed some heat protectant."

I blinked, torn between wanting to scream at him for spending almost five hundred dollars on a hairdryer or crying because he cared enough to buy it.

"Sit down," he said gently, guiding me to the vanity chair. "Let's dry your hair."

I looked at him, speechless, then closed my eyes, silently thanking God for blessing me with this man.

He sectioned my hair with careful precision, spraying heat protectant and working it through with his fingers.

"Where did you learn to do this?"

"I've seen my mom dry Emilia's hair," he said with a fond smile.

I smiled, touched. "That's sweet," I whispered.

After blow-drying, he braided—well, did his best to—my hair into four cornrows, then oiled my scalp.

"All done," he said, stepping back.

I looked at him, overwhelmed. "No one's ever done this for me. I'm so grateful," I whispered.

I kissed him, pouring everything into that moment. We spent the rest of the weekend on the couch, watching movies, wrapped in each other's company.

CHAPTER FIFTY

Mikkel

"Love is not just looking at each other, it's looking in the same direction."
~ Antoine de Saint-Exupéry

A day trip to Seattle sounded easy enough. Fly in, shake a few hands, smile for the cameras, cut the ribbon, then fly back. Simple. But by the time I wrapped up the office opening, handled back-to-back meetings, and sat through a dinner that lasted far longer than it should have, I was running on fumes.

Fun? Sure. But exhausting as hell.

The second I stepped off the plane in New York, my body gave up. I barely made it to my bed before I passed out, only to wake up to Abigail scolding me about pushing myself too hard. It would've been cute if I hadn't felt like I was dying. Then she called my mom—who, of course, lectured me on self-care and rest.

Between them, I had no choice but to give in. So, I rested for two days, then got back to work—eating properly, flying to Los Angeles with Arnoldo, Morison, and Sapphire for market scoping, and returning to finalize the acquisition.

The board approved it without hesitation, calling it perfect timing. Photo ops were arranged, final meetings with Cortez were scheduled, and the launch was set for Christmas Eve. I didn't see the need for a launch party, but Morison insisted it was the perfect way to close out the year and celebrate Elite Rides' success.

Tonight, though, was a long overdue hangout at Arnoldo's house. It was good to unwind with them for a change.

Arnoldo leaned back in his chair, one hand gripping his glass of gin, the other gesturing lazily as if the question wasn't about to stir up some kind of debate. "How much money is too much to spend on your woman?"

The room fell silent for a moment, knowing this would be good. Alex leaned back, grinning. "Here we go."

Dillon was first to speak, casual as ever. "I don't put a tally on it. But it's possibly the matching Bugatti Tourbillon for her and the twins."

The guys chuckled, shaking their heads at the opulence. But that was Dillon—never shy to splurge.

Lucio, lounging with his usual smirk, raised an eyebrow. "The *unborn* twins?"

Dillon grinned. "They'll be born soon, and it was necessary."

Laughter erupted at the thought of twins in luxury cars. Arnoldo crossed his leg. "You're insane."

"Insane or prepared?" Dillon shot back, pride in his eyes.

I shook my head, half-amused. "I'd probably do the same."

Dillon grinned. "She's my whole life. If she wants it, she gets it. Simple as that."

The room grew quiet—not out of surprise, but because we'd all seen it before. Dillon didn't play when it came to Azzaria.

"She's worth every cent," he added, his voice softer than expected. "The cars are nothing compared to my love for her."

Arnoldo smirked, tipping his glass toward Alex. "What about you?"

Alex stretched out, taking a slow sip. "European vacation homes."

Arnoldo raised a brow. "Across the continent?"

Alex grinned. "Mara wanted places in Belgium, Amsterdam, France, Italy, Spain. Gotta have options."

I laughed. "Sounds like a property portfolio."

Arnoldo chuckled. "Now we know Alex's been busy fathering Isaiah, flying planes, and collecting homes like souvenirs."

Alex shrugged. "If it makes her happy, I'm good with it."

The conversation shifted, and Arnoldo's gaze landed on me. "Alright, Suarez. What's the damage?"

I leaned back, amusement in my eyes as thoughts of Abigail crossed my mind. "My jet," I admitted, running a hand over my jaw.

Arnoldo raised an eyebrow. "I thought you bought that for the company?"

I shook my head and took a slow sip of water. "She has flight anxiety."

"I'm waiting for you to tell me this is a joke," Arnoldo said, his tone edged with disbelief.

Dillon and Lucio exchanged knowing glances, their smirks speaking volumes.

"Keep waiting, Reyes," Lucio said, his voice laced with amusement.

Arnoldo shook his head, exasperated. "*Eres increíble*."[1]

"The rule," I said simply, letting the words hang in the air, "is whatever she wants, she gets."

He snorted. "The rule? Come on, there's always a limit."

I shook my head. "Not for her. What are millions compared to her?"

Arnoldo let out a low whistle. "Damn. No wonder she's got you whipped."

"When you love a woman, you love a woman, Reyes. And I happen to love mine."

"I'd say you're bordering on obsessed."

"Bordering?" I laughed. "I *am* obsessed with her."

---

1 *You are unbelievable.*

Reyes chuckled, shaking his head. "Lucio, what about you? What's your damage?"

Lucio glanced at his wedding band, a small smile tugging at his lips. "Marina likes the water, so I bought her an island and two yachts."

Arnoldo raised an eyebrow. "An island? Two yachts? Was that really necessary?"

"Does it matter?" Lucio shrugged, smiling as he twisted the band.

Arnoldo crossed his arms. "You guys are wild. All this for love?"

I shrugged. "You'd do the same if you were in our shoes."

"I don't think I'd drop millions on a yacht, let alone three," Arnoldo said, more to convince himself.

Lucio smirked. "It's not about the money. It's about making her happy."

Arnoldo sat back, stunned. "You're telling me you'd drop anything for your women? No questions asked?"

"Yes," we confirmed.

"I'm not even surprised."

"So, what's the most you've ever spent, Arnoldo?" Alex asked, leaning forward, his curiosity clear.

"The Aruban house as a gift to *myself* or one of my cars." Arnoldo sighed, running a hand through his hair. "I don't have any women to spend on."

Dillon raised an eyebrow, a teasing smile creeping across his face. "When do you plan to fix that?"

Arnoldo rolled his eyes, his smirk betraying his discomfort. "I don't."

"Let's hope you catch the bouquet at Dillon's wedding, Reyes," Alex chimed in, his sarcasm thick.

"Very funny," Arnoldo shot back, crossing his arms but failing to hide his grin. "I'm too busy for commitment."

I leaned back, amusement flickering in my eyes. "Busy doing?"

"Running the biggest multi-billion-dollar law firm in the country and keeping you all in business," Arnoldo replied, shrugging it off. "Not every guy needs a partner to feel complete."

"True," I said, keeping it light. "But you might want to reconsider. You're missing out on some good stuff."

Arnoldo laughed, shaking his head. "Why are you all so hellbent on me falling in love?"

My phone buzzed in my pocket, pulling my attention away. I checked the screen—Abigail had texted me. My cheeks flushed as I read her message.

Red
I'm so wet thinking about you.

They caught the look on my face, and Arnoldo raised an eyebrow. "What's that grin about?"

"Just a… message from Abigail." I cleared my throat, trying to keep myself composed. "I should probably get home."

"Damn, man," Dillon said, feigning shock. "Is everything okay?"

I gulped the rest of my water. "It will be."

The guys exchanged glances, amused and curious. But all I could focus on was Abigail and that damn picture.

I pushed back from my seat. "We'll talk later."

As I headed for the door, Arnoldo called after me. "Drive safe, Suarez."

The drive home was unbearable. Every mile, every second, stretched unbearably. Every red light, every delay, tested my patience. By the time I pulled into the parking lot, my pulse was a hammer, anticipation coiling tight in my gut.

I fumbled with my keys, barely getting the door open before stepping inside. The warmth of home wrapped around me, but it wasn't what made my breath catch. It was *her*.

She sat on the counter like a vision conjured straight from my deepest, filthiest fantasies. The soft glow of the kitchen lights kissed every curve, making the sheer lingerie cling to her skin like sin itself. A glass dangled from her fingers, her green eyes gleaming with something wicked.

"You got here quickly," she mused, her lips curving in amusement.

Not quickly enough.

"I couldn't resist," I admitted, stepping closer, every inch closing the aching distance between us. "Not after that message."

Her giggle was low, teasing. "Was it the picture or the words that did it?"

I swallowed hard. *Both.*

She wrapped her arms around my neck, her body warm and pliant against mine. The scent of liquor lingered between us, smoky and rich.

"What are you drinking?" I murmured, pressing a kiss to her jaw, trailing lower.

"Whiskey."

"Are you drunk?" My hands slid down, gripping her lush curves as I kissed her neck, tasting the heat of her skin.

She giggled again, pressing a finger to my lips. "Not really." Then, her hand trailed down my chest, lingering on the chain around my neck before stopping at my zipper. "I'm sober enough for your cock."

A rough sound tore from my throat as my already hardened cock twitched at her words. Her fingers undid my belt with practiced ease, and before I could think, she knocked back the rest of her whiskey and hopped off the counter.

Without hesitation, she grabbed my hand, pulling me toward the bedroom. "I'm all yours, Mikkel."

God, she had no idea.

I couldn't take my eyes off her. The lingerie, the exact shade of her copper-platinum curls, hugged her like it had been made for this moment. The contrast of her bare skin against the sheer fabric made my throat dry. Her flushed face, her glassy green eyes, her cornrows—everything about her was *utterly irresistible.*

She climbed onto the bed, moving with an effortless confidence that sent a fresh wave of heat through me. My body was a live wire, my restraint unraveling by the second.

Then she met my gaze, bold and unashamed.

"Watch me," she whispered, propping herself up on the pillows.

My breath stilled.

"Hm?"

She ran a slow, teasing hand down her stomach.

"Watch me touch myself."

Fuck.

I stood frozen, jaw tight, fists clenched, every cell in my body screaming for her. For us.

I didn't just watch.

I memorized.

I tossed my head back, the sight of her propped up and completely open for me was enough to bring me to my knees.

Giving me a saucy little smile, she pulled the straps down and popped her breasts out, making me moan as her hard nipples were exposed.

"That feels so good, baby," she crooned, grabbing a handful of her breast as her other hand rubbed between her legs. The cycle repeated until I couldn't take it anymore.

"Fuck it," I muttered and climbed on the bed.

"I'm not done yet!" she protested as I slipped my hand up her thigh, the wetness already running down.

"I'm going to finish you. How do you want it?"

She bit her lip and smirked. "How do I want what?"

I moved my hand from her thigh and brought it to her neck, gripping it gently. "How do you want me to fuck you?"

"Y-you pick," she whispered.

"Hold on to the head board and don't let go."

She nodded and did exactly as she was told.

"Like this?" I asked, lining my cock up with her pussy and thrusting in. I groaned and she shrieked as the tightness of her pussy wrapped around my dick.

So fucking wet...

So fucking hot…

"L-like t-that," she stuttered.

She moaned and panted, her body squirming against mine as I rolled her hardened nipples between my fingers. Gripping the headboard for support, she held on tightly as I thrust into her, hard and rough. Her breaths hitched with every stroke, her movements matching my rhythm as her breasts swayed in time with my movements.

"Mikkel! Mikkel!" She shouted. "Right there. Please, please please."

It only took a minute before an explosive orgasm overtook her. The rapture sent her soaring and her body shuddering at the intense sensations ripping through her.

"Hmm," she moaned, bringing her hand to massage my balls.

My cock bobbed in front of me, glistening with her cum. She looked at me, my eyes now glazed with lust.

"Open up, baby. Clean all your cum off my cock."

She quickly went on her knees, and leaned forward eagerly to take me in her mouth. I moaned at the contact, my hand instinctively reaching her hair. Her green eyes were filled with passion as she looked up at me, her lips tightly stretched around my cock and her body on display for me.

"I love when you suck my cock," I praised as she played with my balls, making me groan as I thrust harder and faster.

Sliding my hands into her hair, disheveling her cornrows, I thrusted hard and fast into her mouth as she sucked with even more force.

"Fuck yes, baby."

The muffled whimpers she made vibrated against me, intensifying the pleasure as her fingers gripped my balls. I tightened my hold on her hair, my head falling back as the tension built. Thrusting into her mouth, I held her close, feeling the movements of her throat and tongue as I came. Wanting more, I withdrew at the last moment, releasing the final strands across her breast.

"Clean off your fingers with your mouth, baby," I said, my voice a little hoarse. "And don't touch the cum on your breasts, I like seeing it there."

"Or," she spoke up, a mischievous glint in her eyes, "let's get in the shower."

"Adventurous tonight, aren't you?"

She nodded, a playful smile curving her lips. "You have no idea."

We stepped into the bathroom, but I stopped in my tracks. She stood there, bathed in soft light, effortlessly captivating. The curve of her back, the way her copper platinum curls framed her face—every inch of her held me spellbound. My gaze traced the graceful sway of her hips, the quiet radiance she carried, and for a moment, I forgot everything else.

She turned to look at me. "You coming in?"

"I just needed a minute."

"A minute to?" She asked, picking up a bar of soap and rubbing it over her body.

"Admire you, baby," I finally said and joined her in the shower. "You drive me crazy."

"In a good way, I hope."

"In the best way," I confirmed. "Seeing your wet pussy like that, that text message. The matching lingerie, knowing how your greedy cunt always milks my cock and how fucking sexy your sounds are. I just.... *You're perfect.*"

Her cheeks reddened as her smile reached her eyes.

I took the soap from her, lathering it in my hands before slowly soaping her neck, chest, and breasts. My hands lingered longer than necessary until she moaned softly and gently pushed them away.

"I love your touches," she whispered and grabbed the soap from me, repeating the process on me this time.

She rubbed my neck, trailing down to my chest, then lower, gliding over my stomach to my pelvis before finally wrapping her slick fingers around my hard cock.

"Is that for me?"

"It's always for you, *mi reina.*"

I pulled her closer, kissing her passionately as our wet, soap-covered bodies pressed together. She stroked me, and I ran my hands down her back to her ass. The kiss deepened, and soon we were grinding into each other.

"Another round, Red?"

She nodded, a small moan escaping. "Fuck me till the sun comes up."

She moaned louder as my fingers teased her clit, her grip tightening on me while her strokes became firmer. Our kisses grew more intense, urgent, and hungry. Breaking the kiss, she dropped to her knees, guiding my dick gently into her mouth as her eyes locked with mine.

A deep groan escaped me, and I leaned back against the shower wall, overwhelmed by the sensation. My hand rested lightly on the back of her head, guiding her. Her moans vibrated through me, driving me wild. Unable to hold back any longer, I pulled her up from her knees, adjusting our positions until I slid my cock between her legs.

"Oh my gosh," she whimpered. "*Yes! Yes! Yes!*"

Our hips pressed together, and she moaned as I brushed cock across her pussy lips, teasing her. She squirmed, trying to position herself closer, but every time she got near, I pulled back, savoring the moment. Sliding to my knees, I grabbed the shower head and brought it closer to her clit.

"Fuck," she moaned. "E-everything f-feels better when you do it."

Another moan came, a much louder one, as I replaced the water with my tongue. I licked her outer lips gently, teasing her, feeling her body quiver from my attention. Becoming more insistent, her hand found the back of my head and pressed my face into her. Soon her hips were grinding erratically, and her moans were becoming louder, echoing in space.

"D-Don't stop," she breathed. "P-please."

Gently, I slid a finger inside her, then a second, as I kept working her clit over with my tongue. Her hips moved faster as I found her g-spot, massaging it slowly with my fingers, while pressing my tongue hard against her clit, grinding it. She began to shudder and shake, the vibrations causing me to go even harder.

"Mikkel!" she yelled and came right on my tongue. Her muscles contracted around my fingers, and her entire body pressed down against me. With a final shudder, she relaxed, and we collapsed together on the shower floor. I held her, her head on my shoulder, as her breathing returned to normal. At some point, she must have felt my dick poking at her, because she took it into her hand and looked at me.

"Do you want it like this?" She asked as she stroked me. "Or in my pussy?"

"That mouth of yours," I whispered, dragging my thumb over her lips, "will be the death of me."

She grinned as the stroking continued and my hand found its way to the underside of her breast, my fingers occasionally moving up to lightly pinch her nipple.

Then out of nowhere, she rushed to her feet.

"Come up here and fuck me."

I wasted no time in rising, and soon she was bent at the waist, holding the safety bar. I moved behind her and ran my cock up her thigh, and between her legs then entered in one long slow push. She pushed back into me, and we both groaned as I filled her.

I let her set the pace, and she began slowly rocking back and forth onto me. Before long she started moving faster, and my hips started moving into her.

"*Fuck. Fuck. Fuck!*" she screamed.

We kept a steady pace, but I needed to see her. I wanted to watch her as I filled her with my cock. Pulling out, I turned her around before she could say a word. Pressing her against the wall, I lifted her leg for better access. She wrapped her arms around my neck and leg around my waist as I entered her again.

Our lips met, and her nails dug into my shoulders, fueling my need. Each thrust brought us closer, our bodies in perfect sync. I kissed her jaw, her moans vibrating against me. She hit the shower wall with every thrust, legs tightening as I pinned her, and she moved herself up and down, driving us both higher.

Fucking her was the most out of this world experience.

"Cum inside of me, baby," she whispered. "Be a good boy and do that for me."

I've *never* been called that but suddenly, I wanted to drop to my knees and show her how good I could be. *Repeatedly*.

Putting her head right beside my ear and increasing her riding speed, she whispered, "you're so good to me."

I could feel myself getting close, and held her even tighter. My motions were becoming more erratic, and fuck, I wasn't gonna last. My balls tightened and my brain felt like it was imploding. I turned my head and kissed her hard as I felt my orgasm wash me.

As soon as I came, her legs clamped hard around me, and she moaned into my mouth. Her pussy went into overdrive, trying to milk every drop of cum from me. We trembled against each other, our lips still locked as pleasure consumed us. As the intensity faded, I sank to the floor of the tub, guiding her down with me, holding her close as our breathing slowly steadied.

"Just the way I like it," she whispered.

"The way you like it?" I asked in between deep breaths.

She nodded. "Good boy."

We moved to the tub, my back resting against the side as Abigail settled in my lap. A soft whimper of disappointment left her lips as I slipped out, her hold on me tightening. I pressed gentle kisses to her neck, my fingers threading through her curls as we held each other, letting the warm water wash over us.

Eventually, we separated and I cleaned us up.

"You're the only one," she murmured, her voice a soft caress that wrapped around my heart. "The only person I have ever and will ever let cum inside of me."

I felt like I'd just scaled a mountain, breathless and exhilarated, her words elevating me to heights I never imagined I could reach.

Her eyes sparkled with an intensity that took my breath away. "I trust no one as deeply as I trust you."

"*Te amo*,[2]" I whispered, the words spilling from my lips like a sacred promise.

"*Te quiero mucho*,[3]" she replied softly, and I froze, my gaze snapping to hers. It was the first time she'd ever spoken to me in Spanish.

---

2 *I love you.*

3 *I love you more.*

"Say it again," I murmured, my voice barely audible.

She leaned in, her lips brushing mine. "*Te amo, guapo.*[4]"

"*¿Siempre?*[5]" I asked, my heart pounding.

"*Siempre.*"

---

4 *I love you, handsome.*

5 *Always*

CHAPTER FIFTY-ONE

Abigail-Ann

"One word frees us of all the weight and pain of life: that word is love."
~ Sophocles

The door clicked shut behind us, and I finally exhaled, the sound soft but filled with relief. Dinner had been lovely, and intimate, but now my feet were paying the price for the heels I'd decided to wear. Ten thousand-dollar shoes. For all the luxury they promised, there wasn't an ounce of comfort.

Mikkel, ever perceptive, glanced at me as I hobbled toward the couch. "Tired?"

I rolled my eyes playfully, trying to hide the discomfort in my expression. "Not tired… these shoes are pure torture."

His gaze darkened and his lips curled into a smirk. "Come here," he commanded, his tone making my heart somersault—an order that had my body reacting before my mind could catch up.

As I approached him, he guided me to a high seat near the wall, pulling it out with a firm yet gentle touch.

I sat, and my feet screamed in relief. But that was nothing compared to what happened next. Without a word, Mikkel dropped to his knees before me. My breath caught, and I instinctively reached to stop him.

"Mikkel, wait—"

He silenced me with a single, commanding look. "Stay still." His voice was low, almost a whisper, but it had the kind of power that left no room for argument.

A deep tremor of anticipation rolled through me as I complied, my heart pounding with a mix of shock and desire for him to continue. His hands moved swiftly and skillfully, undoing the straps of my heels in seconds. The pressure around my toes and the balls of my feet eased, flooding me with overwhelming relief.

"Mmmm," I sighed, sinking back into the chair, too lost in the sensation of his hands on my feet to even care about anything else.

"Better?" he asked, his fingers rubbing along the curve of my arch, his touch steady and slow. My body melted further into the chair as I struggled to form a coherent thought. All I could do was nod, but it wasn't enough.

Then, to my shock, Mikkel pressed a soft kiss to my ankle, and my whole body went still. He continued up, placing another kiss on the curve of my calf, sending a wave of heat straight through me.

I had no words, only feelings, the kind that wrapped around my chest, leaving me breathless. "I… I like you doing that." The words were shaky, not entirely clear. "I like you down there."

He looked up, something unspoken flickering in his eyes. His gaze darkened, lips pressing into a tight line before he spoke, his voice making my heart race.

"All you have to do is say the word," he murmured. "I'll stay here, right where you want me—because you don't just have me on my knees, *amorcita*[1]. You own me. In every way that matters."

---

1 *little love*

A hot flush spread across my skin, and the intensity of his words seeped into my bones.

"Mikkel," I whispered, reaching for him instinctively. I needed him closer—needed to touch him, *feel him.*

Before I could reach him, his hand shot out, capturing my wrist. He guided it to his chest, and beneath my palm, I felt the steady, powerful rhythm of his heart.

"I love you." We've said it before—granted, in Spanish—but this time, it felt different. *More intimate.*

He took a slow breath, his chest rising beneath my palm before he stood, leaving me cold. Towering over me, his gaze softened yet intense, as if memorizing the moment.

I swallowed hard, then the words spilled out. "I spent so long convincing myself I was hard to love. That no one would ever choose me, not fully. And then you came into my life, and you didn't just love me, you showed me what love was supposed to be." My voice trembled. "To be loved is to be loved by you, and I've never been happier."

Emotion flickered in his eyes, raw and unguarded, but I wasn't finished. "Thank you," I whispered, my voice unsteady. "For showing me real love—not just helping me, but teaching me how to love myself."

I looked at him, my heart full, but as I opened my mouth to continue, he reached forward, his hand gently cupping the side of my face. His thumb stroked the edge of my jaw as his lips found mine.

When we finally pulled apart, he cradled my face gently in his hands. "I've spent my life chasing success, building an empire, thinking that would be enough. But you—you're the only thing I've ever truly needed." His voice was thick with emotion. "Every choice I've made, every path I've walked, led me to you. You are my joy, my peace, *mi todo*[2]. In loving you, I've found a wholeness I never even realized I was missing, Red."

"*Te amo mucho,*[3]" I whispered back, overwhelmed with emotion.

---

2 *my everything*

3 *I love you so much*

He looked up at me. "*Te quiero, mi vida.*[4]"

This—us—was the kind of love I had always dreamed of, and now, I was living it.

We lay in bed, tangled in cool sheets, my head resting on Mikkel's chest, listening to his steady heartbeat. The air felt softer, more intimate as I breathed him in. In his arms, everything felt peaceful, real, and certain.

I lifted my head to look up at him. "Do you think about our future?"

His gaze softened. "Every day, Red."

"What's it like in your head?"

"Travel, happiness—though not without a little chaos—nights in, nights out and one day, a beautiful family."

I leaned up and kissed him, wanting to hold onto that promise.

When we pulled apart, breathless, I whispered, "Make love to me."

Heat flared in his eyes as he moved to kiss my neck. "Tell me what you want. You want me to eat your pussy? Say it. You want me to slowly fuck you while we hold hands? Say it. Tell me what you want, and I'll give it to you."

"I-I want it all."

"Entonces te daré todo lo que quieras.[5]"

My body trembled at his touch, his intense gaze sending shivers through me. He admired me like art, making me feel priceless. A soft moan escaped as he kissed and licked my neck, his warm breath igniting waves of pleasure.

I reached out and ran my fingers through his hair, stroking the back of his neck while he planted kisses down my body. I felt his tongue flick across my left nipple before taking it into his mouth and sucking it.

"Please," I begged, gasping.

---

4 *I love you, my life*

5 *Then I'll give you what you want.*

He kept moving lower, his head now between my thighs as the heat between my legs turned into a slick, aching need.

"Please don't stop," I begged, once more. *"Please."*

I spread my legs a little wider and felt his tongue flash across my clit.

I moaned loudly, begging him to go on. "Fuck, yes."

A deep exhale escaped, a warm thrill spreading through the body, igniting every nerve, sinking into mind and soul.

"More," I needily moaned, eliciting such a strong reaction in me that I began trembling and twitching uncontrollably as I approached my climax.

"Cum for me, Red." He brought his thumb to violently rub my clit while he continued eating my pussy. "Let me taste your sweet pussy."

I gasped, my body moving uncontrollably, shaking so violently that I felt his free hand grip my thighs to steady me. I thought I might pass out. As my muscles relaxed, the pleasure surged, filling me with a warm, blissful haze that spread throughout my body.

He smiled, lifting his head to take in my fatigued but satisfied expression.

"Are you okay?" he asked, settling beside me and pulling me into his arms.

"Better than ever." My body still trembled, my clit throbbing in the aftermath, but his warmth wrapped around me like a cocoon.

His face neared mine, and as our lips met, I tasted myself on him. His hand moved in slow, soothing circles along my back, while I cradled his face, pulling him closer. I drank in his kisses like a wanderer finding water in the desert—life-giving, essential, everything I needed.

I felt one of his hands gradually travel down and lightly brushed my pussy as we kissed.

He slowly broke from the kiss and looked me in the eyes, his honey-brown gaze filled with warmth and intensity.

"Do you want my cock now, mi amor?"

"Please."

He lifted me into a sitting position and then lay down on his back, his hard cock sticking straight up. I leaned forward and flicked my tongue over the pierced tip before swallowing the entire head and sucking hard on it.

"Spit on it." His voice was rough, the command pulling at something primal in me.

I froze, my breath catching in my throat as I looked up at him, his eyes bright and locked on mine. My pulse quickened, heat crawling up my neck, though I didn't dare break eye contact.

"Red." His tone was softer now, but no less commanding. "I said to spit on it."

I leaned forward, my gaze fixed on his, feeling the power shift as his jaw tightened. I took my time, savoring the moment, a smirk tugging at my lips. Finally, I obeyed, the deliberate act sending chills through me.

"Good girl," he praised, the words wrapping around me like a tether I didn't want to break. "Now suck."

"Fuck, yes baby," he cursed, his hands finding its way to grip my hair, "Me encanta cuando me chupas la polla.[6]"

I met his gaze with a warm grin, locking eyes in a deep, loving glance.

"A little deeper," he suggested and I took more of him into my lips.

"You're so perfect, *mi corazón*,[7]" he exclaimed, appreciating my efforts, "Just like that."

After a few minutes, I carefully climbed on top of him while he grabbed my hips to keep me from falling over.

"You're s-so big," I said in between moans as I sank onto his cock.

"You're so wet," he rasped. "I can't get enough of you."

He reached for my head, pulling me close as he gently kissed my lips, his hand stroking my back slowly. A soft groan escaped me at the powerful sensation washing over me, feeling cherished and complete in a way I had never known. I sat up, glancing down to see myself completely filled, then began moving slowly, his hands guiding my hips.

He gasped. "Just like that, baby."

I slowly clenched my teeth as his cock went deeper and deeper inside of me.

---

6 *I love it when you suck my cock.*

7 *my heart*

As I adjusted to the sensation, I picked up the pace, my walls tightening around him. I rode him slowly at first, then faster, meeting his gaze as pleasure built between us. His hand found my breast, kneading and teasing, his fingers occasionally pinching my nipple, sending shivers down my spine.

"You like riding my cock, don't you?"

I groaned in response, losing all my words.

He slid his thumb in my mouth, compelling me to suck it. "Use your words, baby."

"Y-yes," I managed to say, my brain completely disheveled.

"I wish you could see me fucking you." He took a nipple into his mouth. "How your eyes roll over whenever I touch that spot and how fucking wet your pussy gets at every stroke."

His hands remained on my hips and I reached down to rub my clit with one hand as I felt him slipping in and out.

"I'm gonna cum," he said.

"Cum inside of me."

As I felt the warmth of him explode within my pussy, I screamed with delight and collapsed against him.

His fingers traced gentle circles on my warm skin. "Are you okay?"

"I'm more than okay," I whispered as I savored the moment.

He started to get up, but I reached out, my hand resting on his arm to stop him. "Let's stay here a while."

"But, I need to get–"

"Let's just stay here a while," I repeated, my eyes locking onto his.

He sighed softly, a smile tugging at his lips. "Anything for you, Red."

"Anything?"

"I love you," he whispered, and with that, his lips met mine in a fiery, passionate kiss, igniting the spark between us once more.

CHAPTER FIFTY-TWO

Abigail-Ann

"You have bewitched me, body and soul, and I love, I love, I love you."
~ Jane Austen, Pride and Prejudice.

My phone buzzed with an email, and I clicked it. The subject line made my breath hitch: **Congratulations!** My heart pounded as I read the words glowing on the screen. I'd been accepted into my year-and-a-half apprenticeship, starting in three months. A thrilled laugh escaped me as I quickly texted Mikkel, my parents, and Azzaria. Years of late nights, doubts, and dreaming had finally paid off.

Sliding my phone back into my pocket, a deep breath calmed the flutter in my chest as focus shifted to the task at hand. The stacks of books on the counter wouldn't shelve themselves, and the murmurs of a few customers near the thriller and mystery section already reached my ears. Work first, celebration later.

The morning passed in a blur of book recommendations and helping customers find their next favorite read. Before I knew it, my shift was over, and it was time to meet Azzaria for her first wedding dress fitting at Vivienne Westwood.

Stepping into the boutique, I was immediately struck by its elegance. Crystal chandeliers cast a warm glow over plush carpets, and racks of luxurious gowns awaited their brides.

"Abi!" Azzaria's voice rang out, filled with excitement. She looked beautiful, her baby bump now a soft curve beneath her dress.

"You look amazing!" I said, hugging her gently. "Ready to find the perfect dress?"

She beamed. "Absolutely. This is so surreal. I'm nervous."

The designer, Cara, a poised British woman with short black curls, approached with a warm smile. "Welcome, ladies. Shall we get started?"

She led us into a private fitting room, where twenty dresses—each sketched by Nina Moretti in Italy—were displayed. "We'll go through these to find the styles that suit you best," Cara explained, scrolling through designs on her tablet.

Azzaria's eyes widened. "When Dillon said there were dresses waiting, I didn't expect twenty," she muttered, a hint of irritation in her voice.

I squeezed her arm. "Breathe, Azzy. Dillon just wants the best for you."

"I know, but *twenty*?"

Cara stepped in with a reassuring smile. "This process is about finding the dress that speaks to you. The one that makes you feel unstoppable. Your groom just wants everything to be perfect and stress-free for you."

Azzaria sighed and spent the next forty-five minutes sorting the sketches into three piles—*no way, maybe,* and *definite yes.*

Cara's eyes lit up as she took the final selections. "These are perfect. We'll have the dresses sent over for your fitting."

Azzaria's eyes sparkled with tears. "Thank you, Cara. Also, I have no idea how much more my belly will grow. I'm carrying twins."

"Mr. Xander mentioned that. We'll take care of the alterations."

Azzaria smiled, touched by Dillon's thoughtfulness.

"You're going to be the most beautiful bride," I whispered, my throat tight with emotion. "It's such an honor to be your maid of honor."

Azzaria turned, her smile radiant. "I couldn't imagine anyone else by my side."

We hugged carefully before she went to change. When she returned, we chatted, her hand tenderly caressing her tiny bump.

"How are the other parts of wedding planning going?"

"It's been a lot, but it's good," she shared. "The wedding is going to be magical. I wanted to do it all myself, but pregnancy is kicking my ass, so Dillon hired Celeste Gray."

I raised my eyebrows in disbelief, leaning forward. *"Celeste Gray that designed and planned the Livingston wedding?"*

Azzy laughed, nodding. "I was just as shocked too, but Dillon will not be stopped. Once he gets an idea in his head, there's no turning back. I think he's secretly enjoying all this wedding stuff more than I am!"

Her smile was soft, but you could tell there was an undercurrent of excitement.

"Your wedding's gonna be perfect!" I exclaimed, already picturing the romantic setting.

She sighed happily. "I'm sorry I've been so busy and not really there."

"Don't worry about it," I reassured her. "Life takes us to different places but no matter what, you're my best friend in every lifetime and that will never change."

Azzaria's eyes shimmered with unshed tears as she leaned over to hug me tightly. "In every lifetime, Abigail."

After an hour of intense negotiations with Javier Cortez, the deal was sealed—Luxe Transports now belonged to Elite Rides. Another "competitor" absorbed, another victory secured. As always, Arnoldo had outdone himself, drafting a clause so airtight that any breach would cost them double the sale price. Ruthless. Perfect.

We did the press rounds—photo ops, interviews. The headlines rolled in, the city buzzing with the news, but none of it held my attention. The only thing that mattered was the clock ticking down to Abigail's doctor's appointment. I barely let the cameras flash one last time before I was out the door.

She wasn't sick, but after witnessing how her period drained her—crippling back pain, abdominal cramps, and relentless headaches—I couldn't just stand by. I urged her to see a gynecologist, hoping she'd find a way to ease the pain. To make her feel safer, I had Ronan's team vet the top specialists in the country, then brought them into my conference room on her day off, letting her choose.

Back at the office, the day blurred into investor follow-ups, a GQ feature, finalizing year-end hiring, and approving Christmas bonuses. But my mind was elsewhere. Sitting at my desk, I attempted to fold paper roses which was frustrating as hell, but I kept at it.

The moment the clock hit six, I was gone. I made a few stops—fresh flowers, her favorite snacks, and two special gifts.

When I finally reached her apartment, she answered the door in one of my button-downs, my cologne lingering on her skin. Nothing was sexier.

For a second, I just took her in, then dropped everything onto the nearest surface and kissed her like I'd been starving for it. Because I had been.

After what felt like forever, I pulled back just enough to look at her. "How was it?"

She leaned into my chest. "Not as bad as I thought. Dr. Sang was nice."

"Good." I brushed my lips against her forehead. "And?"

She exhaled, a hint of relief in her voice. "She gave me options. We'll see what works."

I nodded, tension easing from my shoulders. "You tell me the second you need anything, okay?"

"I know, Mikkel," she teased, her grin playful as her eyes roamed over me. "You look so handsome. And thank you for the flowers."

I lifted a bag of chocolates, a ribbon-tied box, and a bag of Lay's. "Got you these too."

Her eyes lit up instantly. "This is perfect! What's in the box?"

"Open it and see."

She untied the ribbon, revealing rows of black-and-white chocolate chip cookies from Levain Bakery. "How did you know I wanted these?"

"You've mentioned it sometime last week."

Her eyes softened, a smile on her lips. "You never make me feel unheard," she said warmly. "I love you even more for that."

As she set the cookies down, I pulled out another wrapped box. "This is for you."

Curiosity flickered in her eyes as she unwrapped it, unveiling a custom-made leather portfolio embossed with her full name and a delicate house-and-key design. Beside it lay an engraved keychain reading *Home Sweet Home,* adorned with a tiny house charm.

"Oh my goodness, this is incredible!" she gasped, tracing the soft leather in awe.

"We're celebrating all your wins, *mi reina*[1]" I said, my heart swelling as I watched her excitement. "I wanted you to have something special for your apprenticeship, a reminder of how far you've come, how far you'll go and how much I believe in you."

Tears glistened in her eyes as she looked up at me. "I love it!"

I chuckled, pulling her closer. "*Te adoro, Red.*[2]"

I pulled her close again, my lips crashing into hers, deep and desperate. *I couldn't get enough of her.* But then, she pulled back with a breathless laugh, her eyes sparkling with something playful.

"You're gonna get me naked at this rate," she whispered with a smile, her fingers grazing the back of my neck.

"Is that a bad thing?"

---

1 *my queen*

2 *I adore you, Red*

"No," she said, a mischievous glint in her gaze. "But I have something to show you first."

I followed her into the bedroom, curiosity piqued. The first thing I noticed was the massage station, then the spread of tostones, barbecue wings, and *croquetas de pollo*. But what stopped me in my tracks was the sign on the wall: *Estoy muy orgullosa de ti, guapo!*[3]

My throat tightened as I turned to look at her, the reality of what she'd done hitting me like a ton of steel. I pulled her into me, wrapping her in my arms. "*Gracias, mi amor.*"[4]

She cupped my face, her touch gentle. "You never need to thank me," she said, her voice soft, but sure. "You're doing amazing things, Mikkel. You work so hard… doing this for you was nothing."

Her words hit me harder than any success I'd achieved. I couldn't even respond right away, just pulled her closer and pressed my lips against hers.

She smiled softly, her fingers tracing the edge of my shirt. "Now, let's get started."

I sat without argument, letting her hands work into my shoulders, the tension melting away under her touch. My eyes drifted shut as she kneaded at the knots in my neck, the warmth of her hands grounding me in a way nothing else could.

After a while, she leaned down, pressing a kiss behind my ear. "You okay?"

I opened my eyes, reaching for her hand. "Better than ever."

She smiled. "Good. Now, come with me."

She led me into the bathroom, nudging me to sit on the edge of the tub. Grabbing the clippers, she sectioned my hair and began trimming with careful precision.

"You're on a roll," I murmured, watching her reflection in the mirror as she focused.

She smirked. "Of course I am. You're my favorite client."

I chuckled. "*I'm your only client.*"

---

3 *I am so proud of you handsome*

4 *Thank you, my love.*

She shot me a playful look. "And that's the way I like it."

After finishing my haircut, she dusted off the loose hairs before tilting my chin up. "Stay still," she instructed, grabbing a trimmer. With gentle strokes, she lined up my beard, smoothing out the edges before moving to my mustache.

I closed my eyes for a moment, enjoying the way her fingers brushed against my skin as she worked.

A few minutes later, she stepped back, admiring her work. "Perfect," she declared, satisfaction clear in her tone.

I ran a hand over my freshly cut hair, smirking. "You're getting better at this."

She rolled her eyes, laughing. "I've always been good."

Chuckling, I dusted the remaining hairs off my shoulders. "I need a shower."

She met my gaze, something unspoken passing between us. Then, without a word, she took my hand and led me to the shower.

Steam curled around us as I turned on the water. She pulled my shirt over her head, revealing bare skin beneath. My breath caught, but she only held out her hand, waiting.

I stepped in, the hot water cascading over us as I pulled her close. We moved in sync, washing each other in silence, our touches slow and deliberate. The intimacy settled deep, reaching beyond words.

Later, tangled in the sheets, she rested her head on my chest, tracing soft patterns against my skin.

I didn't need anything else. Everything I'd ever wanted was right here—with her.

"This is one of my favorite parts of our relationship, Red."

She looked up at me. "What is?"

"Knowing that at the end of each day, no matter how it goes." I paused, gazing at her with adoration. "I come home to the most beautiful woman who makes me the happiest."

Her smile deepened, and she rested her forehead against mine. "And I always will, *guapo*,[5]" she whispered.

"You speaking Spanish makes my dick hard."

She took my hand, guiding it between her legs. "You existing makes my pussy wet. So, we're even."

I grinned. I guess we were.

"*Te quiero*."[6]

She leaned in closer, her fingers brushing mine. "*Te quiero*, to you too."

"*Te quiero mucho*,[7]" I corrected, stretching the words with a playful grin.

She chuckled, squeezing my hand. "I know. It's just funnier that way."

I love this life. I love this woman. And I'd do anything to keep her in it.

---

5 *handsome*

6 *I love you*

7 *I love you too*

CHAPTER FIFTY-THREE

Abigail-Ann

"Where there is love, there is life."
*~ **Mahatma Gandhi***

The week had drained me—early mornings for book signings and the looming start of my apprenticeship made it hard to shake the feeling that I'd miss the bookstore. Outside, snow blanketed the streets, the cold seeping in despite my layers. But the real weight pressing down on me wasn't the weather—it was the quiet hum of anxiety beneath the surface.

Mikkel had been in Los Angeles for work the past few days, but he was back now. Earlier, I'd rushed from work to my gynecologist appointment, relieved by the good news. I ended the day with a check-in with Dr. Green, reflecting on how far I'd come.

The last thing I remembered was Mikkel typing beside me in bed. Now, I woke up alone.

Where was he?

Sliding out of bed, I pulled on his hoodie and padded barefoot through the penthouse. My first stop was his study, but it was empty—neatly organized as always, but eerily still. I frowned, my curiosity piqued.

I made my way down the staircase, the quiet tapping of my steps the only sound in the vast space. As I reached the lower level, I noticed a door slightly ajar—one I'd never seen open before, and I gently pushed it open and stepped inside.

I gasped. *What the hell?*

The room was straight out of a dream. It *heavily* resembled the enchanted West Wing from *Beauty and the Beast.* Tall glass cases lined the walls, each housing delicate flowers frozen in time. Golden light spilled from the chandeliers and the centerpiece of the room was a pedestal in the middle, like the one that held Beast's rose.

I blinked, unsure if I was dreaming. My voice came out in a reverent whisper. "I never knew this was here."

"That's because it wasn't," came a deep voice from behind me.

I turned, my heart skipping a beat as I saw Mikkel standing in the doorway. He was holding a glass dome with a rose inside.

"*Mikkel,*" I breathed, taking a step toward him. "*Mikkel Andrés Suarez.*"

His lips curved into a soft smile as he stepped closer. "*¿Sí, mi amor?*[1]" he murmured, carefully placing the dome on the pedestal. "*Beauty and the Beast* is your favorite movie, and this room is inspired by the West Wing. I may not be the *Beast*, but you…" His light eyes softened as they met mine. "You're definitely *Beauty*. The most beautiful, actually."

I blinked back the sting of happy tears.

"I can't believe this is real."

"I've been meaning to do this for you. Something that felt magical." He reached for my hands, threading his fingers through mine. "You spend a lot of time here, and I hope one day it becomes permanent. But for now, this rose….this room…it's yours."

---

1 *Yes, my love.*

I glanced at the rose under the glass, captivated by its delicate petals.

He continued, "Each time you tap the glass, a petal will fall. But every petal has something I love about you written on it and a quote I thought might help for the days you need it."

I stared at him, my heart thundering in my chest. "You made the rose?"

He nodded, his gaze unwavering. "It took me a while, but it was worth it."

He. Made. The. Fucking. Rose.

Tears slipped down my cheeks as I closed the distance between us and kissed him gently. When I pulled away, I whispered, "You're beyond amazing."

"Tap it," he urged, nodding toward the rose.

With trembling fingers, I reached out and lightly tapped the glass. One of the petals inside fluttered down slowly, landing softly at the base of the dome. I picked it up eagerly, grinning as I read it.

"I love the way your laugh lights up a room," it read, followed by a quote: *'Just because you feel afraid doesn't mean you aren't brave.'*

I stared at the petal, my throat tightening as emotion surged. "Baby…"

"You're worth it."

I turned to him, threading my arms around his neck and drawing him into a deeper kiss, surrendering all my love and appreciation.

This was magic. He was magic. And somehow, I'd been lucky enough to call him mine.

I pulled back, breathless, his gesture sinking in as I clutched the petal, holding onto the moment.

"*Beauty and the Beast* is everything to me," I said, my voice trembling with excitement. "It's not just my favorite movie, it's the story I've always dreamed of. The magic, the love, the way Belle saw the good in the Beast before anyone else; it's shaped how I see the world. How I see love. And you—" I paused, shaking my head as my smile widened. "You made this. *For me*. Mikkel, this is like stepping into my own fairytale."

His smile deepened. "That was the point."

I twirled around the room, my fingers brushing over the glass cases that lined the walls, marveling at the assortment of yellow flowers inside.

Each one seemed to glow, like they were lit from within.

He grinned, his eyes locked on me with a depth that quickened my pulse. "I wanted to give you something that felt as special as you make me feel."

I practically bounced back to the pedestal, tapping the glass again just to see another petal fall. This one drifted down even slower than the first, as if teasing me. I picked it up eagerly, grinning as I read it.

"I love the way your eyes sparkle when you're eating Lay's or chocolate cake," it said, followed by another quote: *'Even the darkest night will end, and the sun will rise.'*

A laugh bubbled out of me, pure and light. "You know me too well."

"Of course I do," he said, stepping closer until his hands rested gently on my hips. "I know what calms you when you're overwhelmed, what makes you smile when you think no one's watching. And I know how much this story means to you. It's not just a room, Abigail, it's a reminder of how much I see you. How much I'll always want to show you how loved you are."

I couldn't hold it in any longer. I wrapped my arms around his neck, laughing and crying in a rush.

He chuckled, tightening his hold on me.

I pulled back just enough to tap the glass again, grinning like a child on Christmas morning as another petal drifted down. It read: "I love how you always see the beauty in the little things," followed by: '*Sometimes, the smallest step in the right direction ends up being the biggest step of your life.'*

I held it up to him, still in disbelief. "Mikkel, you're everything I never dared to dream of."

"And you're every dream worth having." He kissed me softly, a promise in that kiss. "Tap it again."

I did, knowing with every petal and every moment with him, my heart would keep deepening.

"Abigail-Ann," he whispered, his voice tender. "Your fairy tale was never too much to ask for. This life, this love—it was *always* meant for you. Not as a luxury, but as something you were born to have. I'd give you anything your heart desires because you deserve it all. And I'll spend every moment proving it—showing you just how precious you are. With you, it's about making dreams come true. Without you, my world is incomplete."

His hand gently brushed a curl from my face. "It's always been about you. You make everything more vivid, more meaningful."

His words hit me, and I met his gaze, my hand on his chest. "You've already shown me," I said, my voice trembling. "You make me feel like I'm enough."

The tears ran free, and I didn't try to stop them.

"And on the days you can't hold on, I'll hold on for you," he said firmly. "When you don't feel like fighting, I'll fight for you. When you need space, I'll give it to you. This is about more than just me—it's about us, building a life of living, not just surviving. Even in my darkest moments, you were there, reminding me of what I didn't know I needed. When I think of yellow, I think of you—your warmth, your light."

I swallowed hard, overwhelmed by the depth of his commitment.

"This might be your favorite fairytale, but you…" Mikkel leaned in, his lips brushing my forehead. "You are by far my favorite princess—*my queen*—and I'll spend every day proving that you're worth more than any story ever written."

Warmth spread through me as I turned back to the rose, mesmerized by the delicate petals inside the glass dome. My heart swelled.

"You have no idea how much I love you," I whispered.

Mikkel's hand brushed mine, grounding me.

A thought struck me, curiosity bubbling up. "How many petals?"

His lips quirked. "A thousand."

I blinked. "A thousand? That's impossible."

Mikkel's grin softened. "When you're in love, the impossible becomes possible."

I gasped, my chest tightening. He meant it. It wasn't just the rose. It was the way he saw me, believed in me, and loved me more than anyone ever could.

"This is surreal."

He brushed a kiss against my temple. "I'd do it a thousand times over to see you smile like this."

"You're my everything, Mikkel."

"And you're my infinity, Red."

WARNING

The following chapter contains heavy mentions of mental health/physical health issues. Please refer to the content warning list to be reminded of any potential triggers. Your well-being is important to me, so please take care of yourself while reading.

CHAPTER FIFTY-FOUR

Abigail-Ann

"If I know what love is, it is because of you."
~ ***Hermann Hesse***

The week passed in a blur. If anyone asked me about love, I'd tell them about Mikkel—how he turned my world upside down, how deeply he loved, and how he took the time to understand me. I spent an entire day crying, overwhelmed by the West Wing he built for me, the thousand-petal rose in a glass dome filled with everything he adored about me, and the quotes meant to brighten my day. He mended a heart he hadn't broken and never made me feel like I owed him anything.

But, beneath all that love, a strange restlessness lingered—a quiet hum under my skin I couldn't quite place. Maybe it was exhaustion. Maybe everything was finally catching up to me. I exhaled, trying to shake it off, as the scent of garlic and rosemary filled the room. From my spot on the sofa, I watched Mikkel move effortlessly in the kitchen, stirring with practiced ease before sending me a soft smile over his shoulder.

"Feeling any better?"

I managed a small smile. "Hmm?"

He turned off the burner, sat beside me, and set down a bowl of salad. "You're anxious. You slept under the weighted blanket, clung to your knitted flowers, then bit your acrylics off before I left for my meeting."

I chuckled, embarrassed. "That obvious?"

"I pay attention to everything about you, baby." He nudged me with a reassuring squeeze. "What's on your mind?"

I sighed, facing him. "I just feel on edge."

His gaze softened. "I'm here with you." He took my hand, squeezing gently. "Tonight's just us—good food, no pressure."

"*Te amo.*[1]" I gave his hand a squeeze in return. "You should cook more often. This is working wonders."

He chuckled, eyes gleaming with pride. "Just a little something. But if it helps you relax, I'll keep cooking."

Mikkel plated the steak, perfectly seared, alongside roasted vegetables and a drizzle of barbecue sauce. My stomach grumbled in anticipation. *Was there anything this man couldn't do?*

Just as I speared a bite, my phone buzzed. Expecting a message from Azzaria, Aurora or my parents, I glanced at the screen.

And my heart sank.

Unknown number.

Maybe: Joshua Milton.

Well, fuck. At least I knew that off–feeling wasn't in vain.

"Everything okay?" Mikkel asked casually, his brows furrowed.

"Yeah… just reading something." I tried to keep my voice steady as I opened the message.

The words on the screen hit me like a punch to the gut.

---

1 *I love you.*

I'm in NYC. We need to talk. Meet me at Ginjan cafe tomorrow. Noon.

Or your little boyfriend sees how much of a slut you are.

Attached to the message was a file. My hand shook as I opened it, my worst fears confirmed instantly. *Thank God the volume was down.* It was the sex tape Joshua swore he'd deleted, now a weapon in his hands.

Panic tightened my throat, my chest constricting as I fought for breath. I quickly shut off my phone, forcing a smile as I tried to compose myself. Mikkel, sensing my distress, rushed over, concern clouding his face.

"What's wrong?" he asked, his hand hovering over my shoulder.

"I'm… not feeling well," I muttered, swallowing hard.

Mikkel studied me, his eyes searching for the truth. He nodded reluctantly, but doubt lingered in his gaze.

Dinner passed in strained silence, my mind racing with the terrifying consequences of what Joshua might do next. The thought of the headline—*Mikkel Suarez's Girlfriend's Sex Tape Leaks*—clawed at me. *What would it do to his reputation?*

To his company?

How could I protect him from this?

How could I protect myself?

What would Joshua demand this time?

And, most painfully, why couldn't I find the words to tell Mikkel?

I pressed my fork into my palm, feeling the prongs dig against my skin.

"*Mi amor,*[2]" he said gently, taking the fork from me. "Breathe, I'm here with you."

That one sentence melted the knot in my chest, softening the ache that had built up with my fears. He was here, *truly here*, and there was no rush, no anger waiting to catch me off guard.

After dinner, we went to bed, Mikkel's warmth offering a brief comfort against the fear gnawing at me. But no matter how tightly I held onto him, my mind kept drifting back to Joshua—the five years of pain, the way a single action could unravel everything I'd worked so hard to heal.

---

2 *My love*

Mikkel kissed my forehead, whispering reassurances, and for a moment, I let myself believe everything would be okay. But deep down, I knew the storm was coming.

And then, the dream took me—a warped, sinister version of reality.

A thick fog enveloped me as I navigated through a murky forest, the darkness pressing in on all sides like a suffocating shroud. In the distance, I spotted Joshua standing amidst the twisted trees.

I approached him, my steps heavy with trepidation as a chill crept up my spine. His eyes held a malevolent gleam. When his lips curled into a smirk, an icy shiver ran through me.

"You thought you could escape me?" His voice echoed through the eerie silence, each word laced with malice. "You'll always come crawling back, begging for my forgiveness, whore."

I tried to protest, to assert my independence, but my voice faltered, drowned out by the cacophony of doubt and fear echoing in my mind. Memories of our toxic relationship flooded me—the abuse, the manipulation, the ongoing cycle of pain.

"You'll never be free."

Panic gripped me as I struggled to break free from his grasp, but no matter how hard I fought, I remained ensnared in his web of control. The forest seemed to close in around me, suffocating me with its oppressive darkness.

I woke up with a jolt, heart racing and body drenched in sweat, trying to shake off the nightmare.

"Mikkel?" My voice trembled as I turned to wake him. He stirred, blinking sleepily as he reached for his glasses on the bedside table.

"Baby?" he asked, concern knitting his brow. "Are you okay?"

"I… had a nightmare," I managed, my breath still coming in ragged gasps.

He sat up, brushing my damp forehead. "What happened? Talk to me, *amor*."

"I… d-dreamt about my past," I whispered, trying to stop the shaking.

He nodded, worry in his eyes. "Stay here." He slipped out of bed and returned with water. I drank, the coolness easing my throat.

Mikkel wrapped his arms around me. "I promise, no one will ever hurt you again," he murmured, kissing my forehead.

His warmth settled me, and soon, we drifted back to sleep.

By morning, he was gone, but his embrace lingered. In the kitchen, I found breakfast, a note filled with love, and bouquet of yellow and white roses. A bittersweet smile tugged at my lips as I read his words—touched by his care yet weighed down by the guilt of what I hadn't told him.

I had an early meeting. Hope you're feeling better.

Te amo, mi vida.

—Mikkel.

✿✿✿

Frozen in the café doorway, the heaviness of past pain pressed down on me. Joshua sat at a corner table, his smile a mask for the turmoil in his eyes, a haunting reminder of the past.

I hadn't come here out of desire but out of necessity. I needed this to end. I needed him to understand that whatever he was clinging to was just a ghost of something long gone. This wasn't about closure—at least not for me. I had rediscovered who I was and learned to love myself again, all while the best man I had ever met held my hand. This was about finally putting an end to the shadows he kept casting over my life.

I took a breath, straightening my spine, and walked toward him, each step a silent declaration of everything I had reclaimed since him.

"Hey, love, missed you," he greeted, his voice sweet but fake, a blade twisting in my gut.

"Get to the fucking point. Why am I here?"

His eyes flickered for a second, a flash of annoyance before he masked it. "You wound me, love," he replied, but the charade didn't fool me.

"Why did you want to see me?" My voice trembled with something deeper—rage, sure, but also something harder, something I didn't recognize in myself until now.

"I just wanted to see you one last time," he said, leaning in, eyes intense, searching. "Before I leave for Europe, I had to see my favorite girl—the one who gives the best head—one last time."

The words hit me like a slap, but I held my ground, gripping my bag so tight I thought it would snap. "I'm leaving," I said, standing up, my legs shaking, but my voice strong. "You're fucking disgusting."

"Don't go so fast," he muttered, his voice softening just enough to make my skin crawl. He raised his phone, the screen gleaming like a knife. "Sit down. Let's talk, Abigail."

I didn't move. The blood drained from my face as he hit play. The video began—my stomach lurched, nausea rising.

"W-why do you still have the tape?" I stammered, a tear slipping, but I wiped it away before he saw.

His finger hovered over the screen before he tapped it again, slow and deliberate—like this was all just a game to him. His voice dripped with manipulation as he said, "Why would I get rid of something so valuable?"

A chill ran through me.

"This will always be here," he continued, his smirk sharp and cruel. "You'll always remember who you really are. Not some polished princess with a perfect billionaire on her arm. *The whore* capable of everything and more in that tape."

I could feel the tremor in my chest, but my voice was firm. "I hate you," I spat, the words tasting like acid.

"You loved me once," he said, smug.

"I *thought* I did," I corrected, meeting his eyes without flinching. "You're pathetic."

"And your boyfriend ruined everything. My family's legacy. My dad's company. *Everything.*"

I froze. *What?*

"He tore the Milton Group apart. Demolished our building. He destroyed everything my father worked for. All for what?"

"All for me," I said, my voice steady. "He did it for me. And you don't have as much power as you think you do, Joshua. Send him the tape, I dare you. All your attempts to ruin my life have only ended up ruining yours. You could've maybe gotten to the old me, but this version? This one right here? Fuck no. You spent your life hating your father, but the truth is, *you are him*. And I'm glad Mikkel ruined your good for nothing legacy."

He recoiled, taken aback by the woman standing in front of him—someone he thought he could break, someone he thought would cower. But not anymore.

"You're a fucking psychopath," I spat, disgust flooding my veins.

"I'm leaving," I whispered fiercely, but before I could take a step, his voice slithered behind me.

"One click of a button, and he sees how much of a slut you are. The headlines will destroy hi—"

"Send the tape," I said, my voice low, sharp, and cold. "Fucking send it."

His disbelief was almost palpable. "You don't mean that."

"I do," I said, every word heavy with the weight of everything I'd fought for. "After that, you'll have nothing left."

I pushed my chair back and walked out, head held high, his desperate calls fading behind me. My hands trembled—not from fear, but from triumph. This was for every time I had cowered, every moment he had disrespected and dismissed me.

But now came the hardest part—*telling Mikkel.*

CHAPTER FIFTY-FIVE

Abigail-Ann

"The best thing to hold onto in life is each other."
Audrey Hepburn

Despite being buried under what felt like five billion layers, the cold still cut through me, and therapy did little to ease my anxiety.

I told Dr. Green everything. Joshua's return. The threats about the tape. How I still hadn't told Mikkel. But the words felt strangled, stuck behind a wall I couldn't break. The more I tried to speak, the heavier the silence became, pressing down on me like a weight I couldn't shake.

Dr. Green studied me for a moment, then spoke gently. "What's stopping you from telling him?"

I swallowed hard. "I don't know… Maybe if I don't say it out loud, it won't be real."

Her gaze softened. "Avoidance doesn't erase reality, Abigail. But facing it? That's how you take back control."

I exhaled shakily, nodding. I knew she was right. But knowing and doing were two different things.

Dr. Green's words lingered. *Avoidance won't erase reality. Facing it will.*

But how could I, when the truth felt like a ticking bomb?

I was pushing and pulling Mikkel, trapped in my own turmoil. If Joshua leaked that damn tape… Mikkel's reputation, everything he built, could shatter. I couldn't let that happen. But the more I tried to protect him, the deeper I sank.

Sitting up, I buried my head in my hands, the weighted blanket useless against the storm inside me.

The door creaked open, and I didn't need to look up to know it was Mikkel. His presence grounded me, offering a fleeting sense of calm. He pressed a soft kiss to my forehead, lingering as if he could quiet the storm inside me.

"Hey," I whispered, almost absently.

"How about we go outside?" he suggested, his calm voice offering a sense of safety.

"My feet feel heavy," I mumbled.

"Sit at the edge of the bed." He guided me with a gentle pull. "Open your legs."

His hands gripped my thighs, guiding my legs to wrap around his waist, and for a second, I let myself feel something other than anxiety. *Safe.*

"Now, jump," he said, his smile both playful and reassuring.

I threw myself into his arms, and without a word, he carried me down the hall to the West Wing space he'd designed. As he set me down, I felt lighter. Then I froze.

On the far wall, a projector cast a soft glow. A fluffy floor bed lay on the ground, a blanket like the one I'd left behind draped over it, and movie snacks were scattered around, making it feel like its own little world.

I turned to Mikkel who was already smiling. "A *Beauty and the Beast* marathon in your personal West Wing sounds fitting, right?"

I smiled, the first real one of the day. I nodded and without a word, snuggled into his chest.

"I've noticed how off you've been but, I also know you'll talk to me when you're ready. I'll always be patient with you. In the meantime, I thought this might ease your mind."

I closed my eyes, pressing closer. "You make everything lighter, Mikkel. You quiet my chaotic mind."

He took my hands, grounding me. "*Tu sonrisa*[1] became my sunrise, lighting up even my darkest days. *Vuestra risa*[2] is a melody I carry with me every day. Loving you is as natural as breathing, as vital as my heartbeat. I told you I'd always be here to calm your storms, and I meant it."

"*Te quiero*,[3]" I whispered, my voice unsteady. "More than you can imagine."

He kissed me—slow, deep, and full of meaning. Wrapped in blankets, we let the movies play in the background, but all I felt was him. As night blurred into dawn, one truth settled in my heart—Mikkel wasn't just the man I loved. He was my anchor.

Tomorrow, I'd find the courage to tell him everything. I owed him that.

---

1 *your smile*

2 *your laughter*

3 *I love you*

WARNING

The following chapter contains heavy mentions of mental health/physical health issues. Please refer to the content warning list to be reminded of any potential triggers. Your well-being is important to me, so please take care of yourself while reading.

CHAPTER FIFTY-SIX

Mikkel

"Love doesn't just sit there, like a stone; it has to be made, like bread, remade all the time, made new."
~ Ursula K. Le Guin

Monday morning hit with the weight of responsibility, the kind that settled in my bones before my first sip of water. The usual rush of work felt even more overwhelming this time.

My mind was stuck on Abigail. She wore a mask of despair, and no matter how much she assured me she was fine, I knew better. I just hoped she'd eventually let me in on the burden she carried. There was a hollow silence between us, and it was eating me alive.

As I walked into the office, my phone buzzed with a call from her.

"Hey." Her voice trembled, wrapping around me like a fragile thread, barely holding together.

Why the fuck did it sound like she was crying?

"Hey, baby. Everything okay?"

"Can you come home early tonight?" Her voice was laced with an urgency that set off alarm bells in my chest.

"I was already planning to, *mi reina.*[1]"

"Good. I just need to talk to you about my anxiety, about everything."

The way she spoke, so carefully, made my heart clench.

"Who hurt you?" The question slipped from my lips, sharp and desperate.

A pause hung between us, thick with unspoken pain, and I could almost hear the cracks in her heart. Then came the hitch in her breath, a sound that shattered me. It was as if I could feel her tears, and my resolve wavered.

"Mikkel…" she whispered, and the sound wrapped around me like a vice.

"So help me God," I vowed, my voice low and fierce. "Whoever hurt you won't get to do it a second time."

"I don't want to talk about it over the phone." Her voice quivered, and I could picture the tears glistening on her cheeks. "Tonight, when we're together."

"Okay." My heart thundered in my chest. "But remember, I love you."

"I don't think you love me as much as I love you." Vulnerability dripped from her words, and I felt the air thicken with her despair.

Impossible. *How could she think that?*

"No one could ever love you more than I do." My voice burned with urgent conviction. "You are *mi todo*[2], Abigail. Never forget that."

The moment I came off the phone, Morison approached me and the air felt heavier, as if it knew something I didn't. As long as my girlfriend wasn't happy, there was nothing to fucking smile about.

"Good morning, Mr. Suarez," he greeted me warmly. "How are you today, sir? Sapphire will be out of the office today."

"Morning," I replied, barely glancing at him, and I entered my office, the door shutting a little more aggressively than I had intended.

---

1 *my queen*

2 *my everything*

My eyes landed on a brown envelope lying dead center on my desk. There was no indication of its origin or stamp, just my name and office address scrawled in an unfamiliar handwriting. My heart sank, a sickening premonition twisting in my gut.

Have fun with her. I sure as hell did.

Who the fuck was this?

I ripped it open, hands trembling, and pulled out a thumb drive and two glossy photographs. The first one hit me like a punch to the gut—Abigail with Joshua. But this was from the past. Her nails were almond-shaped, not coffin-shaped. Her hair was more burgundy than copper.

But fuck, none of those details made this any easier to stomach.

What kind of man would do something like this to a woman?

I put the thumb drive in my laptop and before it hit the ten second mark, I knew what it was. A sex tape. Then, another small note fell out from between the photos. I unfolded it, my breath catching in my throat as I read the words.

Get out before she finds another cock to suck.

The world tilted, and I grasped the edge of my desk to steady myself. The words seared into my brain, each letter a brand of agony.

I felt an anger so fierce it seared through my veins, leaving a trail of bitterness. But above all, it was the hurt that drowned me, a suffocating wave of anger that left me gasping for air. My office felt like a prison, the walls closing in on me.

"*Tienes que estar de coña,*[3]" I cursed. "*Este hijo de puta.*[4]"

Was this why she was off? Had Joshua threatened her?

---

3 *You've got to be kidding me*

4 *This son of a bitch*

Without thinking, I shot to my feet, the chair screeching against the floor. There was no way I could focus on work while rage burned through me, hot and unrelenting. Grabbing my keys, I stormed out, my pulse pounding so hard it drowned out everything else.

"Cancel everything, I'll be out of office."

"Sir," Morison called after me and I didn't even stop. *I couldn't stop.*

The drive to Xander Tower was excruciatingly slow, and for the first time in my life, I broke every fucking stop sign. My heart raced as my thoughts pounded in my head like a drum. As I finally pulled up outside the building, I took a deep breath, trying to steady myself.

I strode into Dillon's office, a storm brewing inside me as I saw him, Azzaria and Arnoldo seated. Arnoldo looked up from his phone, his expression shifting from pleasant to concerned in an instant.

"Mikkel? You look—"

"No digas ni una palabra más, Reyes,[5]" I interrupted, brushing past her.

Dillon leaned back in his chair, raising an eyebrow at me as he rubbed Azzaria's stomach. "You're speaking Spanish," he said, stating the fucking obvious. "Who pissed you off?"

I turned to Azzaria. "Can you please stay with Abigail?"

She crossed her arms, suspicion flickering in her eyes. "What did you do?"

"*Nada.*[6]" I tossed her my apartment keys, the gesture almost frantic. "Just... please."

"What happened to my best friend, Mikkel?"

Dillon cleared his throat, sensing the tension. I shot him a look, and he shrugged, his expression unreadable.

"Precious," he said, looking at Azzaria.

She opened her mouth to protest, but Dillon leaned in. "My love, please. This… this looks serious."

---

5 *Don't say another word, Reyes*

6 *Nothing*

Her gaze flickered between us, then she softened, nodding slowly. "I'll go, but if I find out you did anything to hurt her, there will be one less Hispanic billionaire in the world."

"I wouldn't dream of hurting her," I promised, sincerity pouring from me as she left.

Dillon looked up, his expression now hardened. "Please tell me what the fuck is happening."

I took a deep breath, glancing at Dillon and Arnoldo then launched into the chaos of the past few weeks: her anxiety, sadness, the sex tape, the messages, the notes. As I recounted each detail, I could feel their disbelief and anger growing. Dillon's jaw tightened, and when I finished, he ran a hand through his hair, frustration radiating off him.

"The last man who did that with Azzaria is rotting in his grave," Dillon said, his voice low and fierce.

Arnoldo nodded, processing. "What do you want to do about it?"

"*Homicidio*[7] isn't far from my mind," I admitted, the rage simmering beneath the surface.

Dillon's eyes glinted with a dark humor. "Chris!"

His assistant appeared at the door, looking puzzled. "Yes, Mr. Xander?"

"Clear my schedule for the weekend," Dillon ordered, a dangerous smile creeping onto his face.

Chris blinked, clearly caught off guard. "Uh, all of it?"

"Yes," Dillon replied, his tone brooking no argument and Chris walked out.

Arnoldo's brows raised in surprise. "What are we going to do?"

Dillon leaned back in his chair, a wicked grin spreading. "We have a young man to find before he sets foot outside the country."

Arnoldo glanced between us, skepticism etched on his face. "Are you sure about this?"

Dillon turned sharply to me, intensity in his gaze. "Suarez, what would you prefer? Mope or fucking do something?"

"Option two, Xander."

---

7 *Homicide/Murder*

"Then let's fucking go," Dillon said, his voice a rallying cry.

Arnoldo pushed back his chair, determination creeping into his features. "Alright, then. At least you have the best lawyer representing you."

WARNING

The following chapter contains heavy mentions of mental health/physical health issues. Please refer to the content warning list to be reminded of any potential triggers. Your well-being is important to me, so please take care of yourself while reading.

CHAPTER FIFTY-SEVEN

Abigail-Ann

"For it was not into my ear you whispered, but into my heart. It was not my lips you kissed, but my soul."
- Judy Garland

I have to tell him.

The words felt heavy in my throat, like stones bringing me down. He deserved to know the reason behind my vagueness, I kept reminding myself, but what if he ended up hating me for keeping it from him?

I'd seen him angry before—the kind that shook the ground—but this would be worse.

What if this shattered everything? What if this was the thing that pushed him too far?

No, I couldn't think like that. We'd been over this. He was gentle in a way that made me feel safe, but even that reassurance felt fragile, like a thread ready to snap under my fears.

What if I was wrong? What if the truth pushed him away instead of drawing us closer? The thought sent a wave of nausea rolling through me.

Just then, my phone buzzed on the counter, jolting me from my spiral of anxiety. It was a message from Mikkel.

Baby, I'll be home a little late.

My heart sank. A simple text, but it felt loaded with implications. *Why was he going to be late? Did he not want to see me? Did something terribly wrong happen?* Suddenly, my mind was a whirlwind of dramatic scenarios, each one more alarming than the last.

Panic clawed at my chest, tightening like a vice and strength felt so far away. With a shaky breath, I typed a response, my fingers hovering above the keyboard.

Okay, be safe. I'll be here.

I walked into the living room, the weight of his text pressing on me like an anvil. My vision blurred with tears, the uncertainty flickering on the screen. Today couldn't get worse, but the thought twisted in my stomach like a knife.

I exhaled, forcing myself to breathe deeply. The anxiety gripped me, but I closed my eyes, counting my breaths—*inhale, hold, exhale*—until my heartbeat slowed.

Then, I walked into the next room, where the rose sat and tapped the glass, watching a petal fall. The words etched on it read: *Your laugh is my favorite sound*, followed by the quote: *The greatest glory in living lies not in never falling, but in rising every time we fall.*

I took a deep breath and stepped into the living room just as my phone buzzed, Azzaria's name glowing on the screen.

"Hello?"

"Let me in," she said, urgency slicing through the air.

"What?" I managed, confusion knotting my brow. "I'm at Mikkel's."

"I'm at Mikkel's door. Let me in."

Dread and disbelief coursed through me as I opened the door to find Azzaria, her face a storm of anger and worry.

"Are you—"

"Mikkel asked me to stay with you, in a panicked and angry state, and Dillon and Arnoldo are there. I don't know much about Mikkel's anger, but whenever Dillon's like that, it means he's about to do something *really* bad." Azzaria's voice sliced through the chaos in my mind.

Too many things were happening right now.

"I know how bad your anxiety gets," she whispered. "But tell me what's going on please."

The moment she said it, the dam holding me together broke. I collapsed into her arms, sobs wracking my body as I buried my face in her shoulder. "It's a mess," I cried, my voice muffled against her shirt. *"I'm a mess!"*

Her arms tightened around me, but it couldn't stop the tears or the pain. I cried until my body shook, until there was nothing left.

"What happened?" she asked softly, stroking my hair with a tenderness that only made me ache more.

Through my tears, I told her everything—Joshua's text, the anxiety clawing at my chest. Each word felt like a weight, but sharing it with her eased the burden, even if just for a moment.

Her fingers continued their soothing motion, even as my insides twisted with dread. "I'm calling Dillon. I need answers."

"Az—" I tried to protest, but she'd already pressed the call button, jaw clenched in anger.

"Tell me what the hell is going on!" Azzaria snapped as soon as Dillon picked up.

I heard his deep sigh through the speaker. "We're handling something. Just stay with Abigail until tomorrow, please."

Azzaria wasn't having it. "Dillon Timothy Xander," she growled.

His tone shifted. "Are you alone?"

Before I could say anything, she answered, "Are you trying to upset your pregnant fiancée?"

"Prec—"

"Tell me what happened," she pressed, her voice dangerously calm.

Another sigh. "Abigail's been struggling the past couple of weeks, and it's been weighing on Mikkel. I don't know the full details, but he was at his office earlier when her ex—"

My heart plummeted.

"What?" Azzaria's voice sharpened with alarm.

"Joshua," Dillon continued. "He sent Mikkel an envelope. A sex tape, disgusting notes, explicit pictures."

The world tilted. My chest tightened. The air felt thick, suffocating.

Fuck.

I couldn't breathe. I couldn't think.

"Precious?" Dillon's voice cut through the fog. "You there?"

"I'm here," she choked out. "Where are you? Where's Mikkel?"

"Malen," Dillon murmured.

"Dill—" Azzaria started, but he cut her off.

"I know," he said, his voice weighted with something deeper.

Azzaria exhaled, shoulders sagging. "I was going to tell you to make sure Joshua gets what he deserves. I'll stay with Abigail."

"*Ti amo*,[1]" Dillon's voice softened.

"I love you too," she murmured.

Silence settled between us as the call ended, but the weight of it lingered. My thoughts churned, restless, like an unfinished puzzle with missing pieces.

The words stuck in my head. *Malen.*

"What's Malen?"

Azzaria turned, her gaze stormy but her voice steady. "Abigail, let them handle it."

"No. What is it?" I pressed, desperation creeping in. This was tearing me apart—I needed to understand.

"Matthew," she whispered, her expression darkening.

"Are they go—"

"I don't know," she cut in, voice sharp before softening. "Sorry, my hormones... But he deserves whatever Mikkel does to him. Murder or otherwise."

---

1 *I love you*

I sank onto the couch, grief weighing me down. Azzaria pulled me into a tight embrace as sobs shook my body, each tear carving deeper into the emptiness.

"It's going to be okay, Abi," she whispered. But her words felt hollow—empty against the storm inside me.

I cried until there was nothing left, until exhaustion dragged me under. But even in sleep, there was no escape. Joshua haunted me—the café, the moment everything went wrong, the past refusing to stay buried.

Why couldn't he just stay gone?

When I woke, it hit like a tidal wave, knocking the breath from my lungs. My chest tightened, and I gasped for air, struggling to piece it all together.

Everything was slipping through my fingers, and I couldn't stop it.

The silence, the uncertainty—it was suffocating.

WARNING

The following chapter contains heavy mentions of mental health/physical health issues. Please refer to the content warning list to be reminded of any potential triggers. Your well-being is important to me, so please take care of yourself while reading.

CHAPTER FIFTY-EIGHT

Mikkel

"Love is the whole thing. We are only pieces."
~ Rumi

Hours had passed since everything spiraled out of control, and my anger wasn't fading—it was growing, boiling deeper with each breath I took. Fury coursed through my veins like molten lava, scalding me from the inside out. My fists were clenched so tight my nails were cutting into my skin, the pressure building with every passing second. Dillon had used a favor to put Joshua on the no-fly list before he could even leave the country, and from there, he was brought to Malen.

As we pulled up to the nondescript warehouse, Dillon stopped me with a hand on my arm, his face more serious than I'd ever seen it. "Are you sure *you* want to do this?"

I didn't hesitate. "Of course, I'm sure."

Arnoldo chimed in from the backseat, his voice cautious. "We have people who can take care of this—"

I cut him off, turning my gaze to Dillon. "Did you let people handle Matthew?"

Dillon's expression darkened instantly. The mention of that name sent a flicker of something dangerous through his eyes. "You know damn well I didn't."

"Then let's go."

His jaw clenched, but he gave a single nod. He understood. Sometimes you had to take matters into your own hands and clearly, Joshua didn't understand me verbally and I was sure after today, he'd get it.

The building was cold and unforgiving. Dim lighting barely cut through the thick shadows that clung to the walls like predators waiting to strike. The air was heavy with the metallic scent of old blood and sweat and the cracked concrete floors were stained with years of violence.

There was no pretense of sophistication here—just raw and brutal. A place where rules didn't exist.

The faint clink of chains caught my attention. Joshua hung in his restraints, arms spread wide and limp. His wrists were bound in thick cuffs, chains leading to a hook above. His feet barely touched the floor, bruised and broken, his head hanging low in defeat. The dim light cast harsh shadows, making him look even more pitiful. He had no strength left, every bit of the pussy I knew he was.

I stopped in my tracks, a storm brewing inside me as I looked at him. This was the man who'd tried to humiliate *el amor de mi vida*[1], who'd made a mockery of her, and reduced her to the point she hated herself. All the anger, the hatred that had been building up inside of me, now had a target.

Dillon stopped beside me, his expression unreadable. "Are you sure?"

I clenched my fists at my sides, jaw tight. "Yes."

This wasn't just about revenge. This was about making sure Joshua never crossed another line again. And he was about to learn there was no escape from the consequences of his actions.

---

1 *the love of my life*

Dillon glanced at me, then down at my shirt, his lips twitching into the faintest smirk. "You realize you're wearing a full white shirt, right?"

Arnoldo gave a sharp, incredulous laugh. "That's what you're reminding him of right now?"

Dillon shrugged, his eyes still locked on my shirt, completely unfazed by Arnoldo's reaction. "I doubt he wants to stain *Hermès* with this asshole's blood."

A dark chuckle escaped my lips. "You're right," I muttered, the adrenaline still coursing through me. I unbuttoned the shirt swiftly, peeling it off and handing it to Dillon, now shirtless. "Better?"

"Much better," Dillon replied, his eyes flashing with something between amusement and satisfaction. He slung my white shirt over his shoulder, the casualness of it almost ridiculous given the situation. "Nice physique. My gym really is paying off."

Arnoldo shook his head, exhaling sharply. "Only Dillon Xander would be worried about clothes in a place like this."

I chuckled, then shifted my focus back to Joshua, his body still hanging limp, oblivious to the reckoning that awaited him. I didn't realize I had this level of violence in me. I'd been angry before, lost my temper, and raged. But something about this, *about him*, had triggered something deep inside me, something I didn't even know was there.

It wasn't just that they dated or he was part of her past—I couldn't care less about that. It was the way he talked about her, like she was nothing more than something to use and discard. And yes, the sex tape *burned* me. She trusted him with that, and what did he do? Used it to prove a point. Now, I'd use him to prove mine.

The room felt smaller as I crossed it, my gaze locked on Joshua. For a second, I hesitated. Not because I doubted what I was about to do, but because I knew that once I started, there would be no stopping.

And then it happened—my fist collided with his gut, the impact sending a dull thud through the room.

"That," I shouted, "is for treating her less than she deserves. For making her feel insecure. For using and abusing her for years."

His body jerked in the chains, a groan escaping him, but before he could recover, I swung again, landing a punch square across his face. The force snapped his head to the side, blood spraying from his mouth. His eyes widened with panic, but it was too late.

"This," I muttered, "is for thinking it was okay to share her sex tape."

Another punch. Harder this time. I could feel the bones in my knuckles crunch against his face, the crack of cartilage as his nose gave way beneath my fist. I didn't stop. Each hit was fueled by every insult he'd thrown at Abigail, every disgusting word he'd used to describe her.

"And this," I finally stated, "is to make sure you never so much as breathe near her again."

He tried to speak, maybe to beg, but I drowned him out. His groans faded, lost in the raw fury pumping through me.

His head lolled forward, blood dripping from his mouth and nose, but I wasn't done. I grabbed him by the collar of his shirt, forcing him to meet my eyes. "*Eres patético*,[2]" I spat, my voice low, almost unrecognizable to myself. "A sorry excuse of a human being."

I slammed my fist into his gut again, his body jerking in the chains. The sound of the impact was visceral, a sickening thud that reverberated through the room.

My knuckles were raw, bloodied, and I could feel the sting setting in. Joshua's head hung low, blood dripping from his face to the cold concrete floor. Each breath he took was labored, ragged, but I didn't feel any satisfaction. Just rage, simmering hot and unrelenting.

I stayed there, chest heaving, glaring at the wreck of a man in front of me. He barely stirred, too weak to even respond. My whole body was coiled tight, ready to keep going, but before I could land another blow, I felt Arnoldo's hand on my shoulder. "*Ya basta*, Suarez![3]"

I exhaled sharply, stepping back. "*Tienes razón*,[4]" I muttered, flexing my sore fingers. The adrenaline was still pumping, but I knew I had to stop.

---

2 *You are pathetic*

3 *Enough, Suarez*

4 *You're right*

Dillon turned to Kamadge, the man who apparently cleaned up the aftermath. "Finish this."

Kamadge, a hulking man with a calm, unsettling demeanor but with a face so innocent, you'd never expect this line of work from, stepped forward. "How do you want it done, Mr. Suarez?" he asked, his voice cold and professional.

"Ruin him. I don't care how," I said, my voice low but steady. I looked down at Joshua, his beaten, bloodied form. "Make sure he never recovers and he knows never to mess with her again."

Kamadge nodded, his expression devoid of emotion, just the cold efficiency of a man who had done this a thousand times.

Before I stepped away, I turned back to Joshua. "Not so tough now, right?"

He didn't answer, instead coughed, his head hanging low. *"Eso pensaba yo.[5]"*

I turned to Dillon and Arnoldo, feeling the tension in my muscles begin to loosen. "Let me know how much money to transfer," I said quietly. "Whatever it costs."

Dillon nodded, his usual smirk absent, replaced by a hardened expression. Arnoldo exhaled, relieved it was over. We stepped out of Malen in silence, the cool night air cutting through the lingering tension. Without a word, Dillon handed me a fresh shirt. I slipped it on, discarding the bloodstained one, but my hands still trembled.

"Let's get a drink," Arnoldo said, breaking the silence as we started driving. "You can text the girlfriends later, but we all need something to calm down."

"I don't drink anymore, but sure."

Arnoldo glanced between Dillon and me. "Since when?"

"Since she told me her ex was an alcoholic, Arnoldo."

Arnoldo nodded, his expression softening, and we continued driving in silence until we reached *Vero*, one of his private bistros. At the bar, the bartender began pouring drinks, but I stuck with tonic water.

---

5 *That's what I thought*

I raised my glass, my fingers still sore from the impact of each punch, and took a slow sip that offered some temporary relief.

Dillon's phone buzzed, and he glanced at the screen, his brow furrowing in concern as he typed a quick reply. He slid it back into his pocket then turned to face me.

"Suarez, you should either text Abigail or head home."

I looked at him, confused. "What happened?"

He sighed, his tone serious. "Azzaria said her anxiety's high."

A pang of guilt hit me, cutting through the haze of anger I'd been living in. I finished the last of my drink, the glass hitting the counter harder than I meant. "I'm heading out now. Thank you guys."

Dillon gave a small nod, his eyes understanding. "Arnoldo's got a car coming for us. Take care."

I stood up and, as I turned to leave, glanced back at them. "Thanks for everything," I muttered, the words heavier than usual. It wasn't just about what had happened tonight; it was for always standing by me, for having my back through it all.

Dillon smiled faintly, the edge of mischief still there, but his voice was sincere. "We're brothers, Mikkel. Always."

"Love you too, brother," Arnoldo said. "Take care."

With that, I walked out of the restaurant, my mind shifting away from everything and back to the person who mattered most—Abigail. Whatever was going on in her head, I needed to be there with her, and I wasn't going to waste any more time.

WARNING

The following chapter contains heavy mentions of mental health/physical health issues. Please refer to the content warning list to be reminded of any potential triggers. Your well-being is important to me, so please take care of yourself while reading.

CHAPTER FIFTY-NINE

Abigail-Ann

"The giving of love is an education in itself."
~ Eleanor Roosevelt

The penthouse felt too big. *Too quiet.*

I had been pacing the same stretch of floor for what felt like hours, but time had become a blur. Azzaria sat on the couch eating chips, watching me with concerned eyes. She'd tried talking to me, tried to get me to eat, but I couldn't. My stomach was tied in knots, and every time I sat still for too long, my mind wandered to places I didn't want it to go.

I hadn't heard from Mikkel in hours. That alone was enough to unsettle me. He'd asked Azzaria to stay with me—a thoughtful gesture—but it only made my anxiety worse. And no matter how hard I tried, I couldn't stop thinking about Joshua. About everything he'd done. The violation. It sat like a weight on my chest, making it hard to breathe.

"Mikkel's got this under control," Azzaria whispered from the couch, as if reading my mind for the hundredth time. "He's getting you the justice you deserve. Trust him."

"I do trust him," I said quickly, almost automatically, but even to my ears, my voice sounded shaky.

Azzaria sighed and leaned forward, her voice gentle. "Then sit down and eat something. You haven't had real food since I got here."

I ran a hand through my hair, frustration gnawing at me. "I just—I need to hear from him," I whispered, feeling a tear slip down my cheek before I could stop it.

Azzaria stood up and wrapped her arms around me in a warm, comforting hug. "You will. He'll be home soon, Abi."

I squeezed my eyes shut, trying to calm the storm of emotions swirling inside me. The fear, the anger, the confusion, was all too much.

The elevator dinged, and a second later, the door unlocked. My heart leapt into my throat.

Azzaria and I pulled apart just as Mikkel stepped inside, shutting the door quietly behind him. His hair was tousled, his jaw tight, but when his eyes met mine, something in his expression softened.

He crossed the room in quick, purposeful strides. Before I could process it, I was in his arms, his warmth dissolving the tension, anxiety, and fear that had gripped me all night.

"I'm sorry I didn't come sooner," he murmured into my hair, his voice thick with exhaustion. "I ha-."

"You're here now," I whispered, my voice shaky. I buried my face in his chest, letting the steady beat of his heart calm me.

Mikkel pulled back slightly, just enough to look down at me, his hand coming up to gently wipe away a stray tear from my cheek. "I'll *always* come back to you, Red. No matter what."

He pulled away from me slowly, then with a soft sigh, turned to Azzaria, offering her a hug. "Thank you, Azzaria," he said, his voice quiet but full of meaning. "For everything."

Azzaria smiled, pulling back slightly but still holding onto Mikkel's shoulders. "You know I'd do anything for Abigail." She turned to glance at me, her eyes full of affection and reassurance. "She's my best friend."

Mikkel chuckled softly, nodding. "I know you would, but I'm still grateful."

Then, with a quick glance at the door, she asked him, "Did Dillon leave already? He told me to meet him at home."

Mikkel smirked, shaking his head. "He's on his way."

"Was he drinking?"

"Can't recall," he playfully responded.

Azzaria rolled her eyes playfully. "I'm sure."

She turned and practically darted toward me, wrapping me in a tight, loving hug. "Call me, okay?" she whispered, kissing my cheek softly. "Promise me."

I nodded, my throat tight with emotion. "I promise, and get home safely."

She gave me a final squeeze, love and concern in her eyes, then smiled, waved, and left. Silence settled. Mikkel exhaled, rubbed his neck, and stepped closer, his gaze searching mine.

"*Mi amor*,[1]" he began, his voice gentle but serious. "We need to talk."

"We do," I said softly, cutting him off. "But I need to talk first."

I tried to speak, to explain the web of emotions that had kept me silent. "I was scared," I managed to say.

"Scared of what, baby?"

"Scared of everything," I admitted, my voice shaking. "My anxiety was through the roof, and I didn't even know why. Then Joshua texted about the sex tape—one he made our first year together. It haunted me, weighed on me, and suddenly, my world was collapsing."

I stepped closer, hands trembling. "I just needed him gone."

"Bab—"

---

1 *My love*

"Let me finish," I whispered, cutting him off. "I didn't want him to leak it, to ruin your reputation. I was terrified of how it could hurt you and everything you've built. Every day I kept it from you, my heart broke a little more. I know it was wrong, but when I finally found the courage to tell you, everything unraveled. I thought you'd see the tape and leave me because... I can't even put the shame into words."

My chest tightened, but before I could say more, he silenced me with a soft kiss, his lips full of understanding. Tears filled his eyes as he cupped my face, closing his own to steady himself.

"I would never leave you, Red," he whispered, voice thick with emotion. "I love you like no one else. Seeing those pictures, the notes, the tape... it broke me. I felt rage, but worse, I felt scared. You were falling apart, and I didn't know why. I couldn't help you. I couldn't fix it."

His shoulders slumped as he exhaled. "I couldn't protect you from him before, but he's nothing now. Every copy of that tape will be erased. He's done for good."

Relief flooded me, and I leaned into him, tears slipping down my cheeks.

"Thank you for not thinking less of me," I whispered.

His eyes held mine, steady and sure. "I could never think less of you. You mean everything to me. He filmed you without your knowledge—that's a crime, and he's currently paying for it. None of this is your fault, so don't ever believe it is."

I took a shaky breath, ready to respond, but then my gaze dropped to his hands. My heart twisted at the sight of his bruised and swollen knuckles. I reached for them, fingertips tracing the damage.

"Your knuckles..."

He pulled his hand back slightly, shaking his head. "It'll be fine," he said, brushing it off, though the tension in his eyes betrayed him. "I've felt worse."

I held his gaze, unwilling to let it go. "How?" I asked, though deep down, I already knew.

He sighed, looking away for a beat before turning back. "I punched him a few times," he admitted, voice low as if downplaying what really happened.

A laugh bubbled up before I could stop it. It surprised both of us, but the thought of Mikkel finally giving that asshole what he deserved was too satisfying. Shaking my head, I let out a small, wry smile. "Nothing he didn't deserve."

A faint smirk tugged at Mikkel's lips. "Exactly."

I walked to the bathroom, grabbed the first aid kit, and returned to find him sitting on the couch, his injured hand resting on his thigh, eyes fixed on me. Kneeling in front of him, I set the kit on the table and gently took his hand.

"Let me take care of it," I murmured, cleaning the cuts and wrapping his knuckles. He didn't protest, just watched me in silence.

When I finished, my fingers lingered against his skin, my chest tightening with gratitude. The bruises, the blood—he'd taken them for me. My hands trembled slightly as the weight of it all settled in.

"Thank you," I whispered, though it felt like nowhere near enough.

Mikkel's gaze softened. "When I say I'll protect you, I mean it, Red."

I swallowed hard, emotion thick in my throat. "*Lo sé. Te quiero.*[2]" The words left me instinctively, feeling right.

His brows lifted, surprise flickering across his face before his expression melted into something warmer. "You speaking Spanish is my new favorite thing."

I chuckled, trying to lighten the air. "We have Duolingo to thank, then."

His smile grew despite the exhaustion in his eyes. "I'm gonna have to send them a check. *Te escucho hablar español y me vuelvo loco,*[3]" he teased, though there was a serious edge to his tone.

---

2 *I know. I love you.*

3 *I hear you speak Spanish and I go crazy.*

He cupped my face, his thumb brushing my cheek, making my heart stutter. "I love you."

His words wrapped around me, sinking deep.

I loved him with every fiber of my being.

Every part of me was his, just as every piece of him belonged to me.

CHAPTER SIXTY

Mikkel

"Love is an irresistible desire to be irresistibly desired."
~ Robert Frost

Life felt right when she was with me. It wasn't all smiles or easy days, but that was never what I thought of as "perfect." Perfect never meant a life without storms; it meant that in every life I could live, in every reality that could exist, it would begin and end with her. She was *mi constante, mi cada camino y mi siempre.*[1]

I loved her in every way a woman could be loved—like a whispered secret in the dark, like sunlight catching in her copper platinum hair. I loved her in breaths and in silences, in laughter that lingered and in the quiet ache of longing. I loved her with a fierce tenderness, in every glance,

---

1 *my constant, my every path and my always*

in every touch, in all the ways language failed but the heart remembered. She was my dawn and my dusk, and I loved her endlessly, as though it was the only thing I was ever meant to do.

After everything, I made sure she had weekly at-home sessions with Dr. Green, and as many *Beauty and the Beast* rewatches as she wanted. Slowly, I saw her come back to herself, that spark in her eyes reigniting.

As for me, seeing her heal was enough to lift my own spirits. Nothing made me happier than knowing I'd given Joshua exactly what he deserved, and watching the aftermath made it all the more satisfying.

Kamadge let me know that Joshua wasn't dead—but even better, he was fingerless. Eight fingers, gone. Snapped and severed, one by one. Watching him crumble, reduced to a quivering mess, brought a twisted satisfaction I never knew I was capable of. It was brutal, undeniably drastic, but necessary. And without a doubt, the best two hundred grand I ever spent.

Joshua was handled. Gone from our lives in every way that mattered. And with that weight lifted, I could finally focus on what truly mattered: Abigail and the future we were building.

The launch of my acquisition was fast approaching, and Abigail and I spent the entire week at Celestine Grande Hotel, nestled in the heart of SoHo. We needed a break, and it just so happened that this was where the launch party would be held.

Our suite offered breathtaking views of The Haughwout Building, our mornings began with leisurely breakfasts on our private terrace, overlooking the iconic skyline as the city awakened below, and our nights ended with slow, sensual, passionate fucking.

Life was amazing.

I stood in the ballroom, watching my team ensure every detail was perfect. I didn't have to be here—interior designers had been paid handsomely for this—but everything in my company required my hands-on approach. Nothing was left to chance.

Breaking out of my thoughts, I grabbed my phone and quickly sent a message to Abigail.

Me
Hey. Still at the masseuse?

Red
I just finished.

Going to get a mojito at the bar.

Me
Good. Be up by 7 pm, amor.

Red
I'm intrigued.

Me
You should be.

She was used to my secretiveness by now and by the way the three dots lingered in the chat, I could tell her mind was racing with what I had up my sleeve.

"You should be," replayed in my mind and I wondered, what the fuck he was up to.

I set my empty glass down, fingers brushing through my curls as I caught my reflection in the mirror.

Leaving the bar, I headed to our room, anticipation building with each step.

At the doorway, I took in the scene—the soft glow of bedside lamps, their light diffused through delicate, draped fabric.

Mikkel Suarez always outdid himself.

It took me a moment to realize soft music was playing courtesy of a speaker sitting on a desk in the far corner. Just as I was starting to wonder where the hell he was, my eyes were drawn to the paper folded and placed neatly in the middle of the bedspread.

Take the handcuffs from the bedside drawer and secure your wrists to the headboard. I'll be there soon to enjoy you fully.
No puedo esperar a jugar con ese húmedo coño tuyo.
-Tu amante

A playful smile danced on my lips as I imagined the scene he described. Grabbing my phone to translate what those words meant, the breath I caught almost stopped in my throat.

I can't wait to play with that wet pussy of yours.

I placed the note down and opened the bedside drawer, my breath catching as two sets of yellow padded handcuffs slid forward. The short chains gleamed in the dim light, a small key resting beside them. I picked up a pair, surprised by their weight.

Reaching for the bottle of sparkling champagne, I let the cool glass settle against my palm, the meaning behind the note finally sinking in. I would be bound to the bed, completely exposed.

A slow heat spread through me as I kicked off my boots, undressing with deliberate movements. Standing by the bed, fully nude, I hesitated—goosebumps prickling my skin—before finally cuffing my left wrist and securing the other end to the headboard.

The motion tugged the thick comforter down, leaving my breasts bare against the warm air.

My heart pounded, a pulse of anticipation mixing with a twinge of nervousness. Then, I heard it—a card sliding into the door, followed by the soft whir of the electronic lock. The door swung open.

Then his voice. Deep. Controlled. Seductive.

"Ready for the ride, Red?"

A shiver raced down my spine, heat curling in my belly. My voice trembled, thick with anticipation. "*Sí.*[2]"

---

2 *Yes*

He stepped inside, quietly closing the door behind him. I barely registered the backpack slung over his white, tailored suit, too focused on the way his gaze devoured me—slow and unrelenting.

Setting the bag at the foot of the bed, he prowled closer, bracing his arms on either side of my head. His presence suffocated the space in the best way, his scent—leather, spice, and something distinctly him—clouding my senses.

With effortless control, he tightened each cuff to the headboard, testing them with a slow, deliberate tug that sent my pulse skyrocketing. Finally, he retrieved the small key, his lips curling into a smirk before tossing it into the open drawer and shutting it with a bump of his hip.

"We won't be needing that for a while, will we?" The teasing glint in his eyes made my stomach flip.

My breath hitched. Completely at his mercy. My thighs pressed together involuntarily. I swallowed hard and shook my head.

Mikkel smiled—a wicked thing—his eyes dropping to my peaked, pink areolas, a flicker of satisfaction crossing his face.

His hand found my upturned hip, pressing me firmly against the bed, his touch slow, possessive. He traced his palm down the outside of my thigh, his voice a low hum of amusement.

"You're gonna fuck me with a blindfold on?" My voice was barely a whisper, caught between curiosity and something darker.

His response was a single, devastating stroke between my legs—quick, electric, enough to make me gasp.

"Patience, mi amor." His voice turned husky, full of promise. "But yes, I'm gonna fuck you with a blindfold on."

I nodded eagerly, thrumming with anticipation.

The moment the fabric slid over my eyes, my world shrank to sound and touch. I heard him move at the foot of the bed, the telltale clink of his belt buckle dropping, the rustle of fabric as he undressed.

Then—silence.

I felt his weight settle beside me, the mattress shifting beneath him. My body tensed, hanging on to the growing stillness, when—wait. *What the… fuck?*

A single, featherlight touch traced my throat, gliding lower.

Down.

Between my breasts.

Not teasing. *Exploring.*

Each slow graze sent a fresh wave of goosebumps rippling over my skin, forcing a sharp arch of my back. The air felt thick—humid with desire—as his fingers continued their unhurried path, leaving me aching, gasping, completely at his mercy.

A groan escaped my lips as the feather shifted to one nipple and then the other.

"Fuck," I muttered, involuntarily pulling on the handcuffs.

It never dipped any lower though, despite me instinctively lifting my hips towards the soft tickle to make contact with the area of my body that wanted it the most. *My pussy.*

The feather lifted away from my body and I moaned again, waiting for it to tantalize and tease me once more. I jumped when instead of the feather, the chill of an ice cube kissed my collarbone.

A drop of icy moisture was left behind as the ice cube was drawn across to the small cup of my neck. It traveled across my skin, slowly but continuously, leaving behind a path of cool, chilled flesh in its wake. I sucked in a breath as it worked its way down between my breasts, circling my nipples but never quite making contact.

Then I felt it lower across my belly, and lower still, headed straight for the heat burning between my legs.

I tried futilely to hold my legs together against the onslaught of the ice, fighting Mikkel's attempts to spread them apart until he crawled between my legs and wedged them apart with his thighs.

"Legs open, baby," he said.

He lifted the ice, dabbed my clit three times, then slid down, his warm breath chasing the lingering chill. "*P-p-please*," I stuttered, "Right there."

I moaned as his tongue flicked out and lapped on my clit then jerked again as his hand deftly brought the ice cube back in contact with my sensitive pussy.

"*Mikkel!*" I screamed at the intensity of the coldness.

He continued alternating warm, wet licks of his tongue with the bracing chill of the ice until it started to melt away.

After one last tease, he tossed the melting ice cube and bore down with his tongue, eating me out.

He moaned as he felt my legs squeeze together, pinning his head between them as firmly as my legs would allow. I groaned as he attacked my clit with his tongue, lapping and flicking and teasing as I squirmed against his mouth.

"You m-make-" and I stopped. I couldn't finish my sentence. The pleasure, the pressure was too great.

"I make you what?" He slipped two fingers inside me, my back arched and I bore down against him as much as the handcuffs would allow.

"You m-make," I started but again couldn't finish. I took a deep breath then continued, "you make me feel good."

The constant tease of his tongue, combined with the twisting, twirling fingers inside me, continued to send waves of pleasure outward from my dripping cunt until a body glitching climax left my legs shuddering and my breath hot and short.

He then removed the blindfold and his hard cock instantly greeted me.

I blinked in the sudden light, dim as it was, and my arms twitched as I made an effort to pull his head down for a kiss, only to find my movement impeded by the handcuffs still restraining me.

A moan of desire escaped my lips, bringing a smile to Mikkel's face. With a sign of acquiescence, he leaned in, lowering his head enough to brush his lips against mine, testing and teasing me until my mouth parted and my tongue flicked to meet his.

I felt his cock brush against my clit, and my eyes widened as another flash of pleasure washed over me. I lifted my hips, straining to deepen the contact, but he reacted just as quickly, pulling his hips back slightly, teasing me once again.

"Fuck me please," I cried out, my tone almost a beg.

"Patience, *mi corazón*,[3]" he mumbled.

He reached down and adjusted his dick so that the pierced head brushed against my lips, spreading my moistness across its tip.

My whine of frustration, tinged with lust, made his cock grow even more solid as he continued to work its length up and down my lips.

With a gentle slowness, he lowered his hips towards me, until I felt him slide into me, inch by agonizing inch.

"That's my favorite sound," he groaned.

I looked up. "What is?"

He pulled out, then gently grabbed my jaw. "That," he whispered and slid inside my cunt, causing me to moan. "The sound you make when your greedy pussy is taking every inch of my cock."

I bit my lip so hard I thought it might bleed.

My God, the mouth on this man.

"You're gonna be a good girl and keep taking my cock, Red?"

I nodded speedily, lust written all over my eyes. "Yes."

He groaned.

In a span that seemed both endless and all too quickly over, he bottomed out against my pelvis, his cock buried inside me. He kissed me again, his body remaining completely motionless as he reveled in the feel of my wet pussy wrapped around his achingly hard cock.

Still locked at the lips, he slowly pulled himself out of me, feeling the whimper escape my mouth as my pussy struggled valiantly to hold him inside me.

"Can you take all of it, *mi vida*?[4]"

I swallowed. "I…I don't know."

"Do you want to try?"

I nodded. "Yes."

"Let me know when to stop, okay?"

---

3 *my heart*

4 *my life*

I nodded, and he reversed direction quickly, sliding back into me, angling to force himself as deep inside as he could, until I couldn't take any more.

"I c-can't take anymore," I whispered and he pulled out, bringing his fingers to rub my clit.

"You did so well, baby," he whispered. "Your pussy feels so good wrapped around my cock."

His fingers sped up, and I couldn't think. The pleasure felt overwhelming to the point I felt I was about to pass out, but the sensations overflowing me were too good and another orgasm washed me, hard and fast.

"You look so beautiful cumming all over my fingers, Red," he whispered and suddenly, with no warning, he started driving himself in and out of me, reaching down with his hands to lift my hips slightly to better angle himself.

"Mikkel!" I screamed, unable to keep quiet longer. *"Yes! Yes! Yes!"*

His eyes widened and my breathing turned to rapid gasps as his motion sent jolts of fire through my body. My arms strained against the handcuffs, desperate to pull him closer. My fingers clenched and unclenched, helpless against the inability to grasp his flesh as his body pounded into me.

With each thrust, my moans grew louder until a sudden scream tore from my lips. My body became a live wire under his hands, every muscle spasming in ecstasy.

As my pussy pulsed and clenched around his cock, he slammed into me twice, then quickly three more times, and then came, his cock spurting as he pulled my hips against his and thrust himself as deeply as he could.

Satisfied and arms trembling, he lowered his body, head now resting on my heaving chest, our bodies still intertwined and unable to move as the exhaustion of the dual climaxes set in.

Finally, the clink of the handcuff chain made him raise his head, and he saw me trying, without avail, to pull my arms down from their bound position. Still semi-hard inside me, he reached over and pulled the key from the drawer, gently unlocking both of my wrists.

With a sigh that was part relief and part exhausted pleasure, I pulled my arms down around him, gripping him close, and gathered his head back down to one of my breasts.

As his tongue traced my nipple, I moaned then whispered, "That was incredible. Let me handcuff you next time."

He nodded, possibly too exhausted to speak, and we lay there, wrapped in each other's arms, until we regained enough energy for round two.

CHAPTER SIXTY-ONE

Mikkel

"We loved with a love that was more than love."
~ Edgar Allan Poe

The *Elite Rides x Luxe Transports* acquisition launch party exceeded all expectations, receiving overwhelmingly positive feedback. A few critics lingered, but nothing could overshadow the success, thanks to an incredible team.

I wore a sharp, tailored white suit that fit like it was made for me, paired with a fresh haircut Abigail had given me earlier. But no matter how put together I looked, it was Abigail who truly stole the spotlight—stunning in a long emerald velvet dress, the daring slit a bold contrast to the winter chill.

The ballroom buzzed with media personnel, interviewers, elites, politicians, and industry leaders. My parents had flown in for the event, and my sister surprised me by showing up—though she spent most of the night deep in conversation with Arnoldo about real estate law.

Laughter filled the air as my friends—*my brothers*—reminisced about my journey, turning the night into a celebration of not just success but the people who had been there through it all.

During my speech, I thanked everyone who made the night possible, and in my mind, I knew Morison and Sapphire deserved raises for all their hard work. News outlets like *The New York Times, Forbes, Bloomberg,* and *Business Insider* were in attendance, capturing every moment. The applause that followed marked the culmination of years of effort. With a toast and the clink of champagne flutes, the celebration of new beginnings felt complete.

At five in the morning, despite the chill, I stood on the private balcony, watching the sky. Suddenly, the balcony door slid open behind me. Abigail stepped out and joined me at the railing without saying a word.

"Everything okay?" I asked, turning around to face her.

"I felt you weren't beside me, so I got up."

I stole a glance at her. She was lounging in an oversized T-shirt, no bra, just a thong peeking out underneath. Her bare ass was on display, and damn, I was savoring the sight.

"What were you looking at?" she asked with a playful smirk.

"The sky."

She nodded, sidling closer, slipping under my arm.

"Before dawn?" she asked, a knowing glint in her eyes.

"Your favorite time of day, isn't it?"

She nodded again, a small smile playing on her lips. "Absolutely."

I breathed in her scent—jasmine with hints of coconut, savoring the press of her body against mine. Slowly, my hand drifted to the thin fabric barely covering her backside. I cupped her ass cheeks, pulling her even closer and gently squeezing. Tenderly, I kissed the crown of her head, trailing soft, lingering kisses down to her ears and finally to her neck.

"Right now?"

I flashed a playful, wicked grin. "Only if you want to, *amor*."

Her eyes darted around and she nodded. "Right here?"

I leaned in closer, my voice a low, seductive murmur. "Right here."

I moved my lips from her neck and kissed her hard on the mouth and fuck, *she was intoxicating.*

I pulled her closer, the height difference between us suddenly more noticeable. As we kissed, her hands roamed my body—one sliding up to my back, the other slipping beneath the hem of my boxers, gripping me firmly. Heat surged through me, my arousal intensifying as I hardened even more.

Suddenly, she broke the kiss and guided me back until I was pressed against the balcony rail. Hooking her thumbs into the waistband of my boxers, she nuzzled my neck, trailing slow, deliberate kisses down my body. She lingered on my chest, her lips warm against my skin, before continuing her descent.

"I want your cum down my throat," she said seductively.

"You drive me crazy," I groaned, my voice thick with desire. Just the sight of her before me left me aching with need.

Maintaining constant eye contact, she took my cock in her hand and brought it to her lips. Gently, she ran her tongue up my length, eliciting a low groan from deep in my throat.

"Don't be a tease, Red," I rasped, looking down at her through half-lidded eyes, "Be a good girl for me?"

She smiled and pressed a kiss to the tip. The way her smile reached her eyes told me lust was rushing through her veins as I bucked my hips against her lips. She took me into her mouth, and a deep moan escaped from my lips.

"Fuck," I cursed, tugging her hair especially hard, making her moan involuntarily at the sensation.

"I love sucking you off," she whispered as she teased the tip, her tongue deliberately lingering on the piercing.

"You're so fucking good to me," I rasped as she bobbed her head up and down, blowing me like her life depended on it. My honey-brown eyes hooked on hers as she sucked me off. My lips parted and my chest sighed with heavy, hot breaths.

I moved my hips in harmony with her mouth, and threw my head back in pleasure, hands buried in her hair, pressing her against my cock as I face-fucked her.

"Just like that, baby," I said in between moans, picking up my speed, fucking her throat with deep thrusts. She choked but only sucked harder, flicking her tongue against my relentless speed.

My thrusts into her mouth grew erratic, pleasure coiling tight in my core. My grip on her hair tightened, my head tipping back as a groan tore from my throat. I was close—*so damn close.*

"Tell me how good it feels. I want to hear you say it," she said as her head bobbed up and down and the saliva dripping from her chin was an art to me.

"So fucking good," I growled.

"Look at me," I commanded, making her moan around my dick as our eyes met once again, and with a guttural groan I exploded into her mouth. She took it all, sucking me until the very end and swallowing every drop while I watched her.

"God," she muttered.

"Stand up," I whispered, still ready to go, feeling the lust immediately hardening my dick again.

My cock drifted from her lips, and she stood.

Once she was on her feet, I seized her arms and crashed my lips against hers—a full-blooded, hungry kiss.

As we broke apart, she gasped for air, her chest rising and falling rapidly. Without missing a beat, I spun her around, positioning her to face the city. My hand found the small of her back, applying gentle pressure. She yielded, bending forward until her chin nearly touched the handrail.

I lifted the T-shirt she was wearing and tugged the thong down, exposing her pussy to the cold air.

I pressed up against her as she bent over the railing, my cock sliding between her legs and grazing her clit.

"*Please*," she whimpered, the word dripping with desire.

Reaching around her trembling thigh, I brushed past my cock and slowly began to rub her clit.

"So fucking wet for me already, baby?"

"I'm always wet for you."

My rubbing fastened, her breathing slowed to ragged pants and I dipped my head to suck her neck.

"Mikkel," she breathed.

With a gasping cry that disappeared into the oppressive daze of dawn, she came all over my fingers.

We stood still like statues, as I waited for her to come back down to earth.

"You." She *gasped.* "Surprise." *She panted.* "Me." *She panted again.*

Without any notice, I sunk into her pussy with ease. I saw her eyes roll upwards and her eyelids flutter.

"Oh s-shit," she whispered, her body shaking.

I started to ease out of her, then in again—a slow, metronomic rhythm. Her head dropped, the effort of looking back at me no longer possible with the sensations she was feeling.

"I'm c-cumming again," she choked out.

Her pussy gripped my cock like a hand as she twitched and jerked beneath me as an electric orgasm tore through her.

She shifted, toppled sideways, and ended up in the crook of my arm. We lay there, on the balcony beneath the sky, our skin slick with sweat. She draped her leg over mine. As the snow began to fall, we quickly went inside and curled up under thick blankets, the chill outside making the warmth of each other's embrace even more comforting.

"I can't believe we had sex out there," she whispered, her breath warm against my ear, "I loved it."

"It was perfect," I replied, running my fingers through her hair. "Just you, me, and the sky."

She smiled, tracing circles on my chest. "Do you ever get scared?"

I traced the curve of her jaw, watching her expression soften.

"Are you scared, *amor*?"

She let out a small laugh, almost wistful, and nestled closer, her fingers drawing soft circles on my chest. "Sometimes, yeah. Scared of us... of the future. What if we don't get all the things we dream about?" Her voice trailed off, eyes searching the ceiling like she'd find answers written there.

I let her words settle between us, then tightened my arms around her, feeling the beat of her heart as it steadied mine.

"I'm not scared," I murmured. "We don't have to rush any of it. We have more than enough time. I'll make all our dreams come true, don't you worry about that."

She exhaled slowly then she gave a small, rueful smile. "Time... But we're not getting any younger, you know?"

I chuckled, brushing my thumb over her cheek. "True, but we're building something here—something strong, and that takes time."

She leaned into my touch, her eyes warm and shining. "You know, you make everything feel so much simpler," she whispered. "Like you ease all my worries."

"That's because I know you like that I talk you through everything," I teased gently, feeling her smile against my shoulder. "And because you know I'm always here, listening to everything you say, focusing on whatever you want or need. I'm forever here with you, baby."

"I realize you say that a lot. Here *with* me, and not here *for* me."

I pulled back just enough to look at her, my eyes soft but intense. "There's a difference between the two."

She tilted her head, studying me. "Do tell."

I took a deep breath, my hand moving to cradle her face, thumb tracing her cheek with tenderness. "Saying I'm here for you is me offering you support from the outside, waiting to help if you fall." My voice dropped lower, a gentle strength entwined through each word. "But saying I'm here with you? That's me right by your side, living each moment with you. It means if you're hurting, I'm in pain with you. If you're laughing, I'm right there in your joy. "With you" means every heartbeat, every breath—I'm all in, right here. I don't just support you; I share every part of this life, this love. I'm forever yours, every step of the way."

Her gaze softened, eyes betraying the depth of my words. With a tenderness only she possessed, her fingers traced my face. "Before you came into my life, I forgot what it was like to feel this seen… to be heard…to be loved…to matter."

"I think some part of me has always been waiting for you to slip away, like it was just a matter of time," she continued, voice soft but certain.

"But you're still here, *thankfully* and I love you." She let out a shaky breath, pressing her hand to my chest, right over my heart.

A tear slipped down her cheek, and I brushed it away, but her smile didn't waver. "I used to think love like this was too much to ask for. But you…" She took a breath, and it felt like she was looking right through me, into every part of me I'd only ever let her see. "You've taught me that it's possible to be loved and known and still wanted every day. And I'm still here, right by your side, as *with* you as you are with me."

I leaned in, resting my forehead against hers, feeling the warmth of her words settle into my soul. Her voice dropped to a whisper, but it was as steady as I'd ever heard it. "You're my home, and I never want this love with you to end."

I kissed her forehead. "It'll get hard at times, but it won't end."

She nodded, her eyes shining with emotion. "I'm proud of you, by the way. Last night was amazing, baby."

"I still can't believe it happened."

She looked up at me, her green eyes catching the first light of dawn. "I can, and as of last night, so can *Forbes*, *People*, *The New York Times*, and every other media outlet that came to witness your greatness, along with the thousands in attendance."

I bent down to kiss her, our lips gently brushing. Her hand lay on my chest, above my heart, and I could feel it racing beneath her touch. "I'm overwhelmed," I whispered against her lips.

"You've worked so hard for this. You deserve to be celebrated, and I'm forever proud of you."

The sun broke through the snowy clouds, casting a soft, glowing light in the room as we smiled at each other.

I brushed a stray curl from her face. "It's a new day," I whispered. "A new beginning."

She nodded, resting her head on my shoulder. "A new beginning," she echoed. "And Merry Christmas, baby."

"*Feliz Navidad, mi amor,*[1]" I replied, pressing a kiss to her forehead. "Here's to many more Christmases together."

---

1 *Merry Christmas, my love*

She tilted her head up, capturing my lips in a kiss that felt like home. When we parted, her eyes shone with unshed tears. "*Te quiero,* Mikkel,[2]" she said, her voice trembling with emotion. "*Más que nada.*[3]"

"*Yo también te amo, mi reina,*[4]" I replied, my voice thick with emotion. "*Más de lo que nunca sabrás.*[5]"

---

2 *I love you, Mikkel*

3 *More than anything*

4 *I love you too, my queen*

5 *More than you'll ever know*

WARNING

The following chapter contains heavy mentions of mental health/physical health issues. Please refer to the content warning list to be reminded of any potential triggers. Your well-being is important to me, so please take care of yourself while reading.

EPILOGUE

Abigail-Ann

"Some things are worth waiting for, and love is always one of them."
~ Unknown

THREE YEARS LATER.

Mikkel and I had done it all.

We traveled the world, exploring places that felt like they belonged to another era, untouched by time. We hiked the jagged peaks of Zhangjiajie in China, stood in awe of the endless salt flats at Salar de Uyuni in Bolivia, and wandered through the ancient ruins of Petra. We found serenity on the pristine beaches of the Seychelles and marveled as the sun dipped below the fjords of Norway. Each destination brought us closer together, filling our lives with moments so magical, they hardly seemed real.

Through it all, Mikkel's success never wavered. Elite Rides expanded to every corner of the United States, earning him a reputation as one of the most influential businessmen of his time. But, what amazed me most wasn't his relentless ambition or the empire he built—it was the way he always made me feel like the center of his universe. He balanced his towering responsibilities and our relationship with a precision that left me in awe.

Of course, it wasn't always easy. There were stressful days, moments when our lives felt like they were being pulled in too many directions at once. But no matter how overwhelming it got, we always found our way back to each other.

For my twenty-fourth birthday, Mikkel flew me to the set where *Beauty and the Beast* live action was filmed. Walking through the castle's opulent halls, chandeliers glittering like something out of a fairy tale, I felt like I had stepped into the story I'd adored since I was a child. As if that weren't enough, he took me to Disney World for a week, where we indulged in every *Beauty and the Beast* experience, from dining in the Beast's castle to seeing the characters come to life.

It was a dream brought to life, and Mikkel, ever the romantic, said he wanted me to feel like the princess I'd always deserved to be.

As if the West Wing he'd built for me back home didn't do that every single day.

Becoming an independent realtor turned out to be one of the best decisions I'd ever made. After finishing my apprenticeship, I set out on my own, working from home and building an impressive clientele, some of whom I could hardly believe had chosen me. The road wasn't always smooth. There were setbacks that knocked me down and lessons I had to learn quickly. But the victories? I owned every single one of them.

Even with all this success, there was an emptiness inside me, one that nothing seemed to fill. Not the accolades, not the financial stability. When the world settled at the end of the day, I was still a woman facing battles no one else could see. No one except Mikkel.

We've tried so many times, hoping this time would be different. But each time, it's the same story—a painful cycle of failure. Twice, I got pregnant, only to lose the baby. It's become a cruel pattern of hope and heartbreak, leaving me exhausted and aching in ways I never imagined.

The first time, we weren't even trying. When I saw the word "PREGNANT" appear on the test, a wave of pure, unfiltered joy washed over me. I wasn't scared—shocked, yes—but deep down, I knew I could handle this. And I was certain the man I was about to share this journey with was nothing short of incredible. But then, five weeks later, that joy was ripped away from me in the cruelest way. I woke up in a pool of blood, and panic set in as we rushed to the doctor. The news that followed shattered me—*shattered us.* I had lost our baby.

I hated myself more than I thought possible. I felt like I had failed—like my body had betrayed us, *our future.* But no matter how much sadness Mikkel felt, he never let me feel anything less than his unwavering love. If anything, it grew stronger, as if he were trying to piece together the fragments of my broken heart.

With each failed attempt at conception and the agony of a second miscarriage, I felt myself breaking apart, my hope crumbling into despair. I clenched my fists, nails biting into my palms as I fought to hold it together. I had learned to hide the tears, to bury the anguish threatening to consume me. But deep down, the pain never left—it festered, gnawing at my resolve.

I kept my appointments with Dr. Sang frequent, visited countless fertility clinics, endured endless supplements and injections. Mikkel spent thousands on the best reproductive endocrinologists worldwide, but nothing worked. Nothing eased the pain.

Mikkel had given me a life I never imagined, a love that could withstand anything. But I couldn't give him the one thing I knew he wanted—a child. I saw the pain in his eyes after our second loss, in every negative test. Still, he never blamed me. He held me, telling me it wasn't my fault, that we would get through this together.

My phone rang, displaying Azzaria's name, and I hesitated before answering. "Hey!"

"Abi!" Azzaria's voice was bright and cheerful. "The twins have been asking about you nonstop. They miss their Aunty Abi. They're begging to talk to you."

I forced a smile, even though she couldn't see it. "I miss them too."

Before I could say anything else, I heard the excited voices of her and Dillon's two year old twins in the background. "Aunty Abi! Aunty Abi!" they called out, their little voices full of joy.

A real smile finally tugged at my lips. "Hey, my loves! How are you two doing?"

"We miss you!" Catalina chirped. "When you comin' to pway wif us?"

My heart ached at their innocent question. "Soon, I promise. We'll have lots of fun when I see you."

"Pwomise?" Caiden asked, his voice hopeful.

"Promise," I responded, trying to sound more confident than I felt. "You two be good for your Mommy and Daddy, okay? And I'll bring you something special when I come."

They giggled, and I could hear Azzaria in the background, trying to calm them down. "Alright, say bye to Aunty, so she can get some rest."

"Bye, Aunty! We wuv you!" they shouted together, their sweet, slurred words filling me with warmth and longing.

"I love you both too," I whispered, holding onto that feeling as the call ended.

The silence that followed was suffocating as I thought about how happy I was for Azzaria. But, that happiness was often overshadowed by a sadness I couldn't shake. I longed to be the one with kids, to share in their milestones and laughter. Instead, I was the one who couldn't carry them to term.

All I could do was hope that someday, somehow, this pain would be worth it, but that hope felt so far away.

It had been four and a half months since we last tried—months of waiting, hoping, and battling the fear. But this morning felt different. I was off work, taking a much-needed mental health break, and Mikkel was home with me, rare moments away from his packed schedule.

"Are you okay, baby?" Mikkel asked, his hand wrapping around me.

I sighed. "I'm sleepy."

"Get some rest, *mi amor*," he whispered, kissing my cheek.

I didn't have the words, so I kissed him deeply, then gently fell onto my back, my breasts shifting with the impact.

"I'm going to call Emilia," he informed me. "I'll be back in a few minutes."

I nodded again, my thoughts racing as nausea swept over me. My heart pounded as I quietly got up and headed to the bathroom. I grabbed a pregnancy test, hands trembling as I went through the familiar motions, trying to stay grounded despite the hope building inside me.

When the result appeared, I almost fainted.

Pregnant.

The word stared back at me, and I clutched the test to my chest, not even sure how to process the rush of emotions flooding through me.

I didn't want to get my hopes up but I couldn't help it.

What if we were going to actually have a baby?

"Mikkel!" I yelled, my voice shaky with disbelief. "Mikkel, come here!"

He was by my side in an instant, worry clear on his face as he saw me standing there, sobbing. I held out the test to him, my voice barely a whisper. "I'm pregnant."

His eyes widened, and for a moment, he just stared at me. Then he lifted me into his arms, spinning us around. "We're having a baby," he said, his voice full of awe. "We're going to be parents."

I sighed, thinking of how this may be us getting happy for no reason.

"I don't want u—"

He kissed the words out of my mouth. "I know what you're going to say," he started, cupping my face. "But, let's not be negative. It's okay to have hope, *mi reina*."

Tears streamed down my cheeks. "Okay."

We clung to each other, laughing and crying, overwhelmed with relief and happiness. But we needed confirmation, so we scheduled a doctor's appointment for the next day, too anxious to wait longer.

We sat hand in hand in Dr. Sang's office, the wait stretching endlessly. When we were finally called in, her calm voice and the gentle hum of the sonograph eased my nerves. Mikkel squeezed my hand, his eyes never leaving the screen.

Dr. Sang smiled. "Everything looks good," she said, and I felt a weight lift off my shoulders. "You're about twelve weeks pregnant."

I blinked in confusion. "Twelve weeks? That's three months, right?"

She nodded, adjusting the screen slightly so we could see. "Yes, that's right. Sometimes early symptoms can be missed, but from what I see, you're progressing normally."

I stared at the screen, at the tiny flicker of life that had been growing inside me for three months without me even realizing it. Tears welled up, but this time, they were tears of joy. Mikkel leaned in, pressing his lips to my forehead as we took in the reality of it all.

Dr. Sang spoke again, her tone gentle but serious. "This is the furthest you've made it, so congratulations. However, there are some precautions we need to take to help ensure a full-term, successful delivery."

"Anything," I replied quickly.

Mikkel nodded. "Just let us know, Doc."

She offered a small, understanding smile. "We'll need more frequent check-ups, with ultrasounds every two to three weeks to monitor progress. Managing your stress is also crucial. Emotional or physical strain can have a negative impact, so we'll work to keep that to a minimum."

Mikkel tightened his grip on my hand, his thumb tracing soothing circles on my skin. "We'll do whatever it takes."

Dr. Sang continued, "I'll also recommend certain supplements to support the pregnancy. And if you notice anything unusual—cramping, bleeding, anything—you come see me immediately."

I nodded, absorbing everything she was saying. This was our chance, and I wasn't going to take it for granted.

"I'll give you a detailed plan," she said, "but the most important thing is to listen to your body. Rest when you need to, and don't hesitate to reach out with any concerns, no matter how small."

Mikkel nodded along with me, his eyes never leaving mine. "We'll be careful. I'll make sure of it."

Dr. Sang smiled again, this time reassuringly. "Good."

As we left the appointment, the sunlight seemed to shine a little brighter, but it couldn't compare to the warmth in my chest. Mikkel gently guided me to the car, his hand resting on my back.

"Careful," he mumbled, his voice laced with concern as we neared the curb. His arm wrapped protectively around me, as if the slightest misstep could harm me or our baby.

I smiled, teasing him. "Mikkel, I'm not fragile."

"I know," he said, but his brow furrowed. "I just want to be sure you're okay."

Once inside the car, he carefully adjusted the seatbelt over my belly, even though there was nothing to show yet. His sweet, thoughtful gesture made me reach out and squeeze his hand.

"I promise I'll be careful," I whispered.

He sighed, running a hand through his hair before turning to face me, his expression serious. "I'm happy, but also terrified. We've wanted this for so long, and now that it's happening, I just don't want anything to go wrong."

"I know," I whispered. "But we'll do everything we can to keep this little one and me safe."

Mikkel's gaze softened, and he leaned over to kiss my temple. "We're in this together. Whatever it takes."

I nodded, a swirl of joy, hope, and a little fear stirring inside me. But more than anything, I was grateful to have Mikkel by my side.

"There's one thing, though," I said after a moment. "I don't want to tell anyone just yet. Not your friends, not even our parents. At least not until we're farther along. I just want to be sure."

Mikkel met my gaze, his eyes understanding immediately. He nodded. "Of course, *mi vida.*[1]"

"Thank you," I breathed, relief washing over me. "It's just... after everything, I want to be certain. I know it'll be hard to keep it a secret, but—"

He cut me off with a soft kiss, his lips brushing against mine gently. "We'll wait. We'll do this at our pace."

---

1 *my life*

I smiled against his lips, feeling a sense of peace. "Three years later, and I'm still in awe of everything you do, and every word you say."

He chuckled softly, pulling back just enough to meet my eyes. "I'm doing what any man would do for the woman he loves."

"I love you, too," I whispered, leaning in for another kiss. "So much."

Mikkel exhaled, visibly relaxing. With one last glance at me, he started the car, and we drove in comfortable silence. Everything felt a little less heavy as we faced this new chapter together.

FIVE MONTHS LATER

I'd been planning this for what felt like forever—nearly three years of carefully mapping out every detail, imagining how it would go, and praying for the right time. But how could I ask her when she was already carrying so much? Our fertility struggles had been a heavy burden, and I couldn't bring myself to add to it. I couldn't do that to her.

Then, five months ago, everything changed. She was pregnant. I remember that day so clearly—the shock in her eyes when she saw the test, the way her hand shook when I held it. We just stood there, barely breathing, not daring to believe it was finally happening. That moment made all the waiting and heartbreak worth it.

The pregnancy had been hell for her—sick, constantly nauseous, unable to keep anything down. She was pale and exhausted, and I hated seeing her like that, feeling powerless to make it better. But she stayed strong, pushing through. The mood swings were hard, too—one minute, she was furious, the next, she was in tears. I did my best to be what she needed, even when I wasn't sure what that was.

It started early, just after dawn, when the first light crept into the room. I woke to the sound of her retching in the bathroom, my heart dropping immediately. She'd been sick on and off for weeks, but this was different. There was a desperation in the way she hunched over the toilet, clutching the edge like it was the only thing keeping her grounded.

"Hey," I said softly, not wanting to startle her. "Do you need anything?"

She didn't look up, just shook her head, her tangled curls falling around her face. "I just… I can't," she whispered before another wave hit her.

I knelt beside her, rubbing her back, my gut twisting with each heave. I wished I could take it all away, do anything to make it better. But all I could do was be there. It felt like nothing.

After what felt like an eternity, the sickness seemed to subside, and she slumped back against the wall, exhausted. Her face was pale, her green eyes hollow with strain. "I'm so tired," she muttered, her voice weak.

"I know, mi reina," I whispered, brushing a damp strand of hair from her forehead. "Let's get you back to bed, okay?"

She nodded weakly, and I helped her to her feet. But as soon as she saw the bed, panic flashed in her eyes. "No," she said, voice shaking. "I can't lie down. It'll just start again."

I tried to reassure her, but fear had already taken hold, and it broke something inside me to see her so scared. I finally got her to sit on the edge of the bed, but she was tense, like a coiled spring ready to snap.

"What can I do?" I asked, desperate to help.

She looked at me, tears welling in her eyes, and whispered, "I don't know. I just want this pain to stop. I'm losing my mind."

I'd never seen her so defeated, so worn down. I sat beside her, unsure of what to say. "You'll get through this," I tried, but it sounded hollow even to me. "I'm right here with you."

"How can you say that when I can't even keep water down?" Her eyes searched mine for something—hope, maybe. "I don't feel strong enough for this."

"You are strong enough," I said firmly, trying to will my belief into her. "You're the strongest person I know, even if you don't feel like it right now."

But nothing I said seemed to help. The rest of the day passed in a blur of nausea, tears, and frustration. Every time she tried to eat or drink, it came right back up. By evening, she was drained, both physically and emotionally.

I did my best to stay calm, to be her anchor, but inside, I was unraveling. Every suggestion I made was met with resistance. She didn't want to see Dr.

Sang anymore. She didn't want any more remedies from her best friend or our mothers.

Later in the day, she broke down completely. We were sitting on the couch, her head in her hands, sobbing uncontrollably. Her tears seemed to come from a place of pure exhaustion and despair.

"I don't know if I can do this," she repeated, and all I could do was hold her tighter. "I love our baby, but I'm so defeated."

"You can," I whispered, even though I was terrified she might be right. "You've made it this far. We'll take it one day at a time. I'm here with you, baby."

The day felt endless, each minute dragging by with no relief in sight. By the time night fell, she was barely able to keep her eyes open. I managed to get her to drink a little water and eat half a Chipotle bowl before she finally collapsed into bed.

I watched her sleep, her face still drawn from the strain of the day. And in that moment, I had never felt more helpless in my life. The woman I loved was suffering, and all I could do was be there, hoping that would be enough.

I thought back to how far we'd come—almost full term now, and Abigail was doing so much better. The penthouse had truly become our home. She'd insisted we stay, confident we could grow our family there. The nursery was ready—pastel blankets on the crib, tiny shoes lined up, and a cozy rocking chair by the window.

With everything in place, there was only one thing left to do, and it had to be tonight. My heart raced as the weight of it hit me. I'd planned every detail, but nerves wouldn't let up. We'd come so far, and now, on the edge of the life we'd dreamed of, I knew it was time to take the next step. I'd been ready to marry her the moment I first saw her four and a half years ago.

When I got home, bouquet of primroses in hand, the penthouse was unusually quiet. I dropped my keys and headed upstairs. Pausing at our bedroom door, I took a deep breath before stepping inside. There she was, sitting on the edge of the bed, her head in her hands. She looked exhausted but still the most beautiful woman I'd ever seen.

Her skin glowed, her hair pinned up in a messy bun—the same hair that had caught my attention when we first met. *My Red.*

She wore a simple dress that hugged her curves, showcasing her eight-month belly. I couldn't help but smile at her.

I walked over to her, eyes locked on hers. She looked up, tension evident in her gaze. "*Mi vida,*[2]" I whispered, sitting beside her. "Are you okay?"

She tried to smile, but it didn't reach her eyes. Instead, they welled with tears. "I'm a bit nervous," she whispered, her voice trembling. "It's been so long since we've been out like this. I'm just overwhelmed."

I felt a pang in my chest as I rubbed her belly, feeling our baby move beneath my hand. "You'll be okay." I leaned in to kiss her forehead. "Breathe, okay? Just breathe."

Her body trembled with the weight of it all, and I pulled her closer, resting my hand on her belly. "You've been doing so great," I told her, my voice firm but gentle. "Look how far you've come. Eight months. We're almost there. Just a few more weeks."

She nodded, though I could tell she was still unsettled. "You're a superwoman for carrying our baby and still holding onto hope after everything. I'm so proud of you."

She leaned into me, her sobs quieting as I held her. "I know it's hard," I continued softly, "but we're in this together. We've got each other. We're going to make it. Are you still nauseous?"

"Not nauseous," she murmured. "Thank God."

"Okay, baby."

She was quiet for a moment, tears slowing as she calmed. I kissed her cheek, then her lips—slow and tender, trying to pour all my love into that kiss. When I pulled back, I searched her eyes for any sign of relief. "Do you want to stay in tonight instead?" I asked gently, not wanting to push her if she wasn't up for it.

"I want to go." Her voice was steadier now. "I want to be with you tonight. I'm just… I needed a moment."

---

2 *My life*

I rubbed her belly again, feeling a sense of awe at the life we're so close to bringing into the world. "Our little one will be here soon, and all of this will be worth it."

She took a deep breath and managed a small smile. "Just a few more weeks."

"Exactly," I said, smiling back. "And when the time comes, we'll be ready. You've been incredible, and I know you're going to be an amazing mom."

She nodded again, her smile growing as she reached out to take my hand. "Thank you," she whispered. "I don't know what I'd do without you."

"You'll never have to find out, Red."

As I held her close, feeling the tension slowly drain from her body, the room settled into a peaceful silence. I was about to suggest we take a few minutes to relax together before getting ready when my phone buzzed in my pocket, shattering the moment.

I pulled it out and saw Sapphire's name flashing on the screen. My stomach tightened. *What the hell was going on at the office?*

Abigail noticed it too, and I felt her stiffen in my arms.

"It's Sapphire," I said, hesitation creeping in as I debated whether to answer.

Her lips pressed into a thin line, and her arms crossed protectively over her chest, which only made me notice her belly more.

Fuck, it was hot.

"Of course," she muttered, her voice tinged with frustration.

Without a word, I hit decline and quickly typed out a text: *Is everything good at the office?*

Sapphire replied almost instantly: *Contracts are here for the new contacts, and your call with Singapore is rescheduled for next week.*

I slipped the phone back into my pocket and met Abigail's eyes. She was still tense, a mix of relief and lingering frustration in her gaze. I squeezed her hand, trying to reassure her. "She updated me on the contracts and the Singapore call. I'll handle it next week."

Abigail let out a small sigh. "I know you have to work, and I know how busy you are, but I just—" She paused, shaking her head before meeting my eyes again. "I'm secure, okay? I know you love me, and I trust you, but this pregnancy... it makes everything feel ten times more intense."

I leaned in, brushing my lips against her forehead. "You never have to explain, baby. I understand. You're allowed to feel however you want."

Her body relaxed into me, just a little more. "I know it's silly," she said quietly, "but sometimes it just gets to me. I just want you all to myself."

I chuckled softly, pulling her closer. "It's not silly," I assured her. "Because there's nowhere else I'd rather be."

She looked up at me, a soft smile tugging at her lips as she absorbed my words. "You always know what to say, Mr. Suarez."

I smiled, the warmth of her words sinking in, but it wasn't just that. Soon, she'd be taking that last name too.

"I mean every word," I said, my hand resting on her belly, feeling the baby shift beneath my palm. "You're my world. You and our little one."

"Ooo," she gasped, a giggle escaping her as she looked down at her belly. "You're kicking up a storm for daddy, aren't you?"

I placed my hand back on her belly, feeling another gentle kick. "Daddy's girl, already?"

"Definitely daddy's girl," she whispered, exhaling as the tension in her body eased. She added, barely above a whisper, "Thank you for always knowing how to pull me back when I get lost in my head. For making me feel better, even when I'm being ridiculous."

"You're not ridiculous," I said firmly, my voice steady. "You're the strongest, most incredible woman I know. And if you want me all to yourself, you've got me. *Siempre.*[3]"

"Okay," she murmured, her fingers intertwining with mine. "Let's get ready. I want tonight to be special."

"It will be," I promised, pressing a soft kiss to her hand.

"So, what's the plan for tonight?" she asked, playful despite her exhaustion.

I squeezed her hand, lips curving into a knowing smile. "You'll see."

---

3 *Always*

City lights blurred past as we drove toward the East River. At the pier, I parked and helped her out, leading her down a private dock. She stopped short, eyes widening at the yacht waiting for us.

"We're going on that?" she breathed.

I grinned. "We are. Dr. Sang said it's safe."

She hesitated, taking in its grandeur. Then her gaze landed on the name scrawled across the side: **Red.**

"What's this?" Surprise laced her voice.

I slid an arm around her shoulders. "It's yours. A pre-push present."

Her fingers drifted to her belly, tracing slow circles. "*A pre-push present*?" She glanced between me and the yacht, disbelief flickering in her eyes. "Are you serious?"

"Completely." I watched her, taking in every reaction. "You've been through so much. You deserve something special. Something that's yours. And when the baby's born, we'll bring her here too."

She blinked rapidly, struggling to speak. "I don't even know what to say."

"Come here." I led her onto the deck, settling onto a cushioned bench and gently pulling her onto my lap.

She hesitated. "I'm heavy."

I wrapped my arms around her. "You're pregnant. You're beautiful. And you're perfect just the way you are."

A tear slipped down her cheek. I brushed it away with my thumb. "This is yours," I murmured. "A reminder of how much I love you, how amazing you are. You couldn't go to the beach or the river, so I thought this would be the next best thing."

She nodded, her voice barely a whisper. "It's perfect. Thank you."

I kissed her temple. "I'm glad you like it."

After a moment, she shifted. "I want to look at the water."

I steadied her as she walked to the railing, watching her shoulders relax as she gazed at the moonlit waves. Exactly what I wanted—a moment for her to breathe.

I moved behind her, resting a hand on her shoulder. She turned, eyes filled with curiosity.

Taking a slow, steady breath, I lowered myself to one knee.

"No," she breathed, her voice trembling. "Mikkel, what-"

I looked up at her, my heart pounding. "I've been waiting for this moment since our first date, actually." Emotion thickened my voice. "I knew I wanted to marry you from the very start. I knew we were forever."

A slow breath filled my lungs as I steadied myself. "For so long, I've wanted to show you just how much you mean to me. You've been through so much, yet you've never stopped loving, never stopped being the incredible woman you are. You're everything I've ever dreamed of and more."

I swallowed, my heart hammering as I continued. "It was as if the universe itself whispered that you were meant for me. Every beat of my heart, every breath I take, has led me here—to you." I searched her face, watching every flicker of emotion in her wide, tear-brightened eyes. "With you, I've found the kind of love poets write about, the kind artists try to capture in their masterpieces. You've completed me in ways I didn't even realize I was incomplete."

My grip on the velvet box tightened as I carefully pulled it open, revealing the ring—a masterpiece I'd flown to Switzerland to have made. The flawless diamond caught the moonlight, its ethereal glow accentuating the double-band design. Delicate primroses framed the center stone, and inside the band, our initials, A+M, were engraved.

Her fingers trembled as she stared at the ring, her lips parting in a silent gasp. Tears welled in her eyes, catching the diamond's brilliance, and for a moment, I forgot how to breathe.

I reached for her hands, my own trembling slightly. "Be mine. Will you marry me?" My voice was thick with emotion. "I want to spend the rest of my life with you—to be there with you, to cherish you, to love you through everything that comes our way. You're my everything, and I can't imagine a life without you. I don't ever want to."

Her gaze locked with mine—astonishment, joy, love—all reflected in her eyes.

"Mikkel," she whispered, her voice breaking. "This is…"

I squeezed her hands. "You don't have to say anything. Just know that I love you more than words can express. Will you marry me?"

For a moment, she was silent—overcome, overwhelmed. Then, she nodded rapidly, a tearful laugh breaking through. "Yes." Her voice was full of wonder. "I forgot to say yes! Of course, I'll marry you. That shouldn't even be a question."

Emotion surged through me as I slid the ring onto her finger, its delicate sparkle a mere reflection of the light she'd brought into my life.

She looked down at it, then back at me, eyes shining. "Thank you for giving me my happily ever after."

My chest ached with the weight of this moment. "I've been waiting for this for so long." I traced my fingers over hers, marveling at the way our hands fit together so perfectly. "I needed to give you a ring that shows just how much you mean to me."

She shook her head, a breathless smile tugging at her lips. "It's perfect."

And so was she. Mine. Forever.

I slipped the ring onto her finger, and her eyes widened in awe, tears spilling over her cheeks as she gazed at it.

"It's so beautiful," she whispered, her voice breaking. "I can't believe you went through all this just for me."

"The ring is beautiful, but its value is nothing compared to what you mean to me. The time I spent having it made, the cost—it's all worth it for this moment, for making you happy."

I stood and pulled her into a tight embrace, her warmth making the moment whole. I kissed her deeply, tasting our shared joy. Wrapped in each other, we stood beneath the night sky, ready for the life ahead.

"I thought about proposing before dawn," I said softly, and she turned around to look at me.

"Really?"

I nodded, pressing a tender kiss to her shoulder. "Yeah, but I also thought of how irritated you'd be if I woke you up that early."

She laughed then held her hand out, gazing at the ring. "This diamond is so fucking big."

I smiled, brushing a strand of hair from her face. "Only the best for you, *mi amor.*"

"My new last name is gonna be Suarez!"

I nodded, my heart swelling with pride. "*Sí, Señora Suarez.*[4]"

She took a deep breath, her smile widening even more. "This is an entire dream," she avowed, her voice filled with warmth. "I have to call my parents and my sister and Azzy and—"

"Calm down, baby," I urged. "We'll call everyone in due time. Let's enjoy the moment."

"You're right."

She glanced at her belly, then met my gaze. "I can't believe how close we are to meeting our baby girl," she whispered.

I rested my hand on her belly, feeling the tiny life growing inside. "I keep wondering what she'll look like, who she'll become."

Abigail smiled, her fingers brushing over mine. "And I keep picturing you as a dad. You're going to be incredible. And hot."

I chuckled, pressing a kiss to her lips. "I just want to be the best father I can be. But with you, I know we'll be an amazing team."

She exhaled softly, gazing at the horizon. "It's exciting… and a little scary. But knowing we have each other? That makes it all feel right."

I pulled her close, resting my chin atop her head. "We're stronger together. No matter what comes, we'll handle it."

She nodded, her eyes shimmering with quiet certainty. "After everything we've been through, this—us, our baby—it's everything I ever wanted."

I kissed her temple, my heart full. "This is just the beginning, *mi amor.*"

She smiled, leaning into me. "And I can't wait."

THE END.

---

4 *Yes, Mrs. Suarez*

Thank You!

I want to express my deepest gratitude to each and every one of you for taking the time to read this book. Writing this story has been a labor of love, my true passion project, and my book baby. Your support, your enthusiasm, and your belief in my work mean the world to me.

I truly hope you enjoyed reading it as much as I enjoyed writing it. Your interest in my stories is what fuels my creativity and inspires me to keep writing from the heart.

If you have a moment, I would be so grateful for your feedback. Sharing your thoughts on platforms like Goodreads and Amazon can make a huge difference in helping more readers discover my work.

For those who'd like to stay connected and be the first to hear about upcoming books, exclusive content, and more, you can visit my website and sign up for my newsletter. It's the best way to stay in the loop!

Once again, thank you for being part of this incredible journey. Your support is truly the wind beneath my wings, and I can't wait to share more stories with you in the future.

With all my love and gratitude,
Author Jada West

About the Author

Jada is a 20-year-old book lover with a passion for all things book-related. She is currently in medical and psychology school, balancing her studies with her love for reading and writing. She has an undeniable love for cinnamon rolls and Alfredo pasta—her ultimate comfort foods! Along with caramel coffee, they make her happiest on even the busiest days. Her faith is a cornerstone of her life, and when she's not buried in books, you'll probably catch her rewatching The Vampire Diaries or The Chosen. A hopeless romantic at heart, Jada is known for her warm, caring nature and her ability to make everyone around her feel special.

KEEP IN TOUCH

Want to keep in touch? Stay connected for updates, behind-the-scenes content, and more! Scan the barcode below to get access to my socials.

ALSO BY JADA WEST

Timeless Love Series

After Hours- Book 1 - Available Now

Before Dawn- Book 2

Book 3

Book 4

Book 5: Novella

Snowhaven Hills - Coming Winter 2025

TIMELESS LOVE SERIES BOOK THREE

Did someone say second-chance romance with an unmatched amount of yearning, groveling, and absolutely no third-act breakup? Then you're in the right place! Come along to see which Timeless Love man takes the reins in this book.

Pre-Order Now

www.ingramcontent.com/pod-product-compliance
Lightning Source LLC
Chambersburg PA
CBHW020718310726
48979CB00004B/971